PRAISE FOR *It Begins in Betrayal*

"*It Begins in Betrayal* has a wonderfully complex plot with threads that eventually resolve most satisfactorily. The post-war time period is particularly interesting and well captured."—Maureen Jennings, author of the Murdoch Mysteries series

"Action-packed and emotionally charged from the prologue to the climax . . . it just doesn't get much better than this."—Don Graves, Canadian Mystery Reviews

PRAISE FOR *An Old, Cold Grave*

"A fascinating picture of a life in which many people spent every waking hour working and a disturbing look at the fate of orphaned children raise this mystery above the ordinary."—Kirkus Reviews

"Lane Winslow, the intrepid sleuth of King's Cove, is back in her third adventure and, like the first two, it's a charmer. Once again, British Columbia's own Iona Whishaw's delightful modern gloss on the venerable British cozy provides a perfect weekend getaway . . . a cleverly plotted story with a delightful setting and amusing characters. Once again, Whishaw keeps us guessing to the end."—Margaret Cannon, *Globe and Mail*

"*An Old, Cold Grave*—Iona Whishaw's compelling third novel—gives us a gentle rural setting, a body in a root cellar, and, of course, Lane Winslow, the best new amateur sleuth to come along in quite some time. Plot, dialogue, and place: all the requisite elements for an award-winning novel."—Don Graves, Canadian Mystery Reviews blog

"If you enjoy a puzzle set in a 1947, rural BC community, with dialogue that reaches into the soul and a sense of place that is integral to the mystery, then *An Old, Cold Grave* is a summer read for you . . . In short, sin, plot, dialogue and place: all the requisite elements for an award-winning novel. It's easy to imagine a fourth in this increasingly fine series."—*Bay Observer*

PRAISE FOR *Death in a Darkening Mist*

"The late L. R. Wright's marvellous mysteries set on British Columbia's Sunshine Coast remain some of my favourite Canadian books. But this second novel by Iona Whishaw, also set in BC, is every bit as good. Both writers know how to make a book's setting as important a factor as the plot line or the characters . . . [an] excellent chapter in what appears to be a terrific series."—Margaret Cannon, *Globe and Mail*

"An absolute winner [that] moves the notch up several levels when it comes to mystery writing with a historical twinge. The highlight of the writing is the seamless blend of the sense of place into the storyline. The impact of both world wars settles into the essence of any place, and this is a sterling example of how place impacts both events and people."—Don Graves, Canadian Mystery Reviews blog

"Set in 1946, this series cleverly combines both elements of a cozy and a spy thriller, with a heroine who is tough and independent, but harboring secrets of her own . . . The local townspeople are quirky and a nice addition, reminding the reader of another Canadian writer, Louise Penny, who populates her town with interesting characters . . . a series I hope to continue reading."—ReviewingtheEvidence.com

PRAISE FOR *A Killer in King's Cove*

"A good historical mystery with a cast of characters that will provide plot lines for the series to come. Iona Whishaw is a writer to watch."—Margaret Cannon, *Globe and Mail*

"Exquisitely written, psychologically deft . . . If you miss Mary Stewart's sleuthing heroines, if you loved Broadchurch and its village of suspects, settle in, turn off the phone, and enjoy."—Linda Svendsen, author of *Sussex Drive* and *Marine Life*

"A debut mystery from an author destined for awards. A setting that is ripe for storytelling and a convincing gift for portraying the painful and challenging life for the survivors of the two world wars . . . Whishaw is an exciting addition to Canada's fine roster of mystery writers."—Don Graves, Canadian Mystery Reviews blog

"The writing . . . conjures up nicely the ambiance of a 1940s west Canadian locale and develops in depth both the characters and their interactions."—San Francisco Book Review

A KILLER IN KING'S COVE

IONA WHISHAW

A KILLER IN KING'S COVE

A LANE WINSLOW MYSTERY

Cover illustration by Margaret Hanson
Design by Pete Kohut
Edited by Cat London
Proofread by Claire Philipson

LIBRARY AND ARCHIVES CANADA CATALOGUING IN PUBLICATION
Whishaw, Iona, 1948–, author
A killer in King's Cove / Iona Whishaw.
(A Lane Winslow mystery)

Issued in print and electronic formats.
ISBN 978-1-77151-198-8

Title.

PS8595.H414K54 2016   C813'.54   C2016-903371-6

We gratefully acknowledge the financial support of the Government of Canada through the Canada Book Fund, the Canada Council for the Arts, and the province of British Columbia through the British Columbia Arts Council and the Book Publishing Tax Credit.

Canada Council for the Arts   Conseil des Arts du Canada

PRINTED IN CANADA AT FRIESENS

22 21 20 19 18   2 3 4 5

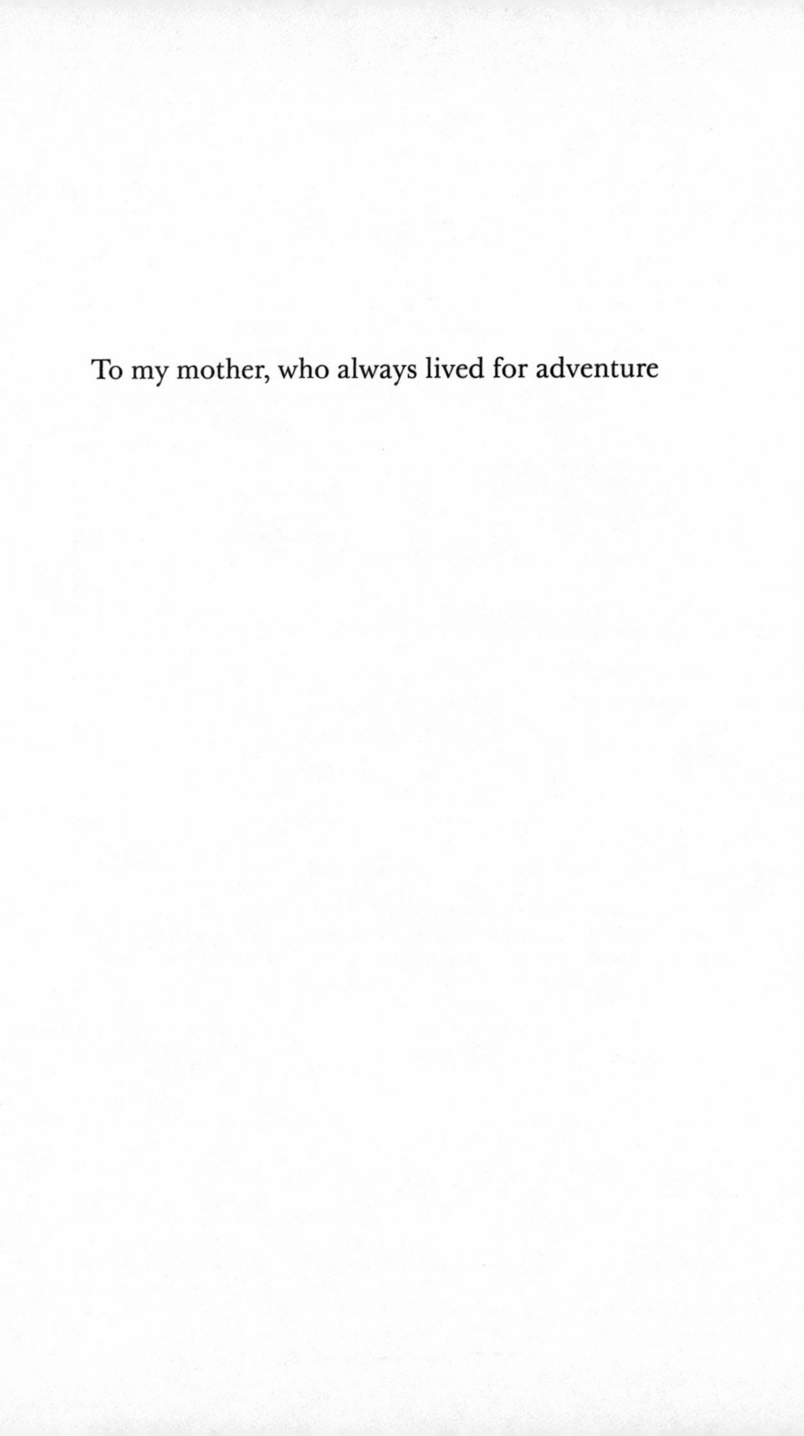

To my mother, who always lived for adventure

PROLOGUE

King's Cove, June 28, 1946

THE BARN WAS A QUIET solace to the old man's agitation. The envelope from His Majesty's Government lay where he had thrown it that morning on the bare kitchen table, but his mind still felt partially colonized by his dark fears. As he cranked the engine, he became aware of another sound. He stopped and listened. A motorcar had pulled up along the front of his fence. Some bloody idiot asking the way, he thought. They weren't going to get it from him. He stayed in the shadow of the overhang and watched the road. Whoever it was would give up.

A young man emerged from the motorcar, and stood looking from the house to a piece of paper. He removed his hat to fan himself for a moment. He climbed the steps of the house and knocked on the door, waited, and then called out, "Hello? Is there anyone here?"

An Englishman! The old man went from irritation to misgiving to stomach-turning panic in one swift moment.

He took a step toward the barn door to go out and confront the man and then changed his mind. If he didn't show himself this person might leave. He waited while the

Englishman called out again, and then muttered "Bugger" under his breath. The old man could hear the other man's progress down the steps and waited to hear the motor door open, but instead heard footsteps come around the house and toward the barn. He looked desperately behind him into the murky darkness of the barn. Not knowing why, he clutched the starter crank in his hand and felt frozen to the spot.

The young man reached the barn and peered in to the dusky interior where he suddenly caught sight of the figure cowering in the shadow and jumped back in alarm. "Oh, gosh, you startled me. Hello. My name is Jack Franks. With whom am I speaking?"

"None of your business," said the old man, scowling.

Misunderstanding him, the young man reached into his jacket and pulled out a billfold from which he extracted a white identity card. "It's quite all right. I'm legitimate. Here, I work for the British government."

Something inside the old man froze. So. They had come.

CHAPTER ONE

LANETTE WINSLOW SAT ON A large wooden box that had miraculously arrived the same day she had and listened to the silence. Old Kenny Armstrong, whose mother's house this had once been, had disappeared along the path to the post office, leaving her with her keys and a plate of cold chicken that his wife, Eleanor, had sent over. Sitting in the shaft of afternoon sunlight that had broken through after rain earlier in the morning, she was grateful not to have to cook tonight.

In the kitchen, true to Kenny's word, all of his late mother's culinary equipment was neatly stored on shelves. Slightly daunted, Lane surveyed the many implements of cookery and wondered what she'd use, after all. After a lifetime of being cooked for, she'd become used to cooking everything in one pan on a single electric element in the shared flat in London. The mysteries of food preparation on any but a wartime, flatmate scale were an opaque mystery to her.

In anticipation of her arrival, Kenny had lit the fire in the Franklin stove in the drawing room at noon, to take down any dampness, and she had only to add to it to keep it going. A neat, fresh pile of chopped wood sat in the basket next to the stove. Looking at the growing swath of sunlight, she thought she would not need to keep it going. She got up and found the kettle, the one implement with which she felt expertise, filled it, and plunked it onto the stovetop. An electric stove in this nearly wilderness setting seemed the ultimate luxury. She wondered if the late Lady Armstrong had insisted on it, or if Kenny had put it in against a future sale of the house. It was very nearly new. She had brought some bags of groceries from Nelson and she stowed them in the fridge, another unanticipated luxury, and then tested the kitchen light several times for fun, because it was hers and she'd never owned one before, attached to a whole house as this one was. After looking inquiringly at the kettle to see if she could hear it heating up, she took a delicious amble through the rooms. She ran her hand along the walls and around the door jambs as she went from room to room.

It was hers. Every board and window and foot of it. She paused in the bedroom and wondered about the north-facing windows. Had she heard somewhere that this was not lucky? Perhaps it was more that she had heard that in some cultures an east-facing room was important.

Her tour took her upstairs next, to the second floor. The fourth stair creaked and she smiled, stepping backwards to hear it again. It was the voice of her house. There was no door at the top of the stairs into what Kenny had referred to as the attic. It was all one large room, occupying the full second floor, with banks of windows on all four sides. It had been equipped with sliding cupboards under the windows, in which, no doubt, boxes of Lady Armstrong's accoutrements, accumulated over her lifetime in two countries, were now stored. She had told Kenny not to move anything on her account; she was quite happy to store anything of his mother's. She wondered about moving some of the cookery items in the kitchen up into storage, but then chided herself. She must learn to use them. That was the meaning of a full life in the New World, where there were neither servants nor war to limit one's experience of it. Light bucketed into the room, making it a canvas of warmth and shadows. She was surprised to find the west-facing windows, which looked out over the lake below her, were standing open. Perhaps Kenny had opened them to air the house out, though it was a peculiar thing to do when rain must have been pelting down in the morning, if the mud in the driveway was any indication.

She closed and latched the windows, looking at the damp on the floor and judging that it would dry all right in time, without damaging anything, and went downstairs to have tea and begin to think about her crate from England. Tomorrow she would explore her outbuilding, a large, weathered but well-constructed barn that was positioned to the left of the driveway that led from the road to the house. The nascent archaeologist in her thrilled to the prospect. Her childhood home had been a rambling of no-longer-used outbuildings and attics, where she had explored with a gnawing feeling of excited dread that these places would all be forbidden to her if her aunts but knew where she went. Perhaps her barn, where she had glimpsed the shapes of things, tools she supposed, hanging in the small dusty windows, would yield that same sense of the now-silent stories of lives lived in an unknowable past, where all the world had smelled of rust and the acrid tang of decaying chemicals and oil. But that was for tomorrow.

KENNY ARMSTRONG KICKED the mud off his boots, took them off, and then stood thoughtfully in the doorway.

"Well, that is a lovely girl!" he declared enthusiastically. "And there's no accounting for tastes, because she took the keys right out of my hands. I thought we'd never sell the thing and we would have to turn it under and plant apples over it to get rid of Mother." He moved in and fell into his chair by the stove and began pulling off his thick wool socks.

Eleanor, his wife of nearly thirty years, smiled and pulled open the stove to push in another stick of wood. "Maybe she'll stop haunting the place now that there's someone in the house. It'll be jolly good having someone else young around here." Aside from the Yanks, who didn't count, the place was turning into a community for superannuated and shell-shocked vets from two world wars, and their mad wives and mothers. "She'll get to meet them all at the vicar's tea. Poor girl! I do hope the Mather boy isn't going to be bothering her. Who knows what she's been through in the old country. I'm sure she'd just like some peace and quiet."

LANE WOULD HAVE been surprised by Kenny and Eleanor's enthusiasm for her looks. She was not vain, having had very little time to develop vanity because of the pressures of her work, which began smartly in 1939 when the war started and she was only nineteen. She was slender but strongly shaped with bigger feet than those of her friends and because she couldn't be bothered redirecting her eyebrows higher up on her brow ridge as many of the girls had done, she was sure she looked a bit like a gorilla. She had been surprised when Angus had run his thumbs gently along the length of her brows that day so long ago and said, "Lovely, lovely!" She had never felt worthy of Angus, truthfully, and he was the furthest thing from her mind now, as was everything from her life in the last seven years, pushed determinedly away by the green presence of this new land.

That was the best thing about relocating an ocean and a continent away. Her whole dark past would recede into the mist, like the skyline of Liverpool, from where she'd embarked. She was here now. She had met no one yet but Kenny and Eleanor, who had been left this house by Kenny's mother but who preferred to stay in their cottage on the other side of the creek. The cottage had been designed before the turn of the century to house the post office for the sparsely populated and far-flung community and it suited their modest view of what was necessary for happiness. It was tiny and comfortable for the two of them and had a big west-facing porch overlooking the garden.

Lane was sure that no matter who lived in King's Cove, she would be happy because she had her house, and it would be possible to begin shaping her life away from the past and into the future, away from the shadows and into the light.

CHAPTER TWO

"CUCUMBERS TODAY," ELEANOR ARMSTRONG SAID a few days later, her warmth intensified by the sheer size of her false-teeth smile. She pushed the mail through the wooden window and followed it up with two long, deep green, spiny cucumbers. Eleanor never just gave out mail. It was accompanied in the spring with flowers, in the summer and fall with vegetables, and in the winter with cookies, generally some Victorian gingery recipe no one had ever been able to duplicate. It was the driest June anyone could remember, and memory here went back fifty years, well before the first war.

Lane still wasn't used to this largesse. "They're spectacular!" she said. "I shall eat nothing else for a week. Do me good."

Eleanor waved a self-deprecatory hand and then leaned forward and bobbed her head, not a hair on her white coif moving out of perfect place. "Has Lady Armstrong been giving you any trouble?"

"She's been very quiet. Perhaps she's left?" Lane said, raising her eyebrows in a kind of shrug they might recognize in France, where she had lived for a brief period after the war.

"Don't kid yourself. She's not going anywhere, though if Kenny fixed the latch on those attic windows, it might take care of most of the haunting. Oh dear," Eleanor whispered suddenly, leaning toward Lane and giving a discreet little point to the door with her chin. Lane turned to the sound of the screen door opening and the little bell tinkling. Mrs. Mather. Lane had seen "Mad Mather," as Eleanor had called her, only from the rear, as she'd made her way up the road the day before. Reginald Mather had collected the mail a few days earlier and she saw now that his debonair, smart presentation was in complete contrast to his wife. Mrs. Mather now stood imperiously in the doorway, her cane momentarily at rest, giving the appearance of being about to thwack someone's calves. Her grey hair had been twisted into a bun, from which much of it now escaped, and contrary to her somewhat military bearing, she was wearing a faded, dark blue dress with a man's belt cinched vigorously about her waist. Her eyes, though a somewhat rheumy and washed-out blue, had a wild and penetrating quality.

"Good morning, ladies," she bellowed. She looked annoyed that there should be anyone but herself in the post office. She eyed Lane critically.

"You'll be the new girl, then," she commented and then turned away as if the addition of a new member to their community were an everyday occurrence, instead of something that had only happened twice in the last thirty years.

Eleanor glanced at Lane, gave an imperceptible shrug,

and then looked pleasantly at Mrs. Mather. "I have some lovely sweet peas today, Alice," she said.

"I'm off!" said Lane, collecting her cucumbers and letters. Mrs. Mather deigned to glance back at her and lifted her cane in a brisk salute.

"See you tomorrow, love!" cried Eleanor.

The screen door swung closed, and the voices of the two older ladies disappeared behind Lane. She took a great breath and walked across the grassy yard of the post office, past Kenny Armstrong's new truck, a gleaming red 1940 Ford. She smiled at it. Eleanor had told her he'd used a horse and wagon until this year and now suddenly he'd precipitated himself into the modern world. It took him twenty minutes now to drive down to the wharf to pick up the mail. His horse, which had retired to the meadow that ran along the roadway to the post office, was tearing up mouthfuls of grass contentedly.

She walked up the dirt road until she came to the little path through the bank of birch trees that made the border between her place and the Armstrongs'. The birches, with their leaves quivering in some almost imperceptible gentle movement of air, looked fragile and incongruous amidst the looming fir that occupied every space that had not been carved away and planted into orchards and gentler, more domestic species. A wooden footbridge carried her over the gully and she emerged from the copse of trees into the sight of her house. She loved this moment. She hoped she'd never stop loving that first sight of the house as she came across the bridge. The White House. Home of Lady Armstrong, late of this Saint Joseph's parish. And sure enough, the windows of the attic were again cast wide open as if an elated young woman longed to see the shadows of the cumulus cross the surface of the lake. She enjoyed the fantasy that Lady Armstrong occupied the hereafter opening her windows. She would set up her typewriter today, she thought. Perhaps the old lady would be something of a muse.

It came to pass that on Sunday, June 16, in weather people declared was more August than June, Eleanor Armstrong made good on her promise to welcome Lane properly to King's Cove by inviting her to the annual vicar's tea party. Perhaps lulled by the general lack of society she had become accustomed to in the days since she'd arrived, Lane stepped into what felt like a hubbub when Kenny swung open the screen door of the little cottage. Where the house was usually quiet except for the crackling of wood in the stove, or the scraping of branches along the roof at the back of the house during a midday breeze, now there was a veritable din of voices, and a loud and vigorous woman's laugh.

"What on earth?" she asked Kenny. "Where have all these people sprung from?"

To which he merely nodded his white head and smiled. "Come on through. Everyone is waiting, and the tea is just at its perfect pitch. Eleanor is about to pour." Befuddled by what she had thought would be an event with about six people, Lane followed Kenny through to the back porch where a comfortable array of rattan furniture and a swing seat were all occupied by an assortment of people. A couple of younger men and three small boys were seated on various levels of the steps down to the lawn. The boys were drinking something cold and iced-tea-looking from glasses and had already gotten hold of some cake.

"Wonderful!" cried Eleanor. "Our new neighbour has arrived! Everybody, this is Lane. She has, I'm sure you have heard by now, settled in to my late mother-in-law's house across the way." All faces turned toward Lane now, except for two of the little boys, who were occupied in a tussle over who got the larger piece of cake. Eleanor showed her to a seat, just vacated by a short dark man, who had jumped up the minute Lane came in. "Tea with?" she asked Lane.

"Milk and sugar. Two. Thank you." This attention was acutely embarrassing, Lane found, used as she was to being, as she saw it, rather unimportant.

Eleanor sensed her discomfiture, and whispered, "Don't worry, my dear. It is the annual summer tea that we throw for the vicar. Have a sandwich. You'll need it!" Eleanor looked at a plate of sandwiches of such beauty, variety, and delicacy that they would be at home at a pre-war tea at her aunt's house in Surrey. Selecting something that looked like it might be cucumber with a few intensely green chives poking out of it, she was just considering a bite when the man with the two children plunged forward, holding out his hand.

"Hi! I'm Dave. Bertolli. The squabbling boys are mine, as is the woman trying to pry them apart. We've only been here three years, so we will count as 'new people' together."

Lane wrestled briefly with the difficulty of balancing her as-yet-untouched sandwich on the edge of her saucer in order to free up a hand, which he took and shook warmly. He looked, she thought, like a good man. His face was open and his dark eyes, given a cast of worry by brows that gathered slightly at the bridge of his nose, looked kindly into hers. She took an instant liking to him, and he had a charmingly American accent.

"Hi, yourself. Lane Winslow. I think Kenny told me you live up the hill toward the east. I'm barely getting a sense of the layout. I can't believe three years would qualify you as a new person. I've only been here a minute!"

"Oh my dear, you have no idea. Though I think people will take to you quicker, being English and all. We Yanks don't rate very highly, and our last name's Bertolli. American Italians. We might as well be from Mars."

"How do you find yourself here? It seems very far away from anywhere, really."

"I'm a composer and I've come out to write, as a matter of fact. I got sick of the rat race in New York, and my old man the shopkeeper died and left me with a bundle and instructions to keep the business going. I figured he wouldn't care where he is now, so I sold up to my brother and came out to the quietest place I could find. We got an old log cabin and have added on to it and stuck a grand piano in it and it's as dandy is it can be. The boys love the country life, and Angela has been doing okay. She's a painter, though it's hard to get much done with that bunch. She's ecstatic to have a friend younger than sixty!"

"Here, Bertolli, make room for the rest of us!" This exhortation came from a man in his early thirties, who smoothed his straw-blond hair back as he approached Lane.

Dave stepped out of the way, his mouth betraying the slightest grimace, and turned to look over the cake tray. Lane took a hasty bite of her cucumber sandwich, as she saw that she might be pinned in this chair for the foreseeable future, her tea getting cold and her food untouched. She had also caught sight of the cake tray, feeling a flicker of concern about the depredations that the Bertolli family as a whole seemed intent on making upon it.

"Sandy Mather, son of the household of the same name. Mater is over there and, between us, is on the eccentric side, and the pater is outside scowling at the way Armstrong has pruned his apple trees, no doubt. How do?" He too, like David Bertolli before him, put out his hand for her to shake. Any resemblance, however, ended here. His hand had a slightly damp feel that instantly caused her to recoil, in spite of its firm grip, and his face seemed to her to loom much too close to hers.

"How do you do?" she asked formally, extricating her hand as quickly as possible. She glanced almost unconsciously toward Mrs. Mather, who was holding forth to a woman with grey hair rolled along the nape of her neck in a style that pre-dated the first war. Seeing the woman's hairdo and even this almost old-fashioned tea made Lane think of the ex-pat British community she'd grown up in. That phenomenon of time stopping for émigrés, while England moved on and was nearly unrecognizable, had overwhelmed her grandmother when she'd had to move to Scotland from Riga in the early months of the war. Lane brought her eyes back to the son. "I do very well, especially now. We haven't had a pretty woman here in an age. Absolutely everyone is over fifty. I've been withering here, socially speaking."

He gave her an ingratiating smile, which caused some inner voice in her to say, Oh dear. She smiled politely and then looked quickly down, feeling more trapped than ever.

"Lane, my dear, please come and let me introduce you to the vicar. Would you mind letting her go for just a moment, Sandy? There, thank you so much." Eleanor had Lane by the hand, somehow miraculously insinuating a plate with a delicious-looking bit of walnut cake into it, and was leading her down the steps toward the garden where two men were standing with their hands behind their backs in unconscious imitation of one another, looking up at a tree. The afternoon was warm wherever the sun fell, and the leaves that had been a suggestion when she had first driven up the hill from the Nelson road in April with the house agent were well on their way to fully clothing their parent trees on this lovely mid-June day.

"Thank you," Lane said to her in a stage whisper before she turned her face brightly to the two men. One she knew was Mather, the other, she assumed, must be the vicar. This proved to be the case and now, not trapped in a chair and having consumed all but the crumbs on the tips of her fingers of the excellent cake, she gave herself with restored equanimity to the task at hand. The vicar proved to be charming and extremely well versed in just about everything. He came originally from Kent, though he had left it as a young man twenty years ago just after his ordination. "Anxious to convert the Canadian heathens!" he laughed. "Do you know Reg Mather?"

"Yes, he's one of the people I do know. We met in the post office here. How are you, Reginald? Your son tells me you are an expert on pruning."

"Oh, I used to toil in the apple orchard like everyone else. I'm hoping to diversify. You know, one thing or another. How are you getting along?" He smiled at her in a pleasant, avuncular way that made her think about how different a father and a son could be. The father, a man in his mid-sixties she estimated, clearly had at one time been a good-looking man. Tall and straight with a bearing that suggested an innate sense of superiority. His hair, thick and just starting to speckle toward grey, was, in a reflection of his personality, the aggressive opposite of his son's thin, fair hair, and made him still a striking specimen. Lane could not shake the feeling, however, that he too was turning his charm on her and seemed intent on managing her in some way. Perhaps father and son had something in common after all.

"I'm getting along fine, thank you. I've settled in and am just keeping an eye on what is coming up in the flowerbeds. Mostly weeds I fear at the moment; it's been five years since Lady Armstrong died. Kenny, I think, has had a hand in keeping the orchard shipshape. I don't know how he does it all!"

"Oh, I think you'll find us like pioneers, Miss Winslow. A strong breed of man grows up out in the British Columbian climate. Some a damn sight too strong for their own good." This observation was delivered suddenly and darkly at the sight of another figure coming off the stairs and into the garden.

Lane couldn't resist asking. "Who is that? I've seen him sort of at a distance once or twice in an orchard adjacent to my place."

"Robin Harris. An unpleasant and taciturn member of this otherwise excellent community. Shell shock, don't you know. I think you will find him a tiresome neighbour, should he ever take a dislike to anything you do. My advice is to avoid crossing his land, gumming up his creek, or otherwise bothering him and you should be fine. I can't think what induced him to come to this. He never sticks his head into the church, so it's certainly not for the vicar. Eleanor must have a remarkable hold on him to get him through that barbed wire fence and into the light of day!"

In any event, the mystery of how Eleanor had gotten Harris off his property and out to a tea, which beverage he didn't touch, was solved by Harris himself when he was introduced to her by Kenny.

"Came to see who you were," he said, his hands thrust into the pockets of a decidedly informal pair of overalls. He wore an expression that Lane would have described as "lowering" except that this was something you'd do when you were angry and clearly his face was set in this growly expression all the time.

Moved by what pain might be encompassed in the term "shell shocked," she put out her hand, saying, "How do you do?" and was obliged to take it back again when he made no move to remove his hands from his pockets.

"You planning to work the orchard?" was his next query.

He could, she decided, be fifty but he looked, perhaps because of his demeanour, closer to sixty. Like nearly everyone she had met, he had a still-discernible trace of an English accent, as though they had all come here as children.

"I'm not terribly sure. At the moment, I'm just getting my bearings. It's been beautifully kept up though," Lane said, taken aback by the question. In truth, she did not see herself in coveralls with pruning shears but perhaps, between writing books . . .

"Oh, do leave her alone, Harris," came the sudden voice of Sandy Mather. He took her by the elbow and steered her away, toward the newly dug vegetable bed. "He's a dreadful old bore," he confided to her. "I felt I was well on my way to finding out what a beautiful young woman is doing burying herself out in this godforsaken place when you were whisked from me."

Lane considered whether the young bore was a good exchange for the old one and tried to decide how to tell him as little as possible about herself, as she was convinced that any information would be unsafe with him. "I'm just seeing how I like it out in Canada," she managed, and then, "I do beg your pardon. I'm just going to help Eleanor." She was sorry to invent this excuse but she didn't think she could bear another moment of being pounced on. Taking refuge in the kitchen, she said to Eleanor, "What a lovely tea! It's like the great pre-war teas of my childhood. What can I do?"

Eleanor laughed. "You mean, whom should you try to stick close to? Tired of the Mathers? Let me recommend the Hughes, mère et filles. They are harmless and wonderful gardeners. They're over there by the lilac." She pointed to a trio of women presided over by the older woman with whom Mrs. Mather had been talking earlier. The chair vacated by Mrs. Mather now beckoned invitingly.

After a much more pleasant interlude with another piece of cake, chocolate this time, and the blameless Hughes, Lane finally made her apologies to Eleanor and was relieved to see that gathered at the front door, also ready to leave, were the Bertollis, whose children had probably reached their limit of exhibiting the behaviour required for one of these formal English teas.

Angela Bertolli turned on Lane with a great warm smile. "My dear Lane. Follow the road up, take a right at the Mathers' imposing stone abode and turn in at the second drive about half a mile along. It is a lovely walk, and I will give you lunch one day soon. I must get to know you without the throng. Agreed?" Lane was delighted to accept this abrupt invitation, and, with a wave, walked the path back to her quiet house.

CHAPTER THREE

IT WAS A FEW DAYS later, after having breakfasted and tidied up, that Lane was trying to decide if she should finally sit down in front of her typewriter and really give some serious consideration to beginning a literary career, or if she should gird up her loins and go into her barn, something she'd avoided thus far, fearing she knew not what. Rodents, she supposed. Standing at her door, she gazed at her bedraggled pond under the weeping willow. It wasn't that she hadn't been writing at all. Her notebook was beside her bed, with a pen and a bottle of ink. That night, she'd had a bad dream in which a bomb had exploded right by her and she knew she was going to die. She had woken petrified and scarcely able to move. There was a grey light coming in the window and she saw that it was four in the morning. Blearily she had reached out for the light, switched it on and had taken up her notebook and pen, holding them on her chest as if still trying to recover her aplomb.

We dropped like ashes out of the night
to settle some secret list of scores

but how we longed for our enemies to take flight
and we to return to the sunlit shores

She often scribbled small poems into the pages of her leather-bound book. It distressed her to fill the pages with what she feared was drivel, and unconnected drivel at that, but she knew that writing anything was better than writing nothing. She'd imagined she would write books about love and war but she found she was too close to it and everything sounded wrong. Only her dreams seemed true to her, as illogical and dark as they were, if she tried to remember them. Having written these words, she put the book aside and said determinedly to herself, "I'm going back to sleep." In the dark, the blankets pulled up around her ears, she did indeed sleep.

The morning streaming through the curtains was so lovely, like the mornings of her childhood—fresh, clean, full of promise—that she decided against the still-unexplored barn just so she could be outside. She would evaluate what it would take to bring her pond back. She went outside and picked her way through the unmowed grass. She was just leaning over the pond to assess its condition when Sandy Mather stepped out from behind the willow, nearly stopping her heart.

"Sorry, Miss Winslow. I was just coming back from the post and thought I'd stop in and see how you were." He was wearing a short-sleeved summer shirt and a well-pressed pair of tan trousers.

Certainly not dressed for any sort of agrarian work, she thought uncomfortably, and he now was standing with his hands in his pockets, somehow managing to look unsure.

Blast, she thought. He must have been hovering there trying to decide if he should come knock. I shall have to invite him in, I suppose, and then wondered if she could get away with saying she was just off to the post herself.

"I'm just off to the post office myself now, actually. But I'm fine, really. It's very kind of you to ask." For some reason she had trouble looking into his face. Instinctively she worried that it would give him ideas. He had come on strongly at the tea and she'd been pleasantly surprised not to have had to deal with him in the intervening days, though she'd seen him twice at the post office.

"Oh, well, that's all right. I'll walk you over there."

They walked in silence for a few minutes. She had absolutely no idea what to say to him that she could trust would not be some sort of encouragement. "Your mother is well?" she asked, and then immediately regretted it. Eleanor had said it was more or less hush-hush that Mrs. Mather had "spells." Now what? So much for her devotion to secrecy.

Sandy coloured. "You've heard then, I suppose. Who hasn't? It's not something easy to hide is it, your mother being mad."

Lane stopped, appalled. "Oh, I am sorry Sandy, I didn't mean . . ."

"No, it's quite all right. Everyone around here pretends that's she's just 'eccentric.' Even I do. It's ridiculous, truth be told. I knew you weren't just asking after her health. You've heard something. That's it, really, isn't it? Everyone pretends to your face, but talks behind your back." Sandy stood on the path with his hands still in his pockets, looking down. Lane was wordless. She felt she ought to put a consoling hand on his arm, but could not. Well, it was out now.

"Sandy, I am really sorry. It's really none of my business. It must be very difficult for you. I, I . . . really didn't know."

"No, of course you didn't. It's what you heard, though, isn't it? That she's mad. I've heard the name, 'Mad Mather.' You can't keep any secrets, even in a place like this where everyone lives a mile away from everyone else. If you must know, she's not actually mad, in the way most people understand. Not crazy. She just gets these terrible moods and she becomes paranoid and angry. Other times she's brilliant. I mean that literally, brilliant, clever, funny, she talks a mile a minute. It's not so bad now, honestly. It was hard growing up. Between Dad thinking I was a total waste of time and her being peculiar, the only relief I had was going away to school in Vancouver."

Lane looked at him and tried for something like sympathy. She did feel sorry for him. All that bravado and annoying male behaviour was covering up this ongoing misery. "Why did you come back from Vancouver? Did you study for a career there?"

He barked an ironic laugh. "You might well ask! I did study for a career. I studied agriculture. I got out of having to enlist just at first on that basis and then I signed up when I'd done my degree. Things didn't quite work out and I was obliged to leave after training, so I never went overseas, for which the pater has never forgiven me. He disowned me for that, you know. He thought I'd done something dishonourable—that I was a coward! Such a funny attitude for a man who didn't serve a day in his war! I was getting the bloody degree to help him, there's the irony! I came back to help him set up a mill for producing board feet of lumber for the war effort; Mum's idea, by the way, and he completely botched the whole thing. So here I am, no prospects and a useless degree. I should leave. I've been planning it." These last words were said in a slightly defiant tone, his chin lifted. "There, I'm being boring, aren't I? Let's get you off to the post office. I'll drop you at the roadway and get back to the madhouse."

They crossed the bridge and he bowed slightly, smiling into her eyes. "Thanks for listening. Sorry about the outburst. I hope you will allow me to make it up to you. I could take you fishing on the lake. I have a lovely little boat. What do you say?"

Lane smiled back at him, still feeling an internal struggle. "That might be nice. Thank you." With a sinking heart she turned off to her little bridge and wondered what she had agreed to. Perhaps he would forget the offer.

THE BUCOLIC ATMOSPHERE of her new community was somewhat shaken a few days later. Lane was pleased to find herself invited to proper lunch with Angela and David Bertolli and their wild brood. She put on a flowered dress that she had bought in France just after the war. It was, one had to admit, outdated now but had been a very expensive dress in the thirties and it had been refurbished by an enterprising French seamstress. She had loved it on sight and its golden calla lilies and blue-hued background set off her dark hair to perfection. Aside from going to church she'd hardly had an opportunity to dress up. Though there was only the lightest breeze, she slipped a yellow cardigan over her shoulders and lifted her foot onto the kitchen chair to tie on her espadrilles. She went into her bedroom to tilt herself slightly before her vanity mirror to try to see the total effect. Her hair hung loose to her shoulders and swung over her eyes as she bent over. Seeing herself in the dress produced a pang of missing Yvonne. They had been together, laughing in delight at the good fortune of finding the dress and Yvonne had told her of plans to hold a party and invite "some people" for Lane to meet. A man was what she meant. But Lane had left France before this party ever materialized. A good thing, she thought. She was unsuitable as a companion for any man at this point.

Now she was at King's Cove where there was hardly any danger of men, only Angela's rambunctious children. Lane left her house and stood for a moment on the porch with her key in her hand, then turned away from the door with a smile. She would not have to lock her house here. She dropped the key into the pocket of her cardigan, wondering at her own deep momentary sense of contentment. The sun, she thought, the green, must scrub and filter away the darkness, as if her fearsome nights belonged to someone else. When she reached the crossroads she saw that there was a path heading into the forest that looked to be going in a direct line to the Bertollis'. Angela had told her about this path. She would take it today, she decided, and, parting the bushy fronds of fern that had grown over the beginning of the path, walked into the muted and dappled light of the forest.

The path was slightly overgrown but it seemed nevertheless to be an old and well-used one, where two could have walked abreast for much of it. It wound downhill and then it met another path that climbed gently toward an opening in the woods. She came out of the trees and was at the edge of a meadow that was alive with fluttering and buzzing insects. Swallows swooped around her out of nowhere as she crossed, skimming through the grass as if they were there to guide her way. Throwing her arms out, she turned and turned, drinking in the warmth and smell of grass and wildflowers, and the intense blissful green silence held in by the forest surround. The path came out through a little border of trees onto the road, she saw the expanded and modernized Bertolli cabin come into view. She came off the path on to the road and walked another fifty yards to their long, winding driveway. Dogs immediately began to give the alarm. She was about to take the whole trip around the driveway when she saw that a little diagonal trail cut directly up to the house. She could hear David shouting, "Shut up, will you?" and Angela saying, "Dave, don't say shut up. The children will learn it," and then from her, "Oh, do shut up, it's only Lane. Lane! Come on up. Don't mind them. I'd be more worried about being bitten by the children than the dogs!"

Lunch was served at a picnic table on the porch. The children, Philip, Rolfie, and Rafe, were allowed to eat in their treehouse just off the kitchen door, and so the grownups sat in perfect contentment eating lovely chicken broth for starters and then chicken salad sandwiches, with a bottle of French wine.

"This is wonderful. I can't quite get used to all the lovely food after years of Spam in my little bedsit. Where did you get this wine? It's heavenly!" Lane said, leaning happily on one elbow, her plate moved to one side. She looked up at the tops of the trees that provided the shade they were enjoying on the porch.

Dave said, "Consider yourself very much honoured. I brought that one out from New York when we moved here. We never had an occasion before now."

Lane had sat up and was about to say, "Well, I am honoured," when a shot rang out.

The dogs leaped into action, and the children began shouting in high-pitched voices, "What's that, Mommy?"

Dave jumped up and took Lane and his wife by the arm and half-dragged them to the door. "Go on! Into the house! Keep down. I'll get the children."

There was another shot that caused Lane to duck automatically and plunge, bent to half her height, into the open door to the living room. Dave had gone around to the other side of the house and she could hear him somehow over the near-hysterical barking of the dogs, exhorting the boys to hurry. Angela knelt on her hands and knees and called out the door to the dogs. "Come on, you stupid mutts! Lassie, stop that racket and get in here!"

Eventually the dogs were got in and shut into the kitchen, where they continued to bark and hurl themselves at the kitchen door. The humans were sitting on the floor against the wall with their feet stretched out before them. There was another shot that sounded as if the shooter had covered a good deal of distance since the first shot, and the direction was toward them.

"For God's sake, Dave, what is it? Can you just peek over the window and see?"

"Thank you very much!" he said acerbically, but he turned and slowly put his head up to the window and then he shot back down with an oath. "It's that bloody Mrs. Mather! She's got a rifle and pair of rubber boots and she is shooting right on our driveway. I should have known. She's as crazy as coot, that one!"

Angela closed her eyes for a moment in something like exasperation. "This is not the first time, I'm sorry to say, though she was not shooting right in our yard last time. Last time it was in the forest. She claimed she was hunting. Dave, phone Reginald. He'll know what to do. I'm going to check on the boys." The boys had been sent upstairs to their room, which was on the other side of the house with a window that looked out on a downward sweep of heavy brush and trees. They could be heard playing with their Dinky cars on the floor, as if gunfire were par for the course, like the barking dogs and their mother's enthusiasms.

Angela hurried on her hands and knees to the stairs while Dave crawled into the hall to the telephone. "What's Reginald again?" he called after his wife.

"Four-four-seven."

Dave, safely in the hall, sat at the little hall table and dialled. "Sandy? Is that you? Is Reginald there? Oh. Listen, your mother is over here with a rifle. She's shooting rather close to the house. I'm not sure why, no. Yes. Oh, I see. Well, we're worried about the boys and we can't really go out of the house. All right. Thanks very much."

He slid back on to the floor with Lane and pulled the bottle of wine toward them, offering her another drink. Angela came and flopped down next to them. Another blast from the rifle shattered her next sentence, which ended, ". . . very quiet for a change."

"Sandy's coming over. He says Reg is out somewhere."

"Honestly, it sounds like she'll be on the porch in a minute," Angela said.

Lane realized they'd been having to speak loudly the whole time because the dogs had kept up a steady protest in the kitchen since the beginning of the drama. This suddenly became louder and more intense and they could hear a car approach, turn in to their driveway, and stop.

"Come on, Mother," they heard through the open window.

"Cougar. Came right through our garden and along here. The Yanks have children, you know."

"Yes. I know. I'm sure they'll send you a thank-you card. Give me that. Thank you, now hop in and I'll make you a cup of tea at home."

Mrs. Mather said something else, but it was lost as she disappeared into the car. The door slammed and in a few seconds they could hear the grinding sound of a car being backed down the narrow driveway to the road.

The lunchers sat for a few minutes in the silence that followed this interaction. The dogs had stopped barking and had settled with an audible humph against the door of the kitchen. Lane suddenly realized that there were lovely paintings on the wall. They appeared to be scenes of farming country, and great trees casting shade across a green landscape. Angela's, she supposed. Finally, Dave spoke, "I brought a case of that wine with me. I think we'd better open another bottle. I had been saving it for an occasion, but I don't think it could get much more occasional than this, do you?"

Later, Dave drove her home against only the weakest protests. Between the admittedly defused danger of being shot by Mrs. Mather and the possibility of meeting a cougar, Lane felt, she had to confess, considerably less brave about the journey home.

CHAPTER FOUR

"YOU KNOW, JUST OUT HERE there's a path that runs up the hill to that fantastic villa of the Hughes' behind us here. You should go up and see the place. Her garden is enormous, and I'm sure they'd be very pleased. They were perhaps slightly put off that they hadn't got to speak to you much at the vicar's tea." It was the day after the exciting lunch with Angela, and Eleanor Armstrong was leaning on the wooden counter of her post cubby. Today it had been sweet peas to make up for there being nothing for Lane in the post.

"I do feel bad about that. I didn't get much of chance, with Sandy hanging about. I sat with them for only a few moments, resplendent in their flowered frocks. I'd like to go see them, though I cannot imagine they have a garden more wonderful than yours!"

"My dear, there's three of them at it all the time and they've got a much bigger space. They also keep chickens. We get our eggs from them. They're quite self-sustaining, that trio. Only one of them drives, Mabel, and they all get into those frocks and go off to town every couple of weeks to get a few supplies. Otherwise they wear trousers and Wellingtons every day but Sunday."

"Why are there no men?" asked Lane, though instantly felt it an inappropriate question, especially given her own status. "Sorry. None of my business!"

"Oh, quite all right, my dear. It's only me you're talking to! It's the usual sad tale, I'm afraid. The old lady's husband died in 1910, of a heart attack. Homesteading in the eighties was very difficult, and I think he just got tired, poor man. Gwen was engaged to Kenny's poor younger brother John." She paused for a moment and then sighed. "Mabel never did seem to find anyone. They're really quite plucky, the three of them. The old lady must be seventy-five if she's a day."

Lane walked home deep in thought about the effect of war on women and then moved on to the effect of war on people in general. Everyone at King's Cove seemed affected somehow by this sense of loss. It made people variously strong and dignified, like the Armstrongs, who had lost a brother, or bitter like Harris. The people who didn't have wars, she decided, could never bridge that gulf of understanding, not really. The Bertollis seemed just a layer lighter than herself.

The sweet peas looked delighted to be in a deep blue, glass vase she had brought from Riga before the war that had somehow survived her wandering course across the world. She wasn't given to nostalgia, but she stroked the rounded bowl of the vase lightly with her fingers when she arranged it in the centre of her kitchen table.

"Right," she said out loud and looked about for what she might bring to the Hughes' house. She had an extra box of English biscuits for tea; they were chocolate-covered fingers and she decided that even self-sufficient ladies who mined their own tea and cookies from the forest would like chocolate.

She put on a clean blouse and, box of biscuits in hand, set off back toward the post office so that she might use the path, as yet unexplored by her, that went up the hill behind their house to the Hughes'. She arrived at the edge of the property quite breathless from both the climb and the sudden beauty before her, looking at a large, rambling wood-frame house painted a deep, old-fashioned green with rich cream trim on the many window and dormer frames. A lawn that seemed endless meandered like a green river around flowerbeds of every shape; islands of riotous colour. Would she ever have a garden like this? Not bloody likely, she decided. A pair of small cocker spaniels came up and sniffed around her feet but, amazingly, did not bark. Finally, one of them trotted away and gave a couple of yaps, as if to say, "We have a visitor, you'd better come along!"

Lane stooped down and patted the head of the remaining creature and then she heard a grizzled female voice halloo-ing. She looked up to see the tall, stringy, elderly woman whom Lane recognized as the Hughes mater, dressed, as Eleanor had said she would be, in baggy, ancient blue trousers and a pair of Wellington boots. She was removing her gardening gloves as she approached, striding with a litheness and speed that completely belied her age. "Hello!" she called out. "Come along, we were about to take a break. We've got some tea on the brew, I think. The girls will have that in hand."

Lane was ushered in through the kitchen screen door to greet the "girls," Gwen and Mabel, both of whom looked very nearly the age of their mother, Gladys, and were dressed in trousers as well, only with slippers on their feet, as the Wellingtons had all been abandoned in the mudroom through which they'd navigated. She noticed that both of the younger women had the nicotine-stained fingers of seasoned smokers and indeed she spotted a can of tobacco and a small rolling machine along the sideboard by the sink. She hoped they were not inclined to smoke with tea. For some reason she had never taken to it herself, though she had tried when she had first moved to London. It was terribly sophisticated, she knew, but she never liked how giddy it made her feel and besides, she got plenty of smoke from those around her in the pubs, and in the noisy plane rides over the water to France, since the men around her all smoked like factories.

The biscuits were very well received, leapt on by the ladies with alacrity. The cocker spaniels benefited as well, as each of the women broke off bits of cookie to drop surreptitiously on to the nose of the nearest dog.

"How are you finding everything, my dear?" asked Gwen, squinting at Lane. She had glasses on a string around her neck.

"Everyone has been lovely," Lane said. "It's such a beautiful place and the Armstrongs' old house is just the ticket for me."

"Harris hasn't been bothering you?" Mabel asked, with a short bark that might have been a laugh.

"I've met him at the post office. He does seem grumpy,

but I can't say he's been bothering me. What sort of bothering might I expect?"

"Grumpy, do you call it? He's got a savage temper and he still jumps at any loud noise. He never tried it on with Old Lady Armstrong because he went off to war with her youngest son, John, and came back without him. I don't know what happened there, but I've always been suspicious because he gets so angry when anyone mentions John. He's never been right since the war."

"Yes, Mother, you're going off track now, aren't you? The question Miss Winslow asked was how might Harris be a bother." Mabel turned away as she said this and her eyes closed momentarily in what looked like tired exasperation.

"If I know Harris, he'll be watching whether your animals wander onto his side of the fence and whether you've done something to the water. You have the misfortune to be on the same creek. Unfortunately, we all get creek troubles from time to time; the screens get clogged and someone has to slosh in and clean them out. He'll get shirty about having to clean it out himself now you're here; he'll want to blame you. It will be most satisfying for him. We, happily, are on the upper creek with the Armstrongs. If you get a dog he'll phone you and demand you keep it from barking. He'll object if you drive back from town too late at night because it wakes him up when people are changing gears coming up the hill here in their motorcars. Well, he comes by it honestly, I suppose."

Mabel shook her head in a way that indicated that she concurred. "He certainly does. It's the shell shock, I expect. He didn't come back till '20, and he was an absolute fright.

And of course that silly woman from town he married had absconded. I've always thought . . ." At that she stopped herself, cleared her throat and had a great swallow of tea. "Would you like to get eggs from us, Miss Winslow? They're lovely layers, our birds."

As Lane was saying, "Please call me Lane and yes, I'd love to get on the egg rota," Gwen said, with a dark expression, "You've always thought what, Mabel?"

Mabel shook her head and moved a frizzy wisp of greying hair away from her face. "Oh, it's nothing. Rubbishy thoughts. Nonsense." She got up and began to clear her cup to the low, battered white enamel sink that sat beneath the window.

"No, I want to know. You were always horrible about John, is this that stupid old story again? That John could even be interested in that pathetic, stupid woman is ridiculous. You never fail to bring it up."

Mabel turned to her and said, "Gwen, darling, it has nothing to do with your John. If anything, she was setting her cap at everyone. I only mentioned once, years ago, that I thought she'd set her cap at him. She wouldn't have had any luck, would she? John only had eyes for you and he was a lovely boy. I only meant that I think she did somehow succeed with someone while Harris was in France with John, because I thought she might have left because she'd gotten in trouble. There, I said it. And it's slanderous, isn't it, because for all I know she is dead. She'd be about fifty-five now, wouldn't she? An old lady. None of it matters now, does it?"

"Do you mean Harris's wife?" Lane asked. Gwen looked guiltily away, but said nothing.

Old Mrs. Hughes stood up and pushed back her chair noisily. "Stop this bloody awful row, would you? What's done is done. I, for one, am going to lie down. Harris is coming later in the afternoon with his noisy, smelly tractor to move the trees he cut out of the orchard last week. There, Miss Winslow, you must be shocked to hear us maligning a man upon whom, I'm afraid, we are rather dependent. He may be bitter but he is not lazy. I doubt, for example, that that idle specimen, Reginald Mather, would come to our aid if we were on fire. He's been here nearly as long as I have and I've never seen him do a hand's turn. Very lucky in his family, that one."

CHAPTER FIVE

JUNE EASED FORWARD WITH A surprising morning of light rain, and then settled back to what it had been: dry, hot, and uncompromising. A frittering wind had picked up, but even at this early point in the day, it seemed only to be moving masses of sluggish hot air from one place to another. Lane had tried to set a routine, but she was struggling to follow it. She was meant to be up with the sun, tea on the porch, and then breakfast and a good two hours of writing. As she had on the previous days, she sat now at the business end of this plan, facing a reproachful typewriter with a blank sheet of paper hanging out of it. She knew what the trouble was: she had no idea what she wanted to write. And she'd had no idea how difficult it was going to be. She had begun to write her poetry when she was young, before the war. She felt vaguely embarrassed now about these early efforts, but had not imagined it would be so very difficult to write something else. Poetry, after what she'd been through, seemed all she could manage. Stories? A novel? When she allowed her mind its freedom, it wandered compulsively back to the war, a subject she daren't tackle. For one thing, she wanted to leave the whole tiresome thing behind, and for another, she'd sworn an oath of secrecy and she did not trust herself to write about any of it, in case she wandered out of bounds.

She rested her fingers on the keys and thought, I'll just start with any old line and see what comes up. Resisting the temptation to write "The quick brown fox," she paused and then wrote:

I can stretch my hand across the fields of time
to pull a child from where she grew alone
and with a breath that might be mine
exhale a garden of her very own.

Well, she could see where that had come from. So much here—the beautiful days, the exuberant gardens of the Armstrongs and Hughes'—had set off explosions of memories of her childhood summers. Hence this drivel of sentiment. Proof positive that this was going to be hard. The alone part was right, she decided. Somehow, though she had been surrounded by people as a child: her grandparents, her nurse, even her distant father, she had always felt alone. Perhaps it was her mother dying, and her father being so forbidding. Or maybe everyone felt they were singular and solitary. The only intrusion into her aloneness had been Angus. She'd let her world expand to include him. When he'd died she had thought she could not go on and yet she found, alone again, that she was on familiar ground. She only thought now how glad she was it had happened. It would not matter that she would not get another shot at love. Some never even got what she'd had. Was it her grandmother or some friend, she could not remember, who had introduced her to that cliché? Yet she saw now that it was true. She stared at the page again. Should she be writing about that? About love? No. Not that either. It was the spaces in between things that she needed to capture and she could not think now what might be there, because what she could not bear to think about was in shadows. Still, she had promised herself she would never reject or erase anything and so she pulled the paper out of the machine and placed it neatly beside the Remington on the table. It would, she decided, soon have chums, and maybe some of them would be better.

Sitting in the sun reflecting on her near-maiden words on her new typewriter, she had just reached the conclusion that the rhyme-bound metre was stultifying when she became aware of the ticking of the clock in the thick silence of the morning. "Gorblimey!" she exclaimed aloud. These four lines and her subsequent ruminations had effectively dispatched two hours of her time.

Sandy would be here to pick her up for the fishing trip. She cursed under her breath and hurriedly packed the lunch she had offered to bring, with some misgivings. This "fishing trip" with Sandy; why had she agreed to it? She'd much rather be at the beach with Angela and any number of noisy boys. What increased her sense of unease, as she wrapped ham sandwiches in greaseproof paper, was that she knew she ought to pay attention to this feeling, not talk herself out of it. But still, she gave her head a little shake and placed the thermos of tea—she had decided against wine, which she would have taken on an English picnic—into the basket with two mugs. She had a fleeting thought that this packing of tea instead of wine was the one reflection of her misgivings. Reluctantly she placed her only remaining box of chocolate biscuits on top of the sandwiches.

She wondered if they would walk to the lake, or drive. She had been down to the lake and the wharf, but could not see where anyone kept boats. She took the filled basket off the table to heft it for weight and then put it back and looked down at her clothes. It was going to be hot and she wanted to wear shorts but, and she blushed at her own vanity, perhaps this would be more provocative than she wanted to be. She opted instead for a light cotton pair of short pants in a pale green, to make a concession to the coming heat, and a sleeveless shirt in Indian cotton with a waist tie. She put on her espadrilles and then worried that they were impractical if they were going to have to scramble along rocks on the shoreline, and ruefully put them away. They reminded her of Yvonne, and she felt a sudden gust of sadness. How she could have used the steadying influence of Yvonne in this crisis!

Tying on her canvas shoes, she chided herself. Honestly, it was all rubbish. She had misread Sandy at the beginning, but he had proved to be a decent fellow after all, and had the added attraction of being hard done by in his mad family. Going out on the lake with him for the day was going to be good fun. She had just completed this mental act of pulling up her socks when she heard the car at the top of the drive.

She took the basket and went to the door. Sandy was coming down the grassy path looking vaguely military in khaki pants and a tan shirt with short sleeves. He smiled broadly at her and reached out for the basket.

"You look nice!" he said.

She smiled, feeling suddenly like even saying thank you might commit her beyond what she felt comfortable with, and she looked past him at the car. A small white rowboat with a wide band of red was upturned and roped to the top of his little Morris.

As he negotiated the turns down to the lake, Sandy looked sidelong at her and asked, "Have you fished before?"

Lane thought about this. Such a common thing, fishing. But she had really done no more than stand by the river in Latvia as a child and throw in a line with her governess. She realized now it was a kind of pretend fishing. An "adventure" you would take a child on. It involved no messy catching or killing of actual fish. "No, not properly, in a boat."

"It's very relaxing. Did you bring a hat, by the way? It can get quite hot sitting on the lake." She hadn't but he had an extra, he told her as they pulled out to the end of the wharf. He untied the small boat and then she helped him lift it off the roof of the car and they carried it between them to the edge of the wharf and upended it into the water. The oars were tucked under the seats, and he fixed the rope into a metal ring. She unloaded the basket and then stood with it at her feet while he backed the car up to the little parking area at the top of the wharf. In the silence of the morning, the rhythm of the car moving over the heavy boards took its place in her mental encyclopedia of sounds.

When the car stopped and its engine was off, she just heard the slight sucking sound of water lapping under the wharf. It was a beautiful morning and she decided she was glad she had come.

Sandy expertly fitted the fishing rods, fish basket, net, and picnic basket into the boat and then held her hand as she stepped into the bow and settled onto the seat. He followed her and locked the oars into place.

"Ready?" She nodded, enjoying the liquid rocking as they pulled away. "We'll row around the point over there and into the next cove. I've had good luck there before."

They moved in silence, with only the sound of the oars hitting the water and the creaking of the oarlocks as Sandy got into the rhythm of pulling them out toward the point that marked the outer edge of the cove and into the open lake.

Lane looked out beyond Sandy, and tried to avoid looking at him as he moved toward and away from her. She found he was watching her, and the sudden intimacy of facing him the whole time made her uncomfortable. "It's beautiful."

Sandy looked at her and then turned away toward the lake and pointed toward the middle. "Did you know the river runs right through the middle of the lake? At the Nelson end it's really a river but here it is a true lake. Lovely fresh water. Perhaps later we'll swim, when we've had our lunch."

Lane felt herself colouring at this and was grateful for the hat she had borrowed, a cotton hat with a low but narrow brim that threw her eyes into shadow. She didn't bother saying coyly, “Oh, but I didn’t bring my swimming costume.” She wanted to glance at him to see if he was being flirtatious, or if he was just reflecting some local habit of going on the lake, having lunch, and swimming in or out of whatever clothes one had. Good God, she thought. How desperately innocent she was! She was alone with a man who knew she didn’t have swimming things. He was pushing to see how far he could go. “I don’t think so, thanks,” she said brightly.

Sandy smiled and shrugged and then looked behind him to adjust the direction of the boat. “Here we are,” he said eventually. Lane looked around and saw that they were in a much bigger curve of the lake and they could see what looked like the whole length toward the north, the blue-green mountains folding down to the edge on either side. The sky took on a deep azure intensity against the green of the mountains. It was mesmerizing. She could feel the weight of the water holding them on its surface and she found she would really like to have been alone and just bobbing and floating, letting her mind melt into the beauty around her. She resolved that she would get her own boat so that she could come here alone. This cheered her.

Sandy was pulling out a fishing rod and preparing it. She was slightly dismayed to see him pull out a jar with worms in it. Impaling worms on hooks was going to be required, she realized. She’d done it once, as a child, and she guessed now that that was probably why all her fishing expeditions with her governess were pretend. Sandy must have sensed her hesitation and competently baited her hook and handed her the rod.

"I'll go off this side, and you off that side," he said and swung his arm to send the line far out into the water. Lane watched his procedure and swung her arm as she'd seen him do, and was pleasantly surprised to see the weighted line sail off, more or less in the direction she'd intended. "Nice work!" he exclaimed, and began to slowly reel in his line.

They sat like this for some time. Lane settled into the quiet of it and wondered again why she had been so nervous, and indeed still had lingering misgivings, about the trip.

"See that long stretch of forest over there, leading up to the rocky outcrop?" Sandy touched her shoulder to make her look where he was pointing. She turned, letting her line go slack. The area he was pointing at was a dark, velvety green from where they were, leading in a long, gentle slope upward. She estimated it was just to the north of King's Cove. "That's going to be mine. My dad bought it. Its lower border abuts onto Harris's bit of forest."

"I didn't know Harris had a bit of forest," she remarked, but was remembering that Sandy had told her he had been disinherited. Did this mean things were better between father and son? Or had that just been a turn of phrase, meaning his father was furious?

"Yes, you know where the prospector cabin is? It's on his land. Father has been trying to buy his forest for as long as I can remember and Harris won't sell, which is ridiculous because he never does anything with it. It got pretty scorched in '19 and there's nice strong wood in there now. I'm having that too." He said this matter-of-factly.

"What are you going to do with it all?"

"Going to log it. There's a building boom on. King's Cove is going to become a real little hive of industry! I just have to get Harris to sell—the old bastard. 'Scuse the language, but he holds on out of spite. When I get my hands on it, things are going to look up around here."

Dismay flooded through Lane. She'd been stuck behind massive logging trucks that lumbered along the Nelson road from farther north, choking on their dust and feeling sorry for the community that was losing its forest somewhere up the lake. The bare patches of mountain where logging had already happened were a blight. She struggled to think of something to say, but could think of nothing but "Are you mad?" and decided against this.

The boat wobbled as Sandy turned full around to look at her. Oh God, she thought, he's going to see what I'm thinking, but to her surprise, he turned on her with a look of full seriousness.

"My father is a remittance man; did you know that? Do you know what that is? It's a useless git that someone in the old country wants to get rid of, so they pay him to stay away. That's my grand old dad! He doesn't want to log all this land he bought. He never had any intention of it. It's his way of pretending he's not useless. That's why he disowned me—because I can make it happen. He just wants to sit on the land and pretend he's a land owner with vast tracts, to show the people back home."

Lane glanced longingly at the shoreline. If this was going to be a long afternoon of Sandy expanding on his theme of being hard done by, all the sunny views in the world would not make it palatable. And she was confused.

She had thought Reginald wanted to log the cove; now Sandy was saying he had been disowned because he wanted to do it. She felt all at once that she couldn't be bothered with any of it. "You know, I'm feeling a little queasy, Sandy. Do you think we might go back?"

He looked stricken and reeled in his line. He laid his fishing rod along the floor of the rowboat, dripping into the puddle gathering at their feet. Reaching around her so that his arm curved around her back, he took her arm, his hand lingering for a moment on it. "Here you go, my girl. Not used to being on the water yet. You'll learn." She could feel his breath on her neck, as he leaned in from behind her. Then he wrenched the oars into place, and they were moving vigorously toward the shoreline, but not toward the wharf.

They crunched on to a small beach of combined pebbles and sand and Sandy leaped out of the boat into the shallow water, pulled it full on to the beach, and then held out a hand for Lane. Chagrined that having feigned sickness, she must now continue to appear weak, she allowed herself to be helped out and then reached in for the basket. Sandy pushed her gently away, his hand again lingering on her bare arm, and took the picnic out of the boat.

"Come, we'll set up here," he said, pointing at a spot under an elm tree that shaded an upper corner of the sandy area. It was lovely. She'd really wanted to go home but here she was on a "date" with a man it turned out she didn't like. It was not the first time. She remembered some wartime outings with men who had bored her rigid within minutes, but she'd had to stick out a whole evening, pretending to enjoy herself. This, she decided, was the rural equivalent. She spread out the blanket she had brought and opened the basket, while Sandy went back to the boat to pull the oars out of the locks.

"No wine?" he asked, when he saw the tea thermos, and then chuckled. "I thought you Limeys liked wine on picnics. Suppose it is early."

Lane was sitting cross-legged on the blanket, arranging the food she'd brought. At least it was beautiful, she thought, but it was going to be a strain if he was going to continue to be offensive. The lake before them was as still as the sky, and the sky was that intense shade of blue that she just could not get used to. In London you never got that kind of sky, even in the summer, when there were few coal fires lit. She remembered it from her childhood and it filled her with nostalgia now. She wanted to lie back, forget the lunch, and just stare upward through the green branches of the trees. The ever-attentive Sandy, however, put paid to this plan. She would, instead, have to think of a topic of conversation.

"You have never gone in for apples, like everyone else?" she said, handing him a paper-wrapped sandwich.

He frowned slightly, as if trying to remember. "My dad never did, no. I'd see all the others going out into their orchards during the season. I even had jobs when I was a teenager working for Harris during the picking season. Dad was always scornful of them. Dad's scornful of everyone." Sandy bit into his sandwich and stared out at the lake. "You know, he never liked me. When I'd done something wrong, he'd stop talking to me. He would act like I didn't exist. Funny thing is, I never knew when I'd done something wrong. I spent my whole life trying to please him, and for what? You know what he told me one time? I must have been fourteen. That he wished he had another son, one that was worthwhile. Can you imagine? I told my mother and she just looked blank, but I heard them shouting later."

Somehow Lane hadn't thought that bringing up the harvesting of apples would lead to another orgy of inappropriate self-revelation. As she had already several times that day, she felt like she was being forced into an intimacy with him. It struck her how far away from anyone else they were and she wondered, frantically, how far the main road was through the bush from where they were sitting. She imagined herself crashing about in the pathless wilderness and chided herself for an overactive imagination. He was harmless and pathetic, really. Still, she didn't know how to respond in such a way that would not lead to more uncomfortable disclosures. And she cursed herself for her curiosity; she was interested in what made people tick.

"I'm sorry. It all sounds difficult," she said, lamely.

"I shouldn't be maundering on about myself," he said, turning on her, suddenly bright. "Tell me about you. You've landed among us like an angel and we know nothing about you!"

With a sinking heart, Lane tried to think of what she could say that would not deepen this atmosphere of camaraderie. Why had she come on this bloody fishing trip? "There's nothing much to tell, really. I've moved here to begin a new life. I'm English, and I hope to be Canadian one day. I was left a little money by my grandmother, I've used it to buy the Armstrong house, and if I use it wisely, I should be able to live comfortably."

"A new life. That's intriguing. What was the old life, I can't help wondering, eh?" He winked at her, causing her to recoil inwardly. "I'd like a new life too," he added, suddenly reflective again. "We could begin a new life, you know." He said this so quietly that it allowed Lane a moment to pretend she hadn't heard it. In the midst of wondering how she could go on pretending she hadn't heard, she found to her horror that he'd reached out and seized her hand.

"I say . . ." she found herself saying weakly, extricating her hand. His hand even in these circumstances had that slightly clammy feel. He didn't try to hold it but he sat up and with his other hand picked up some sand and tossed it along the beach.

"Really," he said, "I've been thinking about this. You and I. Why not? We are young, we could combine our land and really do something."

"Are you proposing to me because I own land?" Lane wanted to laugh. She felt like a character in a Victorian novel. She didn't wait for an answer, but got up and began to pack up the basket. "Come on, get up. I've got to shake out the blanket. I should get back."

It all happened very fast. She was folding the blanket and suddenly he was there in front of her. She instinctively backed away, and found she was blocked by a tree. He pushed into her and seized her chin, pressing his fingers painfully into her face. She closed her eyes for an instant because of the pain, and his mouth was on hers, his tongue trying to pry her lips open. Without thinking, she pushed with all her might into his ribs with both hands, and he sprawled back on to the sand. Wiping her mouth, she looked at her handiwork, appalled.

"You bitch!" he said. "You're all the same, aren't you?"

Well, if that's how you approach women, probably, she thought angrily. With a flood of relief, she saw that he did not seem inclined to come at her again, but had seized the basket and was marching to the edge of the lake, where the boat bobbed gently.

THE CAR STOPPED at the top of the driveway. He said nothing as she got out. She'd held the picnic basket on her lap on the drive back, and she had kept her eyes straight ahead as they climbed the narrow curving road from the lake to the main road and then driven up into King's Cove. The day was now hot and still and they'd met no one on the road, but he had talked. About how he'd been watching her and knew what she wanted. Just another Brit coming out to get a man, he told her. Silent during his tirade, she wondered if the country was flooded with these desperate girls he conjured up. She was a fool. "You wait," he'd told her, "I will be like a god to you." At this she noted with relief that he was slowing the car at the top of her drive, because clearly he was barking mad, and she didn't want to go wherever it was he might decide to take her. "You have no idea," he'd said, "what I will do to get what I want." He stopped the car and sat for a moment staring out the front window. Perhaps he was taking in her barn and through the trees, her house, adding them mentally to some empire he was building.

Safe in her house, she heard him peel angrily on to the road. In the kitchen, she dropped the basket on a chair and looked at it with distaste, as though it had conspired in the events of the day. She would empty it later and then put it away. She would take the next picnic in her French shopping bag and she would be accompanied by a book. Or Angela and her mad boys, but no man. She had gone on this trip because . . . why? Because she had felt sorry for him? Or worse, was curious? She could not tell when a man was dangerous. She was not good at men. Angus didn't count. He had been older and had somehow taken her over. You could not learn from an experience like that how to handle the whole business of men. She threw open the doors onto the veranda and sat heavily in a deck chair that was resting with its companion in the shade of the overhanging roof. She'd put out two deck chairs with a little table for drinks and a book in between, as if there might one day be someone for the second one. She wrapped her arms tightly around herself—even in the heat of the afternoon she found she could not quite stop shivering.

The landscape before her was defiantly and richly beautiful, unconcerned with tribulations of any creatures living upon it. She was one woman, alone, far from anyone who could help or comfort—and, truth be told, she had been in shock before. You do not run messages behind enemy lines for the duration of a war without having memories to cope with. She told herself these things to remind herself that she had been here before and would survive until it passed. The first time it happened was when she had returned safely from a drop, and the plane had limped back to the base and nearly crash-landed after being damaged by enemy fire. Angus had been there then, the first time, and talked her through it, his arms around her. She had not been able to tell him what had really happened, had made up a motorcar accident. She had been horribly unnerved by her own fragility then and had tried to see it as a sort of human and predictable response. She was no more responsible for this mental and physical torment than she would be if she had cut her finger with a knife and it bled. It is what the human body does.

Amazingly, that night she slept a sound and almost dreamless sleep. At one point, she had the impression of a car in the distance and a sense that it was passing along a far road from where she stood in a French field. She woke with the curtains fluttering in a fresh and lovely stream of sun. She lay for a moment, staring at the white ceiling and remembering yesterday. It was as if sleep had washed away all traces but a fleeting memory of it, and a mental reminder to avoid his company whenever possible. She dressed, instead of lounging about in her pyjamas through coffee and toast as she usually did. There were things to do to get the place in hand. This would start with watering the garden before the sun got too hot.

CHAPTER SIX

LANE HADN'T PUT IN MUCH time with the garden, having decided, out of respect, to see what came up on its own, but what there were of Lady Armstrong's phlox and lupines could use some weeding and a drink. The post office first, she decided. She looked nervously at the bushes near the path just to be sure that Sandy was not lurking. All clear.

SHE'D FORGOTTEN IT was Sunday. No sense of time anymore, without the job marking off the days of the week for her. Days of the week seemed to be something she'd left behind in England. Eleanor had been in the garden, and sent her off with some early tomatoes. She had been quite understanding about the mix-up about Sunday. This was the Sunday that the vicar would not be doing a service at St. Joseph's, so quite easy to forget, my dear.

Lane put the tomatoes on the kitchen table and then realized that a slight feeling of letdown had returned with her from the Armstrongs'. She wanted a letter from her grandmother in Peebles, chiding her in the old familiar way. It would be a scent of home. What was it about grannies that allowed them to feel carte blanche to be disapproving? It was in the nature of the love they offered you. You couldn't get their unconditional love. That would be excessive, wasteful. It must come tempered with advice to return home and stop this nonsense. But of course, this was Lane's home. She mustn't engage in nostalgia. Perhaps tomorrow there would be a letter. No. Of course not. Eleanor had told her that July first was Dominion Day. There would be nothing then either. Thinking that a letter from Yvonne would also be nice, she set off to the side of the house where the hose was rolled neatly onto a wooden wheel. It wouldn't, she thought sadly, be neat when she finished with it. She'd love to think of France returned to normal. Perhaps Yvonne was planning a trip to the south in August as they used to do. Perhaps she'd met someone.

The hose, an ancient affair of a heavy, rubbery substance but too good to throw away, was difficult to pull out. It hadn't been used since Kenny, she presumed, had watered before she arrived. She blushed to think that was nearly a month ago. No wonder the beds looked so bedraggled compared to those of her industrious neighbours. She dragged the hose far enough to water the beds directly under the porch, set it down, and walked back to the tap, which was tight and needed oiling. She would get around to it one of these days. There was so much that wanted getting around to. She'd imagined vast swaths of time when she moved out here. She would establish a routine of writing until noon, have a lunch with bread she'd baked and tomatoes from her own garden, and then write for a few more hours in the afternoon.

She turned the tap full on and was dismayed to see nothing was coming out. Now what? The creek was not dried up. She thought she could hear it gurgling exasperatingly in the distance. She ran upstairs to the kitchen and turned the tap. There was a loud, damp, coughing sound, and then waterless silence. She would have to see if Kenny Armstrong had any ideas. The thought of being without water in this heat was daunting.

Just as she was leaving the house, the phone rang. It had a harsh clang that reminded her of the phones of her childhood in the '20s. Two longs and a short. Hers. She lifted the earpiece off the hook and said into the horn, "King's Cove 431."

"Lane, sweetie, is that you?"

"Yes, Angela. How are you?" Who but Americans would call you sweetie? she wondered with a smile. Dave had been right. Their "newness" to King's Cove did give them common cause and the locals had, as Angela had predicted, accepted Lane much more readily for her Englishness than they had Angela and Dave.

"Well, not that great. Something happened to Harris's water and he phoned and stormed at us that it was all our fault. Dave is furious. He was supposed to be spending the day composing and now this has happened. It's put him right off. You'd think Harris'd stop going on about us. It's been three years. It almost makes me want to go back to the States."

"Harris is a bad-tempered git. You know that! But I have no water either, which is a nuisance. The flowers are gasping, and I imagine I'll be wanting a cup of tea at some point."

"You and your bloody tea in the hot weather. If you don't get water back, why don't you come over here and have some down-home iced tea. Now that's a drink. The kids are ecstatic. They see me making iced tea and they think we're going to go camp on the beach for the rest of the summer."

Lane had wondered if the boys were, unwittingly, part of the offence offered by the arrival of this American family. Eleanor had told her there had once been children at King's Cove, enough to fill the small one-room school that still stood up the hill with an overgrown driveway leading to the door. That was before the first war. They had grown up and left to start up lives in cities, or die in the two wars, and now the absence of children was a kind of hollow echo in the long afternoons.

"I'm not sure I can," Lane said. "I think I'll have to tackle this water problem, though I haven't a clue. I'd better phone Harris."

Lane heard a muffled conversation between Angela and someone in her house and then Angela: "Dave will go see what he can do. He'll go help Harris. Let them cope. We've had this sort of thing before . . . I'm sure it's some sort of plugging up of the pipes."

It was thus decided. Lane was relieved. She didn't feel she could manage making the water work, though she never would have admitted it, because she had quite enough of people asking her how a young woman was coping out here on her own, as if she were homesteading in a sod hut in Saskatchewan instead of living in a fully plumbed and elegant, if slightly overwrought, Victorian house with a harmless, fresh-air-loving ghost.

Lane took her bathing suit off the porch railing, where she'd tossed it to dry after her last swim, and collected a towel. What could she bring? She was about to look in her fridge when she heard a sharp bang on the door.

"You were quick!" she called. "Come on in." When she came around the corner from the kitchen, she nearly jumped out of her skin. It wasn't Angela in her hallway; it was Harris who stood glowering in the shadows. "Mr. Harris! You gave me the fright of my life. I'm just off with Angela and the boys. I didn't expect you. In fact, I was just going to phone you." She realized too late it wasn't a very welcoming speech, but he didn't look in the mood for a welcome.

"What have you done to the water?" he demanded. She knew he'd been in the first war on the Somme. Had he been an officer? He still had the power to command attention; a power that seemed intensified by his years. What did he mean, what had she done to the water?

"What do you mean? I haven't any water myself. That's why I was going to phone, to offer to help. I thought Dave was going to help you. I assumed you and Dave were going to investigate." She felt guilty about this, seeing Harris. Of course she couldn't go anywhere. She'd have to help.

"Dave. Pah! He doesn't know his arse from his elbow. You've done something at your end here, where the creek runs down to my place. No bloody idea how to live in the country, that's the trouble," Harris was complaining.

"I've done nothing. I had nothing to do anything with. I got my hose out and turned the tap and nothing but a gasp came out. I hardly think you can say I've done something."

"We've got to go up to the creek. You've obviously balled it up."

"Honestly, Mr. Harris, the agent checked it before I moved in, and I've not been near it since."

"Bloody stupid fellows, the lot of them." He seemed peevish now, and uncertain what to do.

"I'll call Angela and tell her I'll meet her later. We can go across and have a look if you like."

They crossed the back garden and took the driveway past her outbuilding. On the road, they made their way to where a path cut into the woods and up a sharp incline, through a copse of birch trees that, contrary to their usual habit of rustling gently in the slightest movement of air, were completely still in this early mid-morning heat. As they descended, the air cooled slightly, and Lane could smell the water they were approaching. They came to a halt at the creek's edge in a tiny shaded vale. They ought, by rights, to be hearing the creek making a more rushing sound, but it was evident the minute they arrived that something was blocking it and it was overflowing its banks.

Harris whacked irritably at a vast, yellow-green leaf of skunk cabbage, unleashing a strong odour of skunk. A shame, really, Lane thought, as they were beautiful. Being the younger and more light on her feet, she went past him and picked her way down the slippery bank toward the small wooden trough. "It must be full of twigs or something. Or someone's built a nest here. Is the water usually this high? It seems to have turned into a pond."

She suddenly felt a tingle of apprehension. She was surprised at the return of this old, not always welcome companion, and then she told herself that the strong rot smell of the plants was probably making her imagine things.

She'd never given any thought to how the water arrived in her taps, and she was surprised by the simplicity of the arrangement. Above the diversion, the creek flowed in its own natural banks, and here a wooden trough had been constructed into a simple system that diverted the creek into a second channel. There was a natural pool where the water collected just before it poured into the Y-shaped trough. One of the channels going to her, she presumed, and the other to Harris. The water was high, and looked as though it was flooding over what had been grass. She had to lean quite far over to look at where the water ought to be pouring through into the wooden diversion, and pulled back again with a gasp. "Make that someone. Harris, who on earth is this?" she said, keeping her mouth nearly closed in an effort not to breathe. For there, indeed, was an arm encased in a brown tweed jacket, hanging down from where the rest of the body must have been jammed, the water disturbing the arm as it pushed against it, and creating the backup into the pond.

The shock that had left Lane momentarily frozen now spurred her forward in a panic into the water to see if he was alive. Though she could not see his face as it was turned away, water was pouring over his head in a way that could not allow for survival. "He's dead. He's been crammed there by someone." Her instinct to shout at Harris to come help her pull the man out of his watery coffin was nearly overwhelming, but he had been pushed in there. They needed to leave him and call the police. She turned and looked at where Harris stood, and where they had come down the path. What evidence had they destroyed?

She stood for some moments, watching the water swirling the man's sandy, nearly ginger-coloured hair and tried to be perfectly still, to tell memories to stay where they were. Not like she'd never seen a corpse. But still, she battled a dangerous twinge of nausea. She looked up and tried to take in the forest that surrounded them. Who could die here, in this way? It was impossible. How did he get here? His hair moved with the water pouring over it, and she had a momentary and illogical thought that he was alive after all. She felt her ability to act subdued by this confusion.

Into this silence Harris blundered, saying furiously, "What? What? Get out of the way, woman!" He strode brusquely past her and leaned, as she had, and, with perhaps more force than she had done, drew back.

"Bloody hell!" he said. "Bloody hell! This!" As he said "this," his voice rose in a high emphasis, as if this were yet another appalling setback designed to make his life a misery. Lane thought he looked slightly green, but that might have been the green reflection of the great, stinking leaves of skunk cabbage in the mid-morning sunlight.

Back in her kitchen, they sat with glasses of brandy, tea being out of the question. At her insistence they'd phoned the Nelson police and could not expect anyone to be there in anything under an hour, maybe longer, as it was Sunday. She was puzzled by Harris's reluctance to call them and wondered if it was some misplaced sense of independence in longtime dwellers in the country. After all, who else was going to deal with it? He seemed finally to agree with bad grace. Perhaps it was just that he wanted to be in charge of anything that happened.

"Did you recognize him at all?" asked Lane, when they had sat in silence for some minutes.

"No, I bloody well did not! Why do you say that? This is what happens when foreigners start taking over the place." He looked at her darkly, as if she might know who the body had been.

"I rather wish we'd not trampled the place up like we did. It will make it harder for the police."

"Why don't we leave all the thinking to the police, eh?"

Lane thought he must be on the verge of saying "my girl." I should tell him what I did in the war, she thought. That would fix him, self-satisfied old bugger! "I'm sure you're right," she said instead.

She heard the door opening and Dave Bertolli calling in, "Hello? You in here?"

"Come through to the kitchen. We're waiting for the police," Lane called.

Dave tromped in wearing the boots he'd thought he'd need to help with whatever the problem was. He'd gone down to Harris's and, not finding them there, had now made his way to Lane's. "Waiting for the police? Why?" he asked.

"There's a bloody body in the bloody exchange and it's blocked the bloody pipes." Harris's temper seemed to be fortified by the arrival of Dave, whom he consigned to the category of useless Yank who didn't know a Pippin from a Red Delicious and had no business in King's Cove at all.

"Had this sort of thing to deal with in the war, of course. Mind you, I thought you pretty plucky with that body. Most women wouldn't have handled that." His sudden concession surprised Lane, though not his continuing to talk as if Dave hadn't arrived.

"Can I get you some brandy, Dave? It's what we're having. For the shock, don't you know." She held up the bottle. For her own self-respect, she was relieved to observe that her hand had stopped shaking.

"Well, I haven't had the shock you've had but I don't like to be unsociable." He accepted a glass and urged Harris and Lane to carry on. "Now, what do you mean, a body? Whose?"

"We've no idea, evidently," said Lane, looking at Harris.

"Wow," said Dave. "Nothing ever happens around here, and now this. I suppose that's why my water wasn't affected, because I get mine farther up. But what about Reggie and Kenny? Wouldn't it have affected them?"

Lane could see Harris bridle, possibly, she thought, at what Harris probably assumed was the Yank familiarity of adding a diminutive to everyone's name. "On a different creek," he barked.

David nodded and sipped his brandy.

"You were on the Somme, weren't you?" Lane asked Harris, hoping to get him on to something that would keep him from disapproving of them until the police arrived.

"That's right, a lieutenant, not that it's any of your lookout."

"Oh, that's right. Old Mrs. Hughes told me you'd served with John Armstrong, Kenny's brother."

Harris directed a thundering look at her. Too late,

Lane remembered that he became angry at any mention of serving with Kenny's brother.

"What I can't make out is who the heck it could be," Lane reflected, hurriedly giving up on diverting Harris. "We're miles from anywhere, and there are only nine families here. Unless he's one of us, someone's come a long way to get plugged."

"I don't think you have to look far to figure it out, do you? Bloody Americans." Harris looked darkly at Dave. "It'll be one of them. Who knows where those people have come from and what they're running away from? You mark my words. They've run away. The rest of us came out here to grow apples. What's he here for? The climate? Rubbish!"

This appalling breach of good manners dismayed Lane. She cast an anguished look at Dave, who merely waggled his fingers in a "don't worry, what more can you expect from Harris?" sign.

It was true enough about the apples. There were orchards arching over the hills all around the community. She had a whole basement full of wooden boxes and labels ready for the fall pick, and a good half-acre of Delicious apples to contend with when the time came.

Lane sighed and looked back at Harris, who was glaring at Dave. "Really, Lieutenant. We'd best leave all the speculation to the police, as you yourself said, don't you think?"

CHAPTER SEVEN

THEY HEARD THE CARS LONG before they pulled into the grassy driveway. Traffic was so rare that she could hear cars climbing the hill from the main road as a sudden interruption of a silence she wasn't really aware of until someone pushed through from the outside world.

She had expected police cars but, instead, two men were getting out of a maroon, four-door Ford and behind them, an ambulance van was pulling up. Lane and Harris waited outside the door to the house. Dave hovered behind them, aware of his status as a non-witness. Both men had suit jackets, ties, and hats. Lane thought they must be expiring in the heat. She moved toward them.

"Hello. I'm Lanette—Lane, actually—Winslow. I made the call. This is Lieutenant Harris. We were together when we found the body, and this is Dave Bertolli, who lives farther up the creek and has come to help."

The foremost man took his hat off to reveal a head of thick russet hair, which Lane thought must be a little long, strictly speaking, for the police. But of course, she was new and had never met a Canadian policeman. He was clearly young, but had something about him that was old, or maybe weary. She'd seen the look so often, and it was not surprising. The war had ended only one year before. She wondered if he'd been a fighter pilot, though she could not have said why she thought this. His eyebrows had a worried set to them over an intelligent face.

He reached out his hand. "Inspector Darling. This is Constable Ames. You live far enough out, don't you? I don't think anyone from our department has been out this way since before the war, if then. We have some medicos with us to move the body. He is dead, I suppose?"

"As a doornail," Lane said, before she'd realized it might not be so appropriate to word it just that way. Her "Brit" way of dispelling unpleasantness with language might be frowned on here. After all, they still didn't know who it was and, in spite of Harris's protestations, the dead man's face had not been visible from the angle at which they'd seen him, so it might very well be a member of a local family. "Sorry," she added hastily. "Yes. Quite dead." Had the inspector's mouth twitched slightly? The constable cleared his throat in a way that suggested the suppression of a laugh. He was certainly not the stolid, middle-aged, constable sidekick of English detective fiction. He looked to be in his early twenties and had the untroubled, alert air of the young, scenting adventure. He will not have been in the war—at least not in the fighting, Lane thought.

"What's that?" Harris asked, his irritation seeming to take hold of him again. "Yes, course he is. Drowned. You'd better let me show you the way. You can stay here," he said to Lane. "No need for you to go through it all again."

Inspector Darling glanced at Lane, a tiny spark of a glance. He was reassuring her, she thought, and then felt a quick flush and looked down. She reminded herself that she had long ago learned that you cannot assume what someone else is thinking. Where she'd been, such assumptions could be fatal. He could quite easily have been glancing at her to agree with Harris that she should stay.

What in fact he was saying was, "Since you both found him, I'd sooner you both came along. You may have observed different things. I'll ask you to stay behind, Mr. Ber . . ."

"Bertolli," Dave said helpfully. "No problem. I'll go off home and wait to hear the results."

"You can't put a woman through this sort of thing, Inspector. I can give you any information you need," Harris said, his commanding way in full sail.

The inspector nodded, as if to indicate he understood, and said, "Nevertheless, if it's not too much trouble. The young lady looks quite capable of handling this. No one need be present when we remove the body. Do we need to drive the van somewhere?" he asked, indicating the ambulance men.

"Yes, I suppose. It's up the road just by the junction," Lane said, "The body is well in along a path at the creek, so the van will have to just stay on the road by the path."

Darling lifted his chin at the ambulance men, who returned to the van, ready to follow them to the junction. "Ames, camera?"

"Yup," said this young man, holding up the apparatus.

Harris led the way, with Lane directly behind him. The two policemen drew up the rear. As they approached the beginning of the path upward through the birch trees, Lane stopped. "I'm sorry, we walked here earlier and I'm afraid we were not thinking so much of finding a body as finding out why we'd got no water. We've trampled the place up. If there is evidence to indicate how the body got here, I'm afraid it will be a mess."

At this point the inspector, who was carrying his hat in his right hand, waved it over his head and called out irritably, "Lieutenant Harris, could you stop please?"

Harris, who was a good ten feet ahead, pulled around and called out, "What?"

"Stop please. Right there. Thank you. Miss Winslow was just telling me something. Yes, go on," he said, turning to her. He was very close, and she saw that his eyes were charcoal; but perhaps they were black and picking up the slight green that seemed to suffuse the copse in the reflected sunlight.

"When we went up earlier there was a very strong smell of the skunk cabbage. It grows along the banks of the creek. Lieutenant Harris broke a leaf with his stick, but I noticed that some other leaves had been broken as well, farther along. I noticed it because of the smell and I thought initially that he must have broken several leaves in his swipe but I saw he could not have reached the others, as they were across to the other side. I thought at the time a bear might have gone through. We have quite a few in the mountains just around us and they come down to eat our berries and rifle through the garbage."

"Can you show me?" He led her past the bemused Harris and down to the stand of water with the skunk cabbage.

"The exchange is through there to the right, and the broken plants are just there behind it. You can't really see it as well from there because there is a lot of brush along the edge of the creek. I don't think there is a path on the other side of the creek, so however the body got here, I suppose, it must have come along this same path we're on now." They walked farther and came to the edge, where the creek was rapidly climbing to the level of the clearing where they were standing because of the blockage. The police immediately moved toward where the body was lodged, but Lane was looking across the creek. There was very little by way of a bank on the other side and a forest of dense pines seemed to start up almost immediately. There really didn't seem to be a path on that side. "Now that I think of it, I can't make out why the plants should be trampled over there. Do you see, Harris—there are skunk cabbage leaves broken along that edge."

"Ames, pictures please," said the inspector, looking closely to where she had been pointing.

"Rubbish," said Harris suddenly, from his position behind Ames. "Obviously it's bears. Inspector, Miss Winslow is very new here. Doesn't know the lay of the land. I can't be here all day, I've got to get the water running, get on with my work."

"All in good time, Lieutenant. Miss Winslow, were you first to arrive here?"

"Yes."

"And is this exactly what you found?" He indicated the body. She moved gingerly past the inspector and Harris. The water still poured over the barrier, which was faced away toward the downward flow of the creek, and the body was still there, its trailing arm and the back of its head and upper body the only things still visible.

"This is it, really. When I leaned over enough to see what was blocking the water from getting through, I saw him. The creek bank was a little lower, of course."

"Do you know him?"

"No. I mean, I've never seen the back of that head before, I don't think. I was talking about it with the lieutenant. He must be someone from somewhere else, but how he came to be murdered here . . ."

Darling, who'd been leaning forward to have a look, stood up and turned to her. "So, you think it's murder, do you?"

"Inspector, really," she said, waving her hand at the impossibly placed corpse.

Darling smiled slightly and looked up to where Ames was waiting with his camera at the ready. "Ames . . ."

"I know," said the constable. "Pictures, please!" And he got to work.

CHAPTER EIGHT

"MISS WINSLOW, COULD I TROUBLE you to return carefully up the path with Lieutenant Harris and wait at your house? Ames and I will need to go over the scene, but I should like to ask a few more questions."

Harris frowned at this. "How long are you going to be? I've a busy day."

The inspector looked around, as if calculating the time it would take, and then said mildly, "I don't think we will detain you too long. Will you excuse me now?" He turned away and stood with his back to them on the path, gazing at the body, the arm of which still delivered a stream of water musically into the creek, as if it were some macabre limb on an Italian fountain.

"Come on, Lieutenant. There's still some brandy. We both need something," Lane said, starting back toward the road. Harris gave a last dark look at the two policemen and followed her.

AMES, IN THE meantime, had been snapping photos, and was now crouched near the body, shooting the details of its insertion into the wooden structure. "It would have taken work to get the heavy, limp, dead weight of a body into this position," he observed.

"You don't think he died here, then?"

"Very funny, sir. At the very least he would have to have been unconscious when he was put here. No one would willingly get into a thing like this."

"In an amazing turn up for the books, you could well be right, for once, Ames. Further to the work of stuffing him into this wooden whatever-it-is, there would have been the work of carrying him here, presumably from that road. Nothing much left of footprint detail with all the tramping back and forth, but I think we would see a different pattern on the path if he'd been dragged here." Darling gazed at the path leading to the edge of the water, which was creeping ever higher because the outflow was being dammed by the corpse.

"I'm not sure about that, sir. It's been very dry and that path is quite grassy. The problem is that we don't know how low this part of the creek normally is. The normal bank of the creek might have shown us something but it's completely under water now."

Darling grunted agreement. "What about Miss Winslow's skunk cabbage? Didn't she say plants had been trampled along the far edge?"

On the far edge of the pool that had formed by the backed-up water, the ground sloped gently down from what appeared to be dense forest. There was no immediately evident pathway emerging from the underbrush and trees, but it was certainly the case that there were some large, yellow-green leaves lying with their tips now trailing in the water, still wafting a vague, skunky scent of protest. Darling wondered momentarily if he should direct Ames to remove his shoes, roll up his pant legs, and wade across to investigate. As much pleasure as this would have given him, he decided against it. Feeling a slight sense of anxiety that he might be missing something by not going over, he decided in favour of the odds that a person wanting to get rid of a body would be more likely to take an easy, established route than crash about through the underbrush. In a community like this, you could, he reasoned, probably carry bodies around at all hours of the day and not risk being seen. If it had been done at night, it was even less likely that one would take a difficult route to get rid of a body. "Perhaps Lieutenant Harris was right; maybe it was bears. Let's get the van boys to pack him out. Take some more snaps, Ames, as that is happening."

Ames, innocent of the near-plan to make him take off his beautifully polished brogues, already insulted by having to walk about on the dusty road and so dangerously near water, bolted up the path to where the two men in charge of the van were smoking and talking quietly. "Okay, boys, you can fish him out now."

Darling and Ames stood back at the edge of the road watching the anonymous folds of canvas be carried past them to the van. The body seemed scarcely to have shape, though the two men tasked with carrying it were clearly hot from the exertion of bringing it awkwardly up a small path. When the body had been stowed for its final ride back to Nelson, Darling banged a couple of times on the back of the ambulance van to send it on its way. Dangling his jacket over his shoulder, he said, "Shall we go along to Miss Winslow's?"

A rhetorical question, Ames decided, if he had ever heard one. "First ones at the scene, and a fairly out-of-the-way scene at that. What are the odds one of our two is behind this?" Darling mused as they walked. Ames was momentarily distracted by the growing accumulation of dust from the road on his shoes, but then he looked sharply at his superior.

"An old man and that slip of a girl? Neither one of them could manage hauling the dead weight of the corpse of a healthy young man across the country and jamming him into that contraption."

"Maybe not either one . . . but both together."

Ames shook his head. "What circumstance could ever bring those two together to commit a murder? It's ridiculous, if I may say so, sir."

"That, and many other questions, are yet to be answered, Ames. That's where we come in; two open-minded investigators. Or rather, one open-minded investigator and a second, blinded by the sight of a pretty face. Get out your notebook, Ames."

"Aha, then you agree she's pretty!"

Darling had no response to this but a disapproving pursing of his lips, a comment lost on Ames, who in spite of the deteriorating condition of his shoes was cheerful again after scoring, he believed, a point on the inspector.

Lane greeted them at the door, upon which they had knocked though it stood open, and led them to the kitchen, where Harris sat gloomily on a chair that seemed too small for him. She pulled a bottle of beer out of the refrigerator and held it up. "I'm sorry, we've no water just now. This at least will be cold and not full of germs."

"Yes sirree!" said Ames. "I'd love some beer." He looked at Darling, wondering if he was going to stand on a point of drinking on the job . . . in this heat! Thankfully Darling gave a nod. Lane indicated the chairs and the two men sat down while she cleared the brandy glasses off the table. "Unless you'd like some of what we had earlier?" she said, indicating the brandy glass.

"Beer will be fine, thanks. And then I think I'll need to just collect some information from each of you separately. Is there a place Ames and I can ask each of you some questions?"

Thus it was that Lane found herself outside on the porch on a canvas deck chair watching the play of the changing shades of water on the lake, with a copy of *Leave It to Psmith* in her hand. She needed something amusing to read just now. It would be her turn when they had finished asking Harris whatever it was they needed to ask. She imagined him answering in his brusque "you've got no business asking me these things" tone of voice. But in fact, Harris was on very good behaviour, perhaps because he liked talking about himself and had precious little opportunity to do it anymore.

"How long have you lived here, Mr. Harris?"

"I came over when I was a boy, just after the Armstrongs came. My parents were dead so I was sent to live with them. Lady Armstrong was my aunt and Kenny and his brother were my cousins. 1903, I think. I was ten."

"Do you have a family?"

Harris shifted in his chair. "No. I was married. My wife buggered off in 1918 just at the end of the war while I was still overseas. I've managed perfectly well on my own. Keep to myself, pick my crop, ship it off, live off the proceeds. Get a small . . ." And here he stopped.

"A small what, Lieutenant?"

"Pension. Army pension."

Ames glanced up from his notes. Harris seemed uncertain, suddenly. "I see. I'm not meaning to pry; I'm just trying to get a complete picture of the community. Did most of the original people come around that time?"

The gruff demeanour was back. "Between 1888 and about 1904. Then this last crop that arrived just now. The Yanks. God knows why they are here. Running from something, I shouldn't wonder."

"Was your family running from something?"

"Certainly not! My relatives were fascinated by the thought of the Dominion of Canada. They wanted a more adventurous life. In the end, after trying logging, they settled on apples. They grow best around here—pears as well. You need to go farther west for peaches and cherries. A bloody fire in 1919 wiped out the forest and most of the orchards before it stopped. I wasn't here. I was late getting back. Wounded. Found the wife gone, the orchards gone, most of the forest gone. Lucky to still have my house."

Ames, ever relegated to taking notes, was scribbling shorthand across the table from Darling. "Can you tell me, Lieutenant Harris, how does the business of the creek work? How many households obtain their water from the creek?"

"There are two creeks in King's Cove. One feeds the north side, that's this creek, and one feeds the south side, that'll be the Armstrongs, the Hughes up the hill, and Mather, up the other way. This creek I'm on feeds the Bertolli crowd, this house, and myself. There's a family that had the place at the very top of the road, but they left, oh, before the Great War, to sort out some family matters. Haven't seen hide nor hair since then."

"I see. That's why only you and Miss Winslow noticed anything wrong with the flow of the water. How is the water diverted to the different households?"

"It's pretty simple really, there's a wooden trough constructed, almost like a small dam, and water is collected and then diverted into where it needs to go. The diversion where the body was found divides in two and sends water off to the two places. The Yank gets his water farther up the creek. Usually there's more water in the creeks but it's been pretty hot, so the creeks have gone down a bit. That's why the body there affected the supply."

"You must have to worry about that sort of thing—dry spells, overly rainy spells, silting up, and so on?"

"Generally it's not been bad. We have screens as the water gets near the houses, and larger screens near the top to stop leaves and so on. But I usually go up a couple of times a year to clean the place up. Now with this Miss Winslow, I can see I'll be looking after hers as well. Can't think what possessed a woman to come out here alone. It's madness. She'll be gone by next spring, I'll bet any money. Won't stand the winter!"

Ames smiled behind his notebook. He would bet money

she could stand any amount of winter. He looked across at Darling, but the inspector seemed to be thinking of what more he ought to ask.

"You say you do not know this man, Lieutenant Harris. Did you see him arrive here? Hear any cars you didn't recognize?"

Harris gave a long sigh, suggesting, Darling thought, that he'd had enough. He followed this with a pause, indicating what? Darling wondered. "I did not get to see his face, did I? Anyway, this seems to have happened at night. I'm afraid I sleep like a log, Inspector."

"What makes you believe it happened at night?"

"It's obvious, isn't it? Anyone dragging bodies around would be seen during the day." Ames scribbled. Darling took a moment to look in silence at Harris. "Have you, during the course of the day, run across a car parked or abandoned anywhere?"

"Really, if I had, it's the first thing I would have said, isn't it? A strange car here is very rare and we'd notice it, any of us, right away."

Darling stood up. "I expect you're right. Thank you, Lieutenant. If you think of anything further, would you call the police station in Nelson? The exchange will put you through. Ask for me or Ames here." His stance suggested to Harris that he was being dismissed.

"It's the bloody Yanks, you mark me!" Harris grumbled as he left.

Darling watched him until he had passed the barn, and noticed he favoured his left leg. He felt almost a kinship with him for a fleeting second. Back from a war and nothing much to show for it all. He certainly seemed to have it in for the American, however. Darling made a mental note, in case it mattered later.

He stepped on to the porch and was taken by the view, as everyone was the first time. The overwhelming impression was one of multiple shades of blues and greens: the intense blue of the cloudless, now mid-afternoon sky. The layering of sunlit and shaded greens of the mountains rolling down toward the far shore of the lake. The water glinting and shimmering emerald and turquoise reflections of the sky and mountains, and the near, brighter greens of the lawn and shrubbery of Miss Winslow's garden. Darling, who lived in a small house in town with, admittedly, a nice view of Nelson and the lake from his hillside vantage, took his eyes from this much grander display of nature at its most beguiling and turned back to the task at hand. Miss Winslow had been sitting in a green canvas deck chair with a Penguin book, which he was tempted to try to identify, and now she looked up at his appearance.

"Ready for me?"

"Yes, if you don't mind. It shouldn't take long." He was reluctant to go back in to the kitchen, which had now taken on the air of an interview room. But they did and when they had settled and Lane had her hands folded in front of her and was looking at him expectantly, he began again. Ames had dropped his chair back on to four legs from the two he'd leaned back on in the interval, and was now poised with his pencil. "You've been here how long, Miss Winslow?" asked Darling.

"Barely a month. I came out to see the place in April and bought it without a second thought."

"Where had you been living before?"

Lane considered this question. She did not really think of herself as living anywhere. More just staying places, trying them on to see what fit. "Just before I came out to Canada, I was in France for about six months, and before that I was in London, where I worked during the war."

"Are you from either of these places?"

"I'm from . . . well, my family are English, but I was born in Riga. I went to school in England, obviously. My father was in the, ah, diplomatic corps." That had better do, she thought.

"Quite a varied life, Miss Winslow. With all those exotic addresses at your fingertips, what on earth brought you here? You seem to have gone as far away from home as you could get."

Home. That was the trouble, really. Home was elusive. She felt most at home in Bilderingshof where she had been a child, but it was a vanished world. Her mother was dead, she hadn't seen her father since she had gone up to university—she had no idea where he was—and her grandparents had had to share their house with a bevy of Russian officers who gave no indication they'd be moving. Her grandmother and grandfather had finally moved back to an ancient family home in Scotland, a land as unfamiliar to them as Canada was to their granddaughter. Though Lane had been to school in England, it certainly didn't feel like home to her either. She had decided, on the basis of a poster, to come out to British Columbia. It showed a woman standing on a hill with fields and snow-covered mountains behind her and a great, endless blue sky. A new, clean, uncomplicated country with no blood in the soil from centuries of wars. It was ironic that the first thing to confront her was a corpse, bleeding into her water supply. She shuddered. All right, he hadn't been bleeding, but metaphorically, his life had bled away.

"I saw a wonderful poster, if you must know, and thought how beautiful it looked. I was right, I think."

Darling looked at her. He would have liked to ask if she would not be lonely so far from everything she knew and living among what were patently people who were significantly older and by all indications more bad-tempered than she was. Not relevant to the case, he supposed. He also had a nagging feeling about why someone would come this far. Was she running from something?

Like Harris, she had not heard a car at night, and had no idea why a man would come to die in her creek. Then, for a fleeting moment she remembered the car in her dream, and was about to dismiss it. "Funnily, I did dream about a car in the distance. I often dream of that, though, so it probably has no bearing on this."

"What time might that have been?"

She tried to imagine when it might have been. Her nights were such a dark confusion to her. "I couldn't say, I'm afraid. I . . . I didn't wake up from that dream. When I do wake at night I check the clock. A habit I should stop. It doesn't help anything, really."

Darling pondered the troubled look on Miss Winslow's face. Guilt? Or something he himself recognized all too well: trouble sleeping. "Thank you, Miss Winslow. I'm going to go along and talk to some of your neighbours. If we need anything else, we will contact you. Can you write your phone number here, please?"

When Darling and Ames were halfway up the path toward the car Ames said, "Good trick, sir, getting her number like that."

"Shut up, Ames."

Darling and Ames were tucked back into their maroon roadster and about to back the car out onto the road. "Wait," Darling said. Ames stopped the car and the two of them stared at the outbuilding by the gate. "What is that, I wonder? It's not a barn exactly, is it?" He got out of the car and stood gazing at it. "Come on Ames, walkies."

The outbuilding looked grey and brittle in the afternoon heat. The front had a couple of small windows at ground level that were so completely encrusted with dust that you could scarcely see into the place. A second set of windows about fifteen feet up indicated a second floor, perhaps. A door with a rusty padlock stood on the right. It was clear it had not been opened for what looked like years. They walked around the right of the building to the windowless wall that faced the main house. Darling stopped and looked down the slight slope. There were several large trees in the fifty or so yards between this outbuilding and the house. From this angle the large blue spruce nearly obscured the little landing and the door. Around the third side, the building took on more of an aspect of barn. There was a large set of double doors that would open outward and a small side door, and again, a couple of filthy windows. An assortment of unused animal pens was outside, a shed full of wood, and a chopping block.

Darling inspected the ground. "Looking for something, sir?" inquired Ames.

"Yes, Ames. I'm a detective. I am looking for something. You might emulate me in this, if you don't mind. At the moment I'm looking to see if anyone has been moving things in and out of this building. Would you care to speculate on this?"

Ames smiled at this. "Very funny, sir. And no, no one has. The ground has a thick covering of pine needles and dirt and I'd say these doors had not been opened for at least a season."

"Very good, Ames. You may yet turn into a sleuth."

They found they could not walk easily around the fourth side of the building because of a great deal of underbrush, and so retraced their steps to the car.

Once out on the road, the car was facing toward the post office. "We're missing a car at this point, unless Tweed Jacket was dropped off here, or brought here by a local. Let's take a little drive around here and see what we can see," said Darling. The post office lay only two hundred yards down the road, which ended in a large grassy area where it was evident cars would be parked by people visiting or picking up their mail. Armstrong's red truck was parked between the house and an underground outdoor cellar. "You could put a body in the back of that truck quite handily," Ames observed.

An older woman came to the screen door at the sound of the car and waited, smiling, with her arms crossed across her aproned chest.

"Good afternoon, ma'am," said Darling. "I'm Inspector

Darling, this is Constable Ames from the Nelson police. You are?"

"I'm Eleanor Armstrong and Kenny, my other half, is working around the back. Can I help?"

"Perhaps you can. We need to ask you and your husband some questions. Is the truck yours?"

"It's my husband's. Kenny uses it to bring the mail and so on up from the wharf. In the season we help people get their apple boxes down to the boat. Ah, here he is now." Eleanor had by this time been joined by Kenny, who was carrying a small handsaw and wiping his forehead.

"Goodness, what's happened? I heard all the vehicles over the way."

"This is Inspector Darling, and he needs to ask some questions, dear. Won't you come in, Inspector?"

"Thank you, we'll be fine here. Have you heard or seen a strange car at all in the last few days? Anyone come here you don't know? I see you are the local post office. You might be in a better position than most to have seen anything out of the ordinary."

"What's the trouble?" asked Kenny. "And no, I've heard nothing unusual. No new cars. I'd spot those in a jiffy."

"Would you mind if we just had a peek at your truck, sir?"

Darling watched Armstrong's face as he waited for the answer. "Yes, of course." Armstrong began to move toward the truck, his face now puzzled. He pulled open the driver's side door but the two policemen had walked to the back and were peering into the wooden box shoved against the cab, now empty, where he sometimes threw the sacks of mail if the weather was bad. The younger one with the camera was making notes and then took a photograph.

"Can I ask what this is in aid of, Inspector?"

"We were called out by Miss Winslow, your neighbour. She found a body in her creek. Are you on the same creek as she is?"

Eleanor Armstrong had joined them, perplexed by this sudden interest in the truck.

"A body? Whose body? Oh dear, this has never gone and happened in her creek! Oh God, I hope it wasn't one of the neighbours! Was it a suicide, Inspector? Poor Lane! I haven't heard or seen a soul that doesn't usually clutter up this place." Eleanor Armstrong delivered all of this in one breath.

"We do not believe it was a suicide, Mrs. Armstrong. It looks a good deal like murder." He turned to the taciturn Kenny, whose brow was furrowed in what could have been thought or disapproval. "Anything you could add, sir?"

But Kenny was stuck back at Darling's suggestion of murder. "Murder? At King's Cove? It's ridiculous, unthinkable! It wasn't Harris, was it? I know a few that would want to murder him!"

"We're not on the same creek, by the way," said Eleanor.

"Yes, of course," interjected Kenny Armstrong. "Sorry. Bit taken aback by this. Poor Lane. Must go and see to her after this. Let's see. Today is Sunday. I make a run to the wharf three days a week, Monday, Thursday, Saturday, for mail and any supplies that have been sent up from town, but I only go down the road you must have come up and then across the Nelson road, about thirty yards along, to the road that goes down to the lake. I've not gone up any of our other roads for weeks, so things could get past me. Certainly no one strange has been here."

"Unless you count the locals!" Eleanor said.

"What do you mean by that, Mrs. Armstrong?" asked Ames, his notebook poised.

"Nothing, really. Most of the people around here have been here since before the Great War. Some people's peculiarities intensify in a remote region like this after many years."

"She means they're stark raving mad!" snorted Kenny. "But I dare say they are harmless. There has never been a murder here since we were here. I came over with my parents when I was a lad in '92. That house Miss Winslow lives in used to be ours. My mother lived in it till just a few years ago. We're delighted to have her there, I must say. She's improved the look of the place no end! Nice woman too. Writes. Poor thing. Is she all right?"

"She seems fine. It was she who found the body, along with a Lieutenant Harris. He was with her this morning. I spoke with them just now," Darling said, inclining his head to indicate the direction of Lane's house.

"Oh, blimey! Kenny, run over there and rescue her this instant!" exclaimed Eleanor, her hand on her forehead. "Lieutenant indeed!" she added.

Having been given a little hand-drawn map to the rest of the roads and settlements at King's Cove that Kenny sketched on the back of an envelope, Darling and Ames were now cruising slowly along the upper road.

"A useful truck, certainly, but again, dragging a body about the place? Could either of them have managed it?" Ames, as usual, was beginning his list of favourites and non-starters for the crime. Darling, who was thorough and never put anything past anyone, had nevertheless been impressed over the last year by how accurate Ames's instincts about people had been. Grudgingly, he was inclined to agree with Ames's assessment of the Armstrongs as candidates, but he merely grunted noncommittally. The long, rutted driveway that seemed to have experienced mostly tractor use ended in an attractive mock Tudor with flowerbeds around it. A couple of outbuildings were visible, and at least one dilapidated roadster, circa 1920, parked on a lay-by. It looked as if it hadn't been used in some years. There was no sign of activity.

There was a deep silence when they got out of the car and no sign of anyone. "These people are, no doubt, out about the business of their orchards," said Darling.

"What do you have to do with an orchard at this time of year, sir?" asked Ames, peering up the long sweep of orderly rows of trees.

"Spray them? Irrigate them? Weed them? My degree was in literature and history, Ames, and I buy apples out of a wooden box at the greengrocer in Nelson. How they get there, I've no idea." An inspection of the car confirmed that it had not been driven for many years. A rusted gas cap was half-open and grass and weeds had grown up around the wheels and woven through the spokes.

Having found no one at home, as they turned and trundled back along the rutted road away from the Hughes property, Ames wincing at the sound of the scraping along the bottom of the car produced by the centre ridge of the road, Darling mused, "What do you suppose Mr.

Armstrong meant by 'stark raving mad'? Everyone, or just some of the locals?"

"Harris is odd, but more along the bad-tempered lines. I think it interesting that there's never been a murder here."

"Here, Ames. Stop. This, according to the Armstrongs, is where someone called Mather lives." They were at the right-angle turn at the top of the road and, occupying a plot of land that appeared to fan out from the point of a corner, was a long, wood-framed, pale yellow house, a single storey with a porch across the front of it. Either side of the driveway on the other side of the gate was flanked with lawns and flowerbeds that showed evidence of pride and meticulous care. The beds were brimming with the colours of an English perennial garden.

Ames pulled the car out of the road to the front of the gate and they got out. The noise of the doors on the roadster shutting brought a man out on to the porch who shaded his eyes to get a better view of them. He appeared to be in his early sixties, and was now striding down the driveway toward them.

"Jiminy!" muttered Ames. "Everyone here is ancient. Poor Miss Winslow. Whatever was she thinking, coming out here?"

"Good afternoon, gentlemen. What can I do for you? Lost your way?"

Inspector Darling pulled out his police identification. Another English accent, he noted. "Good afternoon. We're wondering if you saw or heard an unfamiliar car or vehicle yesterday or last night, anywhere in the area."

"That is hard to say. Sometimes people turn up the King's Cove road looking for someplace and drive through.

But it's pretty rare. I would have heard. Heard you coming since you left the Armstrongs'. No, I'd say not. Why? What's going on?"

Darling turned to look down the road they'd come up. This corner location certainly afforded a sweeping view of the lower half of the settlement. Sounds must carry nicely up the hill as well. "We stopped by the Hughes' up the hill from the post office, but they weren't there."

"Yup, I heard you do all that. They're in their upper orchard right now. What is this about?" The man was showing a degree of authoritative impatience. Ames imagined he was the sort of fellow who saw himself as the de facto community leader, who thinks he ought to be told things first.

Darling ignored the question. "Does your water come from the same creek as Mr. Harris's and Miss Winslow's?"

"No, it does not. Now what's this about?" The man's eyebrows, just tending to bushiness, now collected themselves into an irritated ridge above his nose.

"A body was found in the creek, Mr . . . ?"

"Mather, Reginald Mather. Whose body? Which creek?" he added as an afterthought, looking nervously up the hill for a minute.

"We don't know who. But it wasn't your creek. And you're sure about the car?"

"Of course I'm bloody sure."

"What do you drive, sir? Might we have a quick look at it?"

Mather glanced back toward his barn. "A Morris. It's in there. Why do you need to see it?"

"Just procedure. Thanks very much," Darling replied pleasantly, starting toward the barn.

The Morris was a dilapidated vehicle of pre-war vintage. Ames asked to see inside the trunk. "This rifle, sir. Why do you have it in the car?"

Mather scowled silently for a moment. "My wife had gone in search of a cougar. Dangerous animals. My son brought her home . . . threw the gun in the trunk. I forgot to take it out."

AS THE POLICEMEN backed out on to the road, Mather stood on the inside of his gate with both his hands resting on the top of it, holding the card upon which they'd written the number for the Nelson police detachment, should he "think of anything else." He watched them drive slowly toward the Bertollis' and felt a slow warming of satisfaction at the thought of the Yanks having to deal with the police. It mingled with a sense of disquiet that Sigmund Freud would have identified as something to do with his ego taking a beating by a policeman who didn't know his place.

"Ames, stop the car." They were a few hundred yards along the road toward where they had been told the Bertolli property was. The vehicle had no sooner come to a stop than the inspector was out and walking back along the way they had come.

"You! Can you stop, please?" he called out toward the field on their right. Ames got out of the car and looked in the direction Darling was calling. A man was looking at them at the far edge of the field, as if deciding whether to disappear into the nearby trees or obey the summons. Slowly he walked toward them. He was young, a fact that surprised Ames, as he'd begun to think the entire place was a retirement community, and he had the impression the man would be surly. He just looked like the kind of man they sometimes arrested after a night of drinking down a paycheque on a Friday. Ready to take offence.

The man climbed over the already broken-down wire and post fencing and stood looking at them. "Who are you?" he asked, as if he owned the place, Ames thought. He took out his notebook and pencil and flipped it open to a new page, a movement not lost on the young man, who cast him a disagreeable look.

"Inspector Darling, Nelson Police. This is Constable Ames. Now, I wonder if I might ask you the same question? Name?"

Ames looked studiously at his notebook. Darling was addressing this man in the meticulously polite voice he used for suspects. It was the first time he'd really brought out that voice on this trip. The surliness of the young man, no doubt, was the reason.

"Sandy. Why do you want to know?"

"Ah. Are you the son of Reginald Mather from just along the road?"

"Yes, for all the good that's ever done me. What's going on?" He was beginning to sound peevish.

"Is this part of your father's land?" Darling waved a hand at the field out of which Sandy Mather had come. This seeming change of tack seemed to irritate the man even more.

"No, it's not. The people who own it aren't here

anymore. I sometimes cut through it. Listen, what is this? I don't have all day."

"A body has been found in a local creek. We are trying to find out what we can. Where were you coming from just now?"

The young man looked behind him. "What creek? What are you talking about?"

"The one that feeds into Miss Winslow's and Mr. Harris's properties." Inspector Darling waited politely. The other man had not asked about whose body it might have been. Perhaps not surprising. In a rural area, the health of the creek would be paramount. "Do you work the orchards hereabout?" Darling nodded his head toward a stand of what he supposed to be apple trees near a greying wood-slat house, which is where he supposed now that Sandy Mather must have been coming from.

"No I don't, as a matter of fact. I'm planning to get a mill up and running . . ." Sandy seemed poised to say something else. "Whose body? Has someone here died?"

"We don't know. Mr. Harris, who found him along with Miss Winslow, did not recognize him."

Mather's face clouded. "Harris? Why would he be stumbling around in the creek with that b . . . that woman?" Ames looked up from his notebook, his hand frozen. He could have sworn Mather had been about to say "bitch," and he didn't much care for it.

Darling, however, went on smoothly. "Have you heard or seen anything out of the ordinary, Mr. Mather? Met anyone you didn't know? Heard or seen a car that would be unusual in this community?"

"No, I haven't. Now I'd like to get home." Sandy looked down the road toward his house. "I suppose you've been bothering my dad with this as well." A slight tinge of satisfaction appeared to creep into his voice at the thought of his father so inconvenienced.

"We've been bothering everyone, Mr. Mather, as we are certain the body was the victim of a murder. Where did you say you were coming from just now?"

Sandy Mather seemed discomfited at this. "There's a patch of timber down behind that house that runs down along the back road. I'm hoping we can get it. I was planning to write to the owners about it. We, I, am trying to identify the best stands of timber for the mill."

IN THE CAR later, as they rolled slowly toward the Bertollis', Ames said, "I didn't like him, sir."

"Nor did I, Ames. Wandering about looking at timber seems scant employment for a man of his age. I suppose we cannot suspect him merely because he is disagreeable."

"He was extremely disagreeable about Miss Winslow; he was about to call her . . ."

"Yes, Ames. Very interesting, that. He's already formed a negative opinion. He could have made some proposition to her about selling her stretch of timber for his putative mill, and she rejected the offer. Or indeed, he could have made advances of a more personal nature and been rejected. That would account for the level of bitterness. Still. One begins to scratch under the surface of a seemingly idyllic community."

"A point in her favour, I must say," remarked Ames.

At the opposite corner of the squared-off intersection of the upper road, before the road turned back down to meet the Nelson road, the Bertollis' renovated log cabin perched on a low hill at the front of their property, surrounded by a shimmering stand of birch trees. Ames nosed the car along a narrow, rutted driveway that curved around a small creek to the back of the house. The cacophony of two un-ferocious-looking collies greeted them. Ames and Darling sat in the car watching them.

"I've never heard of a collie biting, sir," suggested Ames.

"Why don't you hop out and test your theorem?" countered Darling. In the end, they were saved the trouble by the man who exploded out the kitchen screen door onto the veranda.

"Shut up, will you!" he shouted, waving his arms in a shooing motion. The dogs evidently decided they'd done their job and sauntered around the corner to the other side of the house wagging their tails. Darling and Ames got out of the car.

"Sorry about that, Inspector. All done down at the Winslow place?" asked the man.

Now Darling had an opportunity to have a better look at Dave Bertolli. Dark, in his thirties, with the kind of urban vigour of a working-class shopkeeper.

"Come on in!" Dave held open the screen door, using a leg to keep the dogs out. "Get away, you! I was just making myself a cup of coffee, can I interest you in a cup?"

Darling nodded. "Yes, thank you. It's been a long day." They were invited into a narrow living room with an enormous stone fireplace that appeared to be part of the older log cabin. The windows had been enlarged and attached was an airy addition, which contained a wall of bookshelves, a grand piano, and on the outside wall, yet more windows. The sun streamed in, filtered into delicate golden shapes by the trees off the raised porch outside. The two dogs stood by the windows looking in, and then walked out of vision and collapsed onto the porch to await further excitement from another quarter.

When they were seated around the kitchen table, coffee in hand, Dave said, "Angela, that's my wife, and the three boys were going to spend the afternoon at the beach with Lane—you know, Miss Winslow. I need to patch up the roof and I was going to get to work on it without the boys climbing all over everything. In the end, Angela decided to go ahead with the beach plan just to get the boys run down a bit. We'd be having a different conversation if they were here, believe me! They're a handful. They wanted to stay, because they're ghoulish little monsters, and hear all about the body. Once I left you at Lane's I decided to boil up some coffee and enjoy the peace and quiet. "

"What do you do, Mr. Bertolli?" asked Ames.

"I write music. It sounds fancier than it is, trust me! I write commercial jingles and music for motion pictures."

"Excuse me for asking, but this seems a strange, out-of-the-way place to come for that. Should you not be in California, or some other more central place for that sort of thing?" Darling asked.

Bertolli was silent for a few moments. "I have some pretensions to serious composing, I suppose, and I didn't think I could stay on in New York. My late father wasn't keen on my profession and left me the family business, and I saw a chance to get away. We imported olive oil, cheese, that sort of thing. My brother said he was willing to take it off my hands. I used the money to move out here. I like Canada. I used to read boys books about the Mounted Police. You know. Anyway, here I am."

Shortly afterward, as Ames negotiated turning around in the small area where they'd parked the car for their return journey out the rutted driveway to the road, Darling said, "I didn't believe that story for a minute, did you?" He didn't wait for an answer, as Ames seemed to be concentrating on not backing into a pile of garden implements. "I can see wanting to go to Canada, but why not Quebec, or Nova Scotia, even, if you wanted to get well away? Still close to New York. British Columbia, in this case, is an overstatement." He pursed his lips.

Ames seemed to have finally managed the transaction and they were bumping out of the driveway. "I wonder if old whatshisface, Harris, is right: cherchez les Yanks? His station wagon would be convenient for transporting our tweedy friend, if it wasn't so crammed with junk," he observed.

It was late afternoon when they were back in Nelson. They went downstairs to the morgue, to make sure their prize had arrived and take another look at him. The coroner would no doubt provide the details but the abrasion on the side of the head was interesting. They rifled through his pockets and found but one soggy and matted piece of paper, with which Ames was dispatched to the lab.

Now they spread a large piece of paper on the desk and took out the envelope with the hand-drawn map given them by Kenny Armstrong. "Let's redraw this . . . wait. Let's not. Go down to the Land Title office and get an ordnance map of the area. We'll get an accurate look at the layout. There may be back roads, pull-outs, and God knows what-all we didn't see. And pick up see-through map paper."

CHAPTER NINE

"WHAT I DON'T UNDERSTAND IS how the fellow came to be jammed in there. I don't understand any of it! Who was he? Why was he here? And once here, why was he murdered?" Kenny Armstrong was comfortably folded into his favourite chair with his feet propped up on the kitchen stove, onto which he'd just put a kettle. His wife and Lane had put away the dinner things and had joined him in the worn and perfectly bottom-shaped rattan chairs. Lane smiled. Kenny was in a state of sublime happiness. Someone he didn't know had been murdered, right here in King's Cove, and because the Armstrong house was fed from a different creek, he'd not even been particularly inconvenienced.

"I'm sure, my dear, that your mother saw the whole thing," said Eleanor, spooning some black tea into her teapot. She brought out her china, as if a discussion of this dead stranger warranted the good tea things.

"Well, if she did, she won't be saying much. She's not walking about talking to you, is she?" Kenny addressed this question to Lane.

"No. Aside from opening the windows, she's a very quiet house guest. Though when I think of it, she must see me as the interloper. Harris is a handful, isn't he? All that huff and puff. I thought he'd explode when the inspector asked me to go first to show him the scene. He seemed to think I was quite dim. He fumed and fumed and didn't look like he was getting any relief until he was asked to speculate on who it was, which neither of us could have said, as we only saw the back of his head."

"Yes. As stuffed as a shirt can get. You know he fought with my brother in France."

"Mrs. Hughes told me that. When I mentioned it to him, in an ill-fated attempt to make conversation while we waited for the police, he plunged into a dark, moody silence. It was foolish of me to talk about the war. It's so personal. Of course you can't make light conversation on the back of so much suffering. I was very sorry to hear your brother died over there, by the way. It must have been ghastly for you all."

Kenny swung his legs off the stove, something he did with the grace and energy of a young man, though he would surely be in his sixties. He tipped the kettle toward the pot, and then stopped. "You know, she never said a word. I was broken up about it myself. He was a wonderful, gentle sort of chap. I was going to go, but he insisted. He said I needed to stay with our mother and run the orchard. I always felt horribly guilty about the whole thing. Then, after the fire of '19, I couldn't be bothered with the orchards anymore. I just planted a few trees for Mum.

"Harris, to be honest, was more of a mess when he

got back. He had a lot of bad luck on top of just being demobbed and having shell shock. His orchard was all but destroyed in the fire and his wife couldn't cope and left before he even got back. Poor thing disappeared. We thought she'd gone to her people in Nelson but word got back that she'd never arrived there. Perhaps she went to the coast and died of the influenza. He got his batsman to come over and help him get started, and shortly after they'd replanted the orchard, the poor fellow was killed when he got in the way of a tree they were felling. Harris wasn't so difficult before all that. He could be moody when he was young, but his temper after the war was unbelievable. I had to pull him off Reggie one time. I thought he'd kill him, and it was over some imagined slight. Jumpy as hell too. That's what it was! Alice Mather had been going around shooting things and he nearly went crazy. Now he's older, and apt to live on his past glory and think that everyone else is stupid. He's a cousin of mine, as a matter of fact."

Lane frowned. "You know, it's so funny about people like that. I was watching for a minute when we took the police back to the body. Harris looked quite green. He seems so hardened."

"So you didn't get a look at his face? The dead man, I mean," asked Eleanor.

"Sorry, no. He had a nice tweed jacket though. Leather buttons. I don't think he'd be very old. Under thirty-five, to judge by the physique and the hair."

"Stranger and stranger," said Kenny. "Maybe Harris is right. We, aside from your good self, Lane, are all getting pretty ancient. Who but the Yanks, as he likes to call them, would have someone young come see them?"

"Except," said Lane, "and I've just thought of this, I'd have put any money on his being English. I can't even say why I'd say that. The Yanks have no experience with the English at all. They think we are all wonderfully quaint; me especially with my 'cute' accent."

The sky, still light at nine-thirty, was nevertheless beginning to show a slight darkening of the complexion that presaged the coming of full night at ten. Lane wanted to get back across to hers while it was still light. As she was leaving with a couple of corked bottles of water for her morning coffee—she was loath to drink the water, which had finally begun to come through again late that afternoon, until some suitable period of time had passed after the body had been removed—Eleanor and Kenny stood in front of their door waving cheerfully.

"I hope Harris is okay," she suddenly thought to say. "Should I give him a call, do you think?"

Kenny waved a dismissive hand. "I shouldn't bother. He could have come to ours, and he was too bloody proud. Always has to hack through life on his own. He'd just be angry because he'd think you were implying he's soft."

Making a decision, Lane said, "I'm going up to town tomorrow. I think I'm going to splurge and buy myself a new hose. Can I bring you anything?"

"Goodness, yes! I need a sack of flour, if you wouldn't mind," said Eleanor.

"Done!"

It was, she supposed, too sanguine of her to imagine

that this would be a normal night. If she had worried when she was first told that the ghost of Lady Armstrong resided in her attic, and was inclined to the action of opening windows, Lane quickly realized that imagining the ghost there was almost a protection from the internal spirits that haunted her. She had slept well enough on many nights since she'd arrived, though the nightmares were coming somewhat more often, albeit, she noted wryly, taking on a more and more metaphorical character. It surprised her that she was having more nightmares. She had been certain that she would have fewer with increasing distance and time from the war. She wondered if it was because the mind stored up the horrors for later when it was safe. Well, she was no trickcyclist. She couldn't be fussing about with all that psychology business. Millions of people had had a far worse war than she had. She remembered her grandfather saying these things eventually passed. She hoped he was right. Her main thoughts, as she turned on her lamp and put her glass of hot milk on the bedside table next to her book, were reserved for Harris's unsociable behaviour. She thought of him returning from an earlier war—shell shocked, his orchard burned, his wife gone. His age and bitterness seemed to tell the whole of his character, but she imagined him as one of the many young men she had known, early on, when they were still suffused with an eager, conquering spirit. They will all turn into him, she thought, propped up in bed, her book open but unread on her lap—all the ones who made it.

When images from the events of the day intruded, she pushed them back, and allowed only the medical van disappearing up her drive and the policeman with his hat in his left hand as he shook with his right, formal, unsmiling, unlike his constable, who gave her a cheerful smile and a wave as he climbed into their car. She did not even allow Inspector Darling's charcoal eyes.

She always left her windows open. Everything was open. In this she'd taken after the late Lady Armstrong, who was so insistent on fresh air up in her little sphere, the attic. Now the silence gently blew in from the velvet dark outside. The silence was what she loved best. It was the antidote: the healing, green silence. She still had her last lot of letters on the bedside table. They would be neutral enough to read before she went to sleep. There were the two bills—these she put aside—and a letter from Mr. Nesbitt, the house agent from Nelson, asking after her and urging her again to reconsider living in town because, while the summers were lovely, the winters would be intolerable. She laughed at what Mr. Nesbitt must consider intolerable, and opened her last letter from England. It was from the first week in June, a time that suddenly felt months ago.

Darling Laneka, how are you? We are well here, though the rain has been unremitting. We never used to get rain like this in Bilderingshof, did we? Ganf is adjusting well to living here, though he misses the river. He scowls at the mailman with those great black brows of his when there is no letter from you. It is funny to be English but not. We are like strangers here. I have not been here since I was a girl, that dreadful time I came out in '89, or '90, I can hardly remember it seems so long ago, to see your grandfather's sisters and they were so horrible to me. They've all died now, poor dears. It's a good thing they missed this last war; they'd barely recovered from the first one. And we are all dispersed now, your sister to South Africa, you to Canada. I have heard that even the Watsons, who had thought to stay on in Riga, are coming back now. It will be nice to have someone to talk to who remembers our old life, but I suppose Mrs W. will be as tiresome about her health here as she ever was there. You would be pleased with the bed of black-eyed Susans you planted along the south border. They seem to thrive in this wet and are the most brilliant intense yellow, especially on grey days. They remind me of you. Please do not be downhearted, my love. I hope that you are finding ease and rest and forgetting.

Rest and forgetting. Her rest. Her forgetting. She folded the letter carefully back into the envelope, soothed somewhat by the very un-English outpouring of loving words that her grandmother always filled her letters with. This complete lack of the traditional taciturn stiff upper lip comes of being English, she thought, but living your whole life on foreign soil. And now she was doing the same thing. She sipped at her hot milk and thought again about her one great friend, Yvonne. Lane had known, after Angus, that she could not stay on in England and had tried France. Living with Yvonne in her great house in the Dordogne had been lovely, but France . . . too full of memories. Her nightmares were unrelenting there, as if the past could not be made to lie down but must be there with her every night. In the end she had said to Yvonne, who was being Gallicly tragic about not being able to help her, "I really must go somewhere far and new. Look at those posters advertising Canada—the beautiful young woman standing atop a ski hill looking across a range of mountains. That could be me."

"You don't ski," Yvonne had reminded her coolly.

"I can learn. I am young."

She knew Yvonne's life must be busy. Full of her struggles with the local *mairie* over a building permit for an outbuilding for the horses she wished to raise. Yvonne had turned her energies firmly away from the war and thrown herself into horses, an expensive and all-consuming passion that her husband's money allowed her. Lane was secretly pleased her own money allowed her nothing more than what she had: a house, a small living, and time.

SHE AWOKE SLOWLY from the dream, as she always did, rigid with fear that carried into waking and the darkened room. It made her afraid to move, and afraid to fall asleep. She knew that if she did not move, she would fall back into the nightmare as if she had not woken up. She lay with her eyes open, looking into the blackness, still hearing the roaring of the flames. She could not quite place where she was, and this confusion added to her fear. She moved her eyes slowly across whatever scene might be in front of her face, looking for clues—the grey from a window, the looming shadow of her wardrobe—and then she realized the wardrobe had been in her room in her brief childhood home in Kent. The curtains fluttered and seemed to be enough. "I am here," she thought, and knew where "here" was.

It was the same dream again—the one that had so surprised her when it first came. She had abruptly stopped dreaming about the war: the dead faces she could not recognize when she woke but seemed to know so well in her dream; the many manifestations of missions she could not complete because she had lost some tiny piece of paper, or had missed the transport, or could not find the ship. Now it was always a variation on the same dream: she was standing on the road that wound through the wood to her house in Latvia, and the entire road was burning so that she could not get through.

She reached for the pull chain on the light and blinked at the brightness.

CHAPTER TEN

France, May, 1943

LANE BOARDED THE TRAIN, LOOKED right into the next car, and opted for the less-packed other side on the left. She'd only a small shoulder bag and elected to sit with it on her knee. It was funny, in the old days in her trips to France, she'd be wearing a flowered dress and would reach up and toss her bag in the overhead shelf and settle in with a book. Now she was dressed in a dull, and she hoped unremarkable, grey suit and a hat that was compact and businesslike. She put her hands on the bag and kept her eyes down or slanted toward the window. Of course, there was a war on, as they liked to say at home, but the atmosphere that pervaded was so unlike the way she remembered France that though this was her sixth trip in this capacity, she needed to try to identify what the difference was. It was drab, certainly, but there was a heightened sense of alertness. The niceties were more quickly delivered and somehow more strictly adhered to and then people seemed to sink deep into themselves. Even families with children travelling together scarcely spoke. Gone was the loose noisiness of the old train crowds, the careless manners and endless chatter among the passengers. Now everyone was suspicious. And suspect.

It still did not come home to her that she worked for Intelligence. It was a word she'd heard a great deal around her house as a child. Her father had been Intelligence in the previous war. He bashed about pretending to be a smooth, oily British businessman, but was actually sneaking about all over Russia and Germany speaking perfect Russian and German, working for the War Office. It struck her as a cold irony that she had never liked him much and here she was, aping him as if a script had been written for her. But she was convinced this was not the same thing. She didn't have to pretend to be the enemy . . . just a few missions to carry messages. She could pretend to be French.

A man came down the aisle and stood by her seat. Like her, he looked momentarily up at the luggage rack, decided against it, and sat, holding his briefcase on his lap—a businessman going into Lyon. He nodded at her and murmured something she didn't hear. She returned his greeting and then went back to looking out the window. The train started with a lurch. It was too warm and she wanted to open the window, but that would attract too much notice and probably lead to complaints about the through breeze, something continental Europeans in general seemed to fear. Instead she opened her book, *Madame Bovary*, and gave careful attention to appearing to read. What she did, though, was travel quickly down the corridors of her brain, into the place divided into different-coloured shelves, where she stored what she needed to know. This mission was on the green shelf, chosen maybe because it was nearly summer and even the war could not prevent that translucent yellow green that pervaded the trees and bushes of the countryside they were passing.

Mentally pulling each piece of information off the shelf, she reviewed again the codes that represented drop-off times and places. They meant nothing to her. It was coded information she must repeat to British officers, or French intelligence, or the resistance, but could not know the meaning of should she be captured. She didn't think much about being captured. At twenty-four you don't, even in these circumstances, though she had heard it could be extremely unpleasant to be pumped for information. She turned a page in *Madame Bovary* and reached into the green shelf for the map. She would get off at the village of Villeneuve, walk firmly along the road, and turn right up the street she felt she had already seen, as if she were calling on someone, and then continue to the outskirts.

She tried to imagine this arterial road that left the village to the forest northeast of it. She mentally looked up, a technique she had mastered to recall things into her prodigious memory, to see her handler, Bradley, telling her about it. She could see the backs of the heads of the people in front of her, and vaguely sensed the man next to her. Her eyes narrowed suddenly. There was something unusual . . . and she scanned back along the car. There were two men standing in the vestibule. Well, there were no seats, and it was an evening train. The two men were in conversation, leaning into each other in order to hear over the clatter of the metal. Their backs were toward her and their hats seemed to be the ones speaking to each other.

Wondering why she had thought this unusual, she was about to look back at the tiresome Madame B., when one of the men turned slightly and she saw his face.

She felt as though the air had been smacked out of her. It was Angus. She looked away in confusion. How could it be? He had been going back to his base in Ireland the last time she'd seen him. Just a week ago? But here he was in civvies, a nice grey suit and dark tie, in a French train. She glanced at him and he stared blankly back at her. Blankly, deliberately not knowing her. Who was he with? She willed the other man to turn around but he did not. He was dressed in dark blue. He was shrugging in a way that was convincingly French.

Desperately, she wanted to look at the man next to her to see if he'd noticed her shock, her shortness of breath, her confusion; she was aware she'd opened and shut the book several times as she tried to come to terms with what it meant to have Angus on the train when he should be flying over the North Atlantic, or at least getting ready to.

Her neighbour seemed to be snoozing, swaying slightly. She risked another look at Angus. He still looked at her; his face still set in the disinterested lines of a tired traveller whose surroundings mean nothing to him. She looked into his eyes and tried to will his mind to pick up what she was thinking—that she longed to be able to openly know him, say she loved him, and that she could not, could not, understand why he was on a train in the middle of occupied France with her. In this confusing moment she had no way of knowing she would never see him again.

CHAPTER ELEVEN

INSPECTOR DARLING STOOD WITH HIS hands in the pockets of his brown suit pants. He didn't like the brown suit; it had been his brother's. Darling hadn't had a lot of money when he got back to Canada. He was looking with almost expressionless curiosity at the corpse on the slab.

"What do you reckon?" he asked, using an expression he'd heard often on his air base in the north of England.

"Caucasian, thirty-five-ish, relatively fit, but slight. Killed by a blow to the side of the head. Not completely true," the pathologist, Ashford Gillingham, known as Gilly, corrected himself. "Felled by a blow is more like it. Seems to have drowned. No signs of struggle so I'd say he was out like a light when he was shoved in the creek. His feet are scraped and there's skin pulled off his ankle bones—perhaps it happened when he was pushed into the whatever-it-is where the water comes out into the creek. Did you find his shoes?" If Gilly was resentful at being made to work on the Dominion Day holiday, he did not show it.

Darling took his hands out of his pockets and approached the feet of the now-waxy-looking mystery man. "No. Nothing at the scene. I'll have to buzz out there again, I suppose. As it is, we've nothing else to go on. One crumpled bit of paper, soaked through in the pocket. It had something written in peacock ink, almost completely washed out. I've sent it over to Harrison to see if he can decipher anything with his magic potions after it dries. This blow that felled him, the classic blunt instrument?"

"Blunt, yes. No bits of evidence to tell us what, though. Hard, metallic; it could have really shattered the skull, but didn't. The assailant pulled his punch a bit, but it was enough to knock him out. It reminded me of the kinds of wounds you saw in the war in close combat. A rifle butt, say, though this is narrower. Because of the location just here, above and slightly behind the left ear, it would have put him out, but not killed him. Not immediately, that is. I have seen people die from a subsequent blood clotting in the brain from these kinds of blows. So, the person either was not enormously strong or just didn't hit him as hard as he could. As I said, enough to put him out, but not enough to kill him."

"I wonder if the woman is right about his being English?" Darling mused, not for the first time he was ashamed to admit to himself, on the intriguing Miss Winslow with her extraordinary sangfroid in the face of a corpse jammed into a creek on her property.

"She could be," Gilly mused. "There's something in the face that looks a bit toffee."

Darling laughed suddenly, an unusual enough event itself. "You can't tell that sort of thing. He could come from Salmo, for all you know. Now you've interrupted a train of thought. Why would she not seem surprised or distraught? Why the comment that he might be English?"

"You think the girl did it? Ames was complimentary about her. He didn't think she'd whack a guy on the head. Too refined. Too beautiful."

"Why shouldn't she? Being beautiful never stopped a determined woman who wanted to bean a man, and you said yourself it's not necessarily a heavy, masculine blow."

As he left Gilly's dismal little basement kingdom, Darling felt the impact of his last comment. It could have been a woman. He was extraordinarily glum when he got back to his office.

London, England, 1945

Jack Franks sat back in the uncomfortable wooden chair provided by the management at Somerset House. He felt nothing but weariness now that he knew. It was impossible to feel triumphant, or attached, or whatever one was supposed to feel. He had a name now, and it wasn't Franks. He thought about his parents; both dead in the bombing, only they weren't his parents. Someone else was. Elizabeth Conally. He wondered what she'd be like. She would be in her fifties. What would it feel like to see her? Nothing, he knew, like the sorrow he felt every day about the people he had always thought were his parents. It surprised and distressed him that their not being his parents took away none of the misery at having lost them. Outside, summer was trying gamely to assert its magic on the pummelled city. It had only just begun to sink in that the war was over. He'd had not a bad war, really, in Intelligence. Those friends who survived had all begun to realize that they missed the tension, the exaggerated jollity of surviving a mission and fetching up in a pub with plucky WAAFs who laughed at jokes and were less drippy than the pre-war girls they'd hung about with at college. Now they'd have to go back to some sort of lives. They felt too old to go back to finish up their degrees, those who'd left before they'd qualified. Jack was one of these. He was a year short at Cambridge, where he'd been reading history and Russian. Those years in Intelligence had fitted him to keep secrets. What, he'd wondered more than once in the last five months, might he do to make a living with such a skill?

The ultimate irony was, of course, that the whole time the universe had been keeping secrets from him. He'd rushed back when the neighbour had called to say his house had been hit. Stunned, not by the destruction he'd expected to see—after all, it had killed his parents outright—but by the lack of damage that was evident. The bomb had hit the back of the house, right in the garden, and both his parents had been in the kitchen, where somehow they'd been killed by the blast. How? He'd stood dumbly trying to work out how they could have died, and his neighbour, old Miss Pritchett, stood by clucking softly. "They was such dears, your parents. Always a kind word. Your mum used to bring me jam whenever she made it. How she found things during the war, I don't know, but she did. And they was so proud of you." Here she reached over and took his hand and stroked it as if she were rubbing lotion into it. "They always was. Even that first day they brought you home. You were a tiny little mite; couldn't have been more than six months. But she fed you up and soon you were a going concern. You made them very happy."

It took a moment, but then he realized what she'd said. "They moved here when I was six months old? I always thought they'd lived here since they were married."

"Yes, luvvy. They moved here when they were married. The house had been your gran's and she left it him."

"But then I came here when I was born, not six months old. No wonder I looked insubstantial. God, I'm going to have to arrange things. Miss Pritchett, thank you so much for letting me know. I'm glad you weren't hurt. It must have been terrifying for you. I've got to get back to my work, so I'm going to close up the house; I still can't get over there being a house at all."

Miss Pritchett shook her head. "I'm all right, me. But . . ." she hesitated, and then seemed suddenly resolved. "You've had a shock. You'd better come in, and I'll put the kettle on. The arranging can wait." And that's how he'd found out, sitting in his neighbour's parlour, that his parents had indeed brought him home at six months because they couldn't have children of their own, and they were ever so happy. They couldn't, she told, him, have loved you more if you was their own.

Now there was Elizabeth Conally in Cornwall, all the way on the bloody end of the country. As he walked back to the empty house, the kitchen of which he'd begun to repair, somehow feeling he could not let down his parents, who'd done so much for him, who'd saved him from . . . here his imagination gave way. Being an orphan, he supposed. So much about this surprised him. He never had felt, as so many children apparently did, that he was a foundling, that he was so ill suited to his parents that he must have been adopted. He had felt completely theirs, completely a part of them, and in the early years when his dad's parents were still alive, he was sure he could see himself in his granddad, a man who could do anything with his hands, though he'd been a writer who taught him to love history through the stories he told.

Miss Pritchett must be told that he would be going away. Perhaps that nephew of hers could come stay in the house while he was gone.

CHAPTER TWELVE

FINALLY ABLE TO BREAK THE bonds of fear, Lane moved. A surge of impatience and anger assailed her. Could she not have a night now without this? She could hear, she realized, a faint scraping noise somewhere above her and she wondered if this is what had wakened her. There was a kind of translucent, dark light from her open windows that sketched out the shapes in her room: her dressing table, the easy chair Kenny had given her, the bedroom door ajar into a much darker hall. She got out of bed and decided not to switch on her lamp because she'd never get to sleep afterward. She stepped into the hall to better hear the noise. It was definitely coming from the attic. Still feeling her way in the dark, she climbed the attic stairs and pushed open the door. The windows. She'd closed them, most assuredly, before her supper. But here they were, wide open, one of them rocking a little against the frame because of a light wind, causing the noises she'd heard. She really must get the latch fixed. She shivered. It was one thing to think of Old Lady Armstrong ghosting about opening windows in the middle of a sunny day, but at night, alone as she was, she felt a wave of apprehension that made her almost turn and go back down the stairs. But she couldn't have that window scraping all night. It would drive her mad. Resolutely she went to the open windows on the west side of the room, nearest the stairs, and reached up to close them. Even at night, the view from the top of the house was expansive.

She gave up on the closing and leaned out to look across the dark horizon. It was a clear night and the stars gleamed in swirling multitudes. She could see layers of different shades of darkness: the slope of the lawn, the bank of trees at the end, the lake, somehow reflecting light from the faraway universe, and then layers of darker and darker mounds of the distant mountains disappearing to the rim of the sky. There was a kind of beautiful melancholy about the moment, as though the windows stood open, waiting for something that would never happen. She wondered if she could capture this feeling in words. She would try in the morning. No. If she was true to her commitment, she would try immediately when she was downstairs, where her notebook and fountain pen were at the ready. Light be damned. She could sleep when she was dead. She'd heard this often in the sleepless nights of wartime. It was no less true now.

The breeze lifted suddenly, making the window move, and Lane pulled her attention back to the problem at hand. She spoke out loud. "I wouldn't mind getting some sleep, Lady Armstrong."

She reached up to the latch and then felt the strongest urge to look back out the window. Her gaze went toward the almost blacked-out mass of trees that covered the border between her property and Harris's. Her apprehension grew into fear. Night made the forest into an alien and hostile realm. She'd always been a little afraid of the dark. It was why she'd agreed to go into intelligence in the war, in a way: to stand up to the fear. She latched the window and went defiantly to the other side of the attic, where the windows looked out over the blue spruce at her front door, and the sparsely treed space between her house and her barn. Her gasp was involuntary and sounded too loud in the silence of the night. There it was again: a flash of light coming on and disappearing somewhere near the barn. She stood rigid, straining to see, wanting to open the window to lean out but fearing the noise. And as quickly as it had seemed to start, the blinking light stopped and there was only the night to look upon. That light had not been heading toward the road. It was on the other side of the barn, nearer the fence that closed off her small bit of pasture adjacent to Harris's barbed-wire-enclosed land.

Lane sat in her darkened kitchen, now fully dressed, trying to think through what she ought to do. She had decided against turning on any lights in case whoever was out there was alerted to someone knowing they were there, so she had dressed in the dark and found her torch, which was standing upright on the table in the hall. She had an idea that it must be Harris. It was in the direction of his land that the light seemed to be going. But she shook her head, as if to get the nonsense out. What would he be doing, a bit lame and none too young, thrashing about in the bush at, was it nearly three in the morning? If it was he, it was really none of her business. It was his land, and maybe he was having trouble with a mare foaling. On the other hand, it was highly unlikely a mare would be out in the underbrush. Perhaps he needed help? She supposed she could phone him but if he wasn't in trouble, she would wake him and irritate him for nothing.

Not sure why in the end, Lane delivered herself into the frightening world of the nighttime forest, and picked her way up the path at the back of the barn and toward her field. She stood, undecided for a few moments, and then turned off her torch and let her eyes adjust again to the darkness. Before her was the fence between her land and Harris's. She would have to climb over or through it, to get to the other side. The barbed wire was a singular deterrent. Pulling gently on the top strand, she tried to find a way to pull it enough to squeeze through without damaging herself on the barbs. It gave readily and she could just see that the strand directly beneath it sagged downward, as if this had been used before as a crossing point. With care, she bent herself through the gap and swore softly when a barb caught the back of her shirt. Safely on the other side, she surveyed the darkness. Whoever it had been was neither visible nor audible now. She could just see the line of the top of the forest against the sky. If she could make her way through the nearly waist-high grass to the other side of the field, she should be able to look down the slope and see if she could catch any sign of the mystery torchlight. She moved as quickly as she could, hoping the swishing sound she was making in her progress could not be heard. Then she stopped. There was the sound: a stick cracking on the edge of the field before her. She realized that it must be very near the road. Muttering a silent "Damn!" she stood stock still, peering blindly at the wall of darkness. Even as she listened for another cracking twig, her heart pounding out an anxious rhythm, she caught a brief flare of light. She had a momentary flash of the war and Morse code transmissions. Another faint sound, as if someone was moving through the bushes in the distance. There! The burst of light again. She felt the breath catch in her throat. Was the person coming closer or going farther away? When the light reappeared, it seemed to have moved to the left and farther down. Definitely to the road, then. What on earth did she think she was going to do? If she tried to follow the person, it could well put her in danger and, she realized belatedly, mess up any tracks or evidence the person might be leaving.

She knew she was mad to be out here at all, and wanted nothing more than to scurry back across the field to her safe, if haunted, house, but now she had to investigate whatever it was that she thought she'd seen in the underbrush. No she didn't! If it was Harris, however peculiar it was, it was his land and he had a right to smash about in his own underbrush. On the other hand, he'd been smashing around in her underbrush as well, she was sure of it. The light she'd seen from the attic was right near her barn.

She watched the velvety dark for any more signs of the mystery person's receding light and strained to hear any further sound. The person could have continued away from her or turned back toward her, if he'd seen the light she was carrying, or he could be, like her, stopped in the dark, watching and listening for her next move.

The wait was becoming agony and her body felt like it was beginning to congeal into the position she was holding.

Still, there was no sound or repetition of the light across the field. Blast, she thought, I can't slink about here all night. She turned and walked back the way she'd come. She'd become used to the dark, and she could just make out the path she'd made for herself. When she got to her fence, she climbed back through it, this time without mishap, and for the first time wondered why there was no gate into this field near the barn. She would have to look into it. When she was safely over, she turned her torch back on to light her way back to the house. It was in the clearing around the barn that her foot hit something and she shone her torch down to see what it was. There, in the patch of light, was a man's shoe.

Illogically she looked quickly around, as if in the pitch dark, she might see someone or something that had dropped it. Squatting down, she shone the light on the shoe. A light brown leather, the laces still done up. Well polished and slightly worn along the inside of the heel. It was tipped sideways. She could have done that, kicking it. She moved her torch around the perimeter of the shoe to see if there were signs of someone going by. Of course there must be and she was trampling all over them! Though she could not know for certain, she would bet this shoe had not been there before. It looked, well, recent. It wasn't dirty, or looking as if it had been there for some time, enduring the weather that though dry, would still have delivered a nightly dew that might have shown on its otherwise shiny surface.

With some reluctance, she realized it would be more prudent to retreat and wait till morning to call the police out from Nelson. She was sorry about this sensible decision, because for a moment she felt something like the rush she used to feel in the field at night when she hadn't known if she'd find the drop point, or who might find her. She made peace with herself by resolving to come out in the light of the early morning to see what she could see.

GNAWING HUNGER TOLD Darling it was nearly noon, but he was reluctant to give up yet on the survey report for King's Cove he had open on his desk. It appeared to contain not so much nothing as nothing immediately comprehensible to him. He would have to get someone to interpret what it said. It was a faint lead, but he liked to get a sense of everything that might conceivably have any bearing on a case. He was somewhat relieved when a figure appeared at his door.

"Inspector. I think you'd better see this." Darling rubbed his eyes; they tired more easily since he'd come back from his life as a bomber pilot. Charles Harrison, the lab man, was hovering with a look of contained excitement, holding a large photograph by its corner. It was still damp, and so must have been rushed untimely up from the lab for the inspector's perusal.

"Go on, then."

Harrison placed the photograph triumphantly on Darling's desk, the survey having been carefully put back into his in-tray. Darling turned his complete focus on what Harrison had to offer. Initially, he was unrewarded. The photograph before him was of a piece of blurry, damp paper with various stains darkening its wrinkled surface.

"Yes?" said Darling.

"Look closely, sir."

"I am looking closely, Charles. What do you think I'm doing?"

"Sorry, sir. Here." With the back of a pencil, he began to trace the air over the photograph. "It was the piece of paper you found in the victim's pocket, sir. We thought we wouldn't get much, but the enlarged photograph does trace out a couple of partial words. Here, you can see what must be the end of a word, *ane*, and then after this bit of blurring, *ins*, and maybe a *W* here at the end." By this time, Ames had wandered in, sensing excitement, and was watching Harrison's performance keenly, his hands in his pockets.

"What is the name of the girl up the lake?" Harrison asked suddenly. "Winslow is the last name, but what was her first name?"

"Lane," Darling said, leaning closely into the photograph again. "Could that be *Lane Winslow*?" he mused.

"It could, sir, now that you say it. There is only one smudge here in front of the first set of letters. In fact, now that I see it, I can't see how it would allow for another interpretation."

DARLING AND AMES were at the counter of the café on Baker Street that had such excellent ham and cheese sandwiches, and coffee that still tasted good after the swill of the wartime rations in Europe.

Though he felt a small pang, Darling could not keep a note of I-told-you-so out of his voice. "So, it turns out Mr. Tweed Jacket arrived here with her name on a piece of paper and got himself killed. What do you say to that, defender of the too-lovely-to-kill-anyone?"

Ames was gloomy—though, being young, not too gloomy to make inroads on his ham sandwich, and so he spoke with his mouth full. "Yeah. Well. It's still circumstantial, though, isn't it? We don't have any proof that she killed him and while we are on the subject, all that dragging and stuffing of the body into the creek would require more than the usual lady-like amount of strength. She's not that big, if you'll recall."

Darling, who recalled this very well, sighed. Not too big and yet, pleasantly, not fragile either. "Well, it's the only lead we've got, and they're definitely connected, and we definitely still don't have the shoes and no ID for the victim, which it now appears she might be able to help us with after all. And now there's a reason to worry that if she is involved after all, she could be cleaning up the site, which I fear we need to retrace, so we might finish our lunch and have another drive up the lake, eh?"

They had only just got back into the station when a flustered desk sergeant called out, "Ah, Inspector Darling, sir. I took a call very much earlier this morning, sir, and misplaced the slip. A Miss Winslow would be grateful if you could return her call at your earliest convenience."

Darling looked at Ames with raised brows. "Well, speak of the devil, eh? What time did the call come in, O'Brien?"

"I'm sorry sir, right when we opened up at eight-thirty."

"Hell," said Darling. "What's that, Ames?"

"I was saying, sir, I still cannot bring myself to think she is. The devil, I mean," mused Ames.

CHAPTER THIRTEEN

DARLING AND AMES WERE STANDING in the kitchen of Lane's house, Ames poised to take minutes in his notebook. Lane wished she could get them all to sit down.

"Miss Winslow, just out of curiosity, why were you up at three in the morning in the first place?"

Lane hesitated. She was somewhat used to delivering every relevant piece of information to a commanding officer, and Darling felt like a commanding officer, but she thought she could hardly share her little fantasy that Lady Armstrong went about opening windows in a disembodied state. "I have a window in the attic with a broken latch. I went upstairs when the wind made the window scrape against the sill. It woke me."

"I see. So, having seen the light flashing in the field, you went outside to investigate. What I find peculiar is that this is a fairly unusual course of action. Most people, and here I mean men or women, would not go out at three in the morning to see what was going on."

The silence among them after this hung on in a way that was inching toward the uncomfortable, at least for

Lane. She could not explain why she'd gone out into the night.

The only thing she could say concretely was that she was sure it had to do with the murder and she felt it was important. She decided to say this. "I think I just felt it must have something to do with the death of that man. I had this idea that someone was . . . I don't know . . . cleaning up or something and I think I felt I ought to stop it. And considering what I found, I'm worried you left coming out here a bit late."

Her use of the words "cleaning up" was so close to what Darling had been saying earlier in the day that he looked at her sharply. But there was nothing in her face but puzzlement. Her pageboy hair had been pulled back into a ponytail, and a few wisps of auburn were hanging over her eye. She had on a white, sleeveless blouse that seemed to highlight her features: a generous pleasant mouth, eyes that he remembered as green, though in this light they appeared more hazel, and the brow over them just at this moment was furrowed. He brought himself smartly back to the problem at hand. He tried to decide whether he ought to get out with Ames in tow to look at this suspiciously and suddenly produced shoe, or if he should confront her now with the evidence in the photo that she most certainly was connected to the dead man.

Lane was bewildered by the hesitation in the proceedings and wondered if she'd transgressed some Canadian law regarding the scene of a crime, or interference with an investigation. "I realize it must seem strange that I might go out in the dark to investigate. I can only say that I thought it might be important. I felt this very strongly, but once out there, I realized that the figure . . . well the light he was carrying actually, was going further into Harris's land and I just thought if I try to crash about following, I'd mess up any evidence there might be. And to be honest, I was petrified he'd seen me, so I stood like a ninny till I was frozen solid and I was sure he'd gone. It was on the way back that I found the shoe. I was very surprised that it should be on my side of the fence. I didn't want to touch anything but I went down this morning to make sure I'd not been imagining it and it was still there; a nice, if scuffed-up, brogue. I've been quite nervous, waiting, in case the someone who dropped or put it there came back." Here she allowed a slight look of reproof at Inspector Darling.

Darling was experiencing a small internal war. She seemed honest enough, but this could be a colossal game on her part. She knew something about this man, he had the evidence in his manila envelope, and yet she seemed, with complete sincerity, intent on helping their investigation. And quite intelligently, with all this not wanting to mess up evidence. Ames was writing, and the scraping of his pencil went on into the silence when she had finished this explanation.

"Oh, and I called him this morning. Harris, I mean, to see if he'd been out last night for any reason and he asked me what kind of a fool I took him for." Lane smiled at this.

Darling wanted to smile too, but he sighed instead. "All right, Miss Winslow. I think you'd better sit down. In fact we'll all sit down. Not you, Ames." This when Ames made to pull out a chair. "You go fetch the envelope."

"Sir," said Ames, who in truth did not mind being ordered around by Darling, whom he longed to be one day, but he was worried about what he might miss in the minutes it would take him to go out to the car for the envelope. "And the bag," interjected Darling.

And the bag. "Back in a jiff," Ames said, and meant it.

"Something has come up, Miss Winslow, that considerably alters our situation here. I don't mind saying I was very surprised to get your call. You will see why in a moment, but we have reason to believe that you can tell us more about the victim than you seemed disposed to earlier. Needless to say, your banging about outdoors at all hours in this context will strike you, I dare say, as odd." Darling said this in his usual unhurried and calm manner.

Lane wondered, now with some irritation, how he could maintain such a correct tone and demeanour while talking in this slangy fashion. "I'm sorry?" she said.

"I mean, Miss Winslow, that given what we now know, your movements last night might be looked upon as somewhat suspect. Ah. Here's Ames." Darling held out his hand and Ames placed into it the brown manila envelope. Darling unwound the string holding the flap shut, pulled out the eight-by-eleven photo, and placed it on the table, squaring it before Lane. She looked at it and frowned. His last remark had set off a spiral of anxious speculation that made it hard for her to concentrate on the grainy print before her.

It was clearly a photo of a piece of paper; she could see the ridges that were still visible, though someone had tried to smooth them out. She could also see faint traces of what looked like fragments of writing. She felt the constriction somewhere in her chest before she even really knew why, and then her brain caught up. It was the W. The way the end of it curled down into a little drop. But so bizarre was this thought that she shut it out completely. "What is this, Inspector?" She kept her voice completely even. She'd had a good deal of experience with covering anxiety and appearing cool in occupied France. She was surprised by how easy it was to do still, and was possessed now of a caution nearly equal to that which she'd exercised during missions. It seemed vital to her that she keep her wits about her.

The inspector leaned forward. "This is a photograph taken by our lab people, after they'd done work on it, of the piece of paper we found on the victim's body. In the jacket pocket. It was the only thing we found on his person. No identification, no papers, no passport. Just this. If you will see, here," he pointed to the letters that were visible, "are the letters spelling parts of words, we suspect. *Ane*, *ins*, and then this *W* here. I won't keep you guessing, Miss Winslow, about what this suggested to us immediately. Your name."

Lane sat back heavily on her wooden kitchen chair. Of course. She could see this. She would have said the same thing, now that it was put to her. And now, because she was an orderly thinker, she allowed the thought she had torpedoed earlier. The *W*. Angus had written his *W* with this little drop that now seemed to be pulsating off the photograph. But of course, many people might do this. It was only that she was so aware because on the many letters he had addressed to her it was the *Miss L. Winslow* that had made her heart stop every time she saw it. She had developed an affection for the little drop on the *W*.

Her logical approach brought her a small degree of comfort. Since this absolutely could not have been written by Angus, who had been dead since 1944, then it must not have been. Often she would receive letters from him from wherever he was deployed. It had been comforting how they often came before she went out on a mission. As if he knew, which of course was rubbish. He knew nothing about her work. That was what had made their relationship a strain at times, all that subterfuge and pretending to a desk job in the War Office. That life was part of her deep and finished past.

But now remained the problem of her name. This was less easy to explain away and its presence in the dead man's pocket made absolutely no sense to her. But even that thought was wrong. It made a kind of sense, the implications of which made her blood freeze.

"Miss Winslow?" Darling had been watching her.

"Inspector, I see how you have reached that conclusion. I do. But I cannot make head or tail of it. If the man was carrying my name, why was he carrying it? The other explanation is that this is not my name at all."

Ames spoke up suddenly. "I've thought of that, sir. It could be something like *plane window* if that *s* weren't an *s* but a partially erased *d*."

"Thank you, Ames. Always on the job. And what would the meaning of such a note be? Why would a man who ended up dead in the middle of Miss Winslow's water source have *plane window* in his pocket?" His tone was somewhere between repressive and mocking.

"It could have been where he sat on the way over, sir, if he came on an aeroplane. I've had really silly things on pieces of paper in my pockets. The other day I had a note that said *pencil markings* in my pocket. It was really a reminder to get something to remove the pencil markings from my fence that some hooligan put there but if I'd been killed in Miss Winslow's creek," here he grinned at her cheerfully, "it might take on much greater significance. Someone might think it was a dying man's clue to what had happened to him, no?"

"Can I interject at this point that there is no reason to suppose he was killed in my creek," said Lane, a little peevishly.

"You make a point, Ames," Darling conceded, ignoring her.

Lane tried to relax. There was still that *W* with its little downturn, and though her earlier logic had absolutely ruled it out, she could not shake the idea that it was so very like Angus's writing.

"However," Darling continued after a moment, "we must think about probability. It is more likely that a note found near the home of Lane Winslow, which is made up of enough letters to reasonably conclude it has Lane Winslow's name spelled out on it, is more probable than that the note would say *plane window* and only if the *s* were a damaged *d*."

"But what doesn't make sense, to me at least, is that I do not know this man, I could swear to it. He certainly never contacted me before he died. Who was he? I mean, perhaps I should have another look. You still have him, I suppose? Of course. You will. Until you've solved this." She retained her steady calm but she knew now she had to see him. Could it be someone she knew, even slightly, who'd been sent for her? And if it was, what would she do? If she could be traced here, where was left?

Ames, who should have been writing, had stopped and was watching Lane with something bordering on admiration. Here she was, clearly on the verge of being accused of being involved in a murder and she was behaving as if she was completely innocent and offering to come view the body. Perhaps she was innocent. The thought cheered him up immensely.

"I will most certainly take you up on that offer, Miss Winslow. We still have him, yes. On ice, as it were. In the meantime, since we have driven all the way out here, perhaps you could take us back down the garden path, to see what you saw last night."

"*Très amusant, Inspecteur*," said Lane, "but I assure you my story is quite genuine, and I will not be leading you anywhere fictitious."

CHAPTER FOURTEEN

London, June, 1943

MRS. DONALD CALLED UP THE stairs, "The post, Miss Winslow! From your bosses at the Ministry!" She thought Lane was a secretary. Lane, who'd been drinking the last of her tea before she set off to work at that self-same Ministry, was sure she would have a mission in the next week or so and was doing the mental exercises she had early decided helped her to prepare. She had developed her kitchen shelving metaphor for storing information and she was mentally clearing each of the shelves, one by one, taking things out, packaged like groceries from the shop: tins, paper-wrapped sugar, and so on, but were facts, figures, and coordinates to she had no idea what, and she was throwing them into a large metal bin. She'd not been on a mission since May, when she was sure she'd seen Angus on the train. And she'd not heard from him, either. It had been difficult, having no word from Angus and not being able to talk to anyone about him. He had been clear: their relationship must be kept completely hush-hush, mainly, he told her, to protect her work of translation. And reporting to work every day and finding that she was set to translating what seemed to her to be extremely non-essential documents. A report in Pravda about the marriage of a minor government official did not seem to her to be something the security of Great Britain would be hanging on.

The sound of Mrs. Donald's voice calling out the post nearly made her heart stop. Angus! It must be; who else would write to her? She was not deterred by the return address that must have been from one of the government offices. Angus had always written as though he was an official of the government. Well, he was, as a pilot. The letters were always breezy, as if from a friend, but the language they had developed provided them with meeting places, with their chance to be together. Their relationship had needed to be kept secret, but his letters, sent in the often-long intervals between their meetings, kept her alive. She put her cup down with a clatter and bounded down the stairs. The letter was sitting on the landing and she snatched it eagerly.

There was her name, all right, but typewritten, and the envelope looked official. She groaned in disappointment and saved opening the letter until she was back in her room. She leaned against her dressing table and applied the letter opener to the envelope. There was a single sheet, even the signature typewritten. *Dear Miss Winslow, you are asked to present yourself to the Office of Commander R. Fredrickson at 08:00 hours on Wednesday, June 23.* Nothing else. June 23rd was the next day.

At lunchtime, she was at the door of the building she worked in with another of the girls, Betty, who was blowing smoke rings in a nonchalant fashion into the cool drizzle of the day while watching the crowds in the street. "Honestly,"

Betty said, "there isn't a single decent man left in London." In spite of the anxiety that had been gnawing at her all day, Lane smiled at this. While, indeed, not in London—there *was* a war on, as everyone was so fond of saying—her man was decent. She wished sometimes she could babble about how good-looking he was, like the other girls did over their glasses of beer at the pub. Betty waved at a young woman approaching them. "Ah, Mary, there you are. The tea shop today?" The other two laughed at this, as they had never been anywhere else after finding the best lunches for the best price. Sometimes even ham made a rare appearance on the menu, though usually it was thin slices of the ubiquitous Spam. It was too risky to pick somewhere else and miss the rare ham day.

The tea room was steamed up from the damp coats of the girls, who crammed in at lunch from firms all over the area, and the warmth coming from the kitchen. Not a ham day today, but they opted for the bowl of bean soup that was on offer, with a nice roll. Mary was leaning in. "I think something's gone wrong. Everyone on my floor is all quiet and people keep going into closed rooms to confer. I think something's gone west with an operation!" Her two companions looked anxiously around at this revelation. They never, ever talked about operations outside their offices. But Mary was too full of her news to be concerned, though she lowered her voice further. "One of the agents has been killed; not shot down, but on the ground during a pick-up. Angus someone. I heard one of the men talking by the WC."

Lane stopped hearing anything her companions said. Angus. She felt a rush of horror go through her. She forced her mind, which suddenly seemed to be in slow motion, to order the facts. It was not possible that it could be her Angus. He was not an agent, for starters, and he was stationed in Ireland and he flew missions over . . . the North Atlantic, surely. It's what he'd told her. He'd never been in operations. But he'd been on a train in France a month ago and he shouldn't have been there either. She shuddered violently and stood up. "I'm not feeling well. It must be something in the soup. I'm . . . I'm . . ." and she made her way through the suffocating tea room to the door. The other two looked at their bowls with suspicion and then Betty noticed Lane had rushed out without her coat and hat. "For pity's sake! Mary, hold the fort; I'll go after the daft sickie. God, I hope she isn't up the spout!"

She found Lane shivering on the front step, the back of her hand over her mouth, taking deep breaths. "You don't look too clever. Here, put your coat on and get off home. I'll stop on your floor and tell them you're not well." She helped her on with the coat and positioned her hat over her auburn hair. She took Lane's hand, suddenly. "Listen, you're not . . . ?"

Lane looked at her as if she were only just seeing her, and then somehow realized what she meant. She shook her head and turned to go, then she looked back at her friend. "Thank you," she said simply, and walked away, leaving Betty standing ambivalently on the pavement. Betty knew Lane was intensely private and that she would only annoy her by trying to follow and help.

Lane had never received another word from Angus after that, so she knew it must have been her Angus. She had mourned silently and deeply. She could not get past it. There was nothing to help her close the door on her grief; no funeral, no newspaper obituary. She saw only then what an absolute fantasy she'd been living in. She hadn't even known where he'd come from. It was as if he had never existed at all.

LANE WAS GLAD to step outside into the sun. She'd finally stopped mourning for Angus in the last year, but sorrow had ground her down, left a hollow that she had come to expect would be permanent. It was not just the loss of him; it was the strange lack of any trace of him after. She had realized as the weeks passed after she learned of his death that she had not a single token of his. She hadn't even kept the letters, because he'd been so insistent that she burn them. She hadn't questioned him about this, or anything really. It was his physical presence that was everything to her. How young she'd been to have that absolute trust in a man! She had recovered in stages by continuing her war work, then moving to France, and now by moving here. It had been well over two years. But she was oppressed by the memories that had flooded her mind at the sight of that *W*, the sheer inadmissibility of it and yet the too-plausible idea that on that paper, her name must be inscribed . . . by someone. She led the policemen around the house and past the new flowerbed she'd put in. The sun, nearly overhead, cast short busy shadows around them as they walked across to the clearing in front of the barn.

"Please take us only as far as the shoe. We will have to decide what steps to take from there." Inspector Darling was walking directly behind Lane, and his voice sounded sudden in the heavy afternoon silence.

"Yes, of course," she replied. In a few minutes she stopped, relief sweeping through her. The shoe was still there, looking more than ever in the light of day as if it had been dropped. If it had not been there its absence would have indicated that whoever it was had been back again. Just as quickly her anxiety was renewed. Not only did she have to worry about Darling's puzzling attitude to her and this incomprehensible problem of the note, now she realized that she had become used to feeling safe so far from anywhere. But clearly someone had been right here on her land, who might be—no, was almost certainly—a murderer. She could see that the area around the shoe had been disturbed and realized with a sinking heart that the only disturbance visible would be what she had caused. Any ability to follow who might have come there in the night had been eliminated by her own reckless crashing about in the dark.

From where they were standing they could see Harris's field stretching out and then down on the other side of the fence. Ames was already photographing the shoe and Darling was inspecting, Lane assumed, its position or condition or something. She looked across the fence to the other side, but it was impossible to see anything much but deep yellow grass and low fern and the purple spatters of what she thought of as wild sweet peas that tangled around the base of them.

"I think I must have been here and the light I saw was sort of over there, at eye level, and then I saw it moving that way." She moved her arm to the left. "It was going down as well as away, and then it disappeared. I could see even last night that the person would have been heading across the field and down toward the road, I assumed to Harris's house. Though in that case, why not cut down toward the right, which probably leads directly to the back of the house? Much shorter than going by the road. It would surprise me that he didn't know about it, but it was three in the morning."

"Thank you. We'll take it from here. You may, if you would be so kind, return to the house. We will stop by on the way out." Darling touched the rim of his hat, and went past her with Ames at his heels holding the bag and his camera.

Poor Ames, she thought, having to do all the heavy lifting. He didn't seem to mind it. In fact he appeared to like his inspector. She was sorry to be ordered away. The heat of the afternoon filtering through the trees and the immediacy and intrigue of the shoe had begun to keep the other, darker, thoughts at bay. She turned and walked back up the path and down toward the house, gleaming white against the lawn and weeping willow that hung over a long-empty rock pond. She would revive the pond, she thought. Kenny might know how to do that. He'd probably built the thing in the first place. Now though, the security she had felt in this fresh new land was shaken. She would have to face it, have to follow Darling in to town, have to look squarely at the dead man and pray he was no one she knew, because really, no matter what, she was never going back.

"PUZZLING, SIR," AMES declared as he and Darling were returning to where they had parked the car in Lane's driveway.

"Yes, Ames. Well spotted. Murders in which the suspect does not walk into our police station to turn himself in usually are." They had reached the car and Ames was opening the trunk to put away his camera bag and the shoe, which he'd wrapped in his handkerchief. "However, if you mean that the behaviour of Miss Winslow is puzzling, I must concede. Still—" he said this with sudden resolve "—we'd better go down the hill and have a chat with Harris. Run and tell Miss W. that we will be back in due course. Let's see if she does a bunk while we're gone." He didn't really think she would, he decided, which added to every puzzling aspect of the case.

"Now then, Ames. Let us contemplate this shoe business. We have found one shoe on the path but not the other and furthermore, this shoe was not there when we went up to see and retrieve the body. We would have seen it. Well, unless Miss Winslow moved it last night, which she has assured us in her meticulous way that she did not."

Ames had backed the car into the road during this speech and now reflected on Miss Winslow. "You know, sir, she shows some familiarity with policing. Didn't she say she is a writer? Perhaps she writes crime novels."

"Shoes, Ames. Shoes." But Darling made a mental note to ask Miss Winslow that very question.

"Right. Well, are they the dead man's shoes? And if they are, were they taken off after he was killed and if so, why? Where have they been up to now? And this is the part I don't get, sir: why only one?" He drove slowly back toward the Nelson road junction, as if wanting to give this conversation sufficient time.

"Good questions, Ames. A for effort. Let's see what we learn from Mr. Harris."

"GOD, WHAT A depressing place," Ames said, looking around at the neglected garden and peeling house.

"Yes, thank you, Ames," Darling said. At that moment Harris appeared at the door of the barn.

"Mr. Harris, good morning. I wonder if you could spare us a couple of moments?" Darling said.

"I haven't got all day," was the reply.

This caused Ames to look around. Though the house was positioned with a view of the lake and looked like it had been built to house a family, the bleakness of it was the dominant note. Harris, he decided, had nothing but time.

"Miss Winslow has just told us that she saw someone on your property at about three in the morning, walking about in the brush with a flashlight. Can you tell us anything about this?"

"I tell you what I told her. It is absolutely fantastical rubbish. This is a quiet and long-standing community. People do not fumble about in the underbrush in the middle of the night."

Darling switched tactics. He would not, he decided, bring up the fact that a shoe that had not been seen on the path on the first visit to the scene now had appeared there. It was possible that this man, angrily fisting and unfisting an oily cloth in a way that suggested either nervousness or a desire to pop him one, could have been the one moving shoes in the middle of the night.

"Do you live here alone, Mr. Harris?"

"What bloody business is it of yours?"

Darling was pulling for the pop in the nose theory. "We are trying to solve a murder, Mr. Harris, and someone was walking around your property last night with a flashlight, an activity that you have just told us would be nearly impossible to imagine in this traditional, well-run community, and if it wasn't you, perhaps it was someone else in your household."

Harris threw the rag viciously onto the floor of the tractor. "There hasn't been anyone in my 'household' since my slut of a wife left in the first war."

"Did you quarrel?"

"No, we did not quarrel. I was not here; there was a war on, in case you've forgotten. I suppose she got tired of being alone and buggered off."

"So you came back from Europe and found her gone? When did you get back?"

Harris stood squarely in front of Darling and seemed to pull himself up to some new, menacing height. "That question can have absolutely nothing to do with this business. I got back after the thankless job of serving my country in 1920 to find my wife gone and my orchard burned. Since then I keep myself to myself. I was not crashing about in the bush last night and I did not kill that man and I want you off my property. Now clear off!"

Darling tipped his hat and turned back toward the car. "Come, Ames. Please don't leave the area, Mr. Harris. We may have a few more questions at a later date." When he opened the door of the car, he put his foot on the running board and then looked back at the simmering Harris with a pleasant expression. "You've done well, sir, orchard-wise, if you found yourself burnt out. You must have worked hard to put it back together."

And with that he was back in the car. "Back to Miss Winslow's, please, Ames. What did you think of Mr. Harris?"

"Am I right in suggesting he seemed angrier than absolutely necessary? Why all this fuss about when he got back from the front? It's ancient history, isn't it? Nearly thirty years ago. Come to think of it," Ames added brightly, "if he got back in 1920, that is, in fact, late. My dad returned quickly at the end of the proceedings."

Darling turned to look at Ames with interest. He realized with a twinge of guilt that he too often employed his constable only as a foil for his jibes. Ames was quite a good young policeman. Perhaps he didn't give him quite enough scope. "You know something I don't?"

"Well, only this. I happen to know that there was a big fire here in 1919. Quite a lot of orchard burned as well as local forested land, and it set the apple industry back a bit. My dad again."

"Well done. So he makes a large fuss over a couple harmless questions, and he comes back late from the war. Neither one is a hanging offence; nevertheless, it's peculiar. Especially his trying to get us off the activities of last night. Remind me when we get back. I must send a wire to the War Office. There might be something in Harris's war record."

CHAPTER FIFTEEN

The Somme, France, 1917

"HURRY, WOULD YOU? I'M DYING of cold here." Robin Harris flapped his hand at John Armstrong, indicating the thermos of tea John was holding. If he were to put his head over the edge of the trench, he knew he would see a strip of luminescent grey on the eastern edge of the horizon, directly behind the enemy line. Harris had been imagining it with a combination of longing and anxiety. That first light always seemed infused with the freshness of any new day, as if on this day, anything was possible. He used to love the mornings at home. Here the light turned quickly to a grey smudge and today's light promised another "over the top." The prospect made him fidgety and ill at ease with everything.

John took another noisy swig. Steam rose from his mouth in the semi-light. He handed the thermos across to Harris and wiped his mouth. The whistle was blown somewhere nearby in the murky light. "Bugger," he muttered and leaned against the grimy, slatted wall of the trench.

"Bugger indeed," replied his cousin Robin. He put the thermos down and they shook hands. Then they were over.

It seemed there was a long moment of silence, as if they ran in slow motion over a murky landscape, and then a burst of gunfire that exploded as if everywhere at once.

IN LATER YEARS, he would reflect that this was the last coherent memory Harris had of that day. The subsequent hours and weeks and months were lost. When he found himself in hospital in Sussex, he felt that he had literally found himself; that he woke up one day and he was in a strange place and it was a cool, sunny spring day.

He knew he hadn't been unconscious the whole time, because chipper nurses were charging him with things he'd said. "Oh, now, that's not what you said last week, is it?" He was very, very frightened to realize he had no idea. He became afraid that he was mad, or had been, and would not ask how long he'd been there, in case this madness was somehow confirmed on the face of some bemused intern. He found it strange that he knew exactly who he was, Robin Harris, lieutenant, Princess Mary's regiment, King's Cove, British Columbia, and that he had a wife named Liz, but he could not remember anything from the moment he shook hands with John and they were over the trench on that early morning.

Then it happened. He was in a session of "therapy" with a young doctor. He dreaded these sessions because he felt stupid and frightened. Dr. Rich evinced nothing but patience as he tried to tease away at Harris's brain, and this infuriated him. Once Harris burst out, "Just send me bloody well home. What is this costing the British government, eh? What I don't remember isn't worth remembering."

"Usually it will be something significant that is being cloaked by the unconscious. That is what we want to get at, Lieutenant. And as to the expense, don't lose sleep. You are a war hero and were at the Somme, without you lot we'd still be out there or else I'd be conducting this session in German. Now let's go back. John has his hand out toward you with the thermos of tea. Can you tell me what either of you said in that moment?" John's hand is reaching, but there is no thermos. He is reaching up from the ground. Why is he on the ground? Robin feels himself backing away. Mud is grabbing at his boots. He falls and tries to scuttle backward on his behind. John's hand is still there, his fingers splayed out, reaching. Is it John? He tries to stop the memory and see his face, but now it is unleashed, a flood. He has regained his footing and is running away from the hand. He hears John's voice, calling, "Help, please."

It's the "please." Robin slams his hands over his ears and closes his eyes. He can hear Dr. Rich through the blocking of his ears, indistinct. Suddenly it is the present that is fuzzy and the past, that moment, that is terrifyingly present. He can hear and smell and feel. It is mud, blood, a buzzing in his head he cannot shake. He gets the idea that by blocking his ears, he is trapping the memory inside, and he must get rid of it. He pulls his hands away and looks, mouth agape, around the room. It seems to work. The world rights itself slowly, though his heart is pounding as if he has been running.

The fool Rich is there, leaning forward, concerned. "What is it, Lieutenant Harris? Have you remembered something?" His notebook at the ready.

"No," Robin muttered, "not a thing."

London, England, April 15, 1946

Franks sat at his desk wondering, not for the first time, about the relevance of his work. He had the feeling someone up above him was making it all up as they went along. These secretive meetings and speculations about the motivations of a nation that a year ago had been an ally and now suddenly had become a sinister and unknowable threat. He'd understood the work during the war. Intercepting Nazi communications, muddling up their own to keep it from a clearly defined enemy with whom they were at war. He sighed. This made him want to go back to university and try again to become a dentist, or some equally uncomplicated profession. But of course one didn't do that. His course was set and this was it. He'd been asked to go through a pile of "communications" and detect any pattern, to offer up an idea of what might be the underlying meaning. The papers, translations from Russian, had come from some other part of the organization that, again, seemed intent on keeping itself opaque, even to those who worked there.

His mind was not on it; it had to be admitted. When he'd first learned that his parents were his *adopted* parents, his sense of his place in the world had suddenly been rocked sideways and he had not recovered. Everything he did now seemed to have a false note about it, as if he must be living someone else's life, as if he were holding a spot in line for someone he didn't know. He had thought of rushing off to Cornwall to find his birth mother and he had balked at the last minute. It would make real something he couldn't quite accept. He wondered if all adopted people felt this way, or if it was because he found out so late; if he'd known since he was young he'd have had a chance to adjust.

He had been seeing a girl he met toward the end of the war, but even this had faded. She had left in a huff from the café they were at one night, a month before, saying he was obviously seeing someone else, judging by his complete lack of interest in her. He wanted to tell her that the problem was that he *was* someone else, only he didn't know who. Now, sitting at his desk, riffling through these nonsensical papers, he began to feel a tiny seed of resolve. This couldn't go on. He had always paid attention to these small signals from inside and, though he didn't know who he was, he reasoned that he was someone and that the signals, these instincts at least, were real. He would go to Cornwall, find his mother, and begin to make sense of his life. He would go see the director, get time off—explain to him what was going on. The director would probably think him pathetic but there was nothing he could do about that. In fact, the director, who seemed to know everything and had been his mentor, in a way, since he left the college, might know how he could find his mother. In fact, he suspected the man kept information about everyone who worked for him.

CHAPTER SIXTEEN

LANE HAD WONDERED HOW IT would be. Would she be driven all the way into Nelson by Darling and Ames? But then they'd have to get her back. Their whispered conversation outside the door, under her beautiful blue spruce, which suddenly seemed more precious for the sudden threat to her life here, resolved the matter. She would take her little green Ford with the agreeable Ames riding along with her, she presumed, to ensure her arrival at the station in Nelson. She brought her shopping basket with her, to lend some normalcy to the trip. After all, she herself went into town once a week. They were hardly likely to detain her there when she had nothing to do with this increasingly tiresome corpse.

She was going down the King's Cove road, past St. Joseph's, still and empty in the dappled afternoon sunlight, to the intersection of the main Nelson road. Darling was ahead of them. He had become opaque. Since they had returned to the house, the shoe bagged and stowed in the boot of the car, he had, if possible, an increased air of neutral courtesy. Would she mind very much accompanying them to town? She would not. In fact she'd offered to do so in the first place. She didn't say this, of course, but she felt vaguely betrayed by his manner.

She pulled on to the road and struck by a dawning realization that made her feel quite ill. Of course: the sudden appearance of the shoe on her bit of path combined with the note. It wasn't theoretical anymore with him. She assumed that when there was a murder they would review the possible suspects until they had evidence around which their theories could gather. It was gathering right around her. Riding with her was Ames, ostensibly to help her find the station at the other end, a task she felt might be well within her capabilities, as Nelson had only one main street.

Lane desperately wished she were alone. She had to face up to and work through what now seemed to her to be an unfair piling-on of odds. First there was the sheer ridiculousness of her suddenly being put right into the frame for a murder she could never have contemplated committing. And behind that, waiting like a lurking rat, was her greater fear that she had been found and was being called upon when she had expressly asked for, and been given permission for, a complete retirement from her service.

"How often do you run up to town?" Ames asked suddenly, his cheeriness forming a sharp contrast to her dark and foreboding thoughts.

She didn't, she reflected, pick up an ounce of suspicion from him; it was just Darling who seemed to view her with a jaundiced eye. "Once a week," she very nearly snapped and then felt churlish. She added after a few moments, "I might wish it were less, as it seems to take the whole day somehow, though it is less than an hour's drive. I pick up things for the Armstrongs—get in supplies. It's lovely to have all the things one could never get in London during the war. I think that's why I go up so often. I'm like someone who's been starved, I'm constantly afraid it will all be gone by the time I get there."

"Boy, it's bad enough living in Nelson. I couldn't stick it out here, as pretty as it obviously is. Me, I'd like to move out to the coast, but my mother is here and she's getting on, in her fifties, and I don't think I can leave her." This made Lane laugh. She thought of her ancients: Gran in her nineties and various vague sorts of second cousins in their eighties.

"Fifties! I should think you could go away for a bit and she'd just muddle through. Would you still be a policeman if you went to the coast, Victoria, isn't it?"

"Oh, yes. I love the job. But I'd go to Vancouver. That's where all the action is."

"Well, I'm finding I'm getting quite enough action out here," Lane declared. "I came out to get away from people and, well, just get away, and instead I get bodies turning up in the creek. It's not restful. I had hoped to write." She was sorry the minute she'd said it, and more sorry when she glanced over and saw Ames looking at her, interest manifest on his face.

Perhaps, he thought, she will tell me she writes thrillers. "Really! What do you write?"

Bother. She could scarcely answer this question when she asked it of herself. "I used to write before the war. I was reading literature at Oxford and wrote a little poetry. I'd like to try my hand at a novel." It was just as well she didn't tell him she had also been reading languages. That would lead to more curious questions that would potentially lead where she did not wish to take him, or anyone here.

"That's fantastic!" he said, and she reminded herself to take note of the hyperbole in the expression of people in North America. She had met a few Americans in London and they too went in for exclamatory outbursts. "I wouldn't mind writing a book one day. About my work as a policeman, maybe. It'll have to be in a few years. We don't get a lot of what I'd call intriguing crime around here. Mostly homicides after people have been drinking when they come in out of the bush. Mail robbed off the steamboats or trains. Pretty dull stuff."

"Well, now you have a really intriguing murder. Maybe this will make the grade one day." It was certainly intriguing her. Her mind, momentarily diverted by the charming young Ames, went plummeting back to her situation. What if she did know the dead man? It would add to the evidence that he had come out expressly to see her. Curse Darling, she thought angrily. How can he possibly imagine me killing someone? Of course she understood. He was thorough, he didn't know her, it was his job. It was a nuisance because he had a face she trusted. It was an open face, the face of a man who was intelligent. She liked the slightly worried cast of his eyes.

"He's not bad, you know, Darling." Ames said. Lane felt herself flush, as if she'd been caught nosing through someone's papers, something she had, in fact, done in the past, though she had never become comfortable with it. "He's sarcastic at times, usually at my expense, but he's smart. I mean, he really seems to understand how people work. You always know he can get to the bottom of things."

"Well, that's a relief," Lane said, trying to recover from the feeling of having her mind read. "At the moment, it would appear that I could really use someone who can get to the bottom of things."

IN THE POLICE station, Darling was waiting for them, his hat and the manila envelope with the incriminating photo in his hand. "We shall have to go down to the morgue, I'm afraid, Miss Winslow. I'll take over from here, Ames, if you'd be kind enough to take this envelope back up to my office." Darling handed over the manila envelope.

When they were before the sheeted hump that was the body, Darling looked over at Lane, for a brief second held her gaze, as if he was looking for something there, and then he turned back to the body. "I hope you will not find this disturbing, but we must know if you can tell us anything about this man."

"I assure you, Inspector, that I shall only be disturbed if I find I do know him, not simply because he is a corpse. These I have seen before."

"Have you indeed? Nursing?"

"No. Can we get on with this?" She found the room, though it was icy cold, stifling with the smell of formaldehyde. Darling nodded at the attendant and the sheet was drawn back to the man's chest. Lane was surprised to see he was without the tweed jacket that had initially given her that sense that he must be English. But, of course, he was naked because they had done some sort of post-mortem. She didn't know what this would consist of and was grateful she had only to look at his face.

It was difficult to tell the age of a man who'd been dead and kept cold. There was an ageless quality she'd seen on the dead soldiers in France. The faces of the dead seemed to lose all personal character and become almost like clay models of human faces. She'd been afraid she would be startled if she recognized him but it was an enormous relief to realize instantly that she did not. He looked young, thirty or under, certainly, and still, she thought, even without the tell-tale clothes, he looked English. He had a thick head of boyish hair parted on the side like the boys at Oxford had before the war. Had he fought? Her eyes wandered momentarily over the parts of him that were exposed. She couldn't see anything to indicate that he had or hadn't.

"Well, Miss Winslow?" His voice was subdued, cool, like the atmosphere of the room.

"No, Inspector. I have definitely not seen him before. I wonder if he was enlisted."

"We found no evidence of any wounds that might indicate some connection with the military. We were hoping we might send the description and a photo to the War Office. The coroner indicated there was a weakness in the lungs. This might have kept him out, but it will still be worth a try. Let's go back upstairs." He opened the door and stood to let her pass. "Are you all right? I could offer you a cup of coffee, or tea if you'd prefer. You've had a long drive and . . ." He waved his hand at the now-covered body of the mysterious victim.

Lane went through the door and into the murky hallway of the basement where the morgue was. She could see the door leading to the alley at the side of the building, the light coming weakly through the grubby window. But it looked inviting for its sense of escaping from the dense, cold atmosphere of the morgue. As they mounted the stairs, her fantasy of bolting to the alley unfulfilled, she wondered why he was telling her so many details. He was relating them as though to a colleague, yet she knew herself to be a suspect though he had never once said so to her. Perhaps he was letting her know that he intended to follow up on finding out who the dead man was and that she might yet be found to be connected to him. A kind of friendly warning.

When they had gained the main foyer of the station, she sighed and turned to the inspector. "I know you think I have something to do with this. For all I know, you do not believe me even now when I tell you I do not know him. Hence perhaps your kindly musing that you'll be sending his details along to the War Office. If you could but see it, it is as much in my interest as it is in yours for us to discover who he is; why he had a paper with my name ostensibly on it and how he came to be dead in the creek near my property." She clicked open the catch on her handbag to find a handkerchief with which to wipe her hands, which the visit to the dead had left feeling unclean. But in the second after her outburst, she thought she saw a shadow fall across Darling's eyes, as if the reproof had landed home.

"That cup of tea?" was all he said in the end, and his gaze was once again placid when she looked up.

"On the whole, I think not. I will take advantage of my

extra trip to town to pick up some groceries. Thank you. If, that is, I am free to go?"

"You are, Miss Winslow, but I will ask you not to leave the province until this matter has been settled." He smiled at her and thought, as she disappeared down the steps to the street, that he might have just heard her say, "Not bloody likely," under her breath. But maybe not. It's what he would have said in similar circumstances.

SEIZING HIS CUP of coffee, Reginald Mather got up from the table and went out the kitchen door on to the back porch. Irritably wiping the hand on which the coffee had sloshed, he took a deep breath and reminded himself that after all this time, he'd learned to take this business in stride. His wife—he knew people called her "Mad Mather," and in his secret heart he did too—was still holding forth inside, as if he had never left the room. He knew it was her condition, but he still found it unbearable when she went off. The sheer spiteful energy that flamed in her when she had a bad bout was staggering to him.

The theme was familiar. If he had never taken her from her home in England, she would have married someone who would have amounted to something, she would have, she would have, she would have. And now, increasingly, "You and your dreams of millions. We just had a war and you could have made millions if you'd had your famous mill up and running."

"What I could have done if I'd never clapped eyes on you!" he muttered to himself. His Labrador, Rufus, had been on the alert since he stepped out and was up, tail wagging, looking expectantly at him. Reginald gulped the last of the coffee and took his stick out of the umbrella basket. "Come on, then," he said, and the two set off up the path into the forest.

This walk, he thought, was his last comfort, his secret refuge. His escape. He was gratified, as he crossed the upper meadow, a small clearing that had been created when it had been logged sometime late in the last century for the abandoned log house at the edge of his property, to see the cloth markers nailed to the trees up ahead. This is where the mill would go. Turning to look back down the hill, he could see in his mind where the road would wind, bringing logs from all over the properties he had, or would have.

He felt the same surge of excitement at the thought of what he would accomplish and this brought with it the sense of injustice he felt because he'd not been able to get the prime pieces of land he wanted. That's the reason he'd not been able to build the mill. He was beginning to think of it as a chess game between him and the rest of the world. It still galled him that he had lost two prime properties: twenty-five acres on the south slope that had gone to that bastard Harris, who had planted more bloody apples on some of it, and the old homestead land the Yanks had got. There were eighteen prime acres where he had planned to start planting pine in the old orchards and fields. In both cases he'd been outbid. But he still relished what he had, all his original forty acres he'd acquired as a young man when he'd come in 1905, and his quiet additions adjacent to his original property over the years. It was completely unfair of Alice to go on about his failure to have the mill built—to accuse him of being a failure.

He'd never forgotten the shame and fury he had felt when he'd been sent over: a young man disgraced. It had not been his fault the girl had died; he had never asked her to get rid of the baby. He'd been accused of being unfeeling, of bringing shame on the family. Here, surrounded by his growing acres, his plans for industry, he still sometimes felt the agony as if it were only yesterday. He had loved the girl, Emma. Beautiful, unhappy, soft Emma. It was an explosion in him, this love, because he realized he'd had no idea of love before her. Certainly no one in his family: not his brooding, angry father, or the rigid aunts, so full of their theories about children needing to be corrected and civilized.

Some days he sat at the top of the meadow, even forty-five years later, and caressed the agony he had felt, standing in the drawing room, his father and aunts arrayed before him in a phalanx of disapproval. It was early evening, the light beginning to fade, a time of day when he had always sunk to his lowest. It was thus, the light behind his judges and executioners so that they were obscured and menacing, that he had heard of her death, and his supposed complicity in it. His banishment, delivered by his father, he scarcely took in, because he was in the grip of a wave of fear and grief that made him feel as if the floor had opened and he was sinking endlessly downward. Even now, in his sixties, he clung to that first feeling of despair because it disproved the central lie they had told about him: that he was unfeeling. And here was Alice, accusing him of being incompetent.

He had loved Alice, after a fashion. She was something

when she was young! The one and only time he'd been back home, in 1910 to bury his father, he went back victorious, a landowner. The cool reception he received from the aunts almost delighted him. He knew they were afraid he'd come back to stay. That they themselves might now be out of a home. By all rights, his father's house was his now. But he had built his own house, had his own land, all bought with the remittance money they'd sent, which he was sure they thought he'd squandered. He said nothing to ease their minds. Let them suffer their maiden fears of being homeless. And then came Alice—vivacious, forward, strong.

They'd met one windy day when he was walking the coastal path, his usual strategy to get away from the aunts during his long stay. This was the girl for the colonies! She was chafing at the confinement of waiting for marriage or some cataclysmic event to get her out of her overprotective parents' house. The matter was settled within a month and, much to the relief of the aunts, he was back to Canada. It took less than a year for him to realize that it must have been a relief to her parents as well, for lovely Alice began to show mood swings that could not be passed off as normal, or attributed to the depression of being away from home, or to her being pregnant. But when she was up, as he thought of it, the Alice he'd been so smitten by was still there. She was full of ideas and was clever enough to make them happen. In fact, it was she who first had the idea that they should forget the orchards. It was a revelation when she said it. In the horror of the fire of '19, like everyone else, he had lost ninety percent of his crops, and she suggested that the answer was to plant fast-growing evergreens for milling.

And then there was their useless son, Sandy, who couldn't stick to anything. He'd gone out to the coast to do agriculture at the university and had botched it, enlisted in the war and botched that, and had, disgraced and without seeing a minute of the fighting, come back, supposedly to help. In his darker moments he knew he had to face the truth. Sandy had inherited whatever it was Alice had. He had been a little moody as a boy, but now, in his twenties . . .

Barking brought Reginald back from his ruminations. There were bears sometimes that came down to the garbage dump. He whistled to get the Labrador back at heel and turned down the path that skirted an upper orchard belonging to Alec Hughes, as he still thought of it, though Alec had been dead for thirty-six years. This forested sweep was the last strip of property he'd been able to afford. He might as well get down to the post office. This was another day Alice would not be able to go, and just as well. He wanted to know what people were saying about their little murder.

It had been three, or was it four, days since the body had been found on the Winslow girl's property. He'd seen the police arrive the day before, and felt a grim satisfaction. They would go after the Yanks. They had to. No one in his right mind would think she was capable of such an act. He had been surprised to see the car turn south toward her house, but no doubt they were back to look at the scene of the crime. He'd heard the two cars leave an hour later.

Usually he was the only one at the post office, but today the locals seemed to be tumbling out of the small space. A saddled horse that he recognized as belonging to Glenn Ponting, the local prospector, looked up from his attention to the long fronds of grass at the edge of the road as he went by. Old lady Hughes was standing halfway out of the doorway talking to the prospector, who was evidently on his way in. Glenn never seemed to come in from the cabin he had near the road to Kaslo. Angela was leaning on the counter talking to Eleanor and shaking her head. Lane was standing next to her with her arms folded and her mail already in her hand. There was no doubt what everybody was talking about. "Ladies," he said by way of greeting when he got inside. Angela was clearly caught mid-sentence and stopped abruptly.

"Don't stop on my account. I'm sure you are talking of our local corpse. What else is there? Have you reached any conclusions? Eleanor?" he asked, indicating he was ready to receive his mail.

Eleanor leaped away from the window and disappeared into the back where she had, earlier in the day, sorted all the mail into individual slots. "One letter and the paper today, Reg." She handed them through. "Is Alice doing well?"

"Fine." He felt a flash of irritation. He imagined that they thought it was all somehow his fault his wife was unstable. "Well, ladies, what do you make of it?" He turned to Angela.

"If only we knew!" said Angela, clearly still in the grip of the initial thrill of it all. "No one knows the man! Well, I mean, Lane doesn't. We obviously haven't seen him."

"It must have been gruesome for you, my dear, to stumble on such a thing. I'm sure old Harris was no help!"

Lane smiled noncommittally at this. "It was an unusual afternoon; I'll give it that. All I wanted to do was water my flowers."

"Nothing ever happens out my neck of the woods," Glenn Ponting muttered glumly through his old-fashioned prospector's beard, and turned toward the door with his mail.

Reginald lifted his hand in a sort of salute and followed Glenn out the door. "Well, I'm off. Alice will be expecting her paper." They heard him greet the two people still talking outside. Lane leaned back to look out the doorway and saw him walking quickly up the road.

"He seemed to be in a hurry," she commented.

"It'll be Alice," said Eleanor. And because she was meticulous in not gossiping in her post office window, she turned back inside and began to tidy up.

Angela winked at Lane, who looked puzzled, and jerked her head to the outside. "Bye, Eleanor!" she called, and steered Lane out through the screen door. "Do you have a cup of—God, I nearly said tea! You English! Can you manage a cup of coffee at your haunted house?"

Sensing a scoop, Lane said she could also manage a biscuit. "By which you undoubtedly mean a cookie," Angela sighed. They could see Glenn on his brown mare trotting up the road past Reginald as they crossed the garden toward the little bridge leading to Lane's house.

Farther up the road, past the turnoff that took people away from King's Cove and on to the Nelson road, Reginald was looking more closely at the letter he'd been handed. He could not shake his anxiety about the whole business. Somehow he knew he could never discuss it with Alice.

CHAPTER SEVENTEEN

THE COFFEE MADE, THE TWO women settled on the canvas chairs Lane had put onto the porch. Though it was before eleven in the morning, the sun already had a noon intensity, so they slid their chairs and her little French cast-iron table under the wide overhang of the roof. Lane felt a smug delight that she'd had the foresight to pack this little memory of France into her boxes coming to the new world. There was a moment of silence while they both drank and Lane could not decide if she wanted to close her eyes to hear the warm, heavy silence of the day, or keep them open to drink in the rolling greens that reminded her so much of her childhood home. She had wanted to spend this first summer slowly absorbing the *terroir*, as Yvonne would have said, in this new world. That now seemed a distant dream since Tweed Jacket had been found in her bit of creek. She sighed. Even without him, and the appalling implications for her that she tried to keep at bay, she supposed, she would still be here with Angela, and Angela would still be inclined to talk her morning away. The difference now is that she really needed to hear what Angela and anyone else might have to say about the people she'd come to live among. She hadn't done this thing; therefore, that body was connected to someone here. If Darling couldn't, or wouldn't, put in the effort, she could.

"Gosh, you were lucky, sweetie! This view! I ought to be painting it. I love our cabin, don't get me wrong, but we haven't got this outlook." Angela gazed hungrily out across the lawn to the lake in the distance. The morning shadows had lifted off the mountains on the other side, adding a blue-green intensity to the horizon that opened suddenly into an almost inky blue sky. She was right, Lane thought, seeing it as Angela must be seeing it. She was lucky. She'd never thought of herself as lucky, as having anything anyone else would want, but here it was. This house. Old Lady Armstrong and all.

"Hardly a cabin, Angela. You've made a veritable mansion of the place. And no one else in King's Cove has a real grand piano and someone to play it."

"You're darn tootin'!" Angela conceded and settled back. "I bet you are wondering about Mather, and his lovely wife 'Mad.' No, you're probably much too proper to be nosy about the rest of the world. But that family! Their little bit of land borders ours, luckily a mile away from the house. For starters, Reginald is an awful snob. I'm sure he's the one who's led the charge on calling us the 'Yanks.' I can't be bothered explaining that Yankee in the States only refers to northerners and cannot safely be applied to all Americans. When we first arrived he wouldn't acknowledge us at all and when he finally did he seemed intent on persuading us that we wouldn't be able to stomach life in the wild, as he called it. Ha! He should try living in New York. He doesn't know the meaning of wild!

"I heard from old Mrs. Hughes, you know, that Reginald had predicted we wouldn't survive our first winter. He still treats us as if we are beneath his contempt. Kenny told me when I was complaining about it that Reg was probably still angry because he had wanted to buy our land, and he lost to Dave. Only, of course, Dave had no idea he wanted it, so we hardly did it on purpose."

Lane didn't want to stop the flow of Angela's talk. "So what is the story on Reginald's wife? She seems like a military drill sergeant. Was she a WAAF during the war? No, she's much too old. Did they have them during the first war?"

"That I couldn't tell you, but she spent the last war here. Her son, the tiresome Sandy, went to agricultural school and then signed up and did something outrageous, because he got sent back from training camp very suddenly. It doesn't stop him from swaggering about as if he had single-handedly saved a battalion under heavy fire. No, the thing with her is, I don't think she's very well, if you get my meaning." Here Angela tapped her head. "I don't know the whole story, but I can tell you I was at the post office a couple of years ago one morning in November and Alice came pounding in with her stick and began to berate Eleanor out of the blue. I think someone else was there, old Max from the cabin near the lake, maybe. Gosh, I wonder what's happened to him. I haven't seen him in absolute ages! I wonder if he's died, and is moldering away in his cabin? How would anyone even know? Horrors! It doesn't bear thinking about!"

It was a place, Lane realized, where someone could die in a cabin and not be found for years; however, she would, just at that moment, have liked Angela to be the kind of woman who could stick to a narrative without dashing off on every tangent that presented itself. "Why was Mrs. Mather berating poor Eleanor? I should have thought she was the last candidate qualified for such treatment."

"Well, that's the thing. No one could ever be mad at Eleanor, which is how you knew Ma Mather was not all there. She was yelling at her that she'd been hiding her mail, and steaming it open. Spying on her, that sort of thing. After that Reginald started coming more often. Other times she'd come down and she'd be fine. Well, fine for her. Still that brisk barky tone of hers, but she wasn't accusing anyone of anything. It must be very hard for him. I mean, one of the things she said is, 'He's put you up to this, hasn't he?' God knows how she carries on at home. And no one is safe if she's roaming round the settlement looking for cougars. She'd shoot anything that moves."

No wonder people had seemed slightly tentative when Mrs. Mather had come in to the post office that day. No one knew what sort of mood she'd be in. So, she seemed potentially mad enough to whack someone over the head and shove them in a creek. Was she strong enough? And why would she do it? Surely even she would have to have a reason. Lane realized she knew nothing about paranoid conditions.

"You know, Lane, I can't tell you how glad I am you've come." Angela's serious tone brought Lane's gaze and mind back to the present. Angela had reached out and now took her hand. "It's not that we don't love it here; we do. It's beautiful, and the orchard and garden and the three boys keep us ridiculously busy. And Dave, of course, composes when he can find time. He has a few connections in the movie industry in Hollywood. And there's the high school in Nelson. Who has time for anything else, really? But I didn't realize till you came how much one could miss having a friend. Having someone who is my age, and who lives a little in the modern world. It's heaven!"

To Lane's alarm, Angela had teared up. "Oh God, I'm sorry," she said. She took her hand back and fumbled in her pockets for a handkerchief. "I didn't realize how it must have been getting to me. Dave is off to Nelson every day during the school year and meets regular people there every day. I was beginning to get panicked about when the boys have to go off to school. Rolfie is going this year to Balfour. I know it's only three miles away and I can entertain myself driving him every day. But it's the beginning of the end, isn't it? Then it'll just be me and the apple trees." She sniffled and looked moodily at the table.

Lane smiled. "Hardly the beginning of the end, my dear! I'm told children need their mothers well past their eighth year."

Angela giggled at this. She looked at Lane. "Why did you never marry?"

Why indeed? thought Lane. "Well, never is extreme. You are going in for extremes today. I'm only twenty-six. I was working at nineteen. The war came. I didn't have time, really."

"But didn't you have a sweetheart? You must have!

You're utterly gorgeous. My friends in New York tell me lots of the fellows came back with English wives. But here you are all by yourself."

This line of questioning opened up so many paths Lane would have preferred to forget. She tried to form an answer that would satisfy Angela's curiosity and, for that matter, the demands of a real friendship. She too was happy to discover that her new community contained within its strange expatriate, somewhat aging bounds, the vibrancy of an Angela. In London, or France even, she supposed she would have found it difficult to maintain the kinds of friendships she had with the other single girls she worked with as they all married and buried themselves in children and husbands. Here, though, was a woman her own age, with three children, and there was between them almost the energy of teenagers.

"I did have someone," she said at last. "But he died near the end of the war. I suppose you could say I came here to get as far away as possible from all of that."

The smudged photo of the tiny bit of writing came to her mind and she felt a momentary sense of keeping some internal avalanche at bay. She told herself briskly that though the incriminating piece of paper found on Tweed Jacket might be evidence of someone trying to get her back to London, it was certainly not written by Angus—he was dead.

"Oh, gee, of course you did. And here am I pestering you! And, let's be frank, you're not the only one here getting away from things. I sometimes think Dave . . . I . . . well, I should stop yakking on, is what. I'm not from New York originally, you know. I'm from Ohio and I tell you my female relatives set a fine standard of summertime porch gabbing. I better get back. I left Dave with the boys. I'm not sure who I'll still find alive!" Angela pushed herself out of the deck chair and picked up her mail. "It's going to be another lovely, warm night. How about we all go down to the wharf for a picnic supper? The boys are crazy for beachside fires."

They agreed to this plan and Lane watched Angela walk up her treed driveway, past the barn, and through the gate to the road. What had she meant, not the only one getting away from things? Secrets. Everyone had secrets, even a man from his wife. And connected to some secret, somewhere, was the dead man she had seen.

It had been a relief not to know the dead man. It beggared belief that someone here must have known him enough to want to kill him and yet he might have been seeking her. There are coincidences in this world, she assumed, but this was a coincidence that went beyond the pale. The someone who knew him might have followed him here, perhaps. That would make slightly more sense. But if this was the work of her ex-agency it would have been done more neatly. There wouldn't be bodies stuffed in creeks or shoes suddenly appearing. Someone here had to have known him.

With a sigh she turned back into the house. It was cool still, because she'd left all the doors open. She should sit down and write. She'd started a story based on one of her friends in London who'd been in love with a man who died in Burma and she'd been left with their baby.

She felt inadequate, suddenly, to tell that story. She'd never had children, and saw now that at this late stage, she was unlikely ever to have any. Write about what you know, she'd been told by a journalist friend. But her life was such a series of changes and jerks from one world to another, brought up by a hodgepodge of multilingual aunts, governesses, grandparents. There was nothing, not one shred of her life, that was normal, that could translate into something anyone else could begin to understand or relate to.

She felt torn between a desire to avoid writing by reading under the shade of her weeping willow and, conversely, exhausting herself with a long walk along the upper paths of her property. This would take her back to the road and temptingly near the path to the creek. That was it, of course. It wasn't any impulse to avoid writing. Writing was going to be a way to avoid the mess she was in right now. She needed to take that walk. To look again at the scene. To think through what she knew, because after Angela this morning, she was pretty sure she knew more than just that Mather was a snob and had a mad wife and she would need to walk to let her mind assemble the pieces. This much she had learned during the war.

LANE WALKED PAST her great grey barn without giving it a glance. Among the many joys of having something that was truly hers was knowing that she would one day go in there and really have a look. There was still so much to do in the house. When she had first moved in, she'd imagined herself busily painting all the rooms and sewing and changing curtains, and spending hours in furniture stores in Nelson to pick the right furniture. Instead she had found she was the sort of person who liked to be in a place without altering it so she could get a sense of what it ought to be. She had painted one room, the bathroom, because it had been newly plumbed, but they hadn't changed the pale green paint. Now it was a sparkling ivory, a clean white with just a touch of warmth to reflect the warmth of the sun during the day and the electric light at night.

The road, as usual at this time of day, was deserted. As she walked along the road, hearing nothing but the gentle crunching of her own steps, she was thoughtful. Since this whole thing began, she had tried to see it as something that did not concern her. She was new, and though it took place in her part of the creek, it was also Harris's part of the creek, and the Bertollis' part of the creek. Because she had had nothing to do with the murder, she had assumed everyone would see that. The return of Darling with his questions and his photograph of the paper in the victim's pocket had seriously shaken her, and yet she was aware that she had been like someone holding her breath till it all went away. She had been pushing every consideration that the murder could in any way involve her to the back of her mind.

This thing had started—no, ended—in the wooden water diversion and so she must start there. Now, for the first time since the war had ended, she found herself engaged in the kind of mental sorting that had kept her missions clear to her: a place for everything and everything in its place. And so, as she walked, she lined up what she knew. She might not solve anything like this, but by making sure that nothing she knew was left out, the facts might line themselves up and suggest new ideas. It was like poetry—you just wrote the lines and walked away. When you came back, they seemed to form a new entity.

The grassy bank of the creek was dappled with sun and shade, and the water flowed and broke with a subtle music that was soothing in the early afternoon. Lane sat down and leaned back on her elbows with her legs outstretched. The water, now that the impediment to its flow was gone, had shrunk back to its normal banks and was less like a pond and more like a creek. She waggled her feet in a momentary burst of happiness. It was utterly beautiful here. She should be here with a picnic and a good book. She'd found a copy of Maugham's *The Painted Veil* in one of the boxes she had not completely emptied on to her bookshelves yet. Luckily she'd not read it. Why had she packed a lot of books she had already read? It was unlikely, except for the poetry, that she was going to read them again. Except the Wodehouse, of course. She imagined she'd reread P.G. until the last trump. She sighed and lay back, cushioning her head with her arms, and closed her eyes. The sound of the creek and the feel of the soft summer air and the sun on her legs intensified with her eyes closed. A kind of exhaustion overcame her, and she let her mind drift.

There was the photo again of the paper in the dead man's pocket. She could see perfectly the murky writing and though she tried to shove the idea away, she knew. She could not escape the thought. It was her name.

The implications of that knowledge made her feel she was sliding down a long steep cliff of gravel, where she could get no purchase to save herself. She forced herself to look at what this meant. They knew where she was. She could be got at any time. She had thought this, vaguely, when Darling had first shown her the photo but now she allowed it, really allowed it. She tried to imagine herself back in London, at work, but it filled her with a dark sadness. She was happy here, and being back would only remind her of Angus. She realized that two years was not so very long after all. Perhaps her distance from London had given her the illusion that it was so long ago she'd gotten over it. This turmoil in her told her she had not. What it told her was that she missed him still, profoundly, if she but admitted it.

She went back again to that aching day when the girl from upstairs had said he was dead. No one had been able to answer any of her frantic early questions when she first heard, when she realized that she had no way to contact him. It was always the other way around. He always contacted her to make arrangements. Now, in the safety of distance, she wondered at his secrecy. With an angry flush she realized; he had been married. He must have been! Her whole love affair had been a lie.

She felt something hardening inside. Of course. It was her father all over again. He'd never told the truth to anyone. She'd fallen for a man just like dear old dad! She almost wanted to laugh. But now, here was the possibility that the agency was trying to reel her right back in so they'd sent someone here to get her, to drag her back into the world she had wanted to leave behind.

The likelihood of this was so absurd that she shook her head. It was also ridiculous that a man who was a complete stranger to her would have come here to seek her out, especially, only to be murdered by someone else in this tiny, out-of-the way community. It was back to the ridiculous and quite unbelievable coincidence.

She tried to bring her mind back to the problem at hand—the man in the creek and the fact that the police thought it was she who had killed him. She was allowing her mind to run, undisciplined, along the corridors of absurdity. Where had she heard it? From one of her profs: do not throw anything away, not when you're writing, not when you're thinking. Your brain is smarter than you. In the light of this thought, she bundled up all the absurd speculation about Angus and stored it on one of her mental shelves, conceding with some irritation and no little anxiety that it might come in handy. But if this was true, who was the dead man? She scanned his face again in her mind but she was certain she did not know him. Of course, someone in the department might, if he had come for her. She must phone Inspector Darling, she supposed, though on sober reflection, what could she tell him? What could she be permitted to tell him? The Official Secrets Act was a powerful force. This, however, left the real conundrum back in her lap to solve: if he was here for her, who had killed him?

CHAPTER EIGHTEEN

London, England

THE DIRECTOR PLACED HIS HAT carefully on the rack and shrugged out of his wet raincoat. He resented rain in July, but it was London. What did one expect? He'd come back up to town early, leaving his wife with the job of getting the children—well, really, they were hardly children anymore, Wendel was fourteen and Lorraine was twelve—up to their grandfather's small estate in Lake Country. Their long-anticipated summer hols. Jane would come down to London and they would take a small holiday together. Maybe even to France. He'd been to Paris a couple of times since it had all ended, and he was amazed by how quickly the city had fallen back into itself and was embracing a new post-war world, almost as if the whole embarrassment and pain of occupation had never happened, or could be quite forgotten.

He sat at his desk and looked nervously at the pile of papers in his inbox. How could he be sure he'd not made a dreadful mistake? And then the miracle. She had renewed her passport and applied to go to Canada. They knew where she was, of course, in case they needed to get her back. Now the irony, that it was he who was in charge of the department that required her return.

The whole struggle of how to go about it had ended when Franks had come to him. They had only to wait. In fact, he'd persuaded himself that there was something almost theatrical and artistic about this approach. She would find it irresistible. Communication with her, or with any personnel they were to bring back, had to be secretive anyway, so this was perfect.

Smithers, his superior, came into his office. Smithers never knocked. It was his view that all offices were his and their occupants as well. "So? Anything?"

"No, sir. Not yet. But she is a professional."

"It's not wartime, you know, you can't compel people to come and go." He said this apparently completely oblivious to his own penchant for compelling people.

"Yes. Well, if I don't hear from her in another week, I can always go get her." He was only half-joking.

Smithers looked suspiciously at the director. "Yes, no doubt you can. A nice long holiday for you. She lives on the other side of the country, don't forget. Just keep in mind, we haven't got all year. She's the best linguist we had, and she's used to undercover." Smithers turned to go, and then turned back, "I'm bound to say you shouldn't have let her go. It's going to cost the department a lot of money to get her back, if we have to send you swanning off to Canada."

"Sir."

LANE SIGHED AND stretched. The silence, save for the water flowing out of the now unimpeded diversion: returning innocence to a place of death, cleaning with the soothing hand of nature, the way she had seen the countryside in France grow green over battlefields and somehow return order to life and life to order. Standing, she brushed the grass off her behind and turned to follow the path out to the road, and then she froze, every part of her alert.

She was in this state almost before she knew it. She scanned the sounds and turned her head slowly, first one way and then another, trying to see what, in the forest or along the banks of the creek, had pushed her into alert. As her mind caught up to her instinct, she felt it had been a sound that did not belong. She waited, her breath slowing, but she heard nothing but the creek and a slight movement of air in the leaves just above her. Now her body caught up fully and, with her heart pounding, she walked firmly and quickly along the path to the road. It surprised her that it took till now to really register that she herself might be in danger. There was a killer somewhere in King's Cove, and she might want to be careful, especially as the last man he killed had had her name in his pocket.

SHE DIDN'T FEEL like eating that night, but she made a sandwich with Eleanor's cucumbers and a bit of beef she still had left, and a mug of cocoa to go with it. It felt odd to her, on these long summer nights, to settle in for supper while it was still light outside. She sat with her feet up on the ottoman and a book in her hand, and it was from this position that she awoke some time later with a start. Her mug was still in her hand, empty and tilting madly toward the floor. It was dark. She must have gone right to sleep after eating, she decided, groggily peering at the mantel clock, a gift from her aunt. It was bloody nearly eleven o'clock, she grumbled silently. She peeled herself out of the chair and started toward the kitchen, wondering what had woken her up from such a sound sleep. There was never any traffic here at night and yet . . . she had a vague sense of having heard a car. It was a dream. The sound was the sound of being in France, at night, sitting behind a barn in the dark, waiting, and in the distance, a car, the faint whir of the engine rising and then falling away. Her dreams of France were still increasing. She should be having fewer nightmares, yet the safer she was, physically, with all these thousands of miles and worlds between her and Europe with all its memories, the more it all came back in the night when she was most unguarded. With a sigh, she placed her dishes in the sink and then went properly to bed, where she lay, wide awake, wondering what would happen to them all.

CHAPTER NINETEEN

London, England

"SIR." THE YOUNG SECRETARY HELD aloft the receiver of a telephone. He looked nervous, as if he could anticipate a bad-tempered reaction to the interruption. He could.

"What? I've told you. If it's my wife, I will call her back just before I leave." The director was peering at a large map of some obscure part of the eastern Yugoslav frontier through a magnifying glass.

"No, sir. It's not. It's that Livingston at the Yard. I think you'd better take it."

Livingston. Their man at the Yard. Now that was something. They'd not heard from him in weeks. They had almost begun to question the worth of their plant there, designed to give them a quiet word if one of their own fell afoul of the law, either through his own criminal tendencies, or in the service of their nation. The director put down the glass and stretched out his back. Leaning over a map was a young man's game, he thought, and then remembered with some comfort that as a young man his back had hurt just as much when he hunched over for a long time.

"Yes."

"Listen," said Livingston at the other end of the line, "something's come up. We need to meet, say in an hour at the place in Kensington."

The director put the receiver back into the cradle. Now what? Livingston would not drag him out on a whim. So no one connected Livingston to the service, they had "a place" in nearly every borough near central London that they switched around, at least theoretically, but they'd rarely had to use them. Forty-five minutes later he was coming out of the tube station and orienting himself. The Clock, he was relieved to see, was a small pub, rather than the dreary teahouse they'd found themselves in the only other time they'd met. It was, for a change, a sunny day in what had been, so far, a soggy summer and the door was open. A number of patrons had wandered outside with their drinks, so he was pleased to see a small booth unused and in a fairly empty part of the room.

Over a bracing pint of bitter, Livingston pulled out a photo on the front page of an unfamiliar newspaper and tossed it onto the table between them. "I thought you'd want to see this."

The director, who had swallowed a mouthful, put his glass down with a thud that made the contents spill. "Where did this come from?" He picked up the newsprint: *Mystery Man Found Drowned in King's Cove Creek.*

"It was in a nice manila envelope with some photos of a dead man, all the way from Canada. What have you been up to? Canada is part of the Dominion, you know, yet you seem to have flooded it with spies. Oh, and this with it. I wasn't able to spirit out the attached letter, but this is the bit

I thought you'd really like to look at. They are looking for any information about this woman." He placed a slip of notepaper on the table on which was written, "Lane Winslow."

"What's happened? Did you see the photo of the dead man?"

Like a conjurer, Livingston pulled a photo out of the inside of his jacket and plunked it down. It was a small photo of a photo and was grainy, but it was clearly the face of a dead man. "Do you know him?"

As bad as the image was and as dead its subject, this was undeniably a picture of Jack Franks, whom he had seen less than a month ago.

"Yes, I know him. Knew him. He's one of the readers, Russian desk mainly, we used at Hartley House."

"How is he connected to Winslow?"

The director didn't answer. He had to think through what to say, how much he should reveal to the police, even tame police, and he was struggling to imagine how Franks had ended up dead but could reach only one conclusion, a conclusion that was absolutely unthinkable—that Lane Winslow had killed him. The Lane he knew would have been completely incapable of such an act. He swallowed the last of his pint and stood up, collecting the debris that Livingstone had produced. "Thanks. These are for me, I suppose?"

"Yeah, go on. But—you know who these people are and the Yard don't. Are we planning to help them out? I imagine Canada is, figuratively speaking, on the line waiting for an answer."

"I'll let you know," was all the director said.

ROBIN HARRIS WAS putting his tea mug into the basin in his kitchen. The water gushed out of the tap, and he held the cup under the flow briefly and upended it on the counter. There was evidence that the cup had once, years ago, been white, but with years of this treatment it had been stained a mottled and cracked brown. He flicked the envelope with its single thin sheet of paper across the table furiously and, collecting a walking stick, pushed open the screen door with it, letting the door bang on his way out. Eleanor hadn't said a thing when she'd handed him his envelope with its King George British stamp, but she'd been interested. He could see she was. She'd have already asked Kenny what he thought the War Office was writing to Harris about.

"This'll be about my pension, I expect," he'd said.

He wasn't one for going for walks, preferring nowadays to climb onto his tractor and bump up the road to one of his orchards, but today his object was not the orchards. He went onto the path through the forest that led past old lady Armstrong's—he could not think of it as belonging to that girl—and up to the creek.

Reflection was also not one of Harris's habits. He was a man who lived within the actions he took every moment. It was as if he had abandoned thought in favour of action one day twenty years before, when he finally realized that nothing was to be gained and nothing more of interest was really going to happen to him. Now, what he did was who he was, and what he did followed a solitary, seasonal round of the same daily meals, working his orchard, picking and packing apples, sending them off, and going into town to take care of business as needed. He bought most of his groceries just down the road at the little shop in Balfour. He could not remember the last time he'd felt something like what was churning within him now. During the war, his war, that's when. He felt a thrum of anxiety at the thought of it.

He swallowed as he walked along the barbed-wire fence that kept his land apart from Old Lady Armstrong's. His sudden and unusual plunge into thoughts about his war made him realize for the first time the irony of his choosing barbed wire for his fencing. No one else did. Some still had the wood fencing from the previous century and some had upgraded to ordinary wire. He suppressed a grim inner laugh. He must have seen its effectiveness over there. He looked darkly at the unkempt old orchard on the other side of the fence and tried to will himself into his usual state of anger over the orchard being neglected by that girl, but the anxiety pounded on inside him.

He was wearing his heavy black galoshes, perhaps unsuitable for a cross-country walk, but as he wore them every day on his daily rounds, he'd not taken them off. The walk from his house at the bottom of the road out of King's Cove, where it sat on a corner of land directly overlooking the Nelson road, to the exchange in the creek was a good third of a mile, mostly uphill. The path turned through the woods and was a little overgrown. When he was young, before the war, he'd gone many times on the path to meet John and Kenny. Well, John really. They were more of an age. They were cousins, after all.

He reached the clearing by the exchange and realized he was winded. With his hands on his knees, he stopped and bent over to gasp in air. His feet were hot in the rubber boots and sweat was beaded on his face. The sound of the water gurgling seemed to cool him. Recovering, he stood up and looked around him. Why here? was all he asked himself.

Cornwall, April, 1946

The bus let him off in what looked like a great, grassy moorland. He stood bewildered for a moment, looking about at the landscape of green scrub. He was on the brow of a hill down which the bus was now disappearing. No chance to call it back. A grey pall of cloud hung low and seemed to threaten rain. He could see no village, nor even the sea it was supposed to be nestled next to. When he turned around, he saw the signpost pointing to a narrow road that wound down to what he now realized was the sea, though it bore the same dull grey cast as the sky and so had been camouflaged for a moment. Sighing, he adjusted the grip on his small suitcase and started down the road.

It was a good fifteen minutes before he arrived at the upper reaches of the village, which had the air of a deserted town.

His wristwatch told him it was after four. People would be having tea, especially on a threatening day like this. He hadn't thought much about what he'd do when he got here. All he had was the name of the town and the name of his mother. He stopped and put his case down, looking down the turning street, which descended steeply to the sea, a cove, a boatyard. A pub, he decided, would be his best bet. He didn't know what he expected to find, or even why he'd bothered. He told himself that it was just part of his academic approach. Tie all the loose strings. His mother had died in this village giving birth to him. She might have been among relations here. As he neared the bottom of the town, he saw a very small sign swinging overhead with a weathered picture of a wheat sheaf. *The Arish Mow*. This would be it then. He pulled the door latch down and walked into a subdued, squat room that smelled largely of ale and smoke. A lamp burned dimly at the end of the bar and one or two people sat quietly with drinks before them. Franks assumed the afternoon hours had just started. "Good day," he said, putting his case down. Two men in a booth under a tiny, deep-set window looked up at him. They were both wearing dark blue woollen caps and seemed infinitely old. The seafaring life, he thought. He wondered if they'd gotten so weathered fishing or mauling through the loot of ships wrecked along this remote shore. He smiled inwardly. These were stories from his childhood Boys' Own books. Perhaps these two were bankers after all.

One of them nodded at him. Both stared at him, as if expecting him to do something wonderfully foreign like suddenly burst into a dance. "Can we help you?" someone said.

Franks swung around and found he'd been addressed by the publican, who was smiling at him in a friendly manner. "Out here for the fishing?" the man continued, giving the bar a wipe with the cloth he had in his hand.

"No. I mean no to the fishing. You might be able to tell me something. I'm looking for any relations of an Elizabeth Conally. Is there a Conally family in this village?"

The publican shook his head. "Certainly not in my time. You boys know of a Conally family?"

"You don't have to shout, mind. No Conally, no. How did you come to think there might be such a people here?" one of the old men asked.

Frank began to feel a slight sense of despair. He wouldn't be able to leave the town until tomorrow and he quailed at even one night here in what seemed the farthest outpost in the kingdom. "I know that she died here. Her name was Elizabeth. She died in 1917, in November. I thought she might have been here among her own people." Why would someone come here to have a baby and die if she had no people? What if she'd come here because her baby's father lived here? The father could be anyone over the age of fifty. It could be one of these two specimens frowning at him now.

"Oh, well. That were a long time ago. Now, just a minute. Remember that lass that came to Rosemary in the war? That would have been right around '17. Summertime maybe? She were well along, as I recall. Then I heard that she died, poor creature. What happened with that baby? Did it die?"

"Rosemary who?" asked Franks.

"Oh, now, that were Rosemary Trevelyan. She's in the cottage on Copper Lane. She's getting on now."

"Is she on the telephone?" Franks was starting to feel hopeful again. He addressed the question to the publican, who he thought might know and even be able to provide an instrument for him to call her.

"No sir. Not too many of the old-timers are. Why don't you sit down and have a drink? You look all in. It's about a twenty-five-minute walk and all uphill. You'd better rest before you attempt it. She won't be going anywhere. I imagine she could put you up in that great empty house of hers.

I'm sorry I can't offer you anything here. I've only got one room and it's engaged at the moment."

HE HAD IMAGINED a small, thick-walled, whitewashed cottage, able to withstand the sea winds, but the house he found at the end of a little-used drive on the other side of the town was two storeys and made of brick. There was a matted garden at the front and a pre-war Austin that looked as though it was slumped against a small outbuilding. He stood on the stone doorstep and took a deep breath. When he raised his hand to knock, the door swung open before he made contact.

"I've watched you all the way from the village. What do you want, then?" said a woman who could have been any age from seventy to ninety. Her head of white hair seemed to be in permanent surprise, lifted outward by an invisible wind, and her eyes were the watery grey of the sea. She wore baggy trousers and an aged man's cardigan over her thin frame.

"I'm . . . my name is Jack Franks." How could he explain? He stood like a drifter on her doorstep, damp from the mist and the walk, with a small suitcase. He wouldn't blame her if she slammed the door. An elderly lady was unlikely to let a stranger in the door if she lived alone.

"Are you now? Well you'd better come in, Jack Franks. Sit by the stove, have some tea. Nothing but toast I'm afraid, but it will do until supper."

THUS FRANKS FOUND himself in a spare, tidy, rather dowdy kitchen, warming his stocking feet against her ancient

Aga, holding a thick mug of tea with a splash of brandy. Rosemary Trevelyan had evinced no surprise at seeing him; indeed, she had about her an air of having expected him, and being surprised to see him arriving so late.

Rosemary had settled him into a room in the house on the second storey and now they sat in the kitchen in front of the stove, which gave off a soft, deep heat. She had put a stew of chicken into the oven and given them each a good shot of brandy. Franks felt as if he could sink into this stranger's chair and stay forever, protected from whatever the outside world could do to hurt him. Rosemary Trevelyan began to unfurl his own, unknown life before him.

"For starters, your father is my nephew."

"Is? Is he still alive?" Franks had assumed, he realized, that if his mother was dead, his father was either unknown, or dead as well. He was surprised to discover that this woman was on his father's side.

"Yes. He is a stupid man, or was. I assume he still is. You, my dear boy, were not his first mistake. What were your parents like?" She asked this in a kindly manner. "I would love to think that you had been happy. I met your adoptive mother, you know, at the agency. She seemed very happy, even though you were already six months old. We found, you know, when your actual mother died, that we couldn't really manage. I hope you can forgive this. We were not used to children. It would have been, perhaps, not a warm existence for you."

Franks looked into his glass and tried to think of what to say. He could not even identify what he was feeling. A deep well of sadness at the loss of his parents, his real parents as he saw it, who brought him up, was all he could immediately discern. He tried to feel something else.

"My parents were, well, my parents in every way. They were kind and devoted. I believed I was like my grandfather, I played with my cousins on holidays. I have trouble imagining any different family. I suppose I should thank you, really. I did have a very happy childhood, and they sacrificed a great deal to make sure I got a good education. No education can prepare one for this." He fell silent and looked searchingly at this woman who had engineered a life he had believed was absolutely real. "Do you have a picture of her?" he finally asked.

"No. She was only with us a short time, poor love. She arrived when she was seven months gone, and of course died when you were born. She did not seem a happy woman, but of course she was in a strange country, among strangers. He sent her to us because she had no place else to go. Apparently she could not go home to her own people."

"Her own people? But where was she from?"

"Did I not say? She came from Canada. Your father has been out there for years, long before the Great War. To be honest, we didn't know much about her. She didn't say much to us. We think the reason she came out is that she was married to a bloke who was at the front and she couldn't be there with someone else's baby when he got back."

That night Franks lay in the narrow bed on the second floor of Rosemary Trevelyan's house. His great-aunt's house. He had left the curtains open so that he could see outside, but the darkness both inside and outside was complete. Gusts of wind made the windows rattle softly. He tried to imagine his mother, young and dying, with him in her arms for a first and last time, or his father who had sent her away, all the way to this house, from Canada. In that moment he and she seemed like one person to him: strangers in a faraway land, lying in the dark, in this room, alone, alone. He knew he would go to Canada, and he knew he would find his father, but it provided no comfort. He drifted to sleep with his heart aching.

DAVE ALTERNATELY LOVED the sudden silence when Angela and the boys had tumbled off to go to the beach and feared it. As a city boy he had never known silence. It had at first been terrifying, especially at night, along with the utter darkness on moonless nights. He had wondered, when he first got here, if it had been worth it at all. He'd been surprised how enjoyable it was to build the additions to the house and he'd been thrilled to install his piano, after its arduous train journey from Brooklyn, into the large, light-filled place he'd made for it in the living room. Composing again returned his equilibrium, and the job at the high school teaching music, even with the drive back and forth to Nelson every day, was better than he'd expected. The life and noise of a high school seemed to redress the silence of living in the country.

Angela had taken the boys to give him time alone. He was in the middle of a piece for a film, one of his American contracts. He'd told her to just head straight down to the lake and he'd pick up the mail. A walk would do him good before he really settled down. Eleanor had been cheerful, as always, and looked with mild curiosity at the American stamp on the letter she handed him. Curiosity was not what he felt when he saw the writing.

With an increasing feeling of dread, he took the flowers she offered him and trudged back up the hill to the cabin. Now, the flowers languished on the kitchen sink, un-vased, and Dave sat on the piano bench, the single page of the letter he'd received still clutched in his fist. He found himself again turning over in his mind how hard it was to really lose yourself in this world. First a dead body; now this. He might as well be in Brooklyn, he thought bitterly. In his mind King's Cove, so far away, and in another country, had once seemed the safest place on earth. He wished now he'd told Angela the whole truth. She was so plucky and willing to accept whatever life he'd ordained for her. She hadn't even minded the loneliness. The boys, the return of her childhood love of gardens, and her new vocation of painting had made her happier than she had expected to be. Now, she couldn't imagine another life. He couldn't destroy that with his troubles. He threw the balled-up letter in the wastebasket and brought his hands down on the keyboard in a great, crashing minor chord, and wondered what on earth he would do. Of course. The police here would have been thorough. Could he keep it from Angela? This Darling person must know the importance of this. He would have to go in to town, he supposed, to talk with him.

CHAPTER TWENTY

NIGHT HAD CREPT UP ON Lane where she was sitting on the veranda, nursing a scotch. Her father had finished every evening off grimly alone, in the sitting room with a scotch. She looked at the sky, a growing mantle of velvety darkness with stars beginning their appearance. For once, the heat of the day carried over into the evening, so that instead of the dewy cool that usually sent her inside for a sweater, the night seemed dry and warm still. She sighed. Now, it seemed to her, she was much like her disagreeable father, alone with her thoughts and a glass of scotch. Perhaps mulling over the same concerns; he was, after all, a spy. Now she was as well, in a way that had never really sunk in until today. A spy because she could not escape it as she had hoped to. There was no "normal life" for her to return to. She was locked into this as surely as her father had been.

She thought about Angus. She had trusted him completely. But that day on the train, so long ago, had spelled the beginning of the end. She realized that though she told herself over and over that it was work, and that it was reasonable she might not know every facet of her lover's life, there had been growing distrust. She was shaken to realize that she had been deceived, not by Angus, but by herself. What she had thought of as her infallible ability to know whom to trust, who was "one of us." And then he had died and she had ached at his loss, forgotten her misgivings about him, and turned away any notion of love again.

She knew he was dead but now she was forced to think again about what she had been to him; if he had had a whole other life she knew nothing of. She shivered at her own lack of consequence in his life. She felt, here in the dark, the full loss of innocence she had endured; the loss of love, and now, more clearly than ever, the loss of her innocent ability to trust. Well, she had mourned him once. She wasn't going to do it again. What should be the next step in tackling her own situation?

It was a good thing she'd not told Darling more. She wasn't ready in her mind, she realized now. What would she have told him? What could she? What had she sworn to, really, when she'd left the service after the war? Not to talk about her war work, this she understood, but not to say she'd ever been in the service? Under the circumstances, suddenly suspected of a murder, at least this one piece of information might protect her. She got up and stretched. She was glad now to have had the opportunity to think it through. She must tell Darling something and she felt she could at least tell him this. It would have to do.

She woke from a deep sleep, with the vague sense that she had been someplace lovely and hadn't wanted to leave. She widened her eyes in the dark trying to see if even grey dawn was coming through the window yet, but it was pitch black. There it was again. The blasted attic window! "Oh, God!" she groaned aloud. She didn't bother turning on the lights, but felt her way up the stairs. The window stood open and had stopped making noise, as if now that she was here, its job was done. The night air came through like a refreshing drink of cool water, heavy with the smell of the forest just beyond her lawn.

Just as before, she felt no inclination to just shut the window and stagger downstairs to her bed. She leaned on the windowsill, looking out at the dim shape of the lake and the mountains beyond with the diamond mantle of stars above it. Without really knowing why she did it, she said quietly, "What is it? Why have you brought me here?" Last time, she had seen the flashlight making its way through the underbrush. She gazed across the darkened landscape before her, but all was quiet and dark.

"Well, if you're going to be like that, I'm leaving the thing open. It's a lovely night anyway," she finally muttered crossly, and she went back to bed.

She woke the next morning to the sun pouring through the sheer curtains on her bedroom window. She had been in a deep sleep, and she turned slowly to look at the clock. 8:25. That was very late for her. It had been light since before five and she often woke with the sun. In the kitchen, she stretched luxuriously and revelled in the smell of the coffee percolating on the stove. Was there anything lovelier than the simplicity of this moment? The smell of coffee and the clean, clear morning of an as yet unmarked day. In her pyjamas—she had always worn men's pyjamas—with a mug of coffee in hand, she started toward her usual chair on the porch where she could sit and watch the lake, and then changed her mind. She should go to the other side of the house, wander past the pond under the weeping willow, and around the quiet and unused outbuilding toward a small, upper field, which once had been home to horses, if the old salt lick was any indication.

AS ALWAYS, THE whispery silence of the forests and trees around King's Cove gave a sense of deep, still quiet that she loved. No cars, no people talking, even in the distance. She was aware that some people would go mad in this quiet, this lack of diversion and society, but she loved it. She imagined that it must have been like this to live on a distant estate in England in the eighteenth century, before cars and radios, with a manageably small number of completely predictable human contacts. She walked up to the top of her grassy drive and leaned on the fence that ran parallel to it, enclosing the now-unused field. The sounds of nature loomed large. The buzzing of insects, the robins who still had something to say after the early morning sing that usually went on at first light. There were some fifteen trees of, she had been told, Red Delicious along one side of the field, which was now grown high with grass with no animals to crop it. She would have to pick and box the apples, though she had already been told by Harris that if she didn't spray them, they would be in no shape to sell. She had been dissuaded in this by seeing him at the post office in coveralls covered in an acrid yellow dust after one of his sessions in his orchards. She had been told by Kenny that this was DDT, which Harris considered a miracle substance that killed insects and worms that could cut your crop profits in half. She wondered then if everything she bought had been sprayed with some noxious substance like this? Anything smelling that vile could not be good for anybody. She had decided then to go one season without and see how she did. In any case, she had her own money; she would not need to live off the sale of her apples. She'd sell what she could and spend the profit on typewriter ribbons.

Her coffee finished, she sighed contentedly, turned back down the drive, and then stopped. Suddenly unsure, she looked first at the gate. It was closed and the chain was over the post, as she always left it. She looked down and realized what had nudged her unconscious; the grass was flattened, as if a car had driven over it. Had the police driven their car this far in on their last visit? She frowned. The last car had been her own, a day and a half ago, when she'd gone into town to look at the body. There had been a heavy rain since then. The ground in front of the barn doors looked different. It crossed her mind that it had been somehow deliberately arranged to look undisturbed. She had a momentary memory of a book she'd read as a child about Indians in the New World. There was an illustration, she remembered, of a warrior covering his tracks by walking backward, sweeping the ground with an evergreen branch. It was nonsense. Why on earth should anyone want to be covering tracks in her yard, miles from anywhere? Yes, well, why would anyone come here to die with her name in his pocket?

Something inside her chest constricted. She used to get this in the war. That heightened sense of alertness and a kind of fear. She could make no sense of what she was seeing. She'd not heard a car come in the night and now, looking down toward the house, she could see nothing amiss. But she could not shake the feeling that someone had been here. It was like the shoe all over again. That hadn't been there the day they had found the body but someone had put it, or dropped it, there the night she'd madly gone out to see about the flashlight in the dark. Someone was trying to throw suspicion on her. She glanced at the barn doors, but the padlock still hung on them, undisturbed. Feeling suddenly absurdly vulnerable in her pyjamas, she made her way back to the house to change. When she got to the door she turned and looked back up the drive and across the evergreen-strewn part of her yard to the barn. Nothing seemed amiss. She turned back in, saying to herself, "See? Nothing wrong. Pull up your socks!" But the problem was, she knew that something was very wrong.

Lane reached her door by the blue spruce and felt the relief of the relative safety of the house. And anger. Anger that her haven, this little bit of heaven, now felt unsafe. She turned the brass knob on her door and walked inside. She had never locked her doors since she'd been here. Now she felt she had to. It was nearly ten, and the morning was now hanging still and heavy. She propped the door open with the rock she kept for the purpose, and then paused, looking up her drive toward the barn. How beautiful it all was in the still sun. Not a single leaf on the weeping willow moved and the warm greens and yellows of the sun and shade patterns thrown by the trees across the driveway and the grassy verge would, if she were not so shaken, have made her heart soar. It was like being inside the most perfect painting, held forever at this moment. She angrily pushed the rock against the door again. She would not close it. She would not be afraid in her own house.

She walked through to the kitchen and poured a glass of water, reminding herself logically that the body was long gone, and then pushed open the French doors to let whatever air there was move through the house. Well, there was something. She had been leaving the French doors wide open unless it was raining, but she had shut them on the way out the door for her walk. She must unconsciously already have been nervous. She had learned to trust this feeling completely. Any idea or thought that came into her brain had been treated with equal respect. She felt they were messages from her unconscious. The new work in psychology had fascinated her, in spite of her prejudice against newfangled "therapy," and given her a theory on which to hang her practice.

Well, every little piece of a puzzle mattered, however bizarre, and unless this case was solved, she would never feel safe here again. She would have to give Darling every piece of potentially relevant information. Finishing her water with a gulp, she stood up, resolved. She picked up the receiver and spoke into the horn when the operator came on. "Nelson police station, please." She turned and leaned against the wall while she waited, listening to the mysterious faint clicks and fuzz on the line as the call was put through. It was part of the charm, this old-fashioned phone system, and in truth, in spite of the old instrument, which required her to stand and sometimes shout into the horn, it sometimes took this long to put a call through in London. The sound of picking up. "Nelson police station."

"Oh, hello. Can I speak to Inspector Darling, please?"

"One moment, I will put you through to his office."

It was Ames who picked up the phone. She surmised that Darling would probably not answer his own line. "Constable Ames here."

"Good afternoon, Constable. This is Lane Winslow at King's Cove. I'm looking for Inspector Darling."

Ames felt himself brightening up. It was a blistering hot day and he'd had nothing to celebrate on the robbery on 5th Street. "Aren't we all? He's off at the post. Can I help at all?" he said hopefully.

She hesitated. The thought came to her that King's Cove was on a party line. Anyone could be listening. Every instinct she had rebelled at the idea.

"You know, I was just hoping to find out from him about the name of the raspberry variety he was going to recommend. He said he thought they might be available locally. I'll catch up with him later."

"Raspberry variety?" Ames said, genuinely puzzled. And then he thought he saw what might be going on. These country telephone systems were all on party line. Did this mean she'd found something? "Of course. I remember now. I couldn't help you there, but I saw him leafing through a catalogue so he probably has what you want. I'll tell him."

"Thank you, Constable Ames. Goodbye then." She hung the receiver back onto the hook with a feeling of relief flooding through her. Clever Ames! And then further, a feeling of having perhaps nearly made a mistake. What was she going to tell Darling, after all? It had been her intention to come clean about her thoughts about the paper with her name on it. But how much could she really tell him? The Official Secrets Act swore her to silence in perpetuity. And yet her silence kept her on the top of the suspect list. Or would she mention that she had a vague sense that someone had come on her property at night? She cursed inwardly at the impulse to call the inspector, and felt utterly stupid about the raspberry business. It was going on for noon, and though it was a little too early for lunch, she felt in need of head clearing. She would walk over to the post office and see if Eleanor or Kenny were disposed to chat and offer her the ubiquitous cup of tea.

To leave the French doors open or not? It felt a ridiculous question, but Lane's new anxiety, no, her prudent caution, changed everything. She closed the doors and with a slight pang of sadness, threw the bolt and made her way to the front door. She didn't see Sandy until she'd very nearly run into him, where he stood on the landing by the spruce tree.

DARLING, BACK IN his office from a walk to the drug store, and holding a message picked up from O'Brien at the front desk to call New York, was not a little puzzled by Ames's greeting.

"Miss Winslow called about the raspberries, sir. If it is not too much trouble, she would like you to give her the name of the variety you had recommended to her on your last visit."

"Raspberries, Ames? What are you babbling about?"

Ames smiled delightedly and parked his behind on the corner of his superior's desk. "I know, sir; brilliant, isn't it? She's a cool one, that's for sure! Thinking on her feet like that. You don't get that every day from the ladies."

"You don't get anything every day from the ladies, Ames. And you can get off my desk. Now what's this about?" In truth, Darling knew nothing about Ames's private life, where for all he knew, Ames did very well by the ladies. It was a world that seemed so far in his past. He felt old. A war can wear you down, he thought. It was the great divide between him and people like Ames, who, really, was only six years younger than he was, but they could have come from different epochs.

Ames was undaunted by Darling's grouchiness and removed himself to a chair. "It's the party line, sir. All those rural phone systems are set up on a party line. Here in town we might worry about the operator listening in but we don't, because it's a busy system and they don't have a lot of time. But there, they have the telephone exchange at Balfour, and she probably has time to work on her nails all day, and a party line system so anyone can pick up a receiver and have a good listen if they're bored. They're only supposed to pick up the phone if it's the right ring, but heck, why not? Obviously, she heard something on the line and decided to be a spy, and pretend she was wanting something else. It took me a minute to get it, but it was thrilling, I can tell you!"

"You need to get out a bit more, Ames, you're too easily thrilled. Now get out of here." So astonished was he by the raspberry situation that he'd not taken off his jacket and hat, and these he now threw onto the rack before settling into his chair. When Ames had closed the door behind him, Darling picked up the phone and then put it down again. If she was worried about being overheard, he should himself be careful. Up until now they'd not spoken of anything crucial on the phone. In fact, up until now she'd been his number one suspect, and frankly, still was, regardless of what he got back from Scotland Yard. He'd wired a detective there with whom he'd served in the RAF, and told him to expect the envelopes. Why would she be phoning him again? He'd been surprised by her once already, at her quick call at the finding of the shoe, but it was in her interest to look helpful. In fact, it was his experience that sometimes criminals couldn't help being helpful. They deluded themselves into thinking it made them look innocent. Hence the ambiguity in the statement "Helping the police with their inquiries."

He picked up the receiver again and dialed the operator. While he waited to be put through, he worked on the raspberry approach, which he decided would have limitations. Was this going to mean another trip out to the Cove? Ames would be difficult to shut up if it did. He oppressively banished a slight stir of happiness at the prospect of going out there again and then realized he'd been hearing the phone ringing for some moments with no one answering.

"There appears to be no answer at that number. Would you like another?"

"No, thank you." Hanging up, he sighed and scooped up some papers on his desk, lining up the edges, which in truth had already been perfectly aligned. He wasn't bloody well going out there. He'd wait. The corpse was keeping cool. It could wait. In the meantime, he'd put that call through to New York. He didn't really suspect David Bertolli of much, with all the evidence heading so pointedly in the direction of Miss Winslow, but it would be as well to learn what he could.

CHAPTER TWENTY-ONE

"OH!" LANE EXCLAIMED, NEARLY JUMPING out of her skin. "Sandy."

"I was just stopping by to see how you're getting on," he said.

Lane heard a falter in his voice, and thought—no, knew—that it was a lie. She could have sworn he'd had no intention of knocking on her door. He was lurking and she'd surprised him. She felt a swell of anger. Had he done this before? When she thought she'd heard something when she had been by the creek, had it been him? She shook off these suspicions as being unbearable. All this business with the body and people sneaking on to her land. Having the ghastly Sandy lurking would be too much.

"I'm fine, thank you." She locked the door and then said firmly, "I'm going out now to the Armstrongs'. Thank you for your concern."

"Yeah, well. You know. A woman alone with all this going on. It must be hard so I thought . . ." He left his sentence unfinished. He looked peevishly at her as she turned to go.

"I'm only trying to help," he concluded.

"That's so kind. I'll be fine. Excuse me."

She did not hear the exact imprecation he muttered as he watched her walk firmly toward the path across to the post office road, but she imagined it was uncomplimentary. When she was through the trees, she looked back. She could see him moving up her driveway and back toward the road. Her heart was thumping. What did it mean? They had barely been on speaking terms since the godawful fishing trip. She wanted to go back to the house, lock herself into it, and think, but she was committed to going to Kenny and Eleanor's now, and feared Sandy might reach her gate and then look down the road to see if she'd gone into their cottage. She created a shelf in her mind for Sandy and, right next to it, a shelf for the incursions into her property. She must have time to think it all through.

IN THE DAYS since the murder, the residents of King's Cove had gone into a pretense of things being "back to normal." The vicar had asked everyone to pray for the soul of the unknown man during his homily, which had centred largely on the tending of gardens in anticipation of the harvest. Good for the time of year. And for some untroubled residents, it was back to normal, but for others, even the pretense was becoming difficult. Harris had suddenly had a return of the old nightmares and could not sleep. Bertolli had thought he had at last found normalcy, but saw now how it would only take something like this to bring it all crashing down. Reginald, Alice, and Sandy lived in the same household, but in three completely different universes of troubled anxiety. Only Alice's troubles seemed to her to be unchanged.

Reginald had increasingly given himself over to long walks, from which he returned encased in bitterness at the failure of his idea to thrive, all because Harris was being a bastard about the purchase of the land. He should never have lost that bid. And now Sandy was becoming more and more peculiar. The boy had taken to disappearing for long stretches of time at night. No doubt sniffing after that new woman. Well, he might as well. She had a nice piece of property and he wasn't getting one inch of land from him.

AND LANE COULD not settle. She returned from the post office with nothing to show for it. Eleanor and Kenny must have gone together somewhere, as his red truck was gone. She had written to her gran and begun to tell her about her new life, but she had spent ages staring at the blank page, wondering what to say about what was happening now. Of course, she could not worry her. Her gran had no knowledge of what her granddaughter had done in the war. She'd assumed that Lane was just what she said: the secretary to a minor, desk-bound military official in London. Lane couldn't now tell her she was mixed up in a murder. She put down her fountain pen. But she wasn't, was she? The murder had taken place on her land. Maybe, or he'd been dragged from somewhere else. Where else? But now because of the note, she was the one being dragged right into the centre of it.

WHILE LANE WAS glaring at her blank piece of paper, Darling was hanging up the phone with something like a triumphant bang. "Ames, we've got something."

"Have we, sir?" He looked up from his filing.

"None of your disrespectful tongue, my lad. While you've been frittering your time away, I have been gathering information. I think things are looking up. I've been on the phone to New York."

"New York, sir! What time is it there, anyway?"

"Three in the afternoon. I've learned something about that character, Bertolli. But his name isn't Bertolli, it's Agostino. He's a composer all right, but his family harbours one or two malodorous characters. It would appear his clan have some rivals and these same rivals are picking off his relations like cans on a fence because of one of them did in a member of the rival family. He's on the run here. Well, to be fair, in a protection program."

"Your language is very colourful when you are excited, sir. I thought we were pursuing inquiries based on our victim being English. What bearing have New Yorkers to this case, would you say? Well, besides the obvious advantage of their putting Miss Winslow in the clear."

"I'll not be put off by your insinuations today, Ames. Our victim may be English. But he may also be a New Yorker who bought a well-made jacket in a store on Fifth Avenue. We've not heard back from England yet and in the meantime, we've at least one member of the community with something to fear. What if our corpse is someone dispatched to dispatch Bertolli? It is worth a go. Go saddle up the steeds! And while we are there, perhaps you can look into Miss Winslow's raspberry problem."

MEANWHILE, IN LONDON, it had been the end of the day, or the beginning of the evening, if you were at home and preparing to sit down to dinner. Smithers and the director were not. They were sitting glumly together in Smithers's office looking at pros and cons. Franks was dead and there seemed little reason to indulge in an elaborate cover-up. Indeed, it would seem best not to, since they could not be sure his death was random. If it was related to his work, one of them ought to be over there to oversee what was going on. Just in case. The trouble was, Franks hadn't been very important. He didn't speak Russian and had transferred over from wartime communications to peacetime communications. He was an analyst, looking for patterns from translated documents. It was a job any semi-intelligent Oxbridge graduate could do. It seemed inconceivable that anyone would go to the trouble and expense of a trip to Western Canada to bump him off. Unless he'd become entangled with the other side—but would the Russians want an unimportant and somewhat peripheral agent? Yes, why not? He might be disgruntled about being no one special, and would perhaps find an offer attractive.

Even without the presumption that Franks might have been a double agent, it was nevertheless going to be beastly complicated. The fact that Winslow, a former agent, was somehow involved added an unexpected and troubling dimension. The director shifted uncomfortably in his seat. "I don't think, sir, that she did this. But the fact that they are asking about her means that she is a suspect. We don't know what she will say to protect herself. It will look extremely bad for us if there are garish headlines about 'British Spy Murder Mystery' in some local Canadian paper. We'd look like parents who can't control their children."

"You are the one that brought them together in the first place with your scheme to recruit her back to us, and no matter what you say, her reluctance to stay here in the first place was strong enough that she could have killed the messenger to get out of it. All right, I grant you she didn't seem the type, but I don't think we can afford to have Canadian plods stumbling all over the place. You're going to have to go. That's all there is to it."

Which is how the director found himself flying over the pond to Canada.

"WHILE WE ARE out there, Ames, we will devote some more time to looking for the car, if there is a car. And we will ask Miss Winslow a few more questions about her past. I can't help feeling that she is giving us a somewhat rehearsed version of her life story."

Ames said nothing, but smiled slightly. They were a few miles out of town at the point where the road turned, and there was a magnificent lakeside property, with a great sweep of sandy beach. The house itself was mock Tudor and was situated among trees that opened into a lawn that met the sand and the lake. Ames wondered what it would be like to live in that kind of luxury. He still lived with his mother in the house he'd grown up in.

"We don't have any idea how this man got out there," Darling was saying, "but he did, so either he drove himself, in which case someone has hidden his motor, or destroyed it, though that sounds like work, or someone drove him there. He had her name in his pocket. Let's say he comes here with a direct view of meeting her. He calls her from town when he arrives on the train, she comes out and picks him up, waits till his back is turned, and coshes him with a rifle butt."

"Sir, I thought we were driving out there just now to follow your New York gangster theory."

"I'll be following the New York gangster theorem, Ames; you will be following the mysterious English visitor theorem. I'll drop you off at the turn and you pop down to visit Miss Winslow, and I'll go up to Bertolli. When you are done, you can walk up to meet me. It's only a mile. The walk will do you good."

"Here's what I don't understand, sir," said Ames, ignoring the jibe. "If Miss Winslow went to all the trouble you describe, why would she make the mistake of leaving anything in his pockets? Whoever did this clears out the man's wallet, handkerchief, keys, bits of sales slips or whatever else he has in his pockets, and leaves just the one paper. If anything, it seems to me that someone could be trying to throw suspicion on her. What if that piece of paper was never his in the first place? What if it was deliberately put there by the murderer?"

Darling was silent. Ames, in truth, was speaking his own greatest hope. If he was honest, he wanted to believe what his eager constable was proposing. She had seemed genuine in not knowing the victim. He had a hard time believing that she could be responsible for murder, but he distrusted his motives.

She had struck him as intelligent and honest. Someone who knew about the hardships of life; he admired, he had to admit, her striking out to make a life for herself on her own, far out in the country. Still, he would not allow his judgment to be clouded, nor would he be goaded by Ames's insinuations. Ames was young, and he could not imagine admiring a woman without the suggestion of a romance in it. Darling had long ago given up on any idea of romance. That conceit of youth had been blown away by the last few years at the front. He kept firmly away from any thought of Miss Winslow's striking beauty.

"That is why, Ames, we are going to explore all the options. You may be right, in your Pollyanna optimism, but we are policemen, and we must follow every lead—lead where it may."

AMES WATCHED THE maroon car drive up the road and then turned down toward Lane Winslow's house. He was surprised by how the quiet, green landscape seemed to open something in him and free it. Hands in his pockets, he sauntered down the road, practically on the point of whistling, feeling like a young boy again, going out to play on his own. He arrived at the driveway leading down toward Miss Winslow's white house and stopped, wondering for a moment if he should continue down the road to the post office to see who might be gathered there. It was early. They'd made good time out from town. He realized he was trying to avoid going to see her because he didn't feel like interrogating her. It was unnecessary, in his view. Still. Must be thorough.

Taking a deep breath, he lifted the chain off the post and swung the gate open. He could see her little green Ford, parked where he had seen it before, up against the door of the unused outbuilding. He saw that there was an overgrown path on the east side of the weathered grey wooden structure and thought he might go around behind it. They hadn't been able to get around to the back from the other side because the path had been obscured by a sturdy growth of broom, but he saw that it would be easier from this side. He imagined it must simply bring one to the other side of the building and he could walk from there down to the house. His legs swooshed in the long grass that had grown up in the narrow space between the building and the fence along the west side of the upper field, where Lane had been musing that very morning.

He reached the end of the building, pushed through the dense shrubbery, and came out into the open area between the house and the barn he remembered from the first day. There were small, empty animal coops and a woodcutting area. He noticed a little stagnant pond off to the left. A blue jay was making a racket overhead in one of the Douglas firs. Ames was starting down the path to the house when he stopped, frowning. The ground in front of the big doors of the barn seemed to be disturbed. He himself had looked at that ground on their first trip out and he remembered that it had been covered with a layer of evergreen needles that was clearly untouched. Strangely, it didn't look logical. If the doors had been opened, the dust and dried evergreen needles that covered the ground would have been swept into the fan shape by the doors scraping the ground. This just looked as though the ground was disturbed. The evergreen needles were not lying cleanly on the surface as they had been, except, he realized, for when he and Darling had tramped on them in their initial inspection on the day they collected the body. They looked as though they'd been swept up and then somehow spread out again, leaving them covering the ground, but dusty. Perhaps Miss Winslow had thought to sweep them up and then changed her mind.

Almost tiptoeing, as if not to disturb the scene any further, Ames made his way to the dusty window on the right side of the door. He pressed his face to the encrusted glass and used his hands to cup his vision to block out the morning sunlight that streamed through the evergreen stand. His stomach lurched. Even through the grime on the window and the cobwebs growing thickly out of the corners on the inside, he could see that there was a small black roadster inside that had not been there when he and Darling had looked before. He stepped back, looking now toward the house, feeling furtive. He walked carefully back the way he'd come and leaned against the back side of the building.

What could this mean? Don't be stupid, he told himself. It means that someone has put a car in the barn and tried to cover it up. Even a town-bred boy like himself could see that. If it were innocent, he would have seen the marks of the barn doors, some footsteps on that dusty ground. In fact, when he thought of it, even the footsteps he and Darling had left on their last visit had been covered over. He couldn't go see her now. Darling had to know. He felt grimly foolish, taken in. If he was honest, he knew it was because she was so pretty. She just didn't seem like the type.

Now, his anxiety heightened by not wanting to be discovered by her, he moved quickly back up the driveway to the gate and lifted the chain off as quietly as he could. It suddenly seemed as if the heavy chain was the loudest noise in the world. He looked back as he reclosed the gate, but did not see her. She must be in the house or around the front. He hurried up the road, now regretting the jacket and tie. It was warm and he had at least a mile to go to reach the Bertollis', where he would have to tell Darling what he had seen.

"WHY DIDN'T YOU tell me?" Angela Bertolli was leaning against the kitchen sink with one hand over her mouth, looking at the two men sitting at the table.

"I . . . I didn't want to worry you, or the boys. You're happy here, aren't you? The boys love it," Dave Bertolli ended feebly.

"Worry me? Worry me? I'm not worried now; I'm scared to death. I knew your family was a little screwy. But this, the name change . . . How could you lie to me about your real name? How can any of us feel safe now?"

Dave Bertolli had no answer for this. He looked nervously at Inspector Darling, who had been watching the exchange studiously. Then he spoke again. "Look, if you think a guy is going to follow me all the way from New Jersey to this ridiculously out-of-the-way place, you're crazy. And how would he have found me? How do I know? Because I had nothing to do with this! That's how I know. I never saw the guy. I certainly didn't kill the guy. I'm a musician, for heaven's sake. I know I should have told you about what happened with Tony back in New York, but I promise you, it will never put us in danger. No one will come here to find a younger brother that everyone knows had nothing to do with anything. It doesn't make sense!"

"I can tell you one thing, Inspector, he may be a liar, but Dave would never hurt a fly. Why do you think the kids are out there like little wild animals screaming and hanging in trees? He doesn't like to tell anyone what to do." David cast her a grateful look. When the police had gone, he might even tell her about the letter from his brother, saying someone might have found out about his alias. Whoever it was still would have no idea where he was. He knew he didn't have to worry, but there was no point in complicating things by showing the inspector the letter. It was meaningless anyway, because whoever had killed the man in the creek, it certainly hadn't been him. In a way he was relieved to be able to tell Angela the whole truth, though he knew he was in for a rough night.

Inspector Darling, having been forced to write his own notes, closed his little book and was standing up when they heard the hurried footsteps on the wooden porch and looked up to see a winded Constable Ames framed in the open doorway, his tie loose and his jacket slung over his arm.

"Ames. You were quick," Darling said, glancing at his watch.

"Sir. I wonder if you have a moment . . ."

"Lots of moments, Ames, we're done here for now. Could I ask you to stay in the area until this matter is cleared up?" Darling said courteously to the Bertollis, and he stood up to follow Ames back to where he'd parked the car at the top of the grassy driveway by the main road. On the way back to the car they waved at the children, who were taking turns swinging on a rope hanging from a beam in a rickety-looking barn.

"I wouldn't be Mr. Bertolli—or Agostino—for anything just now," Darling commented, settling his hat back on to his head. "Now what's going on, Ames? You look, as they say, as though you've seen a ghost. No more bodies, I hope?"

"No. Not exactly. But I've found the car. I think. I mean, I think I've found the car."

Darling stopped by the driver's side door and looked at Ames, frowning. "And you don't seem very happy about it."

"Yes, sir. No, sir. Not exactly. I found it in Miss Winslow's outbuilding."

CHAPTER TWENTY-TWO

LANE HAD ABANDONED HER LETTER to her grandmother. She could not seem to muster any thoughts that would not alarm her. She been reading Yeats in the hopes that it would inspire her to some useful poetry. Her notebook stood by her, ready with a sharpened pencil set in the dip of the spine. She closed the book with a sigh. For all his angst and beauty, his concerns of unrequited love and the Irish question seemed far from what she had about her right now, and she knew you were to write about what you know. What she knew is that a man had been killed somewhere nearby, by someone unknown, and dumped in her creek, and that in the most bizarre circumstance imaginable, he had been travelling about with her name in his pocket. What kind of poetry would that make? *You lie dead like a fallen leaf trapped in an eddy.* No, that last word cannot be two syllables, it just cannot. Creek. Too matter-of-fact. Water. Two syllables again, but soft ones. Maybe that was the trouble. Eddy was too hard. Water. There.

You lie dead like a fallen leaf trapped in the water
Drifted, danced by the wind off a distant tree
Down like a sinner to a lonely slaughter
With only one word, and it was word of me.

No . . . *for me*. It made more sense.

Not Yeats, but enough to get her going for today. It was as she was settling paper into the typewriter that she heard the knock. "Oh dear." She hoped it was not Angela; she really wanted to work today and she couldn't bear to say no to Angela. She could see through the glass in the door that it was Darling and Ames.

"Inspector Darling, Constable Ames. You got my message! Do come in. Please let me get you a drink of something, Constable Ames. You don't look at all well." But they did not come in. Ames looked down like a guilty child, but Darling, looking down as well, had more the look of a man wondering what his next step ought to be.

"Miss Winslow. I think you'd better come with us for a moment. We've something to show you. Perhaps you should get a pair of shoes," he added, noticing her golden legs ending in bare feet. He wished he hadn't. They waited on the front step for her to return with a pair of gym shoes slipped loosely over her feet. She hadn't bothered to tie the laces.

"Have you found something?" She tried to sound pleased, interested, but there was something in the demeanour of these two that made her feel quite suddenly cold. They walked up toward the barn and then around to where the pens were. "Oh," she said, "I saw this this morning. This is why I called, I suppose."

"What is it? What did you see?" asked Darling, stopping and watching her curiously.

"The way these pine needles are scattered, as if someone did it deliberately. To be frank, it made me extremely nervous, especially after the shoe business. I felt . . . feel like someone has been here . . . at night. I can't see the point of it. Or who would be taking the trouble, unless . . . Well, I wondered if someone were trying to incriminate me."

"Why, I wonder?" His voice retained a calm, steady tone that seemed to be withholding any judgment.

"Honestly, Inspector, I don't know. I don't understand any of it. I've only just arrived here. Am I an easy target? There are people in this community who do not take well to newcomers, but it's a very elaborate way to scare someone off."

"Perhaps we could open the doors now? Ames looked in the window and saw a car parked inside. Can you tell us about that?"

The sense of dread she had felt when she saw the mood of the policemen at her door cascaded into waves of fear. She looked at the barn doors and saw what she had not seen in the morning: the padlock was there but was hanging open. How had she not seen that? She would have looked, seen the car. "I can't believe I didn't see the lock. I mean, it's the reason I phoned you. I was out this morning and I saw what I thought were tracks, only they ended here, so I think I was thinking that someone had driven in last night, messed things about to frighten me, and then left. I did glance at the barn door, but it looked like the padlock was undisturbed." She felt now like she was jabbering. She must seem as guilty as sin to these two men with their carefully non-committal expressions. Feeling suddenly faint, she reached out and leaned against the barn with one arm. Hanging her head, she wondered if she'd be sick, but then decided she would not. That would be feminine weakness taken too far, she thought rebelliously. She was better than that. "If there is a car in there, I did not put it there, Inspector," she said finally. She turned toward the doors and then stopped, looking uncertainly at the policemen, before turning to slip off the padlock and pull the doors open. It surprised her that they came open easily, with only a slight drag on the ground. They had been well made. But none of that mattered because there, with its headlights facing them, was a black DeSoto.

"It's got local plates, sir," Ames said.

June 27, 1946

Franks woke feeling groggy from a deep sleep when the conductor knocked on the compartment door. "We'll be pulling in in ten minutes, sir," he said, touching the brim of his cap.

Pulling himself upright where he had slumped in his sleep, Franks looked blearily out the window at the passing countryside. More trees. What extremes, he thought. All those thousands of miles with no trees, and then nothing but these dense, impenetrable layers of blue-green forests on either side. He had read that travelling across eastern Russia was much like this. With relief he noted that the train was now running along a river on one side, or a lake.

He pulled out his map to look at where Nelson was located. He imagined a primitive mining camp sort of place and sighed. His mother had come from here.

The station was hardly primitive and he was pleasantly surprised. It was late morning and the air had a clean, golden tang to it. Nelson appeared to be built up a long, steep hill, and the road outside the station was bustling with cars, most of them pre-war. He was directed to the YMCA when he asked about a place to stay, and he took his small suitcase and started up the hill. As he walked away from the station and turned back to look at it, in one respect the sight confirmed his prejudice. The station and the rail yards adjacent to it were bustling with activity. Lumber was piled on waiting cars and floating in logjams in the water just beyond. Small tugboats were bustling on the water. It reminded him of the magazine advertisements for immigration to Canada. Great forests and lakes and opportunities. As he reached the top of the hill and was looking down what appeared to be the main drag, he stopped to take off his jacket. It was hot. It surprised him. Canada. Hot. He tried to imagine himself immigrating here.

Established in a small room in the YMCA, he felt himself ironically at home, for he stayed at the Y in London when he was there. A home for the rootless, he thought. He was as without connections here as he was there. He slept well, happy that for the first time in days he was not in a moving train. In the morning, he went to a little restaurant and had a hearty breakfast of eggs and bacon. A full English. With an approximation of the Union Jack flying over what looked like a stone courthouse, he could well be in some rural English town.

He went about trying to hire a car and found a garage just off Baker Street where he was given a bedraggled ten-year-old DeSoto convertible. He was aware that he would have to cope with driving on the right-hand side of the road, but there would be little traffic, he assumed. Leaving his suitcase on his bed, he took some papers and drove carefully to the ferry that crossed the lake to the road out to King's Cove. The few times he passed a car it still startled him to have them racing by on the wrong side, but eventually he settled in to the drive.

He was surprised by the grandeur of some of the properties along the lakefront, and then inwardly chided himself for his prejudices about the colonies. He had expected it to be all rather wild, he supposed. When he arrived at the turnoff that had been described to him at the little store in Balfour, three miles from King's Cove, he turned up the road and suddenly he realized he had no idea what to do next.

NO ONE SPOKE. Finally, Lane walked around the car slowly, looking to see if anything had had to be moved to accommodate the car. Rakes and shovels of various shapes were hung on spikes on the wall, and a rusted horseshoe hung over the inside of the doorway, mocking, she thought, her luck, which seemed at the moment to be going from bad to worse. She had walked around to the driver's side door and was reaching her hand out to open it when Darling stopped her.

"If you don't mind, Miss Winslow, I think we'll handle this." She pulled her hand away, as though from a flame.

"Yes, of course." She stepped back into the light at the edge of the large doors and looked again at the ground around the door, where all that could be seen now were their own scuff marks. "I don't understand this. How could someone get this in here without my knowing?"

Ames looked with interest at Darling, his eyebrows raised as if to say, "Well, how could they?"

Darling ignored him and looked at her. "Are you saying that you have never seen this car before?"

"I certainly jolly well am! And I know it wasn't here before because I've looked in the windows. I was waiting for a good day to get in here and have a real look around. I imagine most of it is forty years old. Except this car. It's probably fifteen years old." She waved a disparaging hand in the direction of the DeSoto.

"Nineteen thirty-three at a guess, not bad on your part, miss!" said Ames, cheerfully, ignoring the repressive look Darling shot at him, his earlier morose mood somehow lifted by Lane's obvious puzzlement about the car.

"Please go and collect the fingerprinting equipment from the car, Ames. Handles, footmarks on the running boards, anything on the dash. Miss Winslow, may we go into the house? I do have a few questions."

"I bet you do!" The whole episode had awoken a contrarian streak in Lane. It was bad enough having a body clogging up her drains and now someone—and she found she had stopped feeling afraid and that her anger was closer to the surface—had moved what was probably the victim's car into her barn. Probably the person who killed him in the first place. She opened the door into the hallway and invited Inspector Darling to walk through with an impatient wave of her hand.

"Miss Winslow," he said, when they were settled at her kitchen table, "I cannot help feeling that you have not been entirely honest with us. Failure to tell us everything you know could seriously hamper this investigation."

"But I have. Everything. I don't know the man, I don't know the car, and I don't know how the car got into my barn. And if you insist on thinking I did this thing, you will be seriously hampering your investigation, because whoever did it is running around out there, no doubt thinking of some other way to place the blame on me." She got up and poured two glasses of water and set them with a bang on the table. The sunlight shone at an angle on them, making them cast a luminous reflection along the white tabletop. "Last night . . . no, it's ridiculous!"

"What is?"

"No. It's nonsense. What else do you want to know?"

"What about last night? Anything, however small, could be of assistance."

"Well, this couldn't."

"Try me."

"Very well. The latch on my attic window is broken, so the windows open on their own. Kenny likes to say his dead mother, Lady Armstrong, lives in my attic and she has a propensity to open my windows. A bit of fun. But the windows opened in the middle of the night a day or two after you found the body, and it was when I was up there that I saw the torchlight in the forest. That was how I found the shoe, as you will recall. Last night they swung open again and the noise must have woken me. I went up, and this time decided not to close them. It was a warm night, and there was no wind to bang them about. I looked out but could see nothing but darkness, so I went back to bed. But someone must have been busy putting the car in barn."

"I'm sorry. I'm just trying to understand how this window business might have any relevance. Are you saying that these windows open when something is going on, or needs to be brought to your attention, or something like that?"

Lane leaned back in her chair. She hadn't made that connection herself, and yet now that he had, she wondered. Was Lady Armstrong helping her? Rubbish. No need to add a supernatural dimension to an already impenetrable problem. "God, it's obviously nonsense. All I can really tell you is that I didn't hear the car going in there, and I have never seen it before. Sometimes I dream of cars in the distance, but I can't even recall if I dreamed that last night, or the night before."

Darling got up and walked to stand in front of the French doors. He was completely puzzled by her apparent surprise at the turn of events. The sun cascaded across the lawn, and he looked at it with longing. The days continued to be beautiful, as if this were some epic summer in a child's memory. He put his hands into his pockets and watched the tops of the trees outside. He loved the way the tops of trees stroked the sky. When he spoke again, it was as if he were musing out loud. "Usually when someone commits a murder, they are finishing a story that began in the past. They are getting, or more likely finding they are not getting, an inheritance, or taking revenge for an old slight. They are someone inconvenient who has turned up. They can come suddenly out of the smoke of the very war we've just been through to finish something or seek justice. This man, in spite of your protestations, Miss Winslow, was very likely seeking you. He had your name in his pocket, unless our beavering murderer put that in his pocket to begin this trail of clues that leads to you. What would your guess be?"

"No. My guess is no. The beavering murderer, clever that, given the dam he created in the creek with the body, did not write on that paper. It is more likely that he took everything out of his pockets if they could identify him, the corpse I mean, and had a bit of luck when he found that paper. He left it in and has been doing his Boy Scout best since then to set it up so I look guilty."

Darling frowned, surprised. "I'm sorry, are you saying that the man, in effect, was looking for you?"

Lane looked past him to the sweep of her lawn and the distant view of the lake. She knew that she was close to losing this view, this garden, this sanctuary from all she'd been through. "The trouble is, I've been wondering if it's possible, but I cannot say anything. I'm sorry, but there is nothing I can do about that. But you must believe me when I tell you, I do not know this man, nor did I kill him."

Darling came away from the French doors and carefully

pushed the chair he'd been sitting in under the table, as though he were cleaning up. "I'm going to see how Ames is getting on with the car you've never seen before. Perhaps in the interim you could pack a bag. I really don't see how I can avoid taking you in."

SANDY CLEARED HIS throat and with only a slight hesitation knocked on his father's small office door. He had rarely gone in there, except as a very small child, and he had been quickly fetched out by his mother. His father was not to be disturbed. He was working. What on earth at? Sandy wondered now. Mather had bought some land, had drawn some sketches, but in twenty-eight years, Sandy had never seen a single result. The war had come and gone, he had gone and come back again, and still his father sat in his office and made plans for a business that never seemed to materialize.

"Yes?" came an almost suspicious answer.

"Father, may I speak to you?" Sandy had determined, absolutely, that he would be calm. He stood with his feet braced behind the still-closed door, as if preparing to weather a blast. He wondered why, at his age, he had to continue to feel like a six-year-old before his father.

"Yes, all right. Come in." It was the voice of a man who could spare only a couple of minutes. Sandy pushed the door open and saw his father, as he had expected, sitting at his desk poring over a map. He had situated his desk so that the natural light from the window illuminated the work surface. He looked up, frowning. "Yes? What do you want?"

Sandy's immediate thought was that his father was too cheap to use a desk lamp.

He stood before his father with his hands behind his back, as if he were in trouble with the dean of the agricultural college he'd attended in Vancouver. "Father, I have a few thoughts about this logging thing."

"Sit down, will you? You're blocking the light. What thoughts?"

Having pulled a chair close to the other side of the desk, Sandy leaned in and pointed at the map. "There really seems to me to be no reason we couldn't get started. Why don't we just begin harvesting the trees? We could truck them in to one of the mills between here and Nelson. That would give us enough capital to build our own small mill in, say, a year's time. The whole province is in a post-war boom. In Vancouver they are building houses a mile a minute. Heck, they're building houses all up and down the outskirts of Nelson. I mean, no one wants to move this far out of town, but lots of servicemen want nice, new little houses for their families near town. We'd be mad not to capitalize on this."

Mather sat forward, his elbows resting on the map and his hands clasped together. He regarded his son silently for a few moments after this speech, and then leaned back. "I know what's behind this, you know. You must think I'm stupid. Or mad. This is a scheme to get your hands on the money. I know you. You think if you work with me I'll reverse my decision—include you in the business. You think I haven't thought of how to get my own bloody business going? Do you think that I need you?" He delivered that "you" as if Sandy were something unpleasant underfoot.

Sandy stood up and stared down at his father. Why had he bothered? He was finished now. Why had he bothered with any of it? He would leave, move back to Vancouver. His father could deal with Mother. He could sit on his useless land making his useless plans. When he finally died, well. We'll see then. He felt himself in the dead, quiet centre of a hurricane of rage. But he savoured the triumph of his next statement. "I just came to tell you that I got Harris to sell."

Mather looked stunned. "What rubbish is this? Why should he suddenly agree to sell after nearly forty years?"

"It doesn't matter why. You should be happy. We can get that damn mill up and running. And if you don't, I will."

"You know," said his father, looking at him coldly, "you are as mad as your mother. I see that now." He resumed looking at his map, trying to hide the elation he felt. Sandy was right. It didn't matter why. It was going to be his, at last. The only misgiving he had was how on earth Sandy had managed it.

Sandy walked out the front door, letting the screen door slam behind him in the thick quiet of the hot afternoon. He was surprised at what he felt. He had imagined that when this moment came, when he finally stood up to his father on an equal footing, he would feel some kind of stormy rage, but what he felt instead was a grim clarity and inner calm. It pleased him to think himself so in control. He walked out behind the house to an upper path that skirted the top border of their property. It dropped down to run parallel along the roadway about where Lane's house was, and eventually joined the driveway to the post office.

He would walk and sort out what his next move would be. He could leave—he should leave. Go back to Vancouver and wait out his father. He didn't know what was in his father's will. But he knew the outcome, didn't he? When all was said and done, he would get the property. His mother, if she survived him, would be completely incapable of running the place. He was initially surprised, he remembered, to learn how much money his father had amassed—but, once he thought about it, he realized it wasn't that surprising. After all, his father was a cheap bastard. He felt an inward tug. He should leave, but he needed to be here to watch over things.

By this time, his walk had brought him parallel to the driveway that pulled into Lane's place. He stopped, half pretending he hadn't come to this spot on purpose. The policemen's car was in the driveway, parked next to her Ford. He could hear voices. He strained to hear what they were saying, but he could just hear the rise and fall of an indistinct male voice. What he saw next was what mattered. Lane was carrying a small suitcase and walking between the two policemen. The door was opened for her and she got into the back seat. Sandy watched without moving until the policemen's car had disappeared around the corner. He could hear its progress right down to the Nelson road.

CHAPTER TWENTY-THREE

THE ROOM WAS NOT SINISTER. This surprised Lane. Interrogation, after all, is a sinister-sounding procedure. She was seated at a small wooden table with Darling opposite and Ames on her right at the end of the table, his ever-present notebook in hand. There was a window behind her with fluttering green curtains, through which a pleasant, herby summer morning smell wafted. Darling had a little sheaf of papers, which he squared the edges of. She wanted to see what was written on them: questions? Results of their investigation to date? She hoped it was facts and not speculation. Facts, she felt sure, would sooner or later result in truth, but speculation could lead to assumptions, and her fear was that in the space between what questions she could answer and what she could not answer, assumptions would result in her being put in the frame.

She looked at Darling now, as he read the first page. Was he the kind of man who would collect facts and assemble them into some kind of truth, or was he already forming questions that would begin with "Isn't it the case that . . ." The former, she hoped.

"I hope you were reasonably comfortable, Miss Winslow?"

"Thank you. Reasonably. And thank you for the breakfast." This had been served to her in this room and the remains had been cleared away.

"Miss Winslow, I will be asking you some questions now. Ames will be taking notes. To begin, can you tell me why you came out to Canada?"

Lane thought about this. She hoped that not every question would be so difficult to answer. Would she tell him of her tiredness after the war, the sadness at the loss of Angus that would not loosen its grip on her, the sheer randomness of picking not only Canada but the farthest reaches of it? "I think I just wanted to start a new life."

"What was wrong with the old one?"

"I found I wanted to get away from bombed-out London and just go somewhere that hadn't seen war, I suppose."

"I see. Did you not leave family behind? It's an unusual move for a young woman to come all this way alone."

"My parents are both gone." Yes, that was easier than *My mother is gone and we don't know about my father. He has disappeared.* "I have grandparents who moved back to Britain and they wanted me to be happy. I seem, at the moment, to be letting them down."

"What do you mean by that?"

She felt her first stirring of anger. "Because, Inspector, instead of unpacking my boxes and arranging vases of wildflowers around my house, I am here, answering questions that seem to be leading further and further away from the dead man in my creek, itself a circumstance that has made me unhappy."

Ames cleared his throat but said nothing.

Darling was unruffled. "I am trying to establish why you have come to British Columbia and how this must connect to that dead man, as the circumstances seem too coincidental to ignore. What did you do during the war?"

"I worked in an office."

"What sort of office?"

"A procurement office."

"Well, that covers a multitude of sins. Can you be more specific?"

Sighing with some impatience, Lane said, "No, I can't. I typed at a desk all day and then went home and hoped a bomb wouldn't fall on me."

"With your international background, do you not have languages that might have been useful to someone?"

"I don't know where you are going with this, Inspector. I speak German, French and Russian thanks only to my early upbringing. No one seemed to be in the least bit interested in this. They only wanted to know how fast I typed."

"A waste of manpower. Do you not have a university education?"

"I do. It is where I learned to type."

Darling made a note on the margin of the first sheet of paper, which Lane determinedly did not try to look at. "You came directly here from England, then?"

"No, I spent some time in France with a friend. I thought I might relocate there, but found I could not. I . . . just wanted something new." Close. She'd been about to say that being in France made her feel still too raw.

Another note. Lane longed to look behind her out

the window but instead sat with her arms folded and waited. She had sat through long episodes of questions by authoritative men during the war. She was used to that, but at least then she was required to recall everything she had seen and heard, and she saw the use of it. There was a war on. She wanted to tell Darling again that he was wasting his time; that while they sat, whoever was responsible was back at the Cove, perhaps covering his tracks or finding new ways to throw suspicion on her, but she was surprised by his pointed determination and did not want to raise his suspicion further by appearing to try to evade his questions.

"In Paris?"

"No, in the Dordogne. My friend breeds horses."

"Your friend, a man?"

"No, Inspector. A woman. A childhood friend." Good God. Was he going to pursue the idea that the dead man was her lover? She hadn't thought of this angle and felt herself colouring from a rush of anger. She waited.

"You have something you wish to add?" He had taken his eyes off the paper and was looking at her closely.

"No, I assure you, nothing whatever."

"I will need her name and address. Ames will collect these from you when we are finished here. Let us move to your arrival in Canada. Why did you come here? It is far from Europe. Quebec might have suited you better. You speak French and it is a shorter journey to visit your country."

"I read books and brochures. And when I visited Nelson I saw the advertisement for the house in King's Cove in the newspaper. I asked the agent to show it to me and I loved it. I am not, before you ask, running from a demon lover or some dark past, though I did fancy a break from war-torn Europe. I consider this to be my country now, by the way. May I have some water?"

To her surprise, Darling looked stricken. "I do beg your pardon," he said. "Ames, could you?" Ames leaped out of his seat as if his young body had been caged in it and disappeared out the door. Darling said, "Miss Winslow, please feel free to stand."

Lane got up, stretched her back, and went to stand by the window.

"It's a pretty little town. Nesbitt, the agent, wanted me to stay here. He said I would be safer. But I grew up in the countryside. I have always felt safe in the countryside. Little did I dream he might be right, though I suppose murders happen even in Nelson."

Behind her Darling made no comment to this but she could hear his pencil scraping over the paper again. The door opened and she turned to see Ames coming in with her glass of water. She felt extraordinarily grateful to him, as if her imprisonment were beginning to take hold and she must hang on to any kindness.

"I have just looked over my notes. Can we go back to the outfit you worked for in London? What was the name of the company?" Darling had resumed his quiet, searching demeanour.

Lane breathed deeply and expelled the breath. She wanted to close her eyes so she could concentrate. Here it was. In all the previous debriefings she'd done during the war, she'd never had to lie. In this moment she understood the implication of the oath she had taken. She was not prepared for it. If she made up a name, it could be checked. If she were vague in her answer, she would sound evasive. Silence seemed the best option. She chose it.

"You cannot remember? Can you tell me who your boss was?"

"Inspector. I had hoped that when your questions brought us all to British Columbia, we might begin looking at the problem at hand. I, though I am innocent in every way of that man's death, had hoped that perhaps skillful questions on your part might get at something I had not remembered, or that I had noticed but hadn't seen the value of. I must confess, I am beginning to feel like poor Joseph K. in Kafka. What you are doing is pointless, Inspector."

"I think you might leave the progress of this interview to me, Miss Winslow. I have made a note that you have refused to answer my questions. I believe these questions to be relevant to the investigation; indeed more so, since you seem unable to answer them. You leave me no choice but to detain you further. I have, incidentally, sent away to my contacts in Britain for any information they might be able to provide. This should be here at any moment. Perhaps we will make better progress then. Ames. Could you walk Miss Winslow back to her quarters?"

In the hallway, Lane muttered, "Pompous ass!" under her breath.

"I know what you mean, Miss. Is there anything you need?"

"Writing paper. I might as well do my correspondence while I am here."

Back in the office, Ames found the inspector sitting gloomily at his desk. "One-nothing to her, sir?" he offered cheerfully. "By the way, who is Kafka?"

"Shut up, Ames."

THE NEXT MORNING the director alighted from the train with much the same relief that Franks had, though he had not taken the train right across the country, but only from Vancouver. He was in a hurry, and he'd flown from London to Montreal and thence to Vancouver. The town looked respectable after all, though being on a train, even from Vancouver, impressed upon him the ridiculous lengths Lane had gone to escape. Escape from what? he wondered now. Perhaps there was something in her family life. He found a small hotel, which provided him with a room on the fourth floor and a view of the mountains on the other side of the lake. Getting instructions from the desk clerk, he walked along the sunny streets until he found the police station. A man in uniform at the long wooden expanse of desk greeted him. "Can I help you, sir?"

"I'm looking for Inspector Darling."

DARLING LOOKED OVER the documents presented to him by the Englishman who had been ushered into his office. He made some effort not to look flabbergasted that the English would have responded by sending a man out. Surely a wire would have answered any questions? The Englishman was a good-looking, tall man with waving light brown hair—in his early forties, Darling would have said. He radiated a sense of confidence and easy power that he had seen sometimes in British officers, who were largely recruited from the privileged classes. "I'm surprised that you have come all this way," he said to the Englishman. "We could have spoken on the telephone."

The director considered this for a moment, as if thinking about how much to say. "The fact is that both parties worked for us. The dead man was called Jack Franks." He left it at that and hoped it would be enough, that this Canadian inspector had enough intelligence to understand, though he realized that was a faint hope. No one on the outside really understood, and while Canada had an intelligence service, it would not be operating in this last-stop sort of place. He looked again around the office and was surprised when his eye lit on a very fine watercolour, obviously of a local scene, judging by the trees and lake.

Darling in the meantime was fighting a deep sense of dismay. The fact that he'd been right to bring Miss Winslow in was little compensation for this knowledge that almost certainly made her guilty, and an expert liar. He supposed that was what people who "worked" for this man were good at.

"Am I to understand by 'worked for us' that they are some sort of operatives? Are you with the British secret service . . . MI6 or something?"

"I see no reason not to tell you. Yes. You can see why this makes it a delicate matter, and requires my presence," the Englishman said.

"I think you'd better understand right away that just because they were both operatives does not mean you will be taking over this case. The murder happened here and is ours to deal with. What exactly is it that you propose?" He had said it, "operative." Now much of what Miss Winslow had said, or not said, made sense.

The director turned and gazed at the man with some respect. He did understand. Looking at him closely he saw what he'd missed, probably because of his own prejudice about colonials. He hadn't looked, as he usually did when he met someone new, for signs of real intelligence.

"I was going to propose that we take Miss Winslow right off your hands. She is a British citizen; she has been accused of the murder of another British citizen. We can try her in Britain."

"She is, I believe, a landed immigrant, and therefore has rights under Dominion law. And, as I said, our case." He considered for a moment. He'd been avoiding saying, or even thinking, the next question. "Obviously, then, Miss Winslow and Franks knew each other?" She had been utterly believable when she had said she had never seen Franks before. But of course, that merely meant she was good at what she did. Funny really, he was seeing it over and over. Something that was an invaluable trait in wartime was an enormous liability in peacetime. How many men had he arrested or dealt with for their violent outbursts in their homes or workplaces whose violent activities overseas had earned them medals? Lying well must be the most valuable asset of a spy, for it seemed to him that this was what he was dealing with and accounted for her unaccountable secrecy, which now was being used for covering a crime.

"No, they didn't, funnily enough."

Darling looked down at the papers under his hands to

cover a flood of relief. Clearing his throat, he asked, "Then can you explain why he appeared to be looking specifically for her?"

The director considered this. If he could keep her in the "guilty" column, he could continue to press for her removal to Britain for a trial. On the other hand, he still felt that she was probably not guilty, and it could be better to clear her and hope that she would come willingly back with him.

"I can tell you that this man, Franks, was coming here for reasons entirely his own. He did not explain these to me when he asked for a leave, but said it was a family matter. I know he lost his parents in the Blitz and for some reason had been quite unsettled since that time. I prefer my people to sort out their personal business and come to work fully committed. I assumed that giving him some time would do this for him. It is a very unfortunate outcome for us to lose him. Tiresome, though I suppose we shall find a replacement with his talents from among the fresh crop of varsity graduates."

Darling kept his face impassive. He found himself in the grip of a growing dislike of this man. Too charming, too handsome, and much too cavalier about his "people." Tiresome indeed to lose someone! He tried to imagine how he'd feel if he lost Ames, for instance. "He told you that he needed to come to King's Cove specifically for a family reason? The difficulty is that whoever killed him took all of his identification, and the only thing on his person was this piece of paper, badly soaked, with Miss Winslow's name on it. On the face of it, that exonerates her, as leaving her name in his pockets is a damn fool thing to do; however, she had the opportunity, found the body, and his missing vehicle was found in her barn. In addition, she produced one of the missing shoes. She has been extremely helpful, but has refused utterly to say anything to help herself, except to admit that this man must have come for her. This has only made her situation worse, since it suggests that no one else at King's Cove, a tiny settlement with a handful of people in it, mostly pre–Great War relics, knew him or had any reason to kill him. And I am at a loss to know why Miss Winslow should kill him, unless he was in a position to reveal that she is a fugitive from British justice, and she did not want to be discovered and sent back. Is she?"

"No." The Englishman again fell silent, trying to decide how much to say. "Look, I will speak where she cannot. It is her very silence in this matter that may explain to you why I have come all the way here. Lane, Miss Winslow, is extremely bright and talented. She speaks perfect Russian and French and has had a peculiar international upbringing that we find most fitting for the work we require of her. She worked for us during the war. She was, and obviously continues to be, extremely loyal."

"And does Miss Winslow," Darling emphasized the name in a tacit disapproval of her first name being used by this man, "wish to return to your service?"

The director stood up and went to look out of the window. The street below had a charming, picture-book feel to it that made him want to disparage its small-town pretensions. This man was proving difficult. He had hoped that he could exert some sense of authority over the situation that would result in them immediately releasing Lane to his care.

This local policeman was more clever and potentially more intransigent than he had expected and he was on delicate ground. He really had no authority here. And now this question. If he was honest, he would have to admit that she did not wish to return. Though he had not spoken with her at the end of the war, she had made it clear to her commander that she was emigrating and had unequivocally refused all offers to stay on in the service.

Finally he turned back to Darling. "Miss Winslow does not know the conditions that I am prepared to offer. I will be frank with you. My knowledge of her absolutely convinces me that she is not guilty of this particular crime. The man, Franks, as I said, was here about his own business. I merely took advantage of his coming here to have him deliver a message to her. If I am . . ."

"One moment. May I ask how you knew where to find her? Did she keep contact with her former employer?" Darling's head was swimming and he was beginning to feel, though he would never have hinted as much to this slippery visitor, as though he was indeed in over his head. What if, in fact, she was still in the service, and was operating under instructions to "eliminate" this Franks, who might have been perceived as some sort of rogue? It would indicate a depth of concealment on her part that made him feel a frisson of disappointment, but it also threw into question whether, under such circumstances he would be able to maintain his local jurisdiction of the case. If this man represented some organ, however secretive, of the British government, then might not the Dominion government also become involved? "Is she still, in fact in your 'employ' and was she acting on orders from anyone in your firm to eliminate this man Franks?"

The other man threw back his head and laughed. "You've been reading too much John Buchan, Inspector Darling. This is not some covert operation we are trying to cover up here. We keep track of all of our former employees, as you can imagine, even when they try to lose themselves at the farthest reaches of the globe." He waved his hand to take in where they were now. "They are obliged to keep the Official Secrets Act and so we must have our ear to the ground, in case someone forgets, or as in this case, sometimes they are so valuable we wish to have them back. I assure you that Franks was here on a personal quest and I asked him to bring a message. I am offering to take the most assuredly innocent Miss Winslow off your hands and I can see, by the way, that in spite of circumstances, you yourself believe her to be innocent, and you can get on with solving your little local crime, committed, I dare say, by little local people for their own little local reasons. And now, if you don't mind, as pleasant as this is, I need Miss Winslow's address, as I would like to speak to her."

Darling, as much as it annoyed him, could think of no immediate reason to deny the request. "As a matter of fact, we have her here at the moment. Please wait here."

CHAPTER TWENTY-FOUR

"MISS WINSLOW." LANE TURNED AT the sound of Inspector Darling's voice. She was not, as she had expected, occupying a cell full time, but had been put back into the room where she had answered questions so fruitlessly the day before. She had books and some writing paper that Ames had obligingly brought her. Because the building was on the corner, she could also see at an angle the street that ran down the hill toward Nelson's main drag. It was treed and pleasant, with rather nice-looking wood-framed houses and little, meticulously cared-for front gardens. Surprisingly, rather than worrying about her situation, she had been spending her time there wondering why she had elected to live on a large unruly piece of land miles from anywhere. She knew she had made the right choice, but what was it in her that craved this independence? Her wild garden and ghost-ridden house, and the darkness of the nights?

Her two nights in the cell had been stressful, and after the unresolved interrogation of the day before, she felt she would continue to be incarcerated for some time. She had tried to bring her centre to a state of calm, as she used to do when she was working. She should be accustomed to these sorts of discomforts. She had found, however, that it was no longer easy, and she was more subject to the fear of any ordinary person.

In a way, she was relieved. It meant that she still was an "ordinary" person. She had not become entirely divorced from the world of real human feeling as her father had. The previous night, she had found she had been able to still her anxiety by looking meticulously at her mental shelving where she had begun to organize information about the murder. She smiled momentarily into the darkness when she realized the shelves were pale green, like the ones in her kitchen at King's Cove.

She had decided to place people and information she felt were less relevant on higher shelves, and anything odd or suspicious on lower shelves, as she would in her kitchen: serving dishes for large parties on the top shelf; mugs, plates, sugar, salt on lower shelves where she would have them available. Once she had neatly arranged the top shelves with the Armstrongs, Kenny and Eleanor, and the cigarette-rolling Hughes women, giving them each a little space, she trolled mentally through the remainder of the residents to decide whom she could arrange on middle shelving, slightly worried that she could not immediately locate the Bertolli clan on the top shelving. As she wondered why, she drifted off and did not wake again until the early sun pooled on her blankets from under the curtains of the cell window. She woke with a feeling of having slept well for some hours, at least. She could not tell what time it was, though standing on the bed and looking out onto what street she could see revealed that some few people were already moving about. She thought it might be seven. What time would the station open? Indeed, what would be the next step? Though she had brought her pyjamas, she had slept in her slip. Putting on full nightwear felt too much like giving up altogether. She had thought that she would, she must, be released any moment. Now she was not so sure. It was absurd for her to be in a jail in Nelson, when she'd done nothing. She defiantly put on her skirt and blouse and a light sweater and then made the bed and sat and waited.

Eventually she heard keys and the door swung open. A young officer asked her to follow him and, as the morning before, she had been put into the interrogation room, as she now thought of it. She had found there a mug of coffee and a boiled egg with a piece of buttered toast, which she dispatched, her heart sinking slightly because she was not being taken to speak to someone about going home. She had thought she would be too distressed to eat, but found that not to be the case. Now, here was Inspector Darling with an extremely professional manner.

"Yes, Inspector. More questions—hopefully more to the point?"

"At the moment, I am proposing to have you speak to a Major Dunn, who has travelled from London to see you."

Lane stared at him and then clutched the chair she had been standing behind. She sat down heavily. "Who? Who?" she could hear herself asking this question as if she were shimmering outside of herself and could not bring herself back into focus.

With some alarm, Darling saw that she had gone quite white. "Are you all right?" He hurriedly poured a glass from the pitcher she had been provided with earlier that day. She drank clumsily and tried to lengthen her suddenly short, shallow breaths.

Drawing in a long breath she asked again, "Whom am I to speak to?"

"A Major Dunn. He's come out from England. He says he knows you. Is this not the case?"

"My God," she whispered, "then he's not dead."

"Why should he be dead? At least, if the man upstairs is Major Dunn. I suppose in your line of work, even that much might not be certain." Darling was surprised, and then instantly sorry, about the bitterness that was evident in his last remark.

Lane drank more slowly and then put the glass down, appearing not to notice Darling's tone. "I, we all, were told he'd died, been shot down. I . . ." She was trying to keep her hand from shaking, and to buy time. What could she say to Angus? Her heart pounded and she felt suddenly ill. What was she so afraid of? That he might be the one sent to take her back? That she might still need him? That she had been deceiving herself about her own newfound liberty? "But why is he here?" she asked, in what she hoped was a calm, untroubled tone.

Darling, who had been taken aback by her reaction, watched her thoughtfully. "I have been given to understand that you worked for him. He has been able to furnish some information that you would not, Miss Winslow, that might exonerate you in this matter. Not, unfortunately, without a price," he added as a bitter afterthought.

"Worked for him. I see. So that's how it was," she said, more to herself than Darling. He could make nothing of this. Then she added, "What do you mean, not without a price?"

"Nothing. I'm having the usual competitive feelings of any policeman when someone tries to come and take over a case. I've told him I'd take you up to my office to see him. Would that suit?"

Lane was almost more troubled by his solicitousness than his officiousness in locking her up for two nights. "I will see him wherever you wish. I wonder . . . no, it's fine."

"You wonder what?"

"I was going to ask if you would mind being present at my interview with Major Dunn, but, well, it's complicated. And perhaps he would prefer to speak with me alone." She suddenly wrung her hands together. "I don't understand. Why is he here? How did he know to come here?" She looked at Darling in some distress and then her face cleared and she became cool. "You did this! This happened because you contacted the authorities in Britain. Of course it would have triggered the firm to get involved." She turned and stood before the door, waiting for him to open it. "We might as well get this over with. It doesn't matter whether you stay in the room or not. I obviously am in the power of everyone else here. How very foolish I was to think I could get away."

When they entered Darling's office, Angus, the director, had his back to them, and the light from the window made him appear as a dark silhouette, but one she would have recognized anywhere. She felt her heart turn over, and she clutched her hands together to try to calm her anxious breathing. She sat down without saying anything and waited. Dunn turned around and smiled at her. She coloured and looked away. She could not take in that he, Angus, was here. Not dead. She was suddenly angry at the mourning she had done. All the innocence and unrecoverable youth she'd lost in her sorrow. The unbelievable depth of his deception.

"Miss Winslow!" he said, "how very nice to see you again." So that's how he was going to play it. She would not join in.

"Back from the dead, Angus. It must be very pleasant for you."

"Inspector Darling, I wonder if you might leave us alone. I promise not to spring her," Dunn said smoothly.

Darling looked at Lane, who gave a slight twitch of the head that seemed to indicate indifference. With a brief hesitation, he turned and stood in the doorway. "You have twenty minutes," he said. He closed the door and had a momentary and irrational desire to get a glass and put it to the wall. He had seen enough, however, to guess at new depths of self-preservation in his prisoner and he felt a certain delight steal over him about it. He didn't have enough to smack down his self-satisfied, arrogant visitor, but she most clearly did. He would go in search of Ames, and bring him au courant.

"Lane, I don't blame you. You are angry. I can explain why that happened. It was necessary . . . there were circumstances." Angus had pulled up a chair and now sat near her.

"Yes, I bet you can explain. Always one of your great skills, talking."

"Lane, this is not like you. This bitterness. You know what kind of business we are in. The fact is, after that mess in France, we had to change our strategy."

"One correction, Angus: you are in the business, apparently, though you never let on, did you? I am not. There is no 'we' here. I was an utter fool. There never was a 'we,' was there? What are you," she looked at him critically, "early forties? I never thought about your age. You must have a wife, children." It was a sudden sickening wave of realization that caused her to add, "You must have had them then."

Angus said nothing.

She felt a sinking rage take her over and set her lips grimly. "You are a bastard, aren't you? Who was this man you sent over for me?"

"Listen, Lane, darling, I would have given anything to change what happened."

She held up her hand, palm warding him off. "No. Stop. Do you want to know what has changed in me? Night after night behind enemy lines by myself, while, it now turns out, you were at home with the wife and family. You dying. And now, when I finally have found a shred of peace and freedom, you come barging back into my life trying to manipulate me. You had no right . . . you have no right. Who was that man?" her eyes widened. "Did you have him killed so that I could be implicated and brought back? Did you do this to me?" She stood up and backed away from him.

Dunn leaped up and took her by the shoulders. "Look

at me, Lane. How mad do you think I am? I cared about you and you were a damn good employee. You're in a spot of trouble here and we need you back. Now stop this nonsense. There is really nothing sinister here."

Lane looked up at him, feeling him holding her by the shoulders, smelling his familiar smell. "You 'cared' about me? 'Cared?' I care about the postman, for God's sakes. I would have done anything for you, and I did, and now I discover that the whole time you were 'handling' me. You were, weren't you? You were never a pilot at all." She pulled away from him and went toward the door.

"Now, Lane, you know how it was in the war. The right hand not knowing about the left hand and all that. It's all changed now. It's a modern operation. You'd be brilliant and we need your skills. Come home. What on earth can there be here for you?"

Lane stood for some moments in silence, her back to him. Was she tempted? She could be back in London, back among her friends, the war over, restaurants brimming, theatres, music. But she had never wanted that life, she decided, and wanted with a passion what she had now. She felt a ferocity about how close she was to losing it and turned to look at Angus, her eyes hard. "I can't really think how that would be any of your business. I loved you. What a fool I was." She turned the handle and pulled the door open. Darling was leaning against the wall, his hands in his pockets. "We are finished, Inspector," she said.

When Darling came into the room, he saw Angus moving away toward the window and Lane sitting, her face impassive, as though she was waiting for someone else to make the next move. He wondered what could have passed between them. He had heard only one sentence: Lane's voice, "I loved you."

"Major Dunn?"

Dunn turned, and Darling saw that his face was set in angry lines. "I have asked Miss Winslow to return with me to London. I assume there will be no difficulty with this?"

Darling did not see the tears of rage spring up in Lane's eyes until he turned to address her. So that was how it was, he thought, seeing the tears. "Since you will be returning with Major Dunn, Miss Winslow, and in light of the information the major shared with me earlier, there is some doubt that you could have been involved. If we can clear you, through fingerprinting and so on, of the car, you will be free to go, and I shall not pursue any further investigation against you. There remains, however, the problem of the corpse, which I have on ice downstairs. I shall need as much information about him as I can get. We will need to continue our inquiry at this end."

Lane angrily wiped her eyes with the back of her hand and looked at Darling. She had an appalling impulse to smile, but instead she said, "On the contrary, Inspector. I shall not be returning with the major. There is nothing for me to return to. And I was just in the process of trying to find out about the dead man myself. I confess, for a minute I thought the worst and assumed that Major Dunn had sent him out here to be killed so that he might have the means of persuading me to return. He has assured me this is not the case, but I'm not quite sure, you know, that I believe him."

She had completely recovered her aplomb, and now sat with her legs crossed in apparent comfort on the chair. She smoothed her turquoise skirt, folded her arms, and waited.

Dunn sighed and pushed his hands into his pockets. "Clearly everyone is reading too many thrillers. The facts themselves are most prosaic. He was a minor operative called Jack Franks who said he was coming out to find something out about his family. When his parents were killed in the Blitz, he somehow found out that he had been adopted. He had traced his roots to this godforsaken place, and I gave him a leave to explore this. It was fortuitous for me that this journey was bringing him here to where Miss Winslow was, as, in the new international climate, I find I need a person with her skills. I asked him to look her up and give her a note."

"You knew I was here? How?"

"Really, Miss Winslow, it surprises me that you have to ask. We know where everyone is." At this Lane turned away from him and then stood up.

"Inspector Darling. You have said you likely have no case against me. You have my fingerprints. You will certainly not find them on the photos taken of those in the car, and therefore I wish to collect my things and make my way home at your earliest convenience. No doubt at some point today you will have contacted any rental agencies in town that might still be missing a black 1933 DeSoto, and you will find it to have been let out to this unfortunate Jack Franks. I promise to stay put in King's Cove, should your assessment change. Major Dunn also, I believe, has no means to compel me to do what he wishes, so I need not be detained on his account." She turned and looked one last time at Dunn. "I most earnestly hope, sir, that you will find it possible to forget where I am from here on out."

Darling called out into the main office. "Ames. Could you run Miss Winslow home?"

Lane walked past him, not looking back, her arms still folded across her chest and said with a tight smile, "How very kind."

Ames drove in silence, contemplating his ill luck. On the one hand he had this opportunity to spend the next hour with this lovely suspect, whom he was relieved to learn was not so much a suspect anymore, but on the other hand, she was in a grim and silent mood. He longed to know what had transpired with the English type who'd arrived at the station in the morning. Something momentous, for certain, or he'd not be driving her home now. They were more than ten miles along the road before she finally spoke and it was not to relieve his curiosity.

"The thing that troubles me is that whoever it is, is still there. And they've gone to a lot of trouble to implicate me. Is it me they are after, or am I just a convenient new expendable person to get rid of? They aren't dead keen on new people there, some of them."

Ames eased off on the gas slightly, as if wanting to slow their progress back to King's Cove. He was frowning. "Are you saying you might be in danger?"

"No, I don't really think so; why should I be? But it's a small place and one of the less than twenty people that live there killed this man. Why? You don't kill people unless you feel threatened. Or you want something. Could it have been a simple robbery? Maybe we should be watching to see who starts living high."

Laughing, Ames asked, "What would 'high' look like out there? The sudden appearance of a new tractor?" This was more like it. She was talking. He clearly wasn't going to get to know exactly what had happened with the man from London or why she'd been allowed to go home, but he was happy. He'd never really believed she could have been in it, though the car had rattled his confidence nearly completely. He glanced at her. She was leaning her elbow on the window and looking out at the passing lake. Her hair was blowing gently off her face, the light of the sun highlighting the beautiful lines of her cheek and nose. Out of his league, completely. He didn't know how he knew that, but he did. She was too old for him, in any case. April at the café was more his speed. Nineteen and a lot less troubled than this glamorous woman. This, he just knew, was the woman for Darling. They had a thoughtful quality in common. And she was smart. He'd like a smart girl. Ames wasn't so sure about a smart girl for himself.

"No. I think not a robbery. This man—his name was Franks, did Darling tell you that?—Franks came out there to find someone. He told Major Dunn that when he asked for leave. Dunn was that insufferable prig that came to see Darling," she added, looking at Ames. She realized he probably hadn't gotten the full story.

Glancing at her, Ames said, "Aha. You knew that man." This whole thing beat the local business they usually had to deal with. "Is he the reason you . . ."

"That I emigrated? I used to work for him, he died,

the war ended, and I left. Only he didn't, obviously. He's certainly the reason I won't go back!"

Died. Wow. Here was a story, surely. He was going to ask about the dying but sensed she would not tell him. "I only was going to ask, is he the reason Darling decided to let you go?"

"Oh. Yes. I suppose so. I'm not one hundred percent in the clear, you know, but there seems to be a reasonable doubt about my motivation to kill a man I've never seen in my life and plant him in my own creek and hide his car in my own barn. Well, the prints will clear that up," Lane said acerbically.

"We are looking a trifle incompetent here," Ames agreed. He chewed his lower lip. "I'll give the car another going over. I might have missed something."

Lane said nothing for a while, and gazed out the window. Some few small farms were beginning to be built on the flats approaching Balfour. They were beautiful, with their green sweeps down to the lake. She wondered if she should have bought a property that would place her right at the lake's edge, but then thought about her house and knew, it had to be that house, with that view, that busy ghost. "I didn't think to ask. Were the keys in the car?"

"No. They're still to be found. And the way things have been going, I bet you anything they'll be found somewhere around your place. Let's have a look when I get you back."

"God, I wish I knew who was doing this. In a way, knowing it's not me means we are ahead of the killer. If we could keep him convinced that you might still suspect me, he might be lured to continue his campaign. That gives me an idea. Since you haven't moved the car, give the car another going over and maybe I'll spread the news that you might have found something—that you'll be coming back out with a forensic kit to check. The person who put the car in my barn may come out of the woodwork to try to cover up whatever he fears is still there."

Ames looked at her with something between admiration and horror. "No, no, no. No. Absolutely not. You should not become involved in this. It is absolutely not safe. If the murderer is keeping an eye on things, he already knows you were 'arrested' and he may be feeling confident. He'll get a nasty shock when he sees you back there. No. I warn you, I'll tell Inspector Darling. He won't have it either."

"I'm not frightened of Inspector Darling."

"Well, I am. He'll have my hide. You've got to promise you won't do anything stupid."

"All right. Relax. I managed to survive the war. I've no intention of getting myself done in now."

This raised a whole new line of thought in Ames.

"Who was that guy, then?"

"Just a man I used to know. Don't bother, by the way. Why don't you tell me about yourself? Do you have a young lady?"

Ames, though frustrated in his attempts to discover more about his mysterious and glamorous passenger, was young and easily brought to expound on his own enthusiasms and so, until they pulled into Lane's driveway, he talked about April and how they'd met when he was investigating a robbery in the winter.

They sat for a minute in the silence of the car's engine

being switched off. Lane looked down the sweep of the grass to the house. She could feel a little pull of anxiety in her. Somehow the situation had turned a corner. It was clear now that it almost certainly was someone right here, around her, who had killed Franks. No one had followed him here. Well, one couldn't know that for sure, she thought, but whoever might have followed him could have just finished him off in England. In her gut, she knew it was someone right here. Someone she met at the post office, perhaps every day, or had tea with, or met on her rambles on the forest paths.

The dead man, Franks, had been here to see someone; was it someone who didn't want to see him? She couldn't immediately see a reason why she should be in any more danger than she was before. After all, whatever motivated the killing really had nothing to do with her. Whatever end had been sought must have been achieved by his death. Yet, she felt somehow as if she were being pulled in. Franks had been in the same business she had. They had a common acquaintance—she would allow no more than this term—in Dunn. Whether she liked it or not, it did involve her, and whether Darling liked it or not, she would work to find out what had happened, if only so she could recover her sense of peace and safety. She sighed and pushed down the door handle. She knew this constant feeling of anxiety. She'd had it all through the war. She had hoped never to feel it again. Well, she wouldn't be telling this fresh young policeman what she was feeling, that was for sure. He'd only go report it to Darling.

"Thanks for the ride. I'm going to make myself a cup of tea. I think you'd better have one before you go back.

I'll put the kettle on and we can search for the keys while it boils."

Ames considered for a moment. "I'd love one but I'd like to get another look at the car, and I think I'll head back. The boss expects me back for three. It doesn't give me much time."

In the house, Lane threw her overnight bag onto her bed and then went to stand in her sitting room. When he was gone she'd wash everything she was wearing and hang it in the sun to clear the aura of her jail cell nights. She pulled open the curtains to look at her beautiful view of her lawn and the lake in the distance. Then she remembered that she had not closed her curtains when she left. She turned to look at anything else that might have been moved when she heard the clanging of her phone.

"KC 431," she said into the horn.

"Lane. Thank goodness! We've all been wondering. Sandy said he'd seen you drive off in that policeman's car. They can't have arrested you for this?" It was Eleanor. Relief coursed through Lane.

"No. Everything is fine. I spent a couple of nights in town. Thank you for tidying up and closing the curtains, Eleanor."

"Well, we didn't know what had happened, how long you'd be gone. You're to come over here this minute for a cup of tea."

"That nice young policeman is just going over . . . some things." She realized they didn't know about the discovery of the car. "I tell you what. Give me half an hour, and then you come over here. And bring Kenny. We'll have a nice cuppa on my porch. I'm sure I have a lovely packet of English biscuits I picked up the last time I did a proper shop in town. We'll have that." She put the earpiece back onto the hook and jiggled it past where it stuck.

Lane couldn't bear the thought of leaving her house now that she was in it. She put the kettle on and then went through the house flinging open curtains and ran upstairs to open the windows, calling out, "There, Lady Armstrong, I've saved you the trouble!"

She could hear Ames at the front door and she remembered that they were going to look for the keys. "Anything new in the car?" she asked.

"Nothing. I looked under it, on the tire rims, under the seats. No keys."

Leaning against the door jamb, she looked out over the yard. If the murderer had wanted to plant them, where would they be? Would he throw them somewhere outside here? No. Too difficult to find. "If I'm the person who wants to frame someone—well, me—I put the keys somewhere they can be found, but somewhere that looks as though they've been hidden. I might even try to get into the house to hide them there." She looked anxiously into her hallway. Could someone have come in? She had locked everything. Except Kenny had come in, hadn't he? No. It wouldn't do. Kenny had come in because he had a key to the house. "Look. I know you want to get back. I will keep my eye open and telephone if I find them." Ames looked at her, his face a picture of worry. "I don't think you should stay out here. It's not safe. Why don't you come back to town till we've sorted this?"

"Thank you, Constable Ames. You are so kind. I absolutely will not be driven from my home. I don't believe for a minute that the killer wants me dead. He just wants the blame deflected to me. Harming me would do him no good at all. I feel quite safe. Please let me know when the fingerprints have been compared. I know you will find nothing, but I will feel grateful to hear it from you, nonetheless. In the meantime, I will keep my ear to the ground and contact you if I learn anything. No doubt you and the inspector will need to retrench and figure out your next moves in this matter. I will be here if you need me." After this deliberately plucky speech she watched Ames back out of the drive. She wished she felt all of the confidence that she had tried to show to him. It was logical, however, that whoever it was would not want to harm her. Nevertheless, it did not take away the anxiety that someone had her in his or her sights.

She set about preparing for the Armstrongs. She spread the little table on the porch with a tablecloth she'd brought from France with blue flowers on it; forget-me-nots. How ironic. She'd come to King's Cove to forget, but now she knew she never would. Perhaps it was better. You don't leave yourself behind. But you can build on what you have. She would not lose what Angus had meant in her life. Maybe it would just soften in time. And then she severely told herself to think of something else. Especially after seeing Angus again. Loving him had been a colossal waste of time.

"Hellooo," came Eleanor's voice from the doorway.

"Come in!" Lane called back happily. A distraction and, she realized, her first proper guest, if you didn't count

Harris guzzling her brandy after they found the body. They peppered her with questions about why she'd been taken away, but she persisted in making light of it.

"But what was the cell like? I can't imagine what a jail cell is like in Nelson. Was if full of the local inebriates?"

"It was very bare, with clean linen and curtains. Curtains in a cell, can you imagine? They let me be in a little office from breakfast on. I had a view out the back window, and could see all the people who were at liberty parading about the street. Now enough about me!"

Eleanor gave up and said, "Well, you'll never guess what's happened! It has burst on the scene like fireworks just this very morning. I so wish you could have been in the post office to see the effect!"

"How could something earth-shattering happen in the time I've been gone?" asked Lane, surprised.

"I'm with you there. I would have said nothing ever happens here, till people began fishing bodies out of the creek! But it is quite shocking, even though it's not a body. Harris has given in to Mather and is selling him that parcel of land up behind the Hughes' that Mather's been trying to get at for thirty-five years! They've been practically at war since about 1910 about it, if not before. Now, suddenly, he capitulates!"

At that moment, there was a knocking at the door and Ames came through the house to the porch. Lane stood up, surprised. "Constable, You're back. You remember Mr. and Mrs. Armstrong? They're just sharing some local news. You've reconsidered about the tea?"

"I do," he said. "Good afternoon. Listen, Miss Winslow,

I just popped back to padlock the door. No, no tea thanks. I have to get back. At this rate I won't be back till four."

"Thank you again for driving me out, Constable Ames. Please let me know if there is anything I can do to help."

"Nope, not a thing. But I mean it, Miss Winslow—no! On that other matter, I mean." He looked severely at her and she covered a smile. A cheerful twenty-four-year-old could only look so severe. She promised him she would do as she was told, but today she had a new consciousness that she had reached her threshold of doing what she was told by men, even harmless young men who really only meant well.

When she and Kenny and Eleanor had sat in silence until they could hear the car disappear up the road, Eleanor turned to Lane. "What did he mean with all that 'no' business?"

"I had this idea that I thought might help to catch our murderer. He wasn't terrifically keen. He thought it might be dangerous, and you know, I believe he is right."

"What sort of idea?" Kenny asked, clumping his cup down into its powder-blue saucer and sloshing tea around. He leaned forward, his medusa-like eyebrows dancing with curiosity.

"It was nonsense, really, and now that I'm here I can see how dangerous it is. I was going to have you let everybody know, in a gossipy sort of way, as they were trooping down to get their mail, that the police had found something in the car and were going back to get their kit to investigate. That might cause whoever it is, if it is someone here, which I have reason to believe now, to sneak back to the car to try to get rid of the evidence. Then I'd see who it was. But really, on consideration, I don't really feel like being confronted with a murderer all by myself."

"We'd be nearby," suggested Eleanor pluckily.

Kenny looked at her with raised eyebrows. "The 'nearby' to which you refer is five good minutes' trot from here. She could be dead by then. And how would we know she was being confronted by the killer; do you imagine she'd ask him to just hold on while she rang up the neighbours? No, Miss W., I must throw my vote in with the police on this. You are not to do anything as stupid as that."

"All right. Keep your hat on. I'll behave. But tell me more about this land business; why is it such a momentous thing?"

"My dear, this whole place has been in the grip of the conflict between these two old idiots since they were young idiots. Mather wanted to build a mill even before the first show, and Harris wasn't going to let him do it with his land. I don't think he's motivated by any love of keeping the countryside green and peaceful, he just couldn't stand Mather getting ahead in any way. No one can think of why he would suddenly change his mind."

WHEN DARLING, FROM his office window, had watched Ames come out onto the street below and usher Miss Winslow into the car and drive off, he wanted to turn around and find that Dunn was gone. But of course, Dunn was not. He was sitting very still as if waiting until Darling could again give him his complete attention. Darling sat down opposite him on his side of the desk, a position that he hoped perhaps would put Dunn into the supplicant position. Dunn seemed as superior as ever.

Dunn had been thinking about Lane. Bringing himself back to life was bringing her back to life, in a way. He'd never meant for anyone to get hurt when it all began. It was work, after all. And it was work now. He thrust to the back of his mind the extraordinary slip of falling for her quite as much as he had. Her loveliness still made him ache. She had been so full of beauty at nineteen. Full of beauty. He meant that. Not just that she was beautiful to look at, to touch, to dream about. She was beautiful in her joyful innocence, her intelligent love of difficult poetry, her optimistic desire to be of use. And even the pain she covered was a poignant attraction to him.

But work was work and now she was needed. She would forgive him, surely. He'd seen her change over the course of the war; the beauty never diminished, but something inside her grew, not hardened exactly, but pragmatic, competent. He sensed, probably correctly, though he'd taken himself out of the picture earlier than he'd have liked, that she had developed a sense of her own independence. She had been slightly clearer about her boundaries with each passing year. One day, he was sure, she would suspect his ease of manner or his absences, and begin to demand the truth. The train incident had cut everything short. He still felt stupid even now. How could he have been careless like that? He had imagined a hundred times meeting her after the war, on a street somewhere, seeing the betrayal in her eyes, having in some way to be accountable for all of it, and having to explain the train.

"It's too bloody bad, really. She used to be quite compliant. And jolly useful."

Appalling. Darling felt his jaw locking, and the word kept repeating itself in his head. He had absolutely nothing to say to Dunn's complaint about the loss of Miss Winslow's compliance.

"Do you think there is anything else you will require of me?" he managed after some moments.

"Well yes, I suppose I'd better see your corpse, just to make sure it is Jack Franks. The photos leave little doubt, but since I'm here I'd better cross the t's and dot the i's." He stood up, making even this movement seem like the upper class drawl with which he spoke.

In the morgue, Darling turned on the overhead electric light and stood back while Dunn surveyed the body. The Englishman reached into his inner jacket pocket, pulled out a fountain pen, and used it to push the head slightly to get a better look at the welt-like stain behind the left ear. He wiped his pen with his handkerchief and replaced it in his inner pocket. "It is Franks, all right. Post-mortem?"

"Struck, likely unconscious, pushed into a creek to drown. We think the business end of a rifle, perhaps pre–first war vintage, or a metal bar, something of the sort. But someone who surprised him. Is there anything else you can tell us about this man? You have been remarkably spare up till now."

"Nothing that will have any bearing on his death. He did not share with me why he wanted to come here, beyond saying he was in search of family, but he was most keen.

He took two months' leave to resolve whatever it was. As I mentioned, his own, or rather his adopted parents died in the Blitz. Perhaps a cousin or an uncle had emigrated and it was his last relation, or indeed, he thought he might find his own parent. I could not tell you more than that."

And obviously don't want to, thought Darling. He'd met people he'd suspected of being intelligence officers from time to time in the course of the war because of his bombing missions. He'd never liked their easy charm and habitual evasiveness.

Even when Dunn had left, Darling still did not know whether he was going to continue to try to recruit Miss Winslow back or not. This infuriated the inspector as well. He sat at his desk, glumly moving his ink bottle and papers around the desk, lining them up this way and that, as he did when he was trying to solve a difficult case. It was a form of doodling, he supposed.

In the end he knew that what he felt was akin to bereft. He could not have said why. He'd had this feeling a few times since he'd been on Civvy Street, and now here it was back. He wondered if it was from spending time again with an English officer. In some ways it brought back the camaraderie he had experienced during the war—the excitement, at least of the early years, before he'd been wounded. He was not one for self-deception. This bout now was about Miss Winslow. If he was truthful, with the hectoring Ames out of the room, he'd confess to himself that he'd been much taken with Miss Winslow. He was relieved to be able to release her, as he hadn't liked her for the crime, but would have been prepared to follow through. Well, there were still the fingerprints to be gone into, but he was certain she was right. Hers wouldn't be there, and likely not the killer's either. Surely he'd have worn gloves, his work till now having been so elaborate.

He imagined her with Dunn and immediately felt his face flush with anger. The English expression "he's queered that pitch" came unbidden into his head and he dismissed it with embarrassment. He didn't know how he felt about Miss Winslow, he decided, but he knew she'd been ill used by Dunn, who talked about her in the most callous terms. Surely she deserved more than that.

CHAPTER TWENTY-FIVE

January, 1915

REGINALD MATHER GOT UP EARLY, as he had all the days since the others had left. John Armstrong and his cousin Robin Harris had gone to join up. He knew it would have broken Kenny up to see his brother off at the wharf, climbing on to the steamboat with a khaki bag slung over his shoulder. He imagined Lady Armstrong putting on a braver face than her eldest son. Elizabeth standing alone to one side, slender and weeping, a shawl wrapped over her coat because the November chill was made colder by this parting, her hair falling out of its knot and across her face. The Hughes girls would have been there as well; Gwen had a thing for John Armstrong. They wouldn't be crying. Their mother wouldn't allow it.

In fact, Reginald had not gone to the wharf that morning to see them off to Nelson; it would have highlighted his own inability to sign up. He really did have a gammy leg, he thought defensively. But he imagined the scene. He knew somehow that it marked a turning point in their lives. The place was quiet enough at the best of times, everyone hard at work on their homesteads and orchards and, let's be frank, avoiding one another. Now the Bentleys, who lived in a damp and somewhat porous cabin on the upper road behind the Hughes', had given up and moved into town. There was more work there now that so many younger men had signed up, and Ted Bentley had never made a success of living out here. The same was true of the Anscombs, with that unhealthy mother and all those children. They had abandoned their draughty, dark house and failing orchard and moved somewhere—to the coast, perhaps—where there was work at the docks.

A thick silent snow had settled on the cove, as eternal as an ice age. The morning unfolded before him as he sat at his table by the window, a mug of tea cooling, the sun coming slowly to light over the hill, sending shoots of pink light along the glistening surface of the unmarked snow. Alice had taken the boat into town and would not be back for two days. A nerve specialist. She had insisted on going alone. He decided he relished the temporary, undemanding solitude. His dog Jonesy lay near him in front of the Franklin stove, head on paws, his eyes fixed on his master. When Reginald stirred, Jonesy's head popped up. This was what he waited for. He stood and stretched, his paws spreading out to grip the dingy hearth-rug, and then waited, his tail swishing with guarded hopefulness. Reginald took up his wool coat and reached for his cane.

He moved first to the barn to see to the horses. They snorted great plumes of white breath at him as he broke the ice on their trough and shovelled out the stalls. It was as he was coming out of the barn and looking across the snow-covered garden that he saw the figure of a woman struggling on the icy surface of one of the ruts on the road. She was encased in a big coat, a wool shawl around her head; she looked drowned in wool, she was so slight. She held her skirts over her boots so that they interfered less with her progress. She stopped when she reached the gate to Reginald's house and stood, panting clouds. She paused indecisively and then she saw him approaching the gate from the barn up behind the right of the house.

"Mrs. Harris," he said, pulling open the wooden gate. Jonesy, sensing traffic was going the wrong way for his walk, sat down in the snow with a humph. Elizabeth Harris hesitated a moment and looked around, as if there might be someone in this empty snow landscape watching her, and walked hesitantly through the gate. Inside the house, she took her shawl off but not her coat and sat nervously on the edge of the chair Reginald offered her near the fire. "Alice is in town for a couple of days. Will you have tea? Or coffee? I've got some on the stove," he asked, and he turned to the kitchen where she could hear him scooping water into a kettle from a metal bucket, so he did not see her shake her head. Jonesy had settled back on to his hearth-rug.

Reginald put the kettle on to the Franklin and opened the grate to push in another piece of wood. Sparks flew out of the embers. Elizabeth Harris sat very still as if she did not dare to look around. "Now then," said Reginald, "how are you getting on down there without Robin? Have you heard from him?"

"He sent one letter from Halifax where they're training. I guess they will ship out soon."

Reginald looked at her, really, for the first time. He knew

she had come from a large, poor, and unhappy family in town. He had seen her father holding forth in the bar on the few trips he had made there. He was a despicable man; an egocentric drunk, roundly disliked. Now here was one of his long-suffering children. She could have been pretty, if she were better fed, or smiled, Reginald decided. She had scarcely improved her lot by marrying Harris! He felt a stirring of protectiveness. She must have staggered up the hill, a mile and a half from the Nelson road where her wood-frame house kept watch at the King's Cove turnoff, for something. "Do you need anything? It's been bitterly cold. Have you enough wood?"

"I have wood, thank you. Robin left me with a big pile and I'm pretty good with an axe. It's just that I haven't got no water. I suppose it's frozen. I've been melting pots of snow." Reginald was about to say that he too was melting buckets of snow, that it was not unusual in the winter, when he saw that her eyes had welled up. She looked down to cover it, and wrung her hands in her lap. She looked small and fragile and utterly alone. For Reginald the moment held an eternal quality. His heart swelled, and his world encompassed, suddenly, only the two of them. He felt a nobility he had not experienced before.

He reached out and took her hand and said, "Come now. Let's see what we can do, eh?"

THE SUN, ABOUT half an hour after Ames had left, was now shining full on the tea drinkers on the porch of the pleasantly haunted house. Eleanor, who had extremely pale skin, in the Edwardian style that must have been the chief influence of her youth, said she thought they ought to go in and sit in the sitting room. It was cool in the house because of the blow-through from the French doors through to the main door of the house, which Lane had left open. She was slightly surprised, but pleased that Eleanor had not said that they'd better leave. She dug her hand into the cookie packet and pulled out another handful to put on the plate. Kenny seemed to be enjoying the chocolate biscuits particularly and she wanted to keep them talking, something they seemed inclined to do. They had moved on from the momentous land-selling news, perhaps because nobody wanted to think about the implications, that Mather might at last build his bloody mill, and they were once again on the murdered man. All the distraction of the conversation suited Lane; she did not want to think about Angus and talking, she earnestly wished, would make him vanish forever from her mind.

"Why would someone come here all that distance, that's what I don't understand," declared Eleanor. "How would he know about this place? Had he bought a piece of property? Was anyone selling anything, Kenny, besides Harris?"

Kenny shook his head. "Don't know of any property for sale."

Lane said, "Maybe we are going about this the wrong way. Let's start with the people here. Maybe the answer is here. Who has connections still in England? Who is selling land, as you asked? Who has secrets?"

"My dear, who does not! But the trouble is, I should think they are boring little secrets. I mean, Mather's wife is mad, we all know that, though we all pretend she's not.

There's the business with Robin's wife, but no one knew really what happened there and it was a long time ago. There's whatever Bertolli might have brought with him, because again, we are all pretending he came out because he could compose in the peace and quiet of our little community. The Hughes are two ladies left maidened by the first war and their vigorous but blameless mother, and could not have one whole secret among them. There's Ponting the prospector in the log cabin out on the Kaslo road. His secret is a claim he's been mining for twenty years with no visible result. There. And of course, Mather and his son don't get along, and none of us is supposed to know about that either. Or that Mather has been planning since before the war, the first one, mind you, to turn his land over to the lumber people. We admit, we were afraid for a few years, but he turned out to be hopelessly bad at business. No one has ever come here to see any of them, and it puzzles me why anyone should have now."

Kenny gazed at his wife after this lengthy speech and said, "Could this be about Robin?"

"I don't see how. It was so long ago. Nearly thirty years."

"What about Robin?" Lane asked.

"Well, it's just that Robin had married a girl from town before he signed up; around '13 or so, and when he came back she'd left. We never really knew why. She was a miserable thing, though pretty in a wet sort of way. I think she resented being left alone with all the work. Did she leave before or after the fire, do you remember?" Kenny turned to Eleanor.

"Well, the fire was in June of '19, you remember, the lightning. She was already gone by then. I think she left right around the armistice. No, I lie, it was earlier. We just noticed she stopped coming to the post office. We didn't think much of it at the time, since we knew Robin had stopped writing to her by halfway through 1917. She just stopped bothering to come there and if anything did arrive, Kenny would drop it off on his way down to the wharf. I can't remember now, was she at the party we had that November for the end of the war?"

Kenny shook his head. "No. Definitely not. Then we had that ruddy fire and we had too much else to think of. I remember Robin coming back, though, and finding her gone and the orchards burned to a crisp. Between that and the war, he never really did recover from any of it."

That night, in the dark, Lane thought about the darkness in human lives. She had locked the door, resenting the need to do it, and now she lay on her side looking across the nearly completely dark space to where the window framed yet more night. Somewhere out of the darkness of someone's life, a young man had materialized and been killed. Why? And, she thought ruefully, somewhere out of the darkness of my life, Angus had materialized. She closed her eyes and journeyed down the pathways where Angus had been in her life, but found she felt nothing. A little hardness perhaps, like the thin crisp layer of salt left on a beach when the sea recedes. And then she slept.

WHEN SHE WOKE she was amazed at the depth of her sleep. She stretched and looked out the window and saw that the light was tempered by cloud. Perhaps today there would be rain. She put on her robe and luxuriated in this feeling of having rested so completely. The kettle made a metallic scraping on the stove and it sounded new and beautiful. The smell of the electric ring had a familiar tang, which she felt at that moment that she loved. Pushing open the French doors into the uncertain weather of the morning, she gloried in the banks of clouds building on the mountain across the lake. They were like Constable clouds. Rich, familiar, eternal in some way. She felt a giddy sense of freedom, as if she had said goodbye to some nameless impediment to her happiness and was beginning a new life.

The kettle screeched and she turned back in to make tea. She would begin in a proper organized way to look at what had happened here. She thought she should begin her day as usual, with poetry, but today it seemed irrelevant, as if it were Aspirin for a fever she no longer had. While the tea was steeping in the dark green pot that Lady Armstrong had kindly left her, she cleared everything off the kitchen table and then stood back and looked at the blank expanse of scrubbed wood. What could she put on there, if this were the plane upon which this human tragedy had taken place? She wondered if this was like Algebra, a subject she had struggled with, while she had mastered all the intricacies of Russian case endings. Did she have enough information to solve for *x*, where *x* is the killer?

Her typewriter was on its little side table with foolscap piled neatly on the shelf beside it. She took several sheets of paper and laid them out on the table until the entire surface was covered. The pencil she wanted, an HB drawing pencil, sat lead side up in the tin by the paper. She sharpened the pencil into the wastebasket by her table, which did not even contain balled-up paper rejections of her own ideas. It waited patiently, and now received the shavings produced by her penknife. She must stop thinking of the things around her as chiding her, she thought, and then she stood before the table.

She pulled forward her stack of foolscap and then decided this was all better accomplished when she had dressed and eaten properly. A faint roll of thunder came across the lake from the phalanx of clouds along the mountain. Perfect! A day to stay in and work on a puzzle. The cozy feeling of childhood rainy days came over her as she went to change.

Back at the table, a warm flannel shirt on to keep out the chill from the rain pelting outside, she gazed at the blank slate before her. Should she work with her shelving? On the whole, though a quick inward glance told her that she had unconsciously continued to place things on the various levels of shelf, this system was more for storing information. What she needed was more in line with a map. Should she start with the dead man? Where would she put him? In the middle? No, that would determine the shape of the connections and they were unknown. If this crime had its roots here, then she must lay out the denizens of King's Cove. It must be a map of the place itself: put people where they lived around the square of road that linked the community, and leave room for information to be written in by each name.

She started on the lower right, drawing a faint line to show the Nelson road, following the lakeshore going north and then, veering sharply left, the road up to King's Cove.

At the intersection of the two roads she wrote *Robin Harris* at the physical spot where his house was, facing onto the Nelson road, this location somehow symbolic of his own angry, isolated distance from the rest of the Cove residents. She followed the road up and wrote in *Church* where it sat at the junction of the corner of the square that made up the complete circuit of the King's Cove settlement; straight ahead led up to the Bertollis', and left led around to the turnoff to her place and the post office. She decided to follow the road up to the Bertollis'. She had never driven up this road, though she had driven down it when she had picked up Angela and the boys for a trip to Balfour for ice cream. She mentally drove it now, and wrote *David Bertolli* and *Angela Bertolli* separately. She continued around, writing everyone's name separately—the connections that had to be written in would be to individuals, because somewhere here was an individual who had killed the man in her creek.

When she had done all of this, she studied it. Now she would need to write in what she knew and find a way to draw out the connections. She would need more space. What she needed was a war room. She'd once been in one when she'd been summoned by her commander, in the middle of a meeting. They had had everything laid out on a massive table. She looked ruefully at her kitchen table. She couldn't leave it here. The wall of the second bedroom? She began to realize she could not leave it where it would be easily seen, as, technically, the crime could have been committed by anyone, and though she hadn't got a lot of visitors, people did come round. She could put it, she decided, on the floor of the attic. No one went up there but her. Well, Eleanor

Armstrong once, to close the windows, but that wouldn't likely happen again.

Lane numbered each of the pieces of paper, piled them carefully in order, and mounted the stairs to the attic, having collected a box of tacks from her work shelf. She was already attached to the creak on the third and fourth stairs. They were like two notes in a song. In the attic, the rain seemed more present, because she could see it pelting outside the windows on all four sides and hear it drumming on the roof. It increased her sense of snugness, of being safely ensconced in her own private aerie. She pushed her remaining unpacked boxes to the edge of the room, clearing an empty space on the floor. Here she laid the pages back out in order. Now she would have room for written pages to be placed near the people to whom they applied. She liked the ability that having the map on the floor gave her to stand above and see it with a bird's eye view, and felt that this would help in her thinking. She remembered very early morning flights into France, when she had memorized the maps of where she would be going, and could look down from the aeroplane and see the features below. For the details of maps, she had a nearly perfect memory. She wondered now if Dunn had even known that about her.

There was something so patronizing about his approach to her even now. She sat down heavily on a wooden crate she'd moved near the window and looked out at her view, green and dripping, the fragrance released by the rain evident even through the closed windows. Low cloud seemed to gather in the basin of the lake and partially obscure the mountains. She would love the ever-changing moods of this place as long as she lived here. She had begun the creation of a world that had nothing to do with him. Could he really have believed she would come back?

Lane remembered herself at nineteen when she'd met him. She'd loved his confidence. She'd put herself entirely in his hands, as though she had found some sort of stability and guidance that had been lacking in her life. She grunted ruefully. Absent father, dead mother, indulgent grandparents, a lengthy series of governesses. She'd practically brought herself up; no wonder he'd been so important. She'd fallen for him completely, and the habit of loving him had never left her during the whole course of their war together.

But now, as she thought of herself in this relationship, she realized she must have been changing where he had not. She was nineteen when she had started with him and twenty-five when the war ended. He always treated her the same way, she saw now. Commanding, indulgent of her, an absolute expectation that she would do what he asked. He had required perfect secrecy of her. She had never questioned it, or doubted him. He must have a good reason. Only his death had freed her from this. She had been devastated and rudderless for a time. But had she not discovered in herself something new? She was strong and self-reliant. And she'd gotten quite clever about the job. She'd been asked to work with some new girls toward the end of the war, and she had realized, as she taught them the ropes, that she had been very good. She taught them how to memorize information and find their way around maps and translate that information into details on the ground and how to avoid detection by the authorities and what to do if they were discovered where they shouldn't be.

These were skills she'd been learning during the length of the war, but Angus had not seen her change. How could he? He had no idea what she did. He thought she worked as a secretary. Flushing, she shook her head. No, of course, he knew all along, just as he'd known where to find her to send Jack Franks after her. She could not completely take in this new knowledge. It was almost more shocking than finding him not dead, knowing that he'd been in intelligence the whole time, no doubt dangling her like a puppet who could not see her own master. But she saw now, as she looked out across the sky over the mountains, where the grey shifted and moved, that if she looked back across her own life, she had always had this core of strength and survival. She had learned self-protection at the hands of a greater master than Angus: her own distant, demanding, self- and work-obsessed father. Angus was just like him, really, only nice to her. Had she read somewhere that women take lovers that mirror their fathers? Freudian trickcycling! She turned and looked back at her map. She hoped that Angus had been taken aback by her self-determination. She felt sure she'd shaken that self-satisfied sense of what the world would do for him.

Now, the rest of her life was waiting for her. Back to work! Lane had index cards piled beside her on the floor of the attic. She moved the original list onto discrete index cards so that she could place them around the map. Her map, she decided, probably wasn't accurate in terms of distances, but it represented a good picture of everyone she knew to be living around her. She began to write. Harris—what did she know about him?

Bad-tempered, she added to her list, and then with a slight touch of remorse, she wrote, *Sad*, because in her heart she felt his temper came out of all his losses. She pinned the card on the floor by the location of his house at the edge of the Nelson road. There was room left on the card and she realized she was letting her emotions dictate the choices. She felt sorry for him; that was not necessarily a good basis for finding a murderer. Then added, *On same creek as I am*.

Next, she drove, in her mind, up the curved road and, after a brief hesitation, chose to turn as if going to her part of the settlement first. She stopped at the church. Should she say anything about it? You never knew what might be important. She wrote, *Vicar does service 11:00 every Sunday, otherwise locked*. Then she followed the road down to the post office but stopped at her own driveway, sighed, and began to write on a new card, *New, British Secret Service, body found on property, car found in my barn, victim was British Secret Service, victim had Winslow name on person*, and punched the pin into the card firmly by her property. No wonder I was arrested, she thought, looking starkly at the facts in this way.

For the Armstrongs she hesitated. Really, as if they could be involved! But she wrote anyway. *Has truck (means to transport body), has control of mail incoming and outgoing*. Here she hesitated. Was there a mail angle here? Had someone in the community received any mail from the victim announcing his arrival? Had someone here sent a letter out that might have brought the man here? Eleanor Armstrong looked at every piece of mail as she put it into the wooden slots; she would notice if there were unusual letters, and while she wasn't a gossip in the usual sense of the word, she certainly would be interested and would remember anything unusual. Lane would need a separate pile of cards; a sort of to-do list. On a separate card she wrote, *Ask Eleanor about the mail.* Anything else about the Armstrongs? She realized she knew little about them really, except, she thought ruefully, that she already loved them. *Brother John died in first war*, she added, finally.

She moved up the hill to the Hughes'. Three old ladies. Really. Still, she took up a card and waited for inspiration. She could not think of anything that would make them in any way likely to be involved. Finally she wrote, *Gwen affianced to John Armstrong* and, as an afterthought, because she realized she was just trying to accumulate what she knew about people, she added, *Thought Harris's wife interested in her John*. It was controversial anyway, though how it could possibly involve a murder thirty years and one war away she could not fathom.

She moved, then, up the road to the Mathers'. Here were some local controversies, surely. To her original list she added *Mather, remittance man*. Honestly, she thought, one of the Mathers ought to be dead, killed by one of the other Mathers, not some complete stranger. She realized she should have a separate card for each member of the family, so under Mrs. Alice Mather she wrote, *Unstable (shoots at imagined cougars)* and then wondered what else she knew. Nothing, she decided. Sandy: also unstable, bitter, self-aggrandizing, made an appalling pass at her. Did he spy on her?

Next to the Bertollis she wrote, *Moved from New York 3 years ago*. It struck her that, in a way, this single statement was the most damning. New York was one of the great cultural centres of the world. Why would an accomplished musician and composer move to an isolated corner of the continent to live in a log cabin, a gussied-up one, to be sure, and teach high school thirty miles away (along a dirt road) every day? Now she realized she did have other facts. She took a card and wrote *Elizabeth Harris; from town, unhappy, set her cap at people? John?* For surely Gwen and Mabel must have meant Elizabeth Harris when they had spoken to her. *Disappeared sometime in, say, 1917?*

By this time her knees were beginning to go from sore to numb from kneeling on the wooden floor. Lane sat back, cross-legged, and remembered that old Mrs. Hughes had had thick sponge knee-pads strapped to her legs when she'd visited them. That's what she needed. She closed her eyes and leaned against the wall. A band of sunlight streamed on to the floor where her map was and the brightness had tired her. There were so few people here, and from the outside, the mysterious Bertollis aside, she was so far above the others on the scale of suspicion, that she thought everyone must be saying so. She imagined a map on everyone's floor, with her name underlined in red grease pen. Of course, people didn't know that she had been in the service, or that the victim had been. Were they all talking about her? The most she had heard is that they were inclined to blame the "Yank," but of course they wouldn't talk about her in front of her. The point was that, as obvious as it must be that she was the culprit, she wasn't, which left someone else.

CHAPTER TWENTY-SIX

WHEN DUNN HAD LEFT, DARLING felt vaguely as if he'd been in some sort of manly competition, only without rules or object. It was an unpleasant reminder of the quiet test of strength that being a Canadian in Britain had been. Most of his comrades had been brilliant fun, but some British officers seemed to think you were something they'd found discarded in a hedgerow. It brought out the masculine competitiveness in him. He'd found ways to subvert the superiority, through under-the-breath comments and a bare compliance with commands. Two hours with Angus Dunn had brought back his natural colonial pit bull.

He sat glumly at his desk and tried to focus on what little new information he had gotten about the dead man, rather than on the words he'd overheard. "I loved you," she'd said. He couldn't shake the feeling of that moment and he couldn't shake the words. A sign of extraordinarily bad taste on her part, he thought petulantly. And worse, he couldn't shake the fury at Dunn's attitude toward her. Compliant indeed. A man who valued compliance in a woman was no man at all, he thought. Dunn was a bastard.

How an intelligent woman like Lane Winslow . . . He pushed back his chair and decided he needed the comfort of whatever Lorenzo had on offer. He didn't expect Ames back for at least two hours, and he realized he was ravenous.

"*Dottore*. Good to see you!" Lorenzo called out through the window from the kitchen. "Today no soup, but very nice pasta with *pomodore*. Sit down." Darling looked about and realized with some delight that all the window seats were taken. Maybe things would look up for Lorenzo sooner than later. The customers seemed to be from the local railway and at least two were speaking Russian. Ah. The English speakers were still not coming in. Well, good for the Russians and anyone else who did. Everyone else was missing a damn good meal.

The cheerful Italian sat down opposite Darling after putting in his order. "How are you doing? You look a little—I like this word I learn today—'discombobulated.' My art teacher give me that one." He rolled the bumpy syllables of his new word around in his mouth with special gusto.

"Nothing gets past you, Lorenzo. I had to let go of my chief suspect today and she is on her way home up the lake with Constable Ames right now. I met a very unpleasant man from England and I am no further along in solving this crime. Discombobulated is a good word. Things are all over the place and I can't put them in any pattern."

"But I see that you are happy to let this woman go, no? I see that. I am not wrong about this sort of thing."

Darling felt himself colouring slightly and cursed himself and Lorenzo. "Do you think women ought to be compliant, Lorenzo?"

Lorenzo sat back in his chair and looked thoughtful and was about to speak when his wife called through the window, "Service!" He smiled at Darling and gave a little shrug as he got up to get the plate of pasta. He placed the steaming plate before his customer and put beside it a bowl of Parmesan cheese. "We just grate this today. Is fantastic." He came back to hover by the inspector. "Now. This compliant business. I don't think so a woman can be compliant. I know, is supposed to be. Obey the husband, all that, but you know what I think? You can't make no life with a woman like that. Look at Mrs. Lorenzo, beautiful and smart. No, *Dottore*. You just gotta be careful *you* not too compliant. It's not good if one person is stronger than another. That's my advice. For when you get a woman, eh?" He winked, a cliché of an Italian waiter.

Inspector Darling was back at his desk when Ames arrived. The food had improved his mood considerably, and he found himself thinking more pragmatically about whatever slim evidence Dunn had given him about the dead man. It wasn't much. Franks had asked for leave to come to Canada, but hadn't said why, except that Dunn understood it was about possibly finding family. Okay, then they'd have to find out who in King's Cove might have been this man's family. And why, if he had family there, they'd choose to bump him off. Dunn would be catching the morning train the next day. Darling wondered if the man had told him everything he could. He doubted it. It seemed beyond belief that someone had worked for Dunn and his people and not been vetted thoroughly. Still. It could happen.

If Franks himself had not known he was adopted until his parents died in the Blitz, it was possible his employers had not known either.

"Sir. Package delivered."

"Ames, could I remind you that we are not in a bad movie, in spite of the necessity of having to deal with that bastard, Dunn."

Ames raised his eyebrows slightly. There was clearly and infuriatingly much that had gone on that day that he didn't know. "Sir?"

"Well, he only came out to make sure no one was breaking his Secrets Act. It's annoying that we've got someone who knew and, indeed, employed the dead man and he's got nothing whatever to contribute. He came to make sure everyone was keeping quiet and to get Miss Winslow back in the harness."

"The harness, sir? Did she work for him as well?"

"Yes, she did, Ames. She was some sort of operative during the war, though she did not realize he was pulling all the strings. This much I got out of Major Dunn, not her. She has proved to be a good little employee and has told no secrets. I'm sure he was very much relieved. Still, he exonerated her, sort of, leaving us suspectless."

"Ah, well that accounts for it."

"Accounts for what, Ames? I'm tired of everyone around me being cryptic. Don't you start!"

"I mean, the operative thing. She's pretty keen to solve the crime because, frankly sir, we've not done much. As she points out, she's worried that someone has it in for her, seeing as they went to so much trouble to pin it on her.

She came up with a scheme, but I said absolutely not. I told her, under no circumstances."

With a tug of anxiety, Darling frowned and said, "What sort of scheme?"

"I thought I'd have another look at the car while I was out there, and she got the idea that if she told the old lady at the post office that I'd found evidence and was going back to get the evidence kit, the old lady could casually tell everyone that came through for their mail, and it would spread like mad and the criminal would come to try to do something to the car, and Miss Winslow would see him and nab him. I told her it was not a good idea, sir."

A wave of panic swept through Darling. "God almighty, you don't think she'd do that do you?" Compliance suddenly seemed to him an ideal feminine virtue.

"I don't think so, sir, but she is very determined to get this solved."

DARLING GRABBED HIS telephone and dialled. "KC 431," he barked at the operator, and then drummed his fingers impatiently on his desk while he waited. "Ah. Miss Winslow. Inspector Darling here." He paused, clearing his throat. "Yes, fine, thank you. Listen, Ames just got back from dropping off the raspberry plant. I find I've sent the wrong one. Could you just hold off on planting it?"

When he had hung up, Ames queried innocently, "Who is in a bad movie, sir?"

"You can laugh all you like, Ames, but as a matter of fact, she understood exactly what I meant. She told me she would wait now before she planted them." He organized papers on his desk to restore his dignity, and sent Ames off to check the day's post.

SHE HAD RUSHED downstairs from her list-making when she'd realized the phone was for her. She was surprised and a little pleased to hear Inspector Darling's voice. Missed me already, she thought. "How are you?" she said into the horn, suddenly embarrassed by this thought. He wouldn't be phoning except about the case. She felt herself both smile and redden at his next comment. Ames had told him what she had talked about doing. When she saw it through Darling's eyes, she saw that out here, alone, trying to trap a murderer was perhaps not the best idea she'd ever had. Raspberries again. She thought she would say, "Don't worry, I won't do anything stupid," but if they were really performing for any listeners on the party line, she'd better play it to the hilt. "I was going to give the shrub to the Armstrongs, but I won't now, I'll wait. Thank you, Inspector." She felt a twitch of regret as she hung up the earpiece and clicked it into place. When this business was over she'd get the hook the for earpiece fixed.

THE DAY OVER, Darling drove back up the hill to his house on 6th Street. It seemed particularly empty as Mrs. Andrews worked only three days a week, and this was not one of them. Usually he loved the emptiness. He would pour a glass of scotch and stand by his large front window and look out at the town descending below to the edge of the water. From where he was he could see the little ferry that constantly went back and forth in the seven-minute ride that took traffic onto the Nelson road. The one that went past the King's Cove turnoff. Today these musings were unsatisfying. He had a constant fear now that Miss Winslow would do something idiotic, and he needed something, anything, that would help them understand why Franks had come to King's Cove.

He had been dozing, after some considerable time of tossing and turning, sleep eluding him, when he'd finally gone to bed after one of Mrs. Andrews's glutinous and tough beef stews, when he woke up fully. Of course. He'd been blinded by fury and hadn't done the most obvious thing! He looked at his bedside clock. It was 2:30. The morning train left at 8:20.

At 8:00 he was pacing in the small waiting room at the station, feeling slightly bleary at the interruption of his night's sleep; he'd tossed until at least 4:00 before he dropped into an uneasy slumber. At 8:10 he saw Dunn approaching the station. He was carrying a small suitcase and looked like someone used to travel. Darling stood up and called out, "Major Dunn. A moment, please."

Angus Dunn raised his eyebrows, somehow conveying a sense that he found it in very bad taste to be accosted at a train station. He paused but did not put down his bag. "Yes, Inspector?"

"You can do something for us when you get back to Britain, if you'd be so good. Franks, you believe, was out here to look up relations. Would you go to Somerset House to look at his birth certificate? If he found he was adopted, he must have gone there himself. There may be something there for us. And could you wire us?"

Seeing Dunn sigh as if he were being unnecessarily imposed upon, Darling added, "Someone has gone to a great deal of trouble to attach Miss Winslow to this business. She lives thirty miles out of town by herself in a small and somewhat isolated situation. If we do not get to the bottom of this and she chooses to go off on her own to solve the problem, we cannot protect her. In any case, I do not like civilians messing about in murder cases. You could be extremely helpful. Otherwise we will be faced with a lengthy process of writing to Somerset House and waiting for an answer you could provide in a fraction of the time."

An "All aboard!" from the platform caused Dunn to look away. "I don't think the Miss Winslow I know would have a go at solving it. A bit too timid, but very good at doing what she's told. But I see your point. All right, then. I'll be back on the eighth, and will wire you shortly after."

Darling pursed his lips thoughtfully. "You know," he said, "the Miss Winslow I know would. I can see that and I've only known her five minutes. Well, thank you, Major Dunn. I shall expect your communication. Good day." He touched the brim of his hat and turned away. Damned if he was going to shake his hand! He left the station without a backward glance, but then stood at the top of the hill watching the train pull away.

CHAPTER TWENTY-SEVEN

TWO DAYS HAD PASSED SINCE Darling had seen off Dunn. He knew it would be easily a week or two before he could hear from him, if Dunn flew to London from Montreal, and that was only if Dunn went to work immediately when he got back and wired the information, or telephoned, though trunk calls had been unreliable lately. The days had continued hot for July, and they were saying August promised to be hotter. The overhead fans in the station were entirely inadequate to the task, even at 9:30 in the morning, providing nothing more than a sluggish moving of hot air in whorls around the sufferers below. Ames was up in the Slocan Valley investigating some livestock robberies and Darling sat glumly at his desk before the neatly organized piles of paper that provided whatever information they had about the King's Cove killing.

His gloominess was intensified by a nagging sense of guilt about having arrested Miss Winslow because he was sure, he did not know how, that she was quite, quite innocent of this crime, despite what the paper in the piles before him said. He mollified his guilt by telling himself crossly that it was his job as a policeman to gather evidence and make arrests based thereon. This he had done. No one could fault him, not even himself.

On the other hand, there was the evidence. It was real, indisputable, and piling up. His old boss MacDonald would have had her trussed up and into court by now. What if she was guilty? He could imagine MacDonald sneering at him right now. He would be telling him he'd been swayed by a pretty face. Was that why he thought her innocent? No, it was, in a way, a greater weakness than that; it was his visceral dislike for Dunn. If Dunn thought her innocent and was abusive and dismissive of her, he could go one better; he could think her innocent and treat her properly.

Disgusted at the boring daily round of this internal struggle, he stood up, pushed his blameless chair roughly out of the way, and went to stand at the window of his second-floor office. From it he could see the street below and, over the two-storey buildings across the way, the top of Elephant Mountain across the river. It rose like a cooling mirage against the azure sky behind it and it seemed to call to him of escape; from the town, from the cares of his world. It spoke of a clean, pristine Eden where sunlight did not fall in leaden streams onto overheated tarmac, but filtered gently through trees that cooled and soothed.

In truth, he knew, in spite of one recent torrent, the lack of rain was causing all that was green to go yellow and that the danger of forest fires was sharply rising in his little Eden across the river but he would, he decided, choose nature over the city this day, at least. He pulled his jacket off the hook and folded it over his arm. It was a formality.

He would not wear it. He pulled his hat onto his head, seized a notebook and a camera, and bounded down the stairs to the main floor.

He told the desk sergeant he would be out for several hours, and soon was barrelling on the open road up the lake with both his windows open, hoping he would not meet much in the way of dust-producing traffic. There was no point in denying to himself that he was going to King's Cove and had been unconsciously planning it all along. There was a murder to solve and he wanted to solve it. Sitting around waiting for telegrams was not the way. He felt an excitement that reminded him of his early days, when he was the Ames of a team with old Inspector Macdonald—young, unruffled by conscience, or a war. The fact of Miss Winslow he tried not to think about, though the image of her thoughtful face and cascades of auburn hair seemed to hover like a backdrop to his musings. He did review many times a day her attack on that prat, Dunn. He told himself that it was because he loved seeing Dunn taken down a peg, but he suspected that what he loved to recall was the pure, sublime outrage on the face of Miss Winslow; it seemed to him, in a world of manners and cloaking of true feelings, a moment of abiding truthfulness. Real outrage, genuinely delivered.

It was nearly eleven when he arrived at the turnoff. He slowed the car, changed gears for the sharp, uphill turn, and caught sight of Harris lumbering along in his tractor, evidently returning from somewhere up the hill behind his house. He must have been out early if he was coming home now. Darling thought of the different rhythms of his urban life. The predictable routine of getting up, walking to a café for breakfast; the noise and early morning energy of others like him, reporting to offices somewhere. Here, he imagined, one's time somehow had an extended shapelessness to it that was dictated by when the sun came up and when it set as its two most determining factors, and not the hour-by-hour consciousness he had developed.

He slowed down as he approached the Winslow driveway. What was his plan? He still wasn't sure. He would present himself, he decided, as wanting to ask a few more questions and look again at the car, which he knew he'd neglected. Thus fortified with a sketch of a plan, he pulled up in front of her gate and wondered at the protocol. Did one leave the car pulled off the side of the road, or did one get out, open the gate oneself, and drive in? Was that like going into a house without knocking? For Pete's sake, he was a policeman! He parked the car, unhooked the gate, and walked down to the house.

The door by the great blue spruce was open. He knocked on the frame of the screen door and called out, "Miss Winslow? Hello?" He waited, listening, and was rewarded by footsteps apparently coming down a staircase. Miss Winslow appeared on the other side of the screen door, and seemed momentarily nonplussed. She was in a pair of khaki shorts and a rumpled, white, cotton short-sleeved shirt. Her hair was drawn back off her face in what looked like a hasty bid to get it out of the way. They looked at each other through the screen for only a moment and then the spell was broken by Lane.

"Inspector Darling! I was not expecting you. Please, come in." She pushed the door open and stepped aside to let him through. Darling felt an uncomfortable momentary turmoil in those seconds of looking at her before she spoke and so he became officious. "I've come out to ask a few follow-up questions, if you've a few moments, and I'd like to go and look again at the car in your outbuilding."

Lane sighed. She had been in the grip of some ungainly feelings for that brief moment as well. These, particularly because she had so recently been reminded of what a dead loss men in general were, made her cross. His pompousness was, in a way, a relief. He too was a dead loss. She turned and led him through to the kitchen and, dutifully but not warmly, asked if he would like some iced tea. She had become addicted to this concoction as made by Angela, with plenty of sugar, and had a glass jug handy in her refrigerator, which she had made for her continued work in the attic. His arrival, in fact, had interrupted a new line of thinking; she had begun to believe that the connections between the residents of King's Cove might hold a key.

It is difficult to keep up a completely official front when one is hot and thirsty. Darling took his hat off and said, "Actually, thank you. That would be lovely." They sat in silence, drinking from blissfully cold, dewy glasses, and Darling realized he hadn't really got any particular questions organized to ask her. He had formulated something finally and began, "I wonder . . ."

But at that moment she too spoke, "I've been doing . . ."

A sputtering of apologies followed and Lane said, "Listen, Inspector. I realize this cannot be comfortable for you, seeing as I am sure I am still your chief suspect, and no doubt you are here finding ways to prove it so that you can put this all to bed. But before you bang me up, as they say, for this, I have worked on trying to figure out the local community. It is possible we could pool whatever knowledge that ass Angus Dunn provided you with and what I might have. As to that car, well, your young Constable Ames kiboshed my plan to draw the murderer out of hiding, so you can do what you want with it."

This speech concluded, she sat back and looked with an uncompromising expression at Darling. He looked down and very nearly smiled. "I believe I have been the ass, Miss Winslow. I should start by saying good morning; that was the bit I missed when I first arrived. Secondly, I appreciate your candour. I do not, as it happens, particularly favour you for this murder, though as you say, the evidence is pretty overwhelming. I am extremely anxious to get it solved, as I am tired of the man's body in the downstairs morgue. I am most happy to look at anything you might have regarding the locals. And, finally, I too was horrified by your plan and for once I agree with Ames. Let's talk no further about that!"

At that moment the phone rang, and both stopped to listen. It stopped at two and a half rings. "It's mine," Lane said, and went into the hallway. Darling tried not to watch her leave the room, but he was intrigued by her old phone. He wondered how many other rural communities still got along with these trumpet affairs. The hall was dark compared to the brightness of the kitchen and, as he watched, she seemed to be consumed by the darkness. He heard her pick up the earpiece and talk loudly into it.

"Hello, KC 431. Oh, yes, hello." There was something hesitant in her manner. "I'm busy just now," she continued to whoever it was. In the dimness, he could see her glance back at the kitchen toward him. There was something in her voice that alerted him, and he did not look away. "Um, yes. It's the police, actually." Her tone suggested she said this very reluctantly. There was another long pause as she listened. "No, I'm not sure. Listen, another time, all right? No, I'm fine, thank you. Yes, bye now!" She reached up to replace the earpiece. He heard her bang it a little. "Bloody thing," she muttered in an unladylike manner, and she came back into the kitchen, looking as if she was trying to recompose herself.

"Are you all right?" Darling asked, watching her face. "You might want to get a new telephone. It's quite quaint, that shouting into a horn. My mother used to do that."

"Yes, quite all right, thank you," she said thoughtfully. "That was, in fact, one of the locals, Sandy. He said he was going along to the Hughes' and saw the car pull up, yours I mean, and he, like you, wondered if everything was all right."

Darling consulted his memory banks. "Isn't he the son of the old gentleman at the top of the hill? Mather?"

"Yes, that's right. I can't make out why he'd be going up to the Hughes'. To buy eggs? That must be it. And is he phoning from home now? He hasn't had time to go up there and come back. You've only been here a short time."

"He could be driving," Darling suggested. "Why does it matter?" But even as he asked, he realized that he had not interviewed Sandy properly, and Lane's concerns seemed to suddenly make him feel he'd been neglectful.

"No. I'd have heard the car. You hear anything moving here because there is so rarely any traffic. And you're right," her face cleared, "it doesn't matter. I'm a little nervy, I think, thinking that someone around here has killed someone. I sometimes think they are just lying in wait, waiting to be discovered, as if it is some sort of cat and mouse game. I hopefully imagine myself to be the cat, but I might well be the mouse." She thought of her bold map on the floor upstairs, with its lines and notations and thought, Who am I kidding? I'm no detective. I'm just doing it to keep from being nervous.

"Is there something about this Sandy that makes you particularly nervous?" asked Darling.

"He's angry, that's all. He feels he's had a rough deal from his father. Sometimes . . . it's nothing. Anyway, it's all fantasy, isn't it?" She brightened. "That man might well have been killed by someone outside. He could have been followed here by some shadowy arm of British Intelligence and done in for something he knows. Or whoever did it could have done it in a passion over an argument, and have no desire to kill anyone else." She did not tell him about the debacle of the fishing trip. Indeed, she was working hard to put it out of her mind, and Sandy's solicitous phone call had not helped. Was he watching her?

"What were you going to say? Any small thing might be relevant."

"This won't be. It's just . . . I sometimes think he's following or watching me. Nonsense, of course. As I said, I'm just a little nervy, I think."

Darling made a mental note—he had stopped making

actual notes when he stopped being a constable—to interview this Sandy. It was disquieting to think of him following Miss Winslow around. "You said you'd been working out something about the locals. Can you tell me about that?"

"It's nonsense too, really. I just realized I'm doing it to keep me from being anxious. I think it's left over from the war. I'm like a commander just trying to work out where an attack might come from by drawing it all out. You can certainly come and see it. I've laid it out on the attic floor because the only long wall I have is in the bedroom and I don't feel like sleeping in a war room." She stood up and led Darling into the hall and up the attic stairs.

CHAPTER TWENTY-EIGHT

THE THING THAT HAPPENED NEXT began quietly enough. In fact, it began just as Lane Winslow and Inspector Darling were on their way up to her attic to look at her map. Mather went to the post office. He had sent Sandy to pick up the mail, but Sandy came back empty-handed because he said he'd found some of the fence on the south side of their property knocked down and had come back to get a hammer. Reginald mentally cursed his son and his wife, who was still not well after the cougar incident and was sitting on the couch staring morosely at nothing. Not well. She was as mad as a hatter. She'd kill someone one day, crashing around in people's driveways after cougars with a loaded rifle.

He pulled his cap off the stand by the door, seized his cane from its peg, and slammed out the door. Sandy, he saw, had been on the telephone. Who was he calling? He was behaving more and more strangely. Alice was mad, there was no point in denying it, and Harris had apparently promised him the land but had made no move to seal the deal. Feeling aggrieved was nothing new to Reginald Mather, but his grievances seemed to be pressing closer, to be more immediate. He no longer had the luxury of being bitter about the thwarting of his ambition to build a lumber empire, which was always somewhere in the future. Now his troubles were moving in.

As he walked briskly down the hill, swinging his cane, he fixed on his wife and the gun incident. It was not the first time she had gone off in this manner and he'd told her before that she'd kill someone someday. But now someone had been killed. Had she shot the man found in the creek? He wished he knew more about how the man was supposed to have died. Drowned, he supposed. That relieved him a little. She would shoot someone in her wild, mad, get-anything-that-moved way, but she wasn't likely to drag a man into a creek. Why? How? And who was the man? He wished now he'd not been so aloof when it first happened. He could have asked the damned police more instead of being pushed around by them.

On a whim, he went to the car and looked through the window onto the back and then the front seat. Hadn't the police found the gun in the trunk where Sandy had put it after Alice's shooting spree? He pulled open the trunk and saw the rifle, broken open and flung into the shadows at the back. He took it out and checked it and then looked around, wondering where he could stow it. He finally decided on the barn. He'd not had horses since Sandy was a boy and Alice never went near the place. He rested it on the shelf created by the crossbeam above the inside of the door, stretching to push it into place. It was dark there. That should put it right out of her reach.

Limping more than usual, he walked slowly down the

road. It was hot now and he stopped when he came abreast of the Winslow gate to wipe his forehead with a handkerchief. The maroon car was pulled up to the gate, and he realized the police were there. He had a small buoyant feeling of relief. If the police were back at the Winslow woman's place, it must mean they were following her as a lead. This relief was momentary, however, because thinking of her led back to thinking of Sandy.

The boy was clearly obsessed with the Winslow woman. Sandy tried to cover it, but Reginald had seen a change in his son since the day he'd met her at the Armstrongs' tea party. Well, she was a murderer and it would serve him right! Idiot. Mather whacked at a fern at the edge of the road with his cane and, with a dark expression, walked the short remaining distance to the post office and pushed open the door. He realized that he did not know who Sandy's friends were, or if he had any—what he thought—where he went. In this maelstrom of unfamiliarity, the question came to him. Where was Sandy when the murder happened? It had been some days ago. Or was it at night? He realized that in his imagination, Sandy was the compliant, if sullen, third member of his household. Always there at the dinner table, always in the sitting room in the evening with them, listening to the wireless or reading. But now, shaken, he realized Sandy was, in fact, often not there of late.

The wooden window slid up noisily and Eleanor Armstrong grinned at him. "Good day, Reginald. I wondered when one of you would get down. I just saw Sandy across the way and I thought he was on his way, but he never got here. I've your paper and a letter. It's from the old country. In fact, I was having a peer at the stamp and the postmark surprised me. This letter was sent in April. I don't know why it's so late. I dare say it got stuck in the bottom of bag somewhere and they've just sent it on." She held out the folded Nelson newspaper and the letter. He looked at the handwriting and recognized, with a shock, that of his aunt. She had not written him in a good twenty years.

"How is Alice?" Eleanor asked, and she reached under the counter and pulled out a bouquet of sweet peas with the stems dripping. "I cut these this morning. I thought they might cheer her up." Mather grunted a near-thanks as he took them. His unsettled mood about his son was replaced first by puzzlement at the letter in his hand, then puzzlement about what Eleanor might have meant by "across the way," and finally, his annoyance that everyone knew his wife was "ill" or needed "cheering up." He put the mail under his arm and, with the sweet peas clutched unceremoniously in his large hand, he started for the door, which he was on the verge of pushing open with his cane, when he turned back.

"What do you mean 'across the way'? Across the way where?"

"I was just coming out of the root cellar this morning and I saw him coming down the road and was just preparing to go into the post to get your mail when he went along that little path toward Miss Winslow's. I was surprised, because he normally would have gone in at the top of the road by her driveway. It looked like he decided suddenly to go see her. The funny thing was, I don't think he ever went right to the house, because in a few minutes he was back out again, and off back up the road toward yours."

Mather grunted and turned back up the road. Eleanor Armstrong watched him for a moment and then called out, "Bye now!" in a cheerful voice and got nothing in return.

So, he was up to something, Mather was thinking. Sandy had stopped at the gate to Miss Winslow's and looked at the policeman's car. Why had he gone toward her house? It wasn't because he hadn't known the police were there and changed his mind at the last minute; he would have seen their car at the top of the drive. Was he wanting to spy on her for some reason? Then he remembered that Sandy had gone straight into the hall and used the telephone for a muffled conversation. Had Sandy called her? He tried to reassure himself by looking up the familiar road he'd walked for forty years, but he could not shake the feeling that he was suddenly not in command of his life. He was certainly not in command of Sandy.

He picked up his speed and arrived home to find Sandy chopping wood with uncharacteristic energy. He experienced again an unfamiliar sense of dissonance. They did not speak; this, at least, was familiar, and Reginald went into the house, hung up his cane, and sat with a grunt in his chair by the window. He now turned to the other mystery. This letter from his aunt in Cornwall. It had been mailed in April; this much was clear from the postmark over King George's face. It occurred to him that someone must have died; perhaps he would get some money? But, of course, there was no one left but her and she'd written the letter. He sliced open the envelope and adjusted his glasses, turning the letter into the light from the window.

Dear Reginald, I hope this letter finds you well. I've not heard from you in some time but I imagine I would have heard if anything had happened. I'm writing to you because I think you may need to be prepared. A young man named Jack Franks is on his way to you in Canada. This will mean nothing to you now, of course, but it will. I suppose that even you will not have forgotten the wretched young woman you landed on us in '17?

He favours her, though she was a most unprepossessing young woman. I don't know if you wondered what became of her, or if you couldn't bother even to do that, but she had a rather bad time of it at the birth and died of an infection. She lived long enough to beg me under no circumstances to tell you where the child was or what had happened. Another convert for you there. Well, that's all water over the dam. The boy, or should I say, man, for he is something near thirty years of age, turned up after he did some sleuthing at Somerset House when his parents died in the Blitz and he discovered he'd been adopted. Don't worry. He doesn't want anything, apparently. Just to look at you. I'll be honest with you, I told him it was a waste of his time, but you know what the young are like: full of ideals.

Reginald slumped back in his chair and stared out the window. His garden gleamed like a show garden, belying the apathy and disorder in the house. Alice had once been the gardener, but increasingly, she could not cope and spent her time when she was there maniacally digging, hurling dirt everywhere, and then storming back into the house with muddy boots. He had to keep up the appearance of his front garden so that his neighbours would not see the disarray in their lives. It used to soothe and comfort him, but he found himself asking, for what? His mad wife, his idiot son? There was nothing worth caring about. And now, suddenly, this. He opened his hand to look at the single sheet of paper that he had crushed in his shock. Smoothing it out on the table, he reread it. This man, Franks, was his son. His first son.

He turned and looked through the door at the couch where Alice still slumped, dozing now, with her mouth open and her lips fluttering slightly with her breathing. Reginald stirred uncomfortably at his desk, wanting suddenly to hide the letter, or to hide from what came flooding back. Thirty years had not altered that memory. He had helped that wretched girl, seen to her wood, her chimney, the state of the house. The rest of that winter after Harris had left for the front, and through the next two years, he had worked Harris's orchard with her, had been surprised at Robin's sparse correspondence, and then the summer of 1917. Funnily, it was water again, he mused. He closed his eyes, thinking perhaps to shut out the memory, but instead he fell into it and could not turn away.

July, 1915

In that year, King's Cove had come on to the telephone, and on this July day, his rang for the first time, startling him. It was Elizabeth. He laughed at the sudden intimacy of her voice in his ear. She shouted, thinking that one had to raise one's voice to be heard so far away. "I've got no water again, Reg." She sounded fed up.

Sunlight filtered through the trees that day and into his memory now. They stood thigh-deep in the icy water, their clothes hiked up as far as possible to keep them out of the way, clearing leaves and sticks away from the wooden pipe's entrance, and then stood, panting as the water began to flow again. After a moment he started toward the bank and then held out his hand to help her up. When she stood on the green verge, she began to pull her skirts out of her waistband, and moved to free her hand, but his grip tightened and with his other hand he reached down past her skirts to her bare leg, moving his hand upward slowly along the wet surface of her skin. She was shivering.

Had she been willing? At this thought his eyes flew open. He frowned. She must have been. But lurking in the memory was a dark moment, when she twisted and pulled. He tried to follow the memory carefully, but only arrived at a vision of her lying on the bank, her head turned away from him, and her utter silence. He saw now, as if for the first time, the tears. Afterward, she would not speak to him. If they met on the road she turned away, or looked at him with blazing eyes if he tried to touch her. He had left notes under her door when she would not answer his desperate knocking, begging to see her. Then one morning she had come up the hill and banged on his door. "You bastard," she'd said. "You have to do something."

LANE STOOD BACK as they reached the top of the stairs so that Darling could see the arrangement. He was, however, momentarily struck by the strange, empty beauty of this attic room. Light poured in from windows on all four sides, and illuminated the soft, variegated pattern of the wooden floor. It was pine, he could see, and finished with an oil that brought out its grain. The room was instantly calming in its emptiness, and he ran through the palette for these colours of light and shadow, with the greens framed by windows.

"Inspector?"

"Yes. I'm sorry. It's such a lovely room. What a complete luxury to keep a room empty like this." He turned to look at the paper taped to the floor. "Explain?"

"I've drawn a rather inaccurate rendering of the system of roads here, marked the houses, and written what I know about the people who live in them. What I see is missing is the connection between them, or indeed, the connection between any one of them and the dead man. I've made a note to myself to ask Eleanor Armstrong about mail coming in. While she is in no way a gossip, or interfering, she will have noticed anything unusual. I say this because perhaps this man sent a letter to let someone know he was coming. I'm sorry about the floor, only I haven't got a table big enough to lay it out on," Lane said, apologetically. His eyebrows furrowed, Darling stood gazing at the map. He saw the juxtaposition of personality on geography; each resident at the end of his or her road with little comments of known facts. Well, known to Miss Winslow, at any rate.

"Interesting approach. What do you think about what you have so far?"

"Well, I've only questions so far, haven't I? It's peculiar; they all seem, on the outside, to have everything in common, because they live in this tiny community with its little, very local history, yet they are as different as anonymous Londoners, all living in a giant metropolis. And of course I don't know enough to really connect them because I am so new here."

"The point being that he belongs to someone here. I see. Why do you think the connections between people here might be important? They've all lived here a long time. There must be myriad connections that have no bearing, I should have thought."

Lane sighed, realizing he was probably right. The connection between the stranger and someone at King's Cove was the crucial missing information. "Perhaps, though, there is something in the connection any of these people had with what they call so affectionately 'the old country,' which, by the way, is to them an Edwardian bastion that no longer exists. You should see teatime around here. There hasn't been a tea like that in Britain since the teens!" She laughed, and Darling, who had been standing with his hands behind his back looking at the map, looked up to catch the loveliness of that sound.

"And do you know what binds any of these people to the old country?"

"Well, that's the thing. I don't really. For example, I know that Mather, up here," Lane pointed to the top of her road, "is reputed to be a remittance man. He's sixty at least. He must have come out as a young man. He has a nearly thirty-year-old son. Would anyone still be remitting money to him? His wife is from there and she's a little off kilter. Either one of them could have relations in England who might come looking for them.

"And Kenny and his brother, John, who died in the first war, came out as children with their mother and father. She owned this house. Harris is their cousin, on the father's side or something. Harris was in France; he shipped out with John, and he was the only one who came back, and he came back pretty late."

"Aha," said Darling, getting into the spirit of the thing. "Did either John or Harris have an entanglement? Is Franks the result of something that went on during the war? It might explain why Harris came back so late. He was wounded, I know that, but that doesn't preclude an entanglement."

"Isn't your corpse about twenty-eight or so? He'd have been born around 1918. That wouldn't have given either one of them a lot of time. That leaves the Hughes. I can't think when the Hughes came out. The two 'children,' who are both in their sixties, must have been born in Britain because they still have traces of nice West Country accents, but I know nothing else about them. Certainly neither of the spinster sisters seems a candidate for having rushed off in shame to have a baby in England, especially with a war on."

"There's quite a lot of scope there. And the Bertollis? Decidedly not old country."

"Yes, well. I'm not in favour of them. I'm not clear why they left Brooklyn, though my brain is full of cliché ideas about Italians from that part of the world. I don't see how they could be connected with an English victim. Besides, I like Angela; she's fun." She was not to know what Darling had discovered, that Bertolli had come from a violent past and had changed his name to escape it.

"I am intrigued with your methodology. It would appear to be a line of inquiry, anyway. Do you have women in your police forces in Britain?"

"There should be more. Lots of women working in offices, though, thanks to the war. We're quite clever, really." Darling smiled at this, but Lane did not respond in kind. She was looking out the window at the sky where clouds flitted past, as hard to pin down as the unknown stories of the people at King's Cove. "The thing about this is that we can only see the most obvious outward connections. What we don't know are the deep rivers of relationship and conflict that exist between people. Why is Harris so bitter, or Mather so angry?" Darling turned his gaze from her profile to the diagram on the floor. These lines of inquiry of a man out to look for family were the very ones he had had. And yet, it was still the case that the only known connection of the victim was, in fact, to her. Was he being hoodwinked? His policeman's instinct that the most obvious answer would always turn out to be the right one was taking a beating. He still didn't think Lane Winslow was a killer. It occurred to him that he could add to the information she had about Bertolli. Of course he could not. They were not, after all, going to pool information. He felt his dishonesty in knowing he would get what he could and give her nothing.

Lane leaned against the door frame with her arms crossed and shook her head. Her hair had traces of shimmering red in the sunlight. Darling looked away. He did not, after all, know she was in the clear, and he didn't want his judgment clouded.

"Oh!" Lane's hand flew to her mouth, as she thought of something.

"You have something?" Darling asked.

"Well, yes, sort of. There are all those connections to

England, but we haven't really listed anyone who was there. Most of them have never been back, but maybe there is something in those who have been there recently, or at all; say because of the war."

"I hadn't thought of that. Who here fought in this last one?"

"That's the problem, really. No one. They're all either too old, or too young, or were excused, like Sandy Mather was to brush up on his agronomy. But Harris was there in the first show, and Kenny Armstrong's brother. He died over there. Could this have anything to do with that?"

"Franks was only a baby by the time that one ended. And I think you are forgetting someone." He wondered when it was out why he'd said it, and was sorry.

Blushing, Lane bent down, wrote, "Old Country," and wrote her own name, followed by Harris's and John Armstrong's. "All right. You've made your point. I'm not out of the woods. Perhaps we'd better go downstairs."

"Perhaps we ought to go and talk to the postmistress, then," he said, ignoring her fit of pique, but he made no move to the stairs because Lane was still in the doorway.

Lane turned as if to go down the stairs and said, "And speaking of not out of the woods, there's still the matter of the car in my barn. How it got there. Who put it there. Whoever put it there is our murderer. I still think we could flush him out if I put it about that you've found some evidence in the car."

"We haven't found evidence in the car," Darling said.

"But we . . . I, could suggest you had," Lane said, starting down the stairs.

"Aside from the fact that it places you in danger, it is unethical."

Lane stopped on the landing at the midway point of the descent and turned to look at him. "Ethics, is it? I'm surprised."

"Why, because I'm a policeman? I don't happen to like lying. Once you start, you can never quite erase the stain and it keeps spreading. I see criminals do it, and they're never very good at it because one lie leads to another. That's how we eventually catch a lot of them."

"That's jolly Baden Powell of you," she said a little crossly, because she was embarrassed to realize that it was exactly because he was a policeman that she supposed he would have no trouble lying. It also made it sticky if she were to tell the lie instead. "I suppose it never occurred to you that we are all in some danger until this man is caught."

Darling laughed. He had moved in front of her and was now holding the front door open for her. "Do your prejudices know no bounds, Miss Winslow? Policemen lie. Men murder. What about Mrs. Mather from up the road? She'd be quite mad enough to kill someone. Indeed, from the stories I've heard, I'm surprised she hasn't managed it yet. Oh. Could you lock your door, please?" He realized that it was unlikely that people locked their doors in King's Cove but he was disturbed by her idea that not finding the killer put them all in danger.

They walked in silence along the path and across the footbridge. Darling felt . . . he wasn't sure what he felt. Perhaps alarmed at how much he was enjoying himself.

CHAPTER TWENTY-NINE

ELEANOR TOOK A MOMENT TO answer the knocking on the frame of her screen door. The house door was open and Inspector Darling and Lane could see through the kitchen to the little hall, where sunlight poured like a river along the floorboards from the back door toward the kitchen where it was swallowed in the shadows. She came in through that back door, wiping her hands on her flowered apron.

"Lane, Inspector! Come in." She was smiling—the smile, Darling thought, of the absolutely innocent. How lovely it must be to have nothing on your conscience.

"Sorry to barge in on you like this," Lane was saying, "but we thought you might be able to help. We've been trying to sort out who might be related to whom, past-history-wise." Eleanor looked at the two visitors, her smile now having a tinge of delight at being in on something.

"I'd put us on the back porch, but the sun is beating down on it just now. Come into the sitting room. It's cool in there. Ah, Kenny, there you are. Will you take our guests into the sitting room while I rustle up some tea?"

Darling put up his hand as if to say there was no need, but Eleanor was already shooshing them through.

Lane had been in this room once before. It had the classic feel of a formal Victorian room that was never used. The air hung as if it were poised to stir again only when someone came in. There was a window bench piled with faded silk-covered pillows and, along one wall, a low bookshelf with books that surely had last been touched the day they were placed there. A glass cabinet displayed tiny figures, a sword, some medals, and a small, silver-framed photo of a beautiful woman in Edwardian dress.

But it was not this picture that arrested Lane's attention. It was the wall of photos she had not noticed when she had last come. She moved closer to look at them.

There were seven in all, placed in a row, as if telling a long-forgotten story. First a picture of a small, wood-frame building, a wisp of smoke rising from the chimney. It was a sunny winter's day, and a small group of smiling children stood, formally posed, before the front steps. They were muffled in thick coats and were all, including two young girls, wearing heavy laced boots. Most looked to be in very early adolescence. Though she wanted to linger on the faces of each of the children, Lane moved to the next photo. It was an unusually unposed and natural scene of a group of people packing apple boxes in front of a large barn. She guessed it would have been before the war, 1912 or so. Were these older versions of the children in the previous picture? She guessed they must be. Beside this was a photo of a house picnic, which she realized had been taken on the lawn in front of her own house. An older woman sat on a rattan chair and younger people were spread about on blankets on the grass. The Hughes girls, a much younger Kenny and Eleanor, perhaps Lady Armstrong in the chair, Harris, and perhaps his wife? A younger Reginald Mather.

The contrast between this happy moment and the next picture made her suck in her breath. It was a stark, almost apocalyptic scene of devastation; a brooding, smoking photo of a burned-out landscape. For a moment she wondered if it was a picture from some European battlefront and then she remembered the fire of 1919. It was incredible to realize that this beautiful community had suffered such devastation only twenty-eight years before. The picture had been taken from the main road and looked up past the Harris house, which stood like a startled survivor among burned-out stumps of trees. No wonder he was so bitter.

Kenny's voice brought her out of her contemplation. "I don't know why that's the only picture I took. The whole place was a mess. It's almost an irony, this picture, because Robin never seemed to get over it. The rest of us, well, moved on, I suppose. I sometimes wonder if he'd have been able to free himself if I'd not captured that particular scene."

Darling was positioned in front of the picnickers. "Why do we not do this sort of thing anymore?" he wondered. "Who is this woman?" He was pointing at the one celebrant who did not look happy to be there. She was slight, and had her hair pulled back in a severe way that emphasized a kind of fragile beauty, but one blighted with permanent distrust. She sat with her legs tucked under her, looking dutifully at the camera, unable, perhaps, to bring herself to obey the photographer's cheerful command to smile.

Kenny peered at the picture, tilting his head back to settle the image into the frame of his glasses. "That is Robin's wife. She'd only married him that year. Miserable little thing. We weren't in the least bit surprised she'd abandoned ship when Robin enlisted. She endured all those winters on her own. No electricity, having to cut wood and live, I dare say, on practically nothing. We tried to help her; Reg did a lot for her, I believe. But it was no life for a young woman. What did surprise me is that she never went home to her people in Nelson. She just vanished."

"Heavens. I thought it must be one of the Hughes daughters. She looks so familiar," Lane commented. "She's quite pretty, really. It must have been tough, a young woman out here on her own."

Inspector Darling laughed. "No irony there?"

"I have a motorcar, electricity, and running water. Hardly the pioneering life!" Lane retorted. She turned back to Kenny. "No children?"

"No, thank heavens. She'd not have managed even what she did, if she had little ones to look after." Eleanor had come in with tea and stood looking at the photo. "Although . . . come, sit. I made some biscuits. Oatmeal with lemon."

Settled onto the settee and chairs, which were surprisingly comfortable, perhaps because they were so rarely used that they didn't have that squashed-down feel the chairs in the Armstrongs' kitchen had, Darling and Lane both spoke at once. "I wonder," said he as she said, "Although?" He courteously waved a hand. Lane smiled and turned to Eleanor.

"You said 'although.' Although what?"

"Well," Eleanor said, drawing out the word, "it's one of those features of a tiny community like ours, isn't it, gossip? At the time we all wanted to help Elizabeth. Even the Hughes, though there were all women in that house. No one in the Cove was alone, except Elizabeth, so naturally we tried to support her a bit. She wouldn't take anything from anyone. She told me one day—she was a very crabby little thing—that everyone laughed at her and treated her like she didn't belong. I was a little cross. There was a war on. Our John was overseas, and Robin of course, and some of the men from families along the lakefront. I can't remember now if I said anything to her but she came up for her mail only every couple of weeks and I was trying to be nice to her, but I did begin to notice that others were giving her a wide berth. The Hughes girls began to be sniffy about her and made remarks about wondering what would happen if Alice and Elizabeth turned up to pick up their mail at the same time. But of course they wouldn't have, because Alice was away in Victoria for much of the war. Reg always said she was in Nelson seeing a cousin, but it was more than that."

"Meaning what, exactly?" asked Darling.

Kenny waved a hand dismissively. "All nonsense, really. Reg Mather used to go round and give her a hand. Especially that first winter. It was bitterly cold. I used to stop on my way down to the lake and try to help and she always sent me away, but Mather did seem to have an in with her. In any case, she was gone by the late summer of 1917. We didn't really know she'd left, except we noticed after a couple of months she hadn't been along to see about the mail. I stopped by Harris's house and the place was deserted. She'd done a decent job of shutting the place down. I found the key under the mat."

Eleanor looked at Kenny impatiently. "Meaning, there was a rumour that Reg had been seen coming back from Elizabeth's place quite late sometimes. No one liked to say it out loud because people here aren't mean-spirited, really, but there always lingered a suggestion that Reg and Elizabeth might have had a fling."

Darling put his cup down, thinking how delicious the tea seemed to be from these fragile "best" cups, in this decorous, time-forgotten drawing room. "What about Sandy?"

"What about Sandy? Oh, might he . . . good grief, no. He's Alice's through and through. She wouldn't put up with that sort of thing from Reg for a second. That's why it's difficult to believe in the fling business. Reg is, if the truth be known, a little afraid of her. Sandy's always been a surly, unhappy boy. I pity any woman who ends up with him!" Eleanor laughed, so that she did not see, in the shadowy room, the slight reddening of Lane's face.

"And just one thing more, Mrs. Armstrong. We were going to ask you about the mail, in case this man was coming here to see someone. You would have noted any odd mail perhaps?"

"It's pretty much what you'd expect. Most people get the Nelson newspaper, a few bills. Harris gets a veteran's pension cheque every couple of months from the old country, Mather has an aunt or something who used to write very irregularly . . . sometimes years apart. He just got one from her today. It was stuck in a bag somewhere because the stamp was franked in England in April. The Hughes ladies used to get mail from the old country but not so much anymore. I expect most of their relatives have died. The only really odd thing is that the Bertollis almost never get mail from the States. You'd think they'd be getting quite a bit, as our most recent residents, but he's only had one letter in the last couple of months."

CHAPTER THIRTY

DARLING HAD LEFT AND LANE was sitting at her little desk just at the time that Reginald was sitting at his. She, at least, had no guilty conscience other than the mild guilt that attends to having puttered away the morning and finding herself trying to write at two in the afternoon, when she knew she was better first thing in the morning. She had typed one line:

Clouds have banked, have banked and rolled

And thundered, she might have written, for at that moment a distant rumble announced itself. She abandoned her poem and gazed with a familiar combination of delight and a slight thrill of atavistic fear as the clouds piled and moved over the lake toward her. They might get a proper storm. Blimey! The windows upstairs. She'd left them open when she and Darling had been going across to the post office. She rushed up the attic steps and arrived just as the first massive drops of rain began to slant into the room. She pulled the windows shut and then stood panting to watch the storm. Lightning added to the theatre and she unconsciously began to count the seconds between lightning and thunder. A wave of nostalgia and sadness engulfed her. Her grandfather had so often rousted her out of bed and made her, with her grandmother protesting in the background, go up to the roof of the house in storms, no doubt risking their very lives. She would stand with her hand gripping his, at once fearful and thrilled while he extolled the wonders of nature at its rawest. These episodes always ended the same way. She was rubbed to a tingling with a towel by her irritated grandmother, put into a new nightie, and given a large cup of chocolate. And then, tucked into her bed again, she felt more wonderful than at any other time; warm, renewed, tranquil, and she slept the sweetest sleep of all.

Reluctantly turning away from the storm and these unrecoverable scenes of her childhood, she turned to go back to the kitchen. Cocoa at least she could have, she thought, for she'd bought a can of Fry's on her last trip to town. She thought about her map, and what needed to be added. In her heightened emotional state, the sudden picture of Darling musing over the map, his face thoughtful, hair falling slightly over one eye, made her chest tighten. "Now then," she said aloud, admonishing herself. Had the ghastly business of Angus taught her nothing? You cannot know another person, she thought, even with years. You cannot know another person enough to trust yourself in his hands. And you cannot trust just because you feel something is right. At nineteen she had believed in the rightness of her passion with every fibre of her being. Love will out.

What blindness it induced! Just like the old saying. Well, not this time. At almost twenty-seven she knew better.

The storm had so obliterated the daylight that even at three in the afternoon it was more like twilight. She switched on the light in the attic room and knelt down before the large sheet of paper, smoothing it out. They had left the pencil on the floor and she took it up, wondering what she could add. Over Harris's name she wrote, *Back 1919, orchards burned, wife gone*. The mousy, unhappy woman who looked so out of place in the picnic group, looking directly into the camera with a kind of challenge, as if suspecting it might pull something on her. Then she paused over Reginald Mather's name. *Helped Elizabeth Harris when husband at front*. This is what Kenny had told them. She wanted to have the picture right here in front of her. Reggie had been in the picture; young and very good-looking. Was he sitting near Elizabeth Harris? Of course not. She'd only just married Harris. But she needed to see that picture of Elizabeth again. She was the one who disappeared. There was a secret no one had plumbed.

The storm seemed to be abating, moving past into the mountains behind King's Cove, leaving behind a drizzle and a blanket of light grey cloud. It was a little before four; she could run across to the Armstrongs' for another look. She stood up and stretched, but she could not eliminate a kind of tension in her that she now identified as excitement.

It was Elizabeth Harris, she was sure of it. It all centred on her. What were the mysteries here? The obvious ones were why had this man Jack Franks come here, and how did he come to be killed, and where did Elizabeth Harris go suddenly in the middle of the war? And of course, why did Harris return a year later than everyone else from the war? Lane shook her head. She knelt down and wrote the questions on the side of the map, but as she stood, she reminded herself that feelings did not equal facts. Feelings of certainty had betrayed her in love, why should she trust them any more in this case?

PERHAPS IT WAS the coming storm and its attendant change in barometric pressure, but the night after the meeting between the Armstrongs, Inspector Darling, and Lane, some people were having trouble getting to sleep. Reginald was worried about the letter he should have received three months ago heralding the arrival of his putative son, only no one had arrived, and now, in this unguarded time, he allowed for the possibility that the man who had been found dead might be his son. Impossible, his mind retorted. Who on earth would have killed a man who was coming to see him? He wished now that he had seen the body. The idea that the dead man might have been his son filled him with a new kind of despair. Every dream unfulfilled and now, here he was, an old man with a crazy wife and a useless son and nothing to show for all his schemes. One thought seized him: he must see the dead man. The police must have taken a picture or something, he reasoned. He would get hold of them in the morning. This led to new worries. Alice had not left the house in days. How was he to get her out so that he might telephone the Nelson police?

SANDY LAY AWAKE in his room at the back of the house. He was thinking about Lane and trying to fight back the deep truth that she did not like him. Alice was awake too. She lay smiling because she'd found Reg's letter and knew she'd been right all along.

NOT ENJOYING HER share of sleeplessness was Lane, who was fighting it unsuccessfully. She listened to hear if the windows in the attic had come unlatched again, but there was only silence that pressed with a ringing in her ears. What had woken her? She opened and then closed her eyes and let her mind wander in the hopes that this would cause her to drift off. Instead of wandering, however, it seemed to focus in on the wall of pictures in the Armstrong sitting room. She felt haunted by that photo of the picnic on her front lawn. When she'd come home from her second visit to look again at the photo, she'd gone around to the front to imagine that afternoon so long ago. It felt so much a thing of the distant past. Two world wars had happened since then. But perhaps there could be another picnic, she decided. Later, when this bloody murder was out of the way. She imagined a photograph of a picnic in which every person at King's Cove was arrayed on blankets. In later years, someone would point at someone in the photo and say, "Oh yes, that is the man who killed that unfortunate stranger who came here back in '46." Or woman, she'd thought glumly. Better wait till it was done.

The flash of the bedside lamp Lane had finally switched on made her shut her eyes. Her clock, as she became accustomed to the brightness, told her it was 2:30 in the morning.

She groaned. The awfullest time. Too early to pretend one was simply an early riser. She sat up and plumped the pillows up behind her. Her book lay on the floor where she'd dropped it. She was reaching for it when she stopped. That picture. There was something in that picture. She tried to reconstruct it. Lady Armstrong, Kenny, Eleanor, the Hughes girls, and Elizabeth Harris. She'd thought Elizabeth must be one of the Hughes girls initially, because she thought she'd recognized her. She'd never seen a picture of her, so why would she seem familiar?

HARRIS, TOO, LAY awake. He was not surprised by this. He had been awake nearly every night since the business began. Suddenly and unaccountably, perhaps because of that interfering policeman, his bitch of a wife, Elizabeth, was on his mind. Where had she gone? She'd not gone home to her brute of a father. He'd checked. It was impossible to imagine her having the wherewithal to go anywhere. She'd just disappeared. Now, he wondered, was everything in his past coming back to haunt him?

The second theme that wove through his midnight thoughts like a strand of curling smoke was wondering what was happening with the investigation. He was paying for his misanthropy now, he knew. He could not bring himself to change his normal pattern of never going to the post more than once a week and avoiding the society of everyone in the community. He had seen the police car coming and going, had seen the Winslow woman drive once in her own car, and once in theirs, and at this, had breathed relief. She had obviously been arrested. Why?

Then he had seen her returned. He could make nothing of this. Had she been arrested because she was new? Nor had he seen the car towed away, though he was certain that the discovery of the car had sealed the woman's fate. The good thing, he supposed, was that no one had come to talk to him after that day when they'd come to ask about whether someone had been in the forest at night. He had been shocked, initially, that someone should be moving about on his land. No one was up at that time of night, for God's sake! His anxiety soared and he turned, irritated, onto his side, somehow hoping a change of position would make him feel better.

What did it mean that that interfering woman thought she had seen him? There was nothing to see. Was she snooping? Had she seen anything? Why had her arrest not stuck? He resolved that, though it was a day early, he would go up to the post office. Eleanor would have news. She would want to know where he'd been. He'd say he'd been sick. It was none of her bloody business, anyway! As he rehearsed in his mind how he might casually ask for the information he wanted—a process that even in his imagination seemed awkward—he drifted, finally, off to sleep.

THE MORNING DAWNED thick. There were heavy clouds massing to the west, but the sun still shone and the temperature was already warm, though it was only seven in the morning; the storm would come later, Lane surmised. She was on the veranda with a mug of coffee feeling sodden herself, with the exhaustion of her late-night wakefulness. She had finally dropped off to sleep, but had never acquired the knack of sleeping in and woke at the usual time. She clutched a mug of coffee in both her hands, looked warily up at the cloud-bank, and sighed.

Was this a writer's life? she wondered. Up early, fill the coffee pot, watch the coffee percolate while studiously ignoring the writing space, deliberately set up in a corner of the kitchen by the French doors so that she must see it every day, and respond by sitting at the desk, ready to work. But she could not shake the image of the picnic.

The lawn swept before her, trees still throwing dark and elongated early morning shadows across its yellow-green surface. She imagined again the picnic scene on her lawn. Old Lady Armstrong seated erect and formal in her rattan chair and the others on blankets around her. The table by which she sat had plates of food, pitchers of something, glasses. Who had brought all this? Did she prepare it? No, it was a rural community. Everyone would have brought something. What was the occasion of the picnic? Dominion Day, perhaps. July first, 1912.

With some determination she went back indoors, put her coffee cup into the sink, and went to her room to change out of her pyjamas. But her destination was not her little desk in the stream of morning sun, which now had a forlorn and abandoned air about it as motes of dust hung suspended in the light over the silent Remington typewriter; it was the attic, and her map of the residents of King's Cove. She would go to the Armstrongs', and she would add her new thoughts about it into the schema. Then she would phone Darling to discuss the picture.

LANE MADE HERSELF a poached egg and watched the clock impatiently so that she could get over to the post office. She told herself it was to look at the pictures again. She reminded herself firmly that they were only pictures. The Armstrongs would think it odd, this third visit to look at the photo. At last, at 9:15, she thought it was late enough not to disturb the morning routines at the cottage, and too early for others to be down for the mail. If Eleanor was surprised to have Lane rapping on her kitchen door instead of coming in at the little post office, she did not show it.

"Tea?" she offered.

"I'm sorry about barging over so early. I wanted to look at the pictures again. Do you mind terribly?"

"Gosh, no. Kenny's up the hill helping Gladys fix her chicken coop roof, so it's just us." Eleanor led the way. "Have you thought of something else? Oh bother, there's the post office. I'll be back in a minute."

Left on her own, Lane stood before the row of pictures again, this time focusing on the picnic. She reached up and took the framed photo off its nail, and walked with it to the window. It was a disappointing exercise. The light seemed to add nothing more to what she'd seen before. But that face, the familiarity of it, still pulled at her. It was as she was putting it back that it dawned on her: Elizabeth had the look of the dead man she'd seen on the slab. She moved quickly back into the light just as Eleanor came back.

"You know, I think this picture of Harris's wife resembles the dead man."

Eleanor came next to her and peered at the picture. "What can that mean?"

"I don't know. But if he were the son of Mrs. Harris, he would not be the son of Lieutenant Harris, is that right?"

"Absolutely right. He'd been gone for two years when she left . . . Oh . . . I say, could she have left for . . . ?"

"And if so, who is the father? It somehow makes it more real that the killer is, in fact, someone from here. And the killer is walking around trying to implicate me. I've a jolly good mind to go ahead with my plan. I feel like we are no closer to catching him."

"You know," Eleanor reminded her, "it is the job of the police to catch him."

"Well, a fat lot of good they're doing. Look at where we are. The inspector came out, did not move the thing one bit forwarder, and has gone back up the lake, leaving us to our fate."

Eleanor looked nervously out toward the kitchen. Kenny had come back and was pushing a log into the stove. "He's not going to like this . . ." she said, in a way that signalled agreement.

"Good! And while you get that round the place, I'm going to telephone Darling about the picture, and then go find that second shoe. It's ridiculous that it should not have turned up yet. It wasn't in the car and it wasn't with its mate and it wasn't on the path to the creek, along which the body had evidently been dragged. I'll come by if I find something!"

After leaving Eleanor to her task, Lane returned to her house. She detected in herself a slight but growing sense of unease. She had been eager, not to say school-girlish, when she and Eleanor had talked about their little scheme, but now, moving across the bridge and through the stand of birch trees that separated her house from the Armstrongs', she felt vaguely vulnerable and caught herself looking around, as if she might see someone sequestered in the trees.

She sighed heavily as she pulled a glass out of the cupboard for some water, her fallback whenever she felt even remotely out of sorts. This was a legacy from her grandmother, who believed a good dose of water was the answer to everything.

First, the telephone. She stood before it, thinking of what she would say to the inspector: that she thought the picture of the young picnicking Mrs. Harris might resemble the corpse. She saw now how unsubstantial this was. So easy to be tricked by imagining one saw resemblances. She should go find the shoe first and then at least she'd have something substantial to say to him. She would not, of course, tell him about the resuscitation of the car scheme. She pushed aside guilt and put her mind to the shoe.

It was nearing noon and at this time of year, night didn't come till a little after ten. No one who would come to look at the car would come before dark, she felt fairly sure, so there would be no point to hanging about at the house waiting. She took off her sandals, found something more suitable for scrabbling about in the underbrush, and left the house, reluctantly locking the door.

Once outside the house she stood, undecided, and then saw the barn through the trees at the top of the yard. That, at least, was a door that she'd better make sure was unlocked for this little ruse. She peered through the window of the door into the side of the barn. The police had wiped some of the thickest layers of dirt and cobweb off the outside surface of it when they came that first day looking for evidence. It was dark inside, though this window, and a couple of windows along the other wall, let in enough light to see the silvery metal bumper of the car and the general outline. It would be impossible to see after dark. She shrugged. She supposed the murderer, should he be a member of this community, would come with a torch. She checked the padlock. It was not locked.

Now, for the first time, she began to reflect on the journey of the car to her garage. Had the car been used to transport the body? It was not clear. She knew from what Ames had said in his unguarded chattering that they had found no evidence of the body having been in the car. The car, in any case, was not in her garage when they found the body, and it wasn't entirely clear the man had not been walloped on his head as he stood by the weir, though why he would have been there, in such a difficult-to-find and out-of-the-way place, was an imponderable question. For a moment, she thought about trying to trace the journey of the car. She walked around to the large doors and looked closely at the ground. How had the car been moved here without her knowing?

Lane walked slowly, looking intently at the ground, along the only path the car could have taken, around the trees that hugged the building, and up the side to where the path met her main driveway and out the metal gate. Her eyes were beginning to water with the effort, and she kept imagining she might be seeing tracks and then doubting what she saw in the blur of needles and grass. She went back and opened the doors to look at the car more closely. Mindful of not touching anything, she looked inside. Had she heard a car that night? With her troubled dreams of fire and the war, she could have dreamed of a car and not known it from reality.

Once she had reached the road, it was impossible to distinguish anything on the now dried and much-used gravel surface. Shrugging, she headed up the road, and then into the underbrush along the path that led to the weir.

She walked along the path, trying to put herself back into that same frame of mind as the very first day she'd made this walk with Robin Harris. It was all new then. She did not want to miss anything because she was making assumptions about having seen parts of it.

She thought about how the first shoe had come all the way into her property: clearly and deliberately brought there. There was some sort of gamesmanship going on here, she thought grimly. First the body being moved, then the shoe, then the car. If the murder had been unpremeditated, the follow-up certainly had not. No good pretending it wasn't. So, back to work. How had the body been brought? She stood up and continued along the path until she got to the creek, which now, returned to its original banks with the removal of the blockage, looked as innocent as any beautiful corner of nature could, as if human shenanigans could come and go, but nature took no interest.

She carefully trod the bank of the creek and along the small stretch of grassy sward that the path issued onto, checking under the ferns and underbrush. Nothing. She looked across the creek, edged with only brush and very quickly becoming forest. There was no path evident on the other side. She assumed people had trod on the other side of the creek when the weir was being built, but that would have been before the first war, maybe during the previous century. It was silly, she knew, but she'd come this far. She considered taking off her shoes, but on reflection thought the canvas would dry and the rubber soles might protect her feet from the rocky bed of the creek, so, calculating that the creek below the weir would be shallower, she plunged in.

The cold gave her a shock and she gasped out loud, a sound that suddenly seemed to reverberate in the thick of the afternoon. Looking around, as if she expected someone might be watching, she waded across toward the opposite bank. The current was gentle enough, but her legs began to lose feeling because of the cold. She grabbed for the tall grasses on the bank, pulled herself up, and stood shivering and looking about. Of course, she could see how foolish this had been. The brush was dense and it seemed no one ventured to this side of the creek. Except, here were the broken skunk cabbage leaves that she had seen on that Sunday. Had the murderer come onto this side of the creek? He wouldn't surely have struggled through the underbrush to get to the wood. She looked again at the wooden diversion. He might have come round this side to gain greater ease of access to the place he was trying to place the corpse. She shuddered at the momentary, almost visceral vision of someone trying to drag and stuff a corpse into the diversion. She looked beneath the underbrush for a second shoe, but found nothing. There were a good fifteen yards of bank before the forest curved in toward the creek, and she could not see herself painstakingly searching every part of it.

Some detective! Lane was about to wade back, regretting now that she would have to squelch home in her wet shoes, when she looked into the trees. What the heck, she was over here. Why not go into the forest and see where it led? She fought her way through the thigh-deep layer of grasses and ferns and was relieved that the ground became more manageable once among the cathedral of trees. It really was lovely. It surprised her to think that she was in Canada and had never ventured into the forest stands, even on her own property. It was a shadowy, silent world. The floor was soft with pine needles—she must find out the proper names of trees—and the sun dappled through like, she thought, the sun coming through the windows of Notre Dame in Paris. She walked in a direction that must be parallel to the road.

The land curved gently downward. If she continued, she must eventually hit the road again, so she proceeded, still in a reverie about the soothing quiet of being among the trees. She was, therefore, the more shocked when the trees cleared suddenly and she nearly tumbled down the bank of a midden. Stepping backward to try to keep her balance, she landed painfully on the sharp edge of a large rock. The whole thing was rocks; it was like an old quarry and into it, long ago, garbage had been tipped on a regular basis.

Looking around in some embarrassment, she hoisted herself up, wiping her behind, and wincing at what she thought would surely become a bruise by the next day. There was, she could now see, a faint trace of a nearly overgrown path going toward the road. This must have been an old garbage dump like the one they all took their garbage to up a hill about two miles toward Nelson, only this one clearly hadn't been used in years. Grasses and ferns grew out from among the rubbish and rocks, and she could see that there were rusted cans and boxes with nearly washed out and torn labels from at least the 1920s. Holding the branch of spruce tree, she steadied herself and stepped a short way down into the dump. There were tobacco tins, and some thick, old, broken bits of glass. She looked along the edges to see if anything, like the damn shoe she was searching for, might have been dropped in. The whole place looked as if it had not been touched in twenty years. Quelling an atavistic childhood desire to explore among the rubble, she turned back the way she had come. Sunlight fell in shards of brightness and shade, and she stopped just near the edge of the trees before the bank of the creek would take her back to another cold crossing. The gentle sound of the water was muffled slightly by the trees and the thick layer of pine needles that she walked on. In truth, though the quiet beauty of the forest was lovely, her heart lifted as the light from the open bank got brighter. She wondered momentarily how terrifying it would be to be alone in that very spot at night, where no light from stars would be visible through the roof of trees. And it was because she was looking up that she did not immediately see the root that almost tripped her. Then her heart nearly stopped and her breathing certainly did. She heard the sound of someone approaching on the path from the road, the very one she had believed was no longer used.

She kept herself absolutely still, her fist closing tightly onto the branch she still held. The noise was most definite. With what she hoped was the utmost stealth, she crept back up to the edge of the dump and then looked around. She could recede back into the bush from which she'd come. Bloody hell, she'd made a path like a rampaging elephant, she thought. Then, when she really felt she'd run out of time, she caught sight of an old stump with a profusion of small branches growing up around it not five feet to the left of her. Making for it, she ducked as low as she could go and prayed she was making less noise than the person approaching. She plunged behind the stump and sat for a few minutes catching her breath. The approaching person could be heard more loudly now. She turned and looked between the branches just as the figure appeared through the trees at the edge of the quarry. God, she thought. God, it's him.

ELEANOR HAD MOMENTARY misgivings as she saw her first customer that afternoon. She and Kenny had very nearly had a genuine row about it, something neither of them could ever remember having. "You're not to do it, d'you hear?"

"Nothing will come of it, anyway," Eleanor had said, though in her heart she did not believe this. "Poor Lane is just tired, in fact we all are, of waiting for the other shoe to drop . . . or be found . . ." Her attempt at humour had not softened Kenny's mood.

"Your policeman is a very decent sort. He also knows a thing or two, I shouldn't wonder, and if he says you're not to do it, why, maybe you'll listen to him, at least."

"Oh, Kenny, stop being such a fussbudget. We're all on pins and needles here, not knowing who did it and, indeed, if we ourselves are going to be murdered in our beds. This way we might find out something and move this thing along," Eleanor had retorted.

"Well, you'll do what you want, I suppose. I'm going to Gladys's." He'd stormed off, avoiding saying something he'd regret, grinding the gears of his beloved new truck in his consternation. Kenny had come back with the mail and had some wooden boxes of groceries for the Hughes.

Eleanor put mail into slots and prepared herself, practising how she might bring it up. Her opportunity came quickly. Angela breezed in with her boys tumbling along behind her.

"Good morning, Eleanor!" she called out, a trifle loudly for the confined space of the post office.

Eleanor chirruped back and bent down to fetch something from under the counter. "Morning, Angela. Would the boys be interested in an oatmeal cookie?" They were, and with their reverberating ruckus temporarily muffled with the chewing, Eleanor turned to get the bundle of mail out of the slot. Here were the usual things in Angela's mail, she always thought, just as she'd told the inspector. The newspaper. Bills. Where were old copies of the *New York Times*, letters with lovely, unusual stamps with everything from Hollywood stars to peculiar paintings? She stifled a disappointed sigh. "Here you go, then. Everything all right up at the log cabin?"

"Oh, yes. Dave is hard at work on some trio, so he's sending us off to the beach. Mind you, I'm a little nervous nowadays, going off there with the murderer not caught. I mean, you never know, do you?"

"I know just what you mean. I've been locking the door for the first time ever. Kenny thinks I'm being a fusspot. He thinks the killer is long gone . . . just followed that fellow up here to do him in. Mind you, I did hear from Lane, and I don't know if I should be saying this, but I understand that inspector is coming back because they've found some sort of evidence in the car . . . it's still in her barn, you know, till they can get a tow truck to take it back to town. Anyway, they're bringing some sort of detective equipment to have a look."

Angela looked with gratifying astonishment at the postmistress. "Really! That's fantastic, isn't it? Boys, outside with you! You're making too much noise." The cookie diversion had run its course and the three boys were now wrestling noisily. In a confined space this sort of activity could quickly end in shouts and tears. "Do you think they'll find anything? What could they find?"

"Now that I think of it, perhaps I shouldn't have mentioned it . . . you won't say anything will you?" Eleanor tried to look earnest, and had the grace to feel a little surge of guilt over her subterfuge.

"Horrors!" Angela cried, "Of course not! I won't even tell Dave. Is Lane all right? It must be terrible having all this go on right under her nose. I'll stop by on my way home."

Letting out a lengthy breath, Eleanor watched four-fifths of the Bertolli household disappear up the road. Not so difficult, really. She'd hold up her end, as it was unlikely Angela would have a chance to tell anyone, unless she met the Mathers on the way home, and they'd been scarce in the last few days. Alice must be having quite a lengthy spell.

Eleanor needn't have worried. Angela thought of stopping by Lane's, but the boys were unruly to the point of being unfit for admission into anyone's house, and she was sure that Eleanor had said she might not be there. The truth was, she wanted to rush home and tell Dave, who she felt sure would welcome a break from the trio. When she met Reginald coming out of his gate as she rounded the corner past his place, she noticed he looked tired. Angela felt a little surge of sympathy. It must be awful having to cope with his wife's moods.

"Good morning, Reginald. How are you?"

"Thank you, well enough," he said through nearly closed lips. Perhaps he was beginning to show his age a bit. "To be honest, I'm a little tired of being on tenterhooks over this beastly murder. The police don't seem to be doing anything."

"Oh, but I think there may be progress. Apparently they've found some evidence in the car and are coming back to look at it." This, of course, had gushed out before she could stop it. "I really wasn't supposed to say anything," she added, a little abashed, but he did look miserable and she'd never seen him look like this.

Reginald contemplated this news on the remainder of his walk to the post office. He felt an impending sense of dread, as if every step closer to solving this murder might bring his lapse all those years ago into the light; as if he might learn that he had lost something irreplaceable. At the same time, what he had said to Angela was true: he felt he could not stand the lack of resolution. He wanted, in fact, for the whole thing to be over and for his life to return to normal.

Mather was sullen when he appeared at the post, not five minutes later, and after a cursory and distracted, "Morning," he said, "the Yank tells me the police might be on to something in the car."

Eleanor had to turn quickly to the mail slots behind her to hide an unbidden smile.

"Well, that's what I hear. I don't know what they hope to find. I don't suppose you have any theories?"

Mather frowned at her. "No, why should I? Whole thing's got nothing to do with me. It's a bloody nuisance. Got everyone on edge. We can't be sure of anything, can we, in a small place like this? Woman we know nothing about moves in. God knows what she's bringing in from the outside world. You should never have sold her that house." And with this declaration he left, banging the screen door behind him.

Well, thought Eleanor. That was a bit strong. There was something bothering him that she was certain he wasn't telling. She'd have to tell Lane. Perhaps later this evening they could sit down and assess their work. She went round to the door and looked up the road. No one on the way.

She might have time for a cup of tea, so she put the kettle on the stove. Kenny should be back any minute from the deliveries. Perhaps he'd be calmer and they could have a biscuit and some tea and discuss things. She'd just poured the water into the brown pot when she heard a tractor. Only Harris arriving.

"Morning, Robin. How's tricks?"

"What?" He was going to be difficult. Taciturn at the best of times. She'd have to be direct.

Reaching into the slot for his mail, in this case a copy of a magazine about farm machinery—he never really did get much besides his vet's pension and a few magazines about farming and machinery—she tried to sound nonchalant. "Looks like we might be having of a breakthrough on this case. I heard the police think they've found something in the car and they're coming back out to have a closer look with their instruments."

Harris snorted. "Police! Ha. Couldn't find their way out of a paper bag." He seized his magazine with his big, gnarled hand and left in much the same way Mather had, banging the screen door.

Back in the kitchen, Eleanor put some cookies on a plate, then realized it was nearly lunchtime, set that aside and pulled a loaf out of the bread box. Kenny would be hungry, and a good sandwich might finish the job of settling him down. She thought about the reactions of the three people she'd told. Angela and Harris were pretty typical. He was non-reactive and she was over-reactive. It was Mather that interested her. He really did seem on edge. Had he got something to hide? Kenny's truck rumbled to a stop outside. Hopefully he was in a good enough mood, because really, she'd like to discuss it with him.

"I'm not upset," Kenny defended himself over his sandwich and a mug of tea, "I just think it's a waste of time, and the fact that it is untruthful, well, it shocks me that you would allow yourself to be involved. You've never told a lie in your life."

"I know, it's rather fun," said Eleanor happily.

Kenny gazed at her as if he was seeing her for the first time. A lifetime of rectitude, and now this. "In any case, what is it going to accomplish? It is ludicrous to think any of the old codgers around here bonked a man on the head for no reason. We know everyone. We've known them all since before the Great War. It's ridiculous." He snorted, and finished up his mug of tea with a long slurp. "Thank you. Lovely sandwich."

Eleanor sat, pursing her lips and gazing thoughtfully at a photograph of Pershing, their inter-war Westie. Though her initial reaction to lying was a kind of delight, she had, during the course of Kenny's discourse, wondered if it were entirely a good thing. And of course, there was the question of whom the subterfuge was being aimed at. Who here, really, he was right, would bonk a man on the head and go to such elaborate lengths to place blame on an innocent young woman. They did know everyone, well, except the Bertollis, and honestly, she didn't see how Dave would have been able to extricate himself from that tumbling family long enough to secrete a car in someone's garage and drag a man to the creek exchange. She doubted he even knew where it was. Still . . . and as for Lane, the only other new person in the Cove, it was impossible to imagine it was she. She knew it was no good.

"It isn't just the bonking, though, is it? It's the dragging the body to the weir. An outsider wouldn't know where that was, and then all the elaborate efforts to blame Lane. You'd have to know the lay of the land here, wouldn't you?"

Kenny remained silent at this.

"Still, you make me wonder if it is worth risking my soul on this little subterfuge."

Kenny pulled the napkin out of his collar. "Especially if the whole thing turns dangerous," he mused darkly, and went out to fiddle with his truck.

HARRIS, UPON HEARING the news, drove his tractor into the middle of his upper orchard, the one from which he could see through a birch break to the Winslow woman's upper field, and turned off the engine. The silence gave him a momentary impression of clarity, a sense that he would be able to sit and think this through. He told himself not to overreact. What could they have found? He had gone over the car himself. No. He hadn't—he'd only looked for a suitcase, but hadn't found one. There was absolutely nothing to link the car to him. Anyway, he'd not touched anything, really. It was that bloody idiot. She'd mentioned equipment. Fingerprints? Had he not been wearing his work gloves? He felt a draining fear. He couldn't remember, now, suddenly. Had he touched anything? He tried to review what he'd done. He'd gone into the house and then gone out and driven the car into his barn. He had a vague sense of himself pulling his gloves off, but was that then?

Or after he'd done work earlier in the morning? When had she said they were coming?

Harris turned on his tractor, and, still unclear about a course of action, moved slowly back to his own driveway. He parked the machine in front of the barn and went into his house through his kitchen door. Perhaps it was his state of mental spareness—all his powers of concentration were focused on one question—but he saw for the first time how his place must look to others. Everything was reduced to the barest needs of one man. One small table, two chairs, two cups, no adornment anywhere, not even a calendar on the wall. He scarcely knew what to make of this sudden vision of his own poverty. He sat down and waited.

CHAPTER THIRTY-ONE

LANE LOOKED BACK TOWARD THE forest through which she had come. She was genuinely afraid now. Could she manage to sneak back? She could hear him and was momentarily relieved because it did not sound as if he were coming any closer to where she was hiding. She risked a look over the stump. Harris's tractor was moving somewhere in the distance, giving a momentary sense of normalcy to the situation. Sandy Mather was walking along the edge of the quarry, evidently looking into it. He had his back to her. What was he up to? The fear that he had followed her began to subside, especially as he had come off the path along the road, though the conviction still lingered that he had seen where she was headed and had decided to ambush her by cutting through from the road.

He suddenly straightened up. He must have seen or sensed something was not right. Lane cowered into a ball behind the stump and waited. There was a loud metallic clang, and then an almost musical sound as whatever it was settled. She cursed herself for a coward. He'd thrown something into the quarry! She came out of her crouch and parted the branches to watch him again. He was standing looking into the quarry, and then glanced around. Satisfied, evidently, that he was unobserved, he turned and started back down toward the road. Lane waited until she could no longer hear his receding footfalls on the soft forest floor and then carefully got into a crouched stand. The forest had fallen back into silence, as if no one were there, not even her. Cautiously, she moved back toward the edge of the quarry. It was impossible, she thought, her heart sinking. The quarry was deep, and the layers of old tins, wooden boxes, old farm tools and the growth of small shrubs and grass that had grown over the now-unused dump made it impossible to distinguish what was in it. Why had she ducked just when he was hurling something in?

"Ninny!" she muttered angrily to herself. Finding a soft patch of moss, she sat down. What had he thrown? Even if she found it, she would not be able to retrieve it; that was police work. She would phone Nelson and tell the inspector. He could come out and cut up his knees looking for whatever it was, or more likely he would deputize that poor sweet constable to do it. What if Sandy was just using the dump for its intended purpose? Tossing out an old bit of machinery or some garbage? Darling would not be amused to have to drive all this way for a rusted hoe. A stab of fear woke her from these coy musings. A rusted hoe—a rusted anything could have been the weapon. She was contemplating going back to the edge of the quarry to look again, this time for exactly that sort of tool. The dizzying understanding of what that would mean made her sit back, her heart pumping in fear again. Was it Sandy?

Had he killed the man, dragged him to the creek, and set her up to take the blame? After the episode on the fishing trip, she felt absolutely certain he was capable of violence; she had been badly frightened by him then but had chided herself later, convincing herself it was just an excess of ardour that drove him to be so forceful. She took two deep breaths and told herself not to let her fear run her imagination.

She reviewed her experiences of him. His smooth insinuations at the tea party, his behaviour on the fishing trip, the fact that it seemed to her that he appeared to be popping out at her nearly every time she left her house. The pattern told her that he was perhaps carrying a torch for her. The stark suggestion that he might be the murderer was a leap. Why should he murder a man he'd never met? What was this man to him? Especially if the dead man was related to Mrs. Harris. Still, she was alone in a forest, far from the earshot of any of her neighbours, and though he might not be a murderer, being alone in a forest with him was an unpleasant prospect, given his recent behaviour. A scream would not be heard unless a handy neighbour happened to be right on the stretch of road where the path emerged, and that was a very long shot. People didn't just go up and down the roads in King's Cove for no purpose; the mail, or a trip to the wharf or to town; otherwise people kept to themselves, attending to their orchards and gardens.

Waiting till she heard nothing more than the whispery silence of the forest, she moved to the edge of the quarry and peered in. It was impossible to see what he might have thrown in. It was a large area and the rubbish was so overgrown with ferns that nothing stood out. There was nothing for it. She would have to tell Darling. She might be wrong, but could not take the risk. Knowing now that she believed absolutely that Sandy was the murderer, she started back in the direction she'd come, through the trees and back to the creek. Then she realized that it would be much quicker to go by the old path Sandy had taken. With some trepidation, she followed Sandy's path out to the road. Though the morning was still young, Lane felt she'd just spent a whole day's worth of anxiety in that forest. She turned briskly home for a cup of tea, rehearsing in her mind what she'd say when she telephoned the inspector.

THE CONVICTION GREW in Reginald Mather that the dead man might be the son he'd been warned about in his aunt's letter. What he could not make out was why he had turned up dead here. This man would be a stranger to everyone. Try as he might, Reginald could not imagine the circumstances in which someone arriving at King's Cove looking for him could meet someone who would kill him. First, no one in the community would do it, and secondly, why should they? Thinking like this he very nearly convinced himself that, after all, it could not have been his son. But the fact was that his son had not turned up.

Glancing at the room where Alice slept, or whatever it was she did now—he'd given up trying to work her out, especially when she went into these long withdrawals—he satisfied himself that the door was shut, and he picked up the telephone receiver and listened. It was silent. He dialled and the exchange came on. "What number please?"

"The Nelson police office, please." He was half-whispering.

"I beg your pardon, could you speak up?"

He let out an exasperated breath. "Nelson police, please," he enunciated, trying to keep his voice down.

To his relief she intoned, "One moment please."

In a moment he was speaking to the desk sergeant. Still in a soft voice, he asked to speak to Inspector Darling. He stood, his chest constricting with anxiety, looking out the window. His view gave on to the garden and beyond that, down along the road right past the old schoolhouse, now boarded up. He looked at his watch. It was just after nine. He could get up to town by ten, ten-fifteen.

"Inspector Darling," came a voice.

"Yes, good morning. I . . ." Now that he had the inspector on the phone he suddenly realized he had no idea what he wanted to say, or indeed, what he could say that wouldn't take too long and risk waking Alice. "This is Reg Mather. I wonder if I might come up to see you this morning before your trip out here?" was the best he could do.

"Certainly, sir. May I ask for what purpose?"

"I'll be able to explain that when I get there. It's . . . it's rather important."

He put the phone quietly back in the receiver, and turned. Alice, her hair sticking out around her head from lying on it, stood in front of her open door, looking at him with an expression of such malevolence that he took a step back, banging into the chair by the desk. "Going to explain, are you? I know, you know. I know all about her. I always have. You must have thought I was very, very stupid." With this she turned and went back into her room and slammed the door.

Reginald, his head a whirl, pounded out of the house and up by the barn where he kept the car. What the bloody hell did she mean by that? He tore open the car door, got in and slammed it after himself. His breath came in gasps as if he had run up a long hill. He felt, at that moment, more exposed than he ever had in his life.

BACK IN NELSON, Inspector Darling sat with his hands behind his head, looking at the papers on his desk. He was running out of patience and time with the King's Cove business. Reginald Mather, he thought, had jolly well better be coming in to town to tell him he'd seen the murder happen, or better yet, had done it himself, because without evidence other than that which implicated Lane Winslow, he was stuck. He was even beginning to worry that he'd let her off the hook. All this cloak and dagger stuff with a British secret service officer! It was becoming more and more difficult to believe that there wasn't a murder in among all that. King's Cove had existed for, what, fifty years at least, with a blameless record; he'd checked. No one had killed anyone for land or money in all that time, though one man had died in an accident felling a tree. Yet in swoops a beautiful ex-secret service woman and she's not there ten minutes and a man from the same part of the world and with, as a matter of fact, the same sort of war record, is struck on the head and stuffed into a creek.

Darling groaned. Was it really just as simple as that? He desperately wished it wasn't. And he desperately wished he'd never met Miss Winslow. He could do without that, thanks very much. He stretched and stood up. Now, what would Mather tell him?

"Ames!" he called into the next room. No answer. He put his head around the door, but the small office was empty. He didn't blame Ames for not being there. Heat seemed to accumulate in this small room on the west side of the building, even with the window pushed up. Downstairs he asked at the desk and was told Ames had gone out to get breakfast. He signed out and went to where he was sure he would be. At the café a block down on Baker, he found his constable propped up at the counter grinning like a Cheshire cat at the pretty waitress. Darling felt a diabolical frisson of delight at the thought of interrupting this courtship.

The inspector perused the tatty cardboard menu. "Scrambled," he said to the girl, Daisy, was it? "And a coffee." He felt in a celebratory mood. The Mather call coming out of the blue was the first indication, he hoped, that someone besides Miss Winslow might have something to say.

"Don't flirt on the company's time, Ames. Let this be a lesson to you."

"I believe I have a right to breakfast, sir?"

"You have indeed, but just breakfast. Now listen," he leaned back to allow the lovely Daisy to place his thick mug of coffee in front of him, and then waited till she'd gone out of earshot. "Daisy, is it?" he whispered.

"April." Ames corrected. Overall, he preferred his inspector dour and serious. Levity in Darling, Ames decided, was always at his expense. "Sir."

"Ah. I thought it was something to do with flowers. Now listen, I think we've some luck. That character from the top of the road, Mather, just called. Seemed in a hurry, wants to see me in an hour's time."

"Did he say why, sir?"

"No. In fact he was whispering." Darling's brow contracted. "It seemed as if he was worried about being overheard. In fact he said something peculiar. Something like 'before you come out here.' Why would he think we were coming out?"

"Because we haven't solved the murder, perhaps?" Was there a touch of sarcasm there?

Darling ignored it. "The point is, it's the first time we've got a rise out of one of the locals. Now, it may end up pointing back at the Winslow woman but the hurried, whispered tone suggests something else to me."

Fighting back an urge to inquire if his boss would always be referring to their attractive suspect as "the Winslow woman" even after, he thought with a dizzying leap into improbability, they were married, Ames said, "Well, the one certifiably crazy person among that odd bunch is Mather's wife. Doesn't she go around the Cove shooting things? Perhaps she's involved. Perhaps he saw her do something and decided to come clean. Mind you, if I were married to her I'd come clean to something she hadn't done just to get rid of her."

Darling nodded by way of thanks to the smiling April as she put his scrambled eggs with four triangular wedges of toast before him, and then paused to think. "Yes. I see the possibility. We could leave the 'why' out for a minute.

I think she would be capable of killing someone, but she's a little mad, and she likes to shoot things. Why would she bang someone on the head? Her excuse for the shooting, I shouldn't wonder, would be that she thought she saw a cougar. To bang someone on the head she'd have to see he was not a wild animal."

"Unless the person attacked her," said Ames, suddenly excited. "Let's say she does her cougar routine and the person, afraid, attacks her and she defends herself. Could that bang on his head have been caused by the butt of a rifle?"

"More likely, apparently, the barrel. But the point is taken. Would she move the body? She's a skinny little thing."

"Ah, but that's where our friend Mather comes in. She breaks down and tells him, and he, anxious to cover up how crazy she is, moves it for her. Now he's coming to tell us it was all a dreadful accident."

"What time is he coming, sir?"

"Ten or so. Didn't we spot a 1930 or so Morris in his driveway? It'll take fifty minutes in that thing. Let's make it 10:30."

It was, in fact, 10:10 when the desk sergeant called up to tell Darling that someone called Mather was there to see him. "Put him in the interview room," the inspector said into the receiver, and hanging up, he barked, "Ames. We're on!"

REGINALD MATHER SAT at the small wooden table, which was placed by a window, saving it, he thought, from being the fictional sealed room with the single hanging light bulb. The view was only of the alley, but real sunlight streamed in and diminished, though only somewhat, his anxiety. He was looking up to see if there was a light bulb when the door opened and Darling and Ames stepped in. Mather stood and offered his hand to Darling. They sat opposite each other and Ames pulled out a chair against the wall and sat with his notebook in hand. There was a longish silence.

"In what way can I help you, Mr. Mather? You seemed most anxious on the telephone to share some information you may have about this matter."

"I . . . er . . . yes. I'm here on the outside chance, you see."

"The outside chance of what, sir?"

"Well, that the man who was killed might be, well, known to me. No, I mean, not really, you see, but he might, if you will, be something to me."

"Perhaps you'd better start at the beginning, Mr. Mather. What has made you think you might in some way know this person?"

"No, don't you see, I don't know him, but if I could see him I might, I don't know. It's so dreadful, and with Alice and Sandy behaving so strangely. And then as I was leaving, Alice said she knew. She knew! And of course she would be happy if he were dead, wouldn't she? And so would Sandy. Oh, I never should have said anything to him!"

This string of seeming non sequiturs looked like it was going nowhere. "Ames, could you fetch Mr. Mather a glass of water?" Darling sat with his hands folded on the table while Reginald looked miserably out the window into the alley. He accepted the glass of water when it came, but then only held his hands around the glass, as if to still the trembling.

"Now then, Mr. Mather, take it slowly, and from the beginning," Darling said soothingly.

Reginald Mather took a deep breath, and as he began talking, Alice Mather was stepping out on to the porch of the house she had shared with him for nearly forty years, flicking her walking stick as if to test its soundness, and walking down the stairs.

SANDY PULLED OFF his gloves and stood for a moment in the road. He considered turning left and going to the post office, then realized he would only do that to walk past Lane's house, and he thought bitterly that he needed to stop that. She was a bitch. He'd known that from the beginning. He still could not make out why the police had brought her back. He would, he decided, go home and look at the plans his dad had for the mill. This at least he had secured for them and his father could no longer ignore him. He heard a car going down the back road; it must be near the church now, obviously heading down toward the Nelson road. It took a moment and then he realized it was his father's Morris. His brow wrinkled and he looked at his watch. Where would his father be going at this time? He'd made a run up to town only two days before. Anxiety crept like an unwelcome visitor into Sandy's gut. He turned down toward the post office. That's when he saw her.

THOUGH SHE KNEW the forest to be empty now, Lane had crept toward the opening of the path onto the road. Ferns curved across the unused path and she pushed them aside, thinking for a moment how like walking in England it was, and then she froze. She heard exactly what Sandy had heard, the car progressing down the road from the direction of Angela and David's. She waited, wondering if it was Angela going to the lake with the boys. No, their car was a station wagon; this was a tinnier sound. When it faded, she started again to the road.

About ten yards from the road, she could just see the top of Sandy's head. Blast! Why was he still there? She should have retraced her steps to the creek! Lane watched him nervously. He seemed to be in the grip of indecision. She waited, barely daring to breathe, and with a sudden nod, Sandy turned, not upward as if to return to his own home but downward, toward the post office and, more unnervingly, toward her house. With a muttered prayer to the gods, she waited, suddenly anxious now to be out of there, to be safe back in her own house.

Sandy watched the house from near her metal gate. He told himself not to be an idiot and kept going to the Armstrongs'. He had an excuse now; his father was off out in the car; he could go and get the mail. Just as he reached the turnoff up to the Hughes', he heard the sound of Harris's tractor behind him. He waited, that anxiety he'd felt at hearing his father's car leaving King's Cove now back. He had a vague sense that he did not have control of events and it was making him jumpy. He must calm down. Nothing unusual in Harris on his tractor at this time of day. He'd be going to his orchard. Adjacent, Sandy thought triumphantly, to the stretch of forest Harris had ceded to him for the mill.

Harris lumbered up and stopped, the engine chugging, and looked at Sandy. "I suppose you heard."

"Heard what?" That stomach-churning fear again.

"There's something in the car. The police are coming out again."

Sandy looked nervously back toward the direction of Lane's barn. "How the hell do you know that?"

"Armstrong said. It's supposed to be hush-hush. What did you do, you infernal whelp?" Harris slipped the tractor angrily into gear. "And now . . . never mind." He started up the hill, and Sandy could hear Harris spit out the word "Idiot!" as he watched him grinding up the hill, the back of his faded work shirt and overalls a contemptuous dismissal.

LANE SAW SANDY leave her gate and go toward the post office. With that relief that comes of nearly being safely home, she ran as quietly as she could down the road to the gate, left the road, and pushed the gate open. She had just done this when she stopped to listen. She could hear the sound of the tractor from the direction of the Hughes' on the hill. Harris, on his way to the upper orchard. She started down the path, the tall grass brushing along her legs as she passed her barn, but stopped again. The tractor had stopped. She was no expert, and certainly had not been here long enough to know the patterns of the daily comings and goings; nevertheless, it seemed strange that the tractor had started up and then so quickly stopped.

It was only when she was pushing open her door that she finally heard the tractor start up again. It was closer than she had thought, maybe at the bottom of the road from the Hughes', where the road divided. The gears ground as he turned the corner, and then the noise began to recede.

Lane washed her hands in the kitchen and poured herself an enormous glass of water. She was surprised to see that her hand shook slightly. She wanted to run upstairs and look at her map again but she thought she should phone the inspector.

A nervous frisson shook her as she stood in front of the phone. Her ridiculous strategy of trying to trap the murderer by putting it about that there was a clue in the car—now that the police were coming back, she could see it for what it was. Dangerous nonsense. Now, having seen Sandy by the old garbage dump, she realized that if she'd trusted to events, a real clue would have come along. Of course, this might not be anything. She shouldn't let her mistrust of Sandy lead her to cast aspersions on him. She could imagine an outraged Sandy, in the full knowledge that she had phoned the police about him. He would be unbearable and she would be stuck in this tiny community with him as a constant neighbour. And then her thinking went the full circle. Her instinctive distrust of him was right and she knew that everything might be of significance.

In the hallway, cast in shadow against the morning light pouring in the front door, she stood in front of her phone and rehearsed what she would say. The line was silent when she picked it up, no one on the party line, so she turned the crank and waited for the operator. "Yes, Nelson police station, please," she said. The phone clicked as the call was being put through. Lane leaned against the wall as she waited. It was very unrestful to talk on this phone, she thought. You had to face the trumpet so you could neither sit down when you used the phone, nor even lean against the wall once you had someone on the line. The romance of its antiquity was wearing off. She should get a proper phone.

"Nelson police," said an officious voice.

"Inspector Darling, please." She waited another long few minutes, aware now of a crick in her back, probably from squatting in the bushes spying on that blasted Sandy. When Darling came on the line, she studiously avoided thinking anything particular about the timbre of his voice, though it had a kind of deep resonance she had earlier found pleasant.

"Inspector. I wonder if you will be out this way?" This sounded a bit wet, but she hoped he would see through it.

"I will, as a matter of fact." He paused. "It is not the first time today this has been suggested to me."

He sounded . . . something . . . cross? Could he have found out about her subterfuge with Eleanor? She felt her face flush, and it seemed clear to her now that she was a first-class idiot for doing it when he'd said not to. "No. It's . . . it's the raspberries. I've planted them. I thought you might like to see them." Now they, or she at least, were being ridiculous, but she could not risk the party line.

There was another brief silence, and then. "An hour and a half, say? I have another interesting variety. Perhaps I'll bring that along as well." She exhaled slowly, relieved. He had understood.

Unless the operator at the exchange in Balfour told all and sundry what calls were being put through to whom, thought Lane, they should be okay if anyone had picked up their receiver during this little conversation. Heartened by not being told off by Darling, and wondering with delicious curiosity what new information he had, she forgave her ancient telephone and, banishing all thought of a lovely, sparkling new instrument intruding perhaps on the sanctity of her sitting room, or taking up space in the kitchen, she climbed the stairs to the attic. She had an hour and a half to figure out why Sandy, if it were he, might have wanted to kill a complete stranger.

ALICE CHOSE NOT the road but the old path that had been used by the Cove's children when they were young and visited each other's houses. It ran behind the fields and along the base of the hill that loomed behind their house and climbed gently until it attained the higher reaches of the fields behind the Hughes' hilltop farm. She knew where Harris would be at this time in the late morning; he worked his upper orchard with that damn noisy tractor. The orchard that Reg had been aching to get off him because it butted up against a good chunk of forest that he dreamed of logging. Dreaming. That was Reg. Her walking cane tangled in the long grass nearly obscuring the now-unused path, and she swished at it impatiently, like a farmer with a scythe.

Somewhat out of breath, she reached the top of the hill, and looked through the neatly planted apple trees. She couldn't see Harris's tractor, but in that moment, a sudden silence told her he'd turned it off, perhaps to have a bite. It was funny, she grumbled to herself, how a steady noise sinks into the background and you didn't notice it till it stopped. She could remember the blessed relative silence of the men using horses to plow their little fields; it was probably the reason they went to apples. Too much work for them. She made her way down the rows until she spotted the yellow tractor at the edge of the field.

Harris was perched on the shaped metal seat with a sandwich in his hand and a thermos of tea at his feet. He was chewing as if he was only given five minutes for lunch, gulping back the food with washes from his thermos. He didn't hear Alice until she was practically upon him and he nearly jumped when he saw her.

"What are you doing here?" he barked.

Alice banged the tractor tire with her cane. "Get off that thing," she demanded, "I've got something to say to you." Seeing that she wasn't actually armed made him feel slightly safer, but he nevertheless got down on the opposite side, so as to keep the tractor between them. "I know what Reg has been up to. He's been at it with your wife."

Harris frowned at her. This declaration was disorienting and he struggled to place what it meant. He looked around, he wasn't sure why, perhaps in the hopes of seeing someone else so he would not have to deal with her alone. He wasn't sure how to respond. Finally he said, "Alice, I don't have a wife. Haven't had one for nearly thirty years. Left me. Remember? '17 or '18."

Alice's face clouded momentarily, and she looked down at the ground. "I've seen the letter," she said. "I've seen the letter," she repeated more strongly, as if on surer footing. "That's why she left. They'd been at it. That trollop of yours."

Harris swallowed, his mouth working. He was beginning see what she might mean, and with it came a dawning, hollow sense of rage. "What are you saying? That they . . . while I was at the front? When? Are you crazy? What letter are you talking about?"

"I've seen it, see. He was out, probably visiting the trollop, and I saw the letter about the baby. Yesterday. It was on his desk."

Feeling like he was going mad, Harris tried to sort out the time scheme. She was obviously mixing up times, memories.

He'd had no idea she was this far gone. Did it mean there was a letter? There must have been; she wouldn't come all the way up here unless there was. He focused on that.

"Alice, tell me about the letter. What did it say?"

"It said that his bastard was going to come here, looking for Reg."

She'd gone then; turned on her heel and walked back through the trees, swinging that cane. She had a vigour that belied the shaky grip she had on reality. Reg, he thought, had better be careful: she could get ugly and she was still strong. Left in the silence, Harris, unused to any complex feelings to deal with, now had what felt like a landslide in him. He leaned forward with both hands on the tractor and put his head down, as if this might steady his insides. He had no coherent thoughts, but only flashes of pictures. Himself in a trench and his wife's letter in his pocket. She'd only sent one. He'd been ashamed somehow when he'd gotten it. The other fellows got letters from home full of love and tales of how the children were doing, or how much their sweethearts missed them. Hers had been two pages of cramped and juvenile handwriting complaining, as if, he thought, he'd started the war himself to make her life miserable. She was alone, she couldn't cope with all the work, no one helped her, how could he leave her to try to manage on her own?

He chewed on the idea of a letter. From Elizabeth? From Reg? From whom? He regretted now that he'd chosen to deal with Alice by not responding in the hopes that she'd take her madness and go away. Was this a letter from the past, or a letter from right now? She had rolled time all together, and he could not sort what was when. Then he moved to her last statement. "It said that bastard was going to come here, looking for Reg."

His next thought made him feel lightheaded, and he crumbled slowly to the ground, and sat, trying to get his breath. He looked up the row of trees, in the direction Alice had gone, and wondered who else she might tell.

THE ATTIC WAS cool because Lane had opened windows on both sides of the room, and a breeze was blowing through. She was sitting with her back against a sealed crate. Perhaps, she thought, when all this was over, she'd get at some of the boxes. She couldn't even imagine now what they could contain that she'd want, she was so used to living in the simplicity of just having the bare minimum around her. The map lay before her, and she wanted to draw other things on it. A suitcase, for example. The dead man must have had one. The murder weapon, which had still not been found. The other shoe. It now felt like days since she'd set off to find the shoe, though it was a matter of a few hours. In her heart, as she looked at the card with Sandy's name on it, she believed it was him. It was all over but the arresting, she thought, and Darling was probably forty minutes away. Her map had had its day. But it was all very unsatisfactory, she thought. She hated guessing. She wanted to know, to have solid proof. Why would Sandy kill Franks? Well, for that matter, why would anyone? There were only two possibilities about this death that might, but only might, suggest some sort of motive. One was that Franks had been an agent of the British government, had blotted his copybook somehow, and been done in by some shadowy agent who'd long since left, and the second, highly speculative, was that Franks had been Elizabeth Harris's son, if the similarities in the photo were to be believed. But neither of those led directly to Sandy. She sat up. Could Elizabeth Harris have been pregnant with Franks when she left here? She did a quick rough calculation, and saw that she could have been. That suggested someone here had made her pregnant. It was 1916 or 17. Who were the eligible candidates? Kenny Armstrong? She thought not, but struggled to keep him on her list, just to be fair. One shouldn't jump to conclusions simply because one liked someone. Reginald Mather. Mather! Mather who had helped Elizabeth get through the winters while Harris was gone. Hadn't Mabel and Gwen said as much? So Franks is making a pilgrimage to find his father, only for some inexplicable reason, he ends up dead before he even finds him. She couldn't see how just yet, but this way of looking at it brought Sandy a little more into the frame. After all, Franks is potentially suddenly promoted from rank outsider to Sandy's brother. But was he the one? Was she overreacting to the business of Sandy being in the forest? Perhaps he'd just thrown out garbage. He did creep about. Was he violent enough to kill someone? He could, she supposed, have had his way with her on that ghastly fishing trip when she rejected his ridiculous proposal. But even in the midst of that incident, she had felt in her heart that what Sandy really was, was pathetic. Could that make him a killer?

But what about Harris? He too, suddenly, began to come into focus as a potential. After all, Elizabeth had betrayed Harris, let's say with Mather. This thought made her stand up and wander across the room to look out her window toward the barn, as if looking outside would open new avenues in her mind. She felt a flush of guilt and anxiety. Though she hadn't told Darling on the phone whom she suspected, she was unnerved by the idea that she might be wrong. She would hate to have made him drive all the way here, when even now she had talked herself into not only seeing Sandy as the man they were looking for, but potentially implicating Harris as well. And why not Mather while we are at it? Perhaps the sudden appearance of a son he didn't know about and didn't want would be extremely inconvenient to him.

And there was the matter of how Franks was killed. Should she be going at it from that angle first, instead of trying to pin it on someone right away? He was hit with a hard, probably metallic object and then, very likely, moved and pushed into that awkward position in the creek, where he died of drowning. It is a fairly elaborate way to get rid of someone, she thought. It speaks of it being unplanned, spontaneous. Someone, say Sandy, gets into an argument with Franks and hits him with . . . the business end of rifle? No, that's not very natural. If you were going to use a rifle to hit someone instead of using it to shoot them, you'd likely drive the butt end of it into a head. If done thoroughly enough, the killer would not have had to resort to drowning. Or did the killer think he'd done the job and was simply trying to get rid of the body?

She wondered how often people would go and check the weir. If it was once or twice a year, it was possibly a reasonable place to hide a body. Could the killer not simply have driven the body down to the lake and heaved it in? Eventually the body might fetch up considerably higher up the lake, carried by the quite powerful river that ran through the middle of the lake. It could have been washed up on a completely deserted shore and never have been found or, if found, it would never have been associated with King's Cove. It would be dismissed as a drowning, resulting from a fall off a cliff or a boat. Did the killer panic and take the first alternative that presented itself? Or did the killer think through the whole thing and deliberately put Franks into the weir. But why? And then, somehow, all the bits and pieces started coming together. Who had been blamed immediately? She had. The paper with the name found in Frank's pocket, the car mysteriously ending up in her garage. Even the fact that the body was in the weir that fed into her property. She felt herself blanch. The killer had targeted her. He wanted her to be arrested. That, without a doubt, pointed at Sandy. He was still furious at her rejection of him. She shuddered at the kind of obsessive arrogance one would have to have to take such revenge on someone.

Well, I've added to the number of possibles, I suppose, she thought, now weary. She hadn't explored the British agent angle. Funnily, they'd be the most likely suspects, if Franks had gotten into some sort of trouble. Angus Dunn hadn't said anything and seemed genuinely puzzled when he identified the body, but he was a master of deceit. She flushed angrily. First Angus and then Sandy. Were there no decent men around? And finally, of course, lest she forget her recent humiliation, there was her very own self, and she had never made contact with him at all before someone had bumped him off. She sighed. At least she knew she hadn't done it. She paced and then leaned back against the window. She would be glad when Darling got there. She wanted to talk through her thinking with him.

She glanced at her watch. Nearly two. She should go down and put the kettle on, but was stopped dead in her tracks, because at that moment she heard a noise through the open window. Suddenly nervous, she stood with her back to the wall between two windows and breathed. There was the sound again. A scraping noise. She risked a quick look into the yard. The near door to the barn was open. So soon! She moved away from the window, her heart banging. She should wait and see who it was. The scraping sound again. With utmost care she turned again to look carefully through the window. Sandy. She heard, and simultaneously felt, a loud crack and a shower of glass. She threw herself to the floor. He had a rifle, and he'd seen her.

CHAPTER THIRTY-TWO

ANOTHER SHOT, THIS TIME EMBEDDING itself somewhere in the wall of her house. She manoeuvred herself to the door on her hands and knees, trying to avoid shards of glass. She must telephone someone. Who? Darling would have left and been on his way. Kenny. No. It would put him in danger if Sandy was running mad with a rifle. Having reached the stairs, she dashed down them, made for the phone in the hallway, and then crouched down in a hurry. Her glass-panelled front door would allow anyone outside to see in. Lane felt a little silly about ducking about in her own hallway in this dramatic fashion. With anxious looks toward the outside, she found Mather's number on the wall and, willing her hands not to shake, she turned the handle; three longs.

"KC 283," she heard.

"Reginald, Lane. Listen . . ." But the line disconnected.

REGINALD HAD ONLY been back ten minutes and had found Alice gone. Now the phone. He shouted, "Hello! Hello!" But he could hear nothing. He slung the receiver back on the phone with another epithet, and strode out the front door, banging it pointedly. He'd heard shots. He knew it must be someone phoning about Alice again. How had she found the rifle? He went into the barn and reached above the door where he'd hidden it after the incident at the Bertollis'. Gone. He looked around, puzzled. How had she gotten it? She'd have needed the ladder, which was in the shed. Alice could never have moved it. He looked quickly around; a chair? And where was bloody Sandy? He usually handled this sort of business with Alice. She seemed to be more docile with him.

He was about to get into the car when the next sound made him stop. It was Alice, calling him from behind the house. He hurried out and around the side of the house. There she was, looking querulous, wanting something. She looked as though she'd been out, an unusual circumstance lately, but she was here now. The relief of this was quickly overshadowed by the next thought. Someone was shooting down the road, near the post office. Who had his rifle and where was Sandy? He had arrived home from Nelson feeling like his insides had been hollowed out. There seemed no doubt that the dead man must be his son. His resemblance to Elizabeth was too striking. It was somehow apt, he thought, as he backed his car, still warm from the trip to town, that the whole world should be upended at this moment, for certainly, his had been.

LANE TOOK A couple of breaths. There'd not been a shot for a few minutes. That was good. But it didn't answer the question of where Sandy would be now. The ringing of the phone startled her, and then she realized it was her number. Praying for she knew not what, Lane picked up the receiver.

"King's Cove . . ." she began but she got no further. She felt something hard pressed into her neck.

"Put that down," commanded a quiet voice. Sandy's quiet voice. Reaching her hand slowly toward the hook, she replaced the earpiece and waited, her heart in her mouth.

He came alongside her and, leaning the rifle against the wall, he pulled her two hands behind her and tied them, she couldn't see with what. It felt like a scarf of some sort. He kept her facing away from him, her head turned uncomfortably and pressed against the wall. Then he took up the rifle and pointed it under her chin.

"Sandy, what . . ."

"Ah!" he cautioned, "I'll do the talking, don't you think? That's the trouble with women since the war. Thinking they're in charge. You want a strong man to take charge of you, don't you? You missed your chance. You could have had me but you were too good for me."

He was sounding mad, Lane thought, ranting, like he had in the car. Maybe ranting was as far as he was going to go. But no. He'd been shooting. He'd seen her in the attic. He had been trying to shoot her. Her eyes swung toward the front door as if she could locate him back out there, still firing at her. He'd been in the barn, looking at the car. She'd been right. It was Sandy. She tried to calm herself, to look again toward the window.

"Don't bother. There's no one there to rescue you. I was just out there, or did you miss me? I know I missed you! I thought I'd better come in and not risk missing again.

Perhaps you would have been happier with that man who came here, eh? One of your own kind. I saw his identification. But you know that, don't you? British. Probably had a fancy accent. Mind you, I didn't get to hear it. That idiot Robin heard it. He had your name in his pocket, like he was looking for you. A boyfriend, was he?"

Lane shook her head in confusion, little convulsive movements, and found Sandy had moved so that he could look into her eyes. She tried to imagine what she could see there; fear? Anger? Triumph? She'd read somewhere during her service that the impulse to kill broke down when you could make a personal human connection with the enemy; look into someone's eyes, see the common humanity. It hadn't worked in occupied France. It didn't seem to be working now. He was staring into her eyes, and she could detect only his obsession with himself. She could see in his eyes the cold calculation that she, in a way she could not yet fathom, was an impediment he needed to rid himself of. And what did he mean, Robin had heard Frank's accent? Somewhere in her head, her brain was carrying on trying to understand the implications of what Sandy was saying. What she couldn't understand was why he was there with her. Why did he want to kill her? He'd said she knew he'd seen Franks' identification.

It couldn't have been long, but already her hands and shoulders were beginning to hurt from the unnatural position he'd forced them into. She waggled her hands to test how tightly they were bound. A faint hope. She could feel no play whatsoever in her wrists. What had he used?

He shook her violently. "I'll let you know when you can

close your eyes, Miss Winslow. Indeed, I will close them for you when the time comes. In the meantime, why don't you tell me about this dashing lover who came looking for you?" He leaned in at these last words, whispering them into her ear. She could feel his breath. Why would he have connected the stranger with her? Of course; the paper with her name.

"I don't know anything about him," she ventured, her voice feeling unfamiliar to her.

"Funny. He knew about you." He let this rest in the stultifying heat of the passageway. Lane could feel sweat sliding from under her hair and down her neck.

"Sandy, did you . . ."

"No, no, no. I ask the questions here. I thought I made that clear." He laughed. "Anyway, I'm just pulling your leg. I know he wasn't your lover. You're too cold for that sort of thing. In fact, I know who he was. He was my dear old father's other son. Now isn't that something?"

So, it was true and Sandy had found out. Then why was he turning on her?

"You'll be wondering how I know this. You'll be wondering how he ended up dead. In fact, it's your bloody wondering that's caused all the problems. This whole thing is your fault."

"Sandy, I don't know what . . ."

"Ah . . . please, no denials. I know you think you worked it out. You followed me in the forest. Yes, you're surprised that I saw you."

He must have seen her coming out of the forest from the quarry, followed her and watched her make the call to the Nelson police station, and she hadn't known. Some spy she was, she thought ruefully. At the same time she could feel the gun at her neck. Would he use it? Could he? Lane wondered if she could keep him talking . . . until what? Perhaps the house agent was right, she should have bought a nice little place in town. Then at least someone would hear if she screamed.

Sandy shook her again like a naughty child. "Come now; I want to know how you worked it out." Everything she said seemed to irritate him. He was looking for a specific answer. He would not be satisfied until he had it but she hadn't got an answer. She felt a surge of rage. His bloody vanity! He had to know, because it was inconceivable to him that he could have made a mistake. He really was quite mad, she thought, her rage contracting into a ball of fear.

UP THE HILL, at the Hughes' house, the nearly religious observance of a regular lunchtime had been complied with and Mrs. Hughes was heaving herself out of her chair to return to the garden. Misunderstanding her intention, her youngest daughter, Gwen, rose quickly and said, "Don't bother, Mummy, I'll take care of the tea things." Mabel, the elder, was already in the kitchen seeing to the bread.

Scooping everything on to a lacquered tray, Gwen scarcely listened to her mother's retorted, "I was going to see to the lupines, if you must know."

Gwen was feeling a degree of rebellion. The electricity in the garage had been on the blink and she'd been finding it a confounded nuisance, for that was where she enjoyed her one little indulgence, wood turning, and it was too dark, even on a summer's day. She was going to phone Robin and get him to come along and look at the wiring. Of course her mother and sister laughed at her, but they didn't mind eating salad out of the bowl she had turned for them! She picked up the phone and was annoyed to find someone was on the line. Gingerly she hung up so that whoever it was might not think she was listening. As she washed the dishes, it occurred to her that she had not immediately heard who it was. There were only two possibilities: the Armstrongs or that new woman, Miss Winslow. Neither of them seemed, as far as she could tell, prone to long chatting. She'd try again in a few minutes.

The dishes upended in the drying rack, and the dish mop wrung out and hung, Gwen went into the hallway again. She had a frisson of annoyance that Mabel was now in the spare room, just off where the telephone was hanging, and seemed to be sorting through piles of mothballed clothes. As soon as Gwen picked up the receiver, Mabel popped her head around the door. "Who are you calling?" she said, but Gwen ignored her.

With the instrument against her ear, she could tell that the phone was still engaged, but it was strange, because the voices seemed to be coming from far away. A male voice. "I'll do the talking," it said. She heard no answer, and in a few seconds, something else, though she couldn't quite make it out.

"Gwenny, you shouldn't be listening to other people's conversations," Mabel said to her. "The whole democracy of this place depends on . . ." but Gwen did something unthinkable, she waved her hand frantically to shush her sister.

Mabel frowned, and advanced toward the phone. "What . . ."

This time Gwen put her hand on the speaking device and said, very quietly and deliberately, "Shh! Please."

The voice was louder now, and Gwen could hear more distinctly. ". . . you'll be wondering how he ended up dead . . ." said the voice. It sounded strident, boastful even. Who was it? There was another long silence.

With her hand still covering the phone, she whispered, "I think there's something wrong. I think . . ." and then she suddenly understood what she thought: "I think someone has their phone off the hook, and they don't know it."

"Yes, well, that doesn't give you the right to listen in. What do you mean something's wrong, anyway?"

"Shh," whispered Gwen once more, and closed her eyes to hear better.

What she heard made her go pale and feel faint. "Sandy, please . . ."

This voice Gwen knew, by its very strangeness to her. She carefully hung up the earpiece, praying that the click would not be audible.

"Mabel, I think Miss Winslow is in trouble and I think Sandy Mather is with her. We've got to do something."

"What are we going to do? We can't telephone anyone."

"Let's go down to Kenny!" Gwen said decisively and hurried to the mudroom to put on her boots. "Come on! There's no time to lose."

Mabel, following her sister in some confusion, said,

slipping into her own boots, "But Kenny can't phone anyone either; he's on the same line as we are!"

"Yes, but he's a man. He'll know what to do."

Mabel stifled a "Ha!" to this last observation and together they descended from their hill along the winding verdant path to the Armstrongs', both of them thinking grimly that they wouldn't be at all surprised if Sandy Mather were up to no good.

PULLING IN TO the gas station at Balfour, Ames was retaining a dignified silence. Any word he said would break the dam and unleash a torrent of recrimination from Darling, he knew. Fred Bales, the proprietor, came out of the shop, wiping his hands on the back of his pants. He leaned down to peer at Ames. "Fill up?"

"Yes please," Ames answered, keeping his gaze on the road next to the station. It was three miles to King's Cove, and he could not wait to get there. Being crammed, for that is how it felt when his boss was in this sort of mood, into the car with Darling for the length of the drive, had been an ordeal. He had meant to gas up the car, but how was he to know there would be this imperious summons to bolt up the lake on a moment's notice? There were other crimes in the district, and he had been attending to them. The robbery of the tobacconist from the night before, for example, which had tied him up for most of the day, since the shopkeeper had been certain, incorrectly, as it transpired, who the culprit was.

Darling, for his part, knew his power was in not speaking. In any case, he would not have known what to say.

He only knew that he had to be in the Cove at once, and the agonizing fifty minutes on the road, followed by the revelation that they were nearly out of gas, had thrown him into an explosive humour. The tension had begun in town, when he had tried, over a period of an hour, to reach Ms. Winslow on the telephone to tell her he was leaving later than he'd planned. The final time he had been certain she picked up the receiver, but no one had answered his anxious, "Miss Winslow? Is that you?" repeated several times. Of course he knew it was the fault of the rickety phone she had, but it had filled him with an urgency he could not explain, which added a savage edge to his order to Ames to get them to the Cove as quickly as possible.

Now they were parked in front of the gas pump in Balfour, waiting for Fred Bales to come back with their change. In the interim, an elderly woman with a shopping basket on her arm and a brown scarf tied around her head had gone into the shop. No doubt Bales was attending to her, thought Darling. Dear God! He pushed open the car door and strode to the shop just as Bales was coming out the door. They nearly collided.

"Did you want something else, sir?" asked the proprietor, surprised.

"Just my bloody change, thank you," and, seeing the slightly wounded look on Bale's face, Darling added, "We're on police business." He took the proffered change and leaped back into the car. A car went by on the road, kicking up a cloud of dust. Shutting the door quickly, Darling barked, "Now get a move on!"

"Sir, I think that's a rental from Nelson. In fact, it almost . . ." but he was cut off.

"I am, as always, astounded by your powers of observation, Ames. Now that we have identified the various motorcars on the road, perhaps you could get us on to it and up to the Cove sharpish?"

"Sir," said Ames.

"WHAT I MEAN, Sandy," Lane had lowered her voice and was trying to force some sort of soothing quality into it. "What I mean is, I think you were very clever because I hadn't worked it out. I hadn't worked it out at all." They had moved to the bedroom just off the hall from the phone. This turn of events had really frightened her but all he had done was throw her roughly to the floor so that she could sit up leaning against the bed. He must have been as tired as she was of the uncomfortable tableau they made leaning awkwardly against the wall. The bedroom was the nearest room. He had taken her vanity chair and he sat on it now, the gun in the crook of his arm, still pointing unnervingly at her. She was more comfortable, but she cursed inwardly that they were so far from the telephone. It was a long shot, anyway. She didn't know if the phone had latched all the way down, or had stuck, leaving the line open as it usually did. Someone would have to pick up their phone, try to make a call, hear the line was engaged, and perhaps even hear bits of this mad conversation. No one had come bursting through the door to rescue her. There would be no chance, now that they were out of earshot.

Sandy's expression didn't change, but she felt a slight, nearly imperceptible shift in the atmosphere. Then she immediately doubted this. In the war she hadn't thought twice, hadn't second-guessed herself. She'd trusted her instincts immediately. She'd never had time to think. It had been too long. Her wartime sangfroid had deserted her. But he really did seem slightly less belligerent with his next question; indeed, almost petulant.

"Why were you following me?"

"I wasn't following you at all. I'd gone back to the creek to try to work out what had happened and I saw the path on the other side of the weir. It looked overgrown, but I wanted to see where it led. I'd found the quarry with all the old rubbish in it and then I heard something . . . you . . . and hid." She was going to stop there, wondering what else she ought to say and then she said, trading on her earlier instinct, "You must have been astonishingly quiet when you were following me. I didn't have a clue."

Her captor smirked. "I'm good at that. I can go anywhere in these forests like an Indian. I know all the secret places." They sat in silence for some moments. She didn't want to encourage any meditation on any secret places in the forest, in case he devised a plan that ended with her being dumped in one of them. She plunged ahead.

"It must have been really shocking to find your father had another son." She was about to add that that was the real thing she'd worked out, because the dead man had looked so much like his mother, but then she worried she would anger him. In his unstable frame of mind it was best if he were in charge of the conversation.

"Nothing my father would do shocks me. But I was pretty mad when I found out about him. I know he was planning to put him in my place. He's a bastard. That's why Harris and my dear old father hate each other. I always thought it was the land that Harris wouldn't sell, but it was because my father had a go at Harris's wife when he was away in the war."

"Are you sure Harris knew about this affair?"

"Of course he knew. My mother knew. That's how I found out. If she knew, he must have. See, that's another thing. My mother is as crazy as a loon. He did that to her. It drove her crazy when she found out. But you know what, dearie? We aren't going to be led down the garden path by you. I want to know why you did this to me!"

Now Lane was genuinely puzzled. What had she done? Or what did he think she had done? She wanted to say "I don't know what you mean" again, and then thought he'd become angry, and she was hoping to calm him down while she thought of a plan. "Sandy, what I don't understand is, why did you kill him? You really don't believe your father would have put you aside for him, do you?" She hoped he wouldn't detect that she was trying another garden path. Anything to keep him talking. To her horror he suddenly sobbed.

"That's the whole point, you stupid cow! I didn't kill him! Harris did. He hit him with his bloody tractor iron; it was hard enough to fell a bull. All I did was get rid of the body. But you, you stupid, miserable, bitch, you've been trying to pin it on me! Me!" Lane lay back and shut her eyes. Harris had hit Franks, then, but Sandy had put him in the creek. She mustn't say the man had died of drowning. She had to keep him talking. "Sandy, look, this is silly. Why do you think I was trying to pin it on you? If you didn't kill the man, then why all this? It's completely unnecessary and if the police . . . well . . . this sort of thing wouldn't help your case at all."

KENNY ARMSTRONG FURROWED his brow, and then wiped it with his handkerchief. "Are you quite sure, Gwen?"

"Of course I'm sure. Go listen to it yourself!" Kenny moved toward the screen door into the front of the house. He'd been under the hood of his new truck. Not that it needed his attention, but he liked being under the hood, sniffing that new engine smell, and fondly wiping away bits of oil.

Eleanor came to the door and threw it open. "Whatever is the matter? You two don't usually clop down here at this time of day in your wellies."

"They think Miss Winslow is in trouble. They think Sandy is with her and . . . what do you think he's doing?" He turned and addressed this to the two maiden ladies.

"I think I heard him threatening her. On the phone, you see. It wasn't hung up properly on her end, and I could hear voices."

Eleanor bolted out of the cottage. "Well, what are you doing standing around?" And she began to walk quickly up the road to the path that would take them to Lane. At that moment, they heard a car changing gear on the uphill just before the fork in the road. They could hear it turn and come down the hill. "That will be the police, maybe. Did one of you call them? That shows some foresight, anyway." But she didn't wait to hear the answer.

AMES TURNED OFF the road to Miss Winslow's driveway, but there was already a car there. "I could swear it is that rental motor that passed us," Ames remarked.

"Something very odd seems to be going on." Darling pushed past Ames and around the gate, striding briskly past the barn and toward the house. But he stopped and turned back. The barn doors were flung open. Had she gone ahead and told that lie about them coming back to inspect the car? As he neared it, the west side of the house came into view, and he stopped as if hit by a jackhammer. "What the bloody, bloody hell is he doing here?" he said grimly under his breath. Ames shook his head. There, peering into the window of what must surely be Miss Winslow's bedroom, was Dunn, who should, by all rights be back in Britain by this time.

"Get down!" Dunn hissed in a loud stage whisper. Ames and Darling scuttled behind him and crouched below the window. "She's in there with some idiot and he has a gun. I'm certain from the way the conversation is going that he was the one who killed our agent, Franks. We mustn't startle him." He looked back and then swore. "They've gone. Why the devil have you turned up here? Now I've lost sight of what is happening!"

Darling, who was pretty certain that he was the one who should be doing all the why-the-devilling here, took command. "They haven't left the house. Ames, take the veranda; I suspect they will have gone into the hall, if he is planning to take her out of the house, or the kitchen. I'll go in the front door. Maybe you could make yourself useful and keep him from escaping out the window," he added crossly to Dunn.

HARRIS HAD SAT still, watching Alice trudging away from him through the orchard and back on to the road. It dawned on him that he didn't know her at all. She was just Mad Mather. Perhaps that is the way everyone thought of him as well: Mad Harris. Well, he had plenty of bloody reason and maybe she did too. Elizabeth. What madness was in his young self that had made him take up with her? He could barely remember now what he must have been like at twenty or twenty-one. He'd seen her . . . where? At the feed store in town? Possibly. She was a dishevelled little thing, her poverty and misery written in her drab clothes and unbrushed hair. But she had some wild energy about her. He remembered his face flaming up as he watched her throwing a bag of oats onto her father's wagon. Something in her physicality, he decided. How had he courted her? He was cheerful and he remembered she laughed. He didn't recall that they went to the pictures. He wasn't even sure there were pictures before the war. Maybe they'd eaten at the soda fountain. Had he had any warning? She was pleasant enough at first. She was used to work, but she'd said she didn't want children. She would never go with him into town after they were married, in case she met her father there; she hated him, venomously, furiously. Then Harris had gone to the war and whatever he had been was burned away at the front. He had been fearful of coming home to her, that much he did remember, and when he finally made it home, her being gone and the land burned to a crisp around them all, in a way, seemed fitting. The whole world he'd known, seared away, but now, suddenly, here it was.

Unbidden, there suddenly sprang up a picture of Reginald Mather and Elizabeth in bed. His bed, no doubt, as Alice would have been back up the hill in Reginald's. The Reginald he saw moving his hands over the body of his young wife was today's Reginald, older; sleeping with the last Elizabeth Harris he ever saw. It was grotesque, and he shivered. Rage was growing in him slowly, like coals catching fire. All at once the life he had constructed out of the nothing that remained him all those years ago after the Great War revealed itself to him in its stark truth: empty, lonely, a terrible gulf between him and anyone else. He got off his tractor to crank it, and looked at the crank, amazed that he had forgotten what he'd done to that boy. He felt a wave of fear sweep over him and he dropped the crank into the grass. His hands were shaking as he picked it up. But it wasn't this one, was it? Sandy had taken the other one. He said he'd take care of things. Just like his bastard of a father then. He'd been taking care of things, all those years ago, too.

He could see Mather in the car, beginning to back it away from the barn. Mather would see him when he turned around. He could wait. He'd waited nearly thirty years, not knowing, not understanding, losing every last thing, and Mather had kept quiet and devoted himself to trying to get him to give up his land for that filthy lumber mill, as if, once he'd taken from him and gotten away with it, he would be easy pickings. That bloody boy had finally achieved what his father never could. He uttered a mirthless laugh. Mather had backed down the driveway without seeing the tractor until he was practically upon it. He shook his head uncomprehendingly, looking back toward the house, where Alice was now standing at the door, watching them. He half got out of the car.

"What the bloody hell are you doing here?" he finally managed.

"You screwed my wife?" Harris said, not really a question, he realized.

Mather looked toward Alice and back again at Harris.

Harris advanced, devouring the ground between them with his strides. "You slept with my wife while I was up to my withers in blood in France. You were here, cozy and warm, 'helping' my wife. And then, when you put her up the spout you made her disappear." Mather had backed away and now stood on the other side of his Morris.

Harris looked around wildly and his eyes lit on a heavy metal-tined rake leaning against a wooden wheelbarrow. He seized it and slammed it down on the car, denting the hood. "If you paid to get rid of her, I should be grateful, shouldn't I? It's the only bloody thing I've gotten from you in forty years!" He swung the rake sideways and slammed it into the windscreen. Mather threw up his arms to shield himself from the shattering glass.

"Harris, I . . . I . . . have to go . . . my boy, he's . . ."

"Oh, yes, your boy. Which boy is that? That useless Sandy, or that other one? If I'm not mistaken that dead boy is yours as well. He looked just like her. I don't know why I didn't see it." Mather looked at Harris. There was something wrong with what he was saying, he knew that, and he was afraid of what Harris might do with the rake, but he was terrified at every moment that he would hear gunshots again.

"Robin, listen please. I've got to get down to Winslow's. I think Sandy is down there with the gun for some reason. We can talk about this later." He pushed past Harris and climbed into the driver's side of the Morris, brushing glass off the seat onto the ground. Harris, with an energy that terrified Mather, darted around the other side of the car and began to break the passenger side window. Yes, it was right, thought Mather, that the whole world should come unravelled, and he slumped over the steering wheel, hoping that there would, at least, be no more shots.

THEY WERE AT the table in the kitchen now. Lane had made tea. She was pushing the sugar bowl toward him, still being soothing, when she caught sight of a figure to one side of the French door on her veranda. She wondered momentarily how it had been accomplished so quietly, and then said, without looking back toward the door, "Sugar, Sandy? It's best to have really sweet, strong tea when you've been upset." Sandy was looking into his cup, his rifle across the table in front of him. Lane was alert now; if someone was on the veranda, someone must be around at the front. Had they come into the hall already? It must be Darling and Ames. She hoped they would not make a splashy entrance; it might spook Sandy, and he still had the gun. She must avoid being in the line of fire or being taken hostage again. Could she get the gun away from him on any pretext? She thought not. He was stirring his tea with his left hand, and had the gun in a death grip with his right hand, and he was still in a volatile mood. She'd only got him this far because she'd pretended to believe that he hadn't killed Franks and that nothing was going to be accomplished with her bound on the floor of the bedroom. They would go and have tea, and they would talk about how to get him out of this jam. After all, as he was innocent, it was no use making his situation worse. To her amazement, he'd bought it.

She heard the creak in the hallway and glanced at Sandy. He didn't seem to have heard; perhaps the sound of the stirring covered it up. Any moment from now someone was going to spring into the room to effect a rescue. She had to keep it calm. Or not. As the door of the veranda burst open, she shoved the teapot so that it rolled onto its side and deposited scalding tea onto Sandy. At once the room was mayhem. She reached for the gun just as someone jumped Sandy and pushed him onto the floor. Ames! She stood back against the stove, holding the rifle in her hands, and did not take her eyes off Ames, who was now snapping handcuffs on the swearing Sandy, until she felt someone gently tugging at the gun.

"There, Miss Winslow. Shall I take that?" And she looked around to see Darling standing next to her, now holding the weapon.

"Ah, you're here about the raspberries" was all she said. How the whole thing ended, Lane would doubtless reconstruct later, with her cup of cocoa. There was a period of businesslike activity: a now mysteriously passive Sandy being led away in handcuffs, the sound of the car backing up the drive.

Lane had reported, a bit shakily, what she had been told by Sandy. She assumed they would take Harris up as well.

It hadn't been difficult. They had met him coming down the road on his tractor. From where they stopped him they could see, near the top of the road, Mather standing looking at his car. They would find out in the course of the afternoon what had happened, and how it had been a corollary to the dangerous events unfolding in Lane's house.

Kenny and Eleanor and the Hughes all came out from behind the weeping willow where they had been hurriedly told by Darling to go, looking suspiciously at Angus as they left, still asking if Lane was going to be all right. Everyone gone but one. It was silent again, and she sat on the veranda with a scotch, deserved, she thought, and looked out at the lake. The light had a particular yellow intensity at this time of the afternoon. Soon the shadows would bleed across the lawn, the forest, the mountains, but the lake would still be reflecting the deep blue sky until the very last minute. She put her glass down on the table, and turned to Angus Dunn, who sat on the other side, his empty glass in his hand, in what she sincerely hoped was an advanced state of discomfort. She laughed inwardly. This sort of thing would never be his style. She was sure now that he must have a family and that that family lived somewhere in the countryside, but an English countryside, especially Kent, or Oxfordshire, or wherever he stashed them, would be nothing like this vast, lonely place.

"Were you planning on staying? Only I've nothing set up. We could ask the Armstrongs if they could put you up."

"How long are you planning to keep up this cool front? You know why I'm here—I shan't go without you. I've gone to a lot of trouble, you know. I was most of the way to Vancouver when I knew I couldn't go back without you. Seems I was just in time to rescue you. It's ridiculous, this colonial cowboy nonsense you're going in for. You don't belong here. You belong in England, putting your talents to use. Your country needs you. There, I've even pulled that one out, but it happens to be true."

Lane stood up. Who had rescued her? She couldn't have said, though she knew she'd had a part in it. She'd seen Ames burst through the door, then Darling, then, even in the state she'd been in after pouring scalding water on Sandy, a kind of shock at seeing Angus. She could scarcely imagine what she was feeling now, with him sitting before her. She had overheard snatches of whispered and angry conversation between him and Darling as Ames was leading Sandy out of the house. They had been talking about her. What could Darling have said to elicit an angry "I have every right to her" from Angus? Now she was exhausted, enraged, she hardly knew.

"Angus, I've had, as they say, a long day. I cannot see what I have done to be plagued by you, in my own home, far from any hope of being rescued. I told you when I met you in Nelson that I wanted nothing more to do with you or the service. You have been gassing on since the police left with that wretched young man about why I should go back and work for you. I don't want to work for you or be like you; to lie so easily, to presume on people, or to use them. I shiver when I think how close I came to staying after the war. Now, please, please, get back in that motorcar and drive away out of my life."

He stood on her doorstep, under the great blue spruce, holding his hat in his hands, looking at the ground. He seemed to have understood that he had lost, yet appeared to be mustering one more plea. Lane was holding the door, waiting for him to turn and walk up the driveway to wherever he'd put his car. When he turned, she would close the door and go back to her drink. She would not stay and watch him leave.

"I loved . . . love . . . you, you know . . ." He left the sentence hanging in the air.

"You are absolutely unbelievable," she said, smiling. "Now, get out." She closed the door and walked back down her hallway, now nearly dark in the late afternoon, toward the light still pouring in from the open veranda doors.

CHAPTER THIRTY-THREE

IT WAS RAINING THE DAY it all ended. It had taken until mid-September for the trial to get underway and now, after all that time, it seemed to end in no time at all. Lane stood on the stairs of the courthouse, struggling to unfurl her umbrella so that she could make her way back to where she had parked her motorcar. She could not wait to be on the road. Rain in town was bleak, she reflected, rendering everything into a landscape of greys, but out in the country it was soft, the greys ameliorated by infinite shades of green as the trees caught the shimmer of light in the drops of water.

She had testified, something she'd been nervous about, fearful that she would get muddled under the badgering of lawyers, but, in fact, both sides had seemed doggedly interested in collecting tiny details: Had she seen what the victim was wearing, could she recall the time when she was on the road, how many minutes, how far, how dark, how light . . . ? These scarcely seemed to add up to the human drama that had unfolded before her in the summer. In the end, Sandy owned that he had gotten the idea to place the blame on Miss Winslow from the papers found in the victim's pockets, all of which he'd burned but the one with her name on it. Yes, he'd planted the shoe in her property and at four in the morning had moved the car from Harris's barn to Lane's. No, he didn't know what happened to the other shoe. Why had he fixed on having her take the blame? A long silence. It was because he'd promised Harris that he'd take care of everything. He got rid of the original crank in the old dump and fixed it so that no one could trace the death to Harris. He'd kept the keys. He'd thought he might have use for the car one day.

Sandy was deemed to be responsible for Jack Franks' death and would likely be sent to the coast to prison, and Harris had been charged with assault, for which he would likely serve very little time because of his age. The whole thing, conducted in a darkly panelled room whose high windows admitted only the dull light from the banks of grey clouds outside, was infinitely depressing.

The umbrella had just sprung into life when she heard her name called. She quelled with irritation the pang she felt at the sound of his voice and turned, lifting her umbrella to address Inspector Darling.

"Yes, Inspector?"

He seemed momentarily at a loss for words, and then, finally, "Thank you for staying on and coming in to town to testify."

"There is no need to thank me. I assure you I was most mindful of the legal consequences of a failure to respond to a subpoena."

Darling looked down, rain beginning to drip from the brim of his hat. "When will you be off back to London?"

She looked away, struggling with an anger she could scarcely comprehend. How dare he assume she would go back? "I'm not sure, you know. In the meantime, I will try, Inspector Darling, to cause no more mayhem in your patch."

The inspector stood for a long moment, but again seemed unable to think of anything to say. Lane wondered what she would say if he suddenly said something ridiculously unlikely like, "Please don't go." Well, he wouldn't, of course, and why should she even think of it? She certainly had no interest in him. She still smarted from the angry conversation he and Angus had had about her as if she were an animal found on the street that had to be put somewhere. It would be good to be at home with her own thoughts, and Kenny and Eleanor's or Angela's if she got bored. Men were a confounded nuisance.

"I'm relieved to hear you say so. My patch, as you quaintly put it, has plenty to occupy me without any contributions from your neck of the woods."

"Right, well. You'd better get out of the rain, Inspector. A sick policeman will do no one's patch any good. Good day."

She began to descend the steps toward the street when she heard him call out. She turned and he came to the step just below the one she was on, so that his eyes were level with hers. "Miss Winslow, he cannot hold a candle to you." And he turned and walked away.

ON THE FERRY across the lake Lane stared at the rain slashing onto her windscreen. What had he meant? He could have said that Angus was not worthy, or not worth it. He could have said she was a fool to go back for a fool, but instead he had said Angus couldn't hold a candle to her. She could not remember ever being compared equally to a man, especially not by a man. Now she felt guilty about how she'd treated the inspector. There was no need to be so cold, and there was no need at all to pretend she might even be thinking of going back to England. She would never go back, would never even consider it. How could he understand that she wanted only to be considered in her own right, and yet not understand that nothing would induce her to go back? Certainly not that prig, Angus. She tried to imagine Angus thinking of her as equal to him—to any man. It would be impossible; he had the superiority of men ingrained in every pore. He would not even think his own behaviour reprehensible, in taking her, young and vulnerable, to be his lover while he had a wife somewhere. With a shudder she realized there must have been others before her, and would likely be others after. Girls fell for that sort of confident domineering. She tried to forgive her young self for falling for him.

Well, she thought grimly, putting her car into gear and driving off the wooden ramp of the ferry onto the road for the long drive home, there will be no danger of any sort of falling. King's Cove would be a guarantee of that, and she was, she decided, satisfied with this.

EPILOGUE

October 11, 1946

"NOW THAT IS LOVELY!" EXCLAIMED Angela, who had walked into the church carrying a thick bundle of golden grasses for the pots at the front of the church by the first pews. Eleanor had produced a beautifully embroidered white silk cloth for the altar, and they had piled apples and gourds in among the flowers and a few sheaves of barley. There were two bushel-baskets of vegetables just inside the door. Lane and Eleanor beamed at the compliment and stepped back to look.

"Your first Harvest Festival, my dear. The vicar will do a very nice service. I think we need this just now, don't you?" Eleanor brushed the detritus from organizing the barley off the front of her apron. "The tea afterward is always lovely. I'm so pleased that Gladys and the girls decided to throw it. We used to have the loveliest teas in their garden before the war. It'll be quite like old times."

Lane thought about Sandy, away in Vancouver in prison, and the wreck that was Robin Harris, back in his house, more embittered, unreachable. Put that against Alice Mather, who suddenly appeared to be quite normal, while Reginald seemed to shrink inside himself. "Perhaps not altogether like old times," she said. "Listen, I must get back. I promised myself I'd work today."

Angela protested, "You said you were coming up to my place for a drink!"

"I know, I'm so sorry, Angela. It'll keep. Tomorrow, yes?" She felt, in the crisp, autumn chill of the afternoon, that she wanted to be alone. She felt the most haunted during this season, she decided. When the past and present lingered together, when she felt pulled to solitude.

The air was clean and cool, and though the leaves had not yet started their autumnal journey to the ground, the smell of smoke from the chimneys foretold the coming of she knew not what, in the way of winter. Perhaps it would be like Latvia: encased in white, clean, and quiet. As she walked up the hill, buttoning up her red and black lumberman's jacket, a purchase she'd delighted in on her last trip into town, she wondered how she would be when the snow came; she recoiled a little inwardly at the prospect that the snow would plunge her into homesickness. Now then, she thought, you didn't come all the way out here to wallow in nostalgia.

In the house, she lit the fire and made herself a drink. With a book in hand she sat in her armchair and put her feet up on the grate. She tried to imagine writing about the war, tried to imagine what she would say. But it was impossible—too close, too incomprehensible, especially here. Of course, she thought ruefully, the war does come all the way here. People like Harris carry it around inside them, where it still has the power to strike. What did she carry?

Nothing like Harris, she decided; his must have been a bloody awful war. She couldn't imagine any more what it was like to be at war.

The fire was blazing, and it was late, nearly six, when Lane woke with a start from her slight doze. Someone was knocking on her door. She pulled her feet off the grate, her legs stiff, her feet over-hot, and glanced at the clock and then outside. It was beginning to get dark; she felt a slight sadness at the memory of the long days of summer, but at the same time an exhilaration at the prospect of the coming winter. She could see a man's figure through the panes in the door, and though he was obscured by the coming night, she thought for a moment it had the air of Inspector Darling, and then dismissed that as impossible.

"Inspector," she said, surprised, looking past him up the drive. She'd not heard his car. "I hope you've not found new evidence that puts me in the frame after all."

"I had a matter to see to in Adderly, so I thought I might drop by. I brought you this." He held up a large paper bag. Nothing in his face betrayed that last moment they'd been together on the steps of the courthouse.

She looked with surprise at the bag, but did not take it. "You'd better come in." She stood aside to let him in, and then watched him as he moved down the hall to the sitting room. Her heart was pounding, probably, she told herself, from suddenly jumping up out of a doze.

She moved the second armchair to a position by the fire. He took off his hat and coat and then stood with them, unsure. "Here, I'll take those. Please sit down. Scotch?" Lane put the hat and coat on the couch and then occupied herself getting a glass and a bottle of scotch from a cabinet by her partially filled bookshelf. She had her back to him and fumbled with the stopper in the bottle. She poured a splash of scotch into the glass and, with a deep breath, took it to him. "I should have asked if you wanted water." He shook his head and took the glass.

"Are you having one?"

"Yes, all right, why not?" She made her own drink, still waiting to know why he had really come.

"I thought you might have left, you know, gone back to England. My constable is your slave and he has been pining for you, so you can imagine that when he saw you in town at the dry goods store last week, I was obliged to hear all about it."

"Ames? Really? How extraordinary. I should have paid him more attention." She settled in to her armchair, stretching her legs toward the fire. "So you've come to see if it's true? That I'm still here, I mean."

"I've come to bring you these blasted raspberry canes, since you are still here and possibly staying after all. I have also come to see if you've any insight into the whole business of your countryman's untimely death. Aside from Harris's confession that he poleaxed him with his tractor crank, we got very little else on why—except that he thought he was a British agent. I've wanted to kill a few British agents myself, but the prosecutor seemed uncurious about why and I was sorry he dropped his line of questioning when he got his man, as it were. I thought, you know, you living here among the natives, might be in someone's confidence and have found out more than we got at the trial. And, of course, perhaps the inestimable Director Dunn told you something about the fellow's life prior to his arrival here."

In the flickering firelight dusk of the sitting room, Lane felt herself smile and then crossly stopped herself. It would not do to be pleased to see this slight evidence of Darling's—could she think it?—jealousy of Angus Dunn. If only he could know the depth of her utter indifference to Dunn and the relief she felt when he finally agreed to leave. Or the fervour of her hope that she would never see or hear from him again.

"I did learn a bit from Kenny and Eleanor. It's really a story about war. Amazingly, Harris, who has been an absolute recluse since he was released from hospital after his heart attack in the jail . . . you know the doctors said he should stay in town and they offered him a little bedsit or something so he could be near care. He wouldn't have it. I can't help feeling he just wants to die. He's been in a kind of purgatory for nearly thirty years, living with this. Anyway, he made his way up to Kenny and Eleanor's one evening; I've been taking whatever mail he has and dropping it off at his door, because he never comes out of the house. On that night, he seems to have made a confession of sorts. He and Kenny are cousins, you know, through old lady Armstrong's brother who died in South Africa before Harris came out. He was very young; maybe ten. It must have been a frightful trip for a young child to undertake, but he was sent here to live with the Armstrongs. He was always dour, according to Kenny, even as a child."

"I shouldn't wonder, losing his parents and being packed off to a strange place at such an age." Darling was leaning back in his chair so that he was angled toward her, and she could see the gentle flicker of the fire reflected on his left cheek.

"I have some sense of such strangeness. I lost my parents, well, the one that mattered, when I was very young, but thank God I was raised by my grandmother who had been with us the whole time. Anyway, according to Kenny, Harris became more standoffish as he got older and they were all very surprised when he turned up with a wife whom he'd married by special licence in town. She was the daughter of the man who ran the dry goods store and was a very undernourished and overworked specimen, by all accounts. She was not more than eighteen and arrived in the spring and could not have known what trading her town life for a rural life was going to mean, especially in the winter. Though they all knew her father seemed intent on working his children to death; perhaps it was her chance to get away. Then that summer, war was declared and Harris and John Armstrong signed up and were gone. So then the details get scarce, but when Harris came up to see Kenny last month, suddenly out of the blue, this is what he told him. He and John were in the same regiment. I think it was mostly made up of experienced soldiers, but John and Robin were no doubt tough young men because of their work here. Anyway they survived to the Somme and then, during a charge, John was struck down. It was dark, early morning I suppose, and they were under a brutal barrage. Robin stopped, of course, and saw that John was wounded, not dead, and could hear him saying 'please.'" Here Lane stopped and tried to stop herself from tearing up. She had imagined it so vividly as Kenny told it and he too had barely been able to continue past this moment. She took a breath and continued, "But they were under such fire and he could feel the press of men charging up behind him that he didn't stop, you see. He kept going. He thought somehow he could go back for him later, but at the end, John was found where he had fallen, in the mud, among the dead."

She stopped. Dusk had turned to darkness and the only light now was that of the fire. She was acutely aware of Darling sitting in the next chair, watching her. He had not interrupted the story but the one time, and now sat in silence. She glanced at him and then away again quickly. "They were victorious that day and Harris was wounded, shot in the leg and, like all the survivors, got some sort of a service medal for taking down a German machine gun blind. Then things got peculiar. Everyone was demobbed in the winter of '18, and they all came pouring back. Kenny and Eleanor and poor Old Lady Armstrong had gotten the official notification of John's death, but there was nothing whatever about Harris. He had been taken to a hospital on the south coast somewhere to recover and then had disappeared, and he didn't come back till nearly 1920. When he did come back, the fire of '19 had just happened, and his orchards had been hit particularly hard and his wife had disappeared. In fact she'd left in '17, telling no one where she was; just vanished one day without a word. Here they all thought she'd gone back to her family, but Kenny didn't see her when he took the steamboat up to town, as he wanted to offer her some help, though she had refused this throughout the war. When Harris did get back, he became positively misanthropic and had bad shell shock. He never spoke of the war, or told anyone where he'd been for so long. It turned out, though, that he had been full of fear that one day someone would come and take him because he'd left John dying and had done nothing for him. He would pick up his vet's cheques at the post office every quarter, apparently always afraid that one would not be a cheque but a warrant of some sort. In all those years he must have been wracked with guilt and this blind, unreasoning terror that this one act, this failure to act, I suppose, would catch up with him.

"He couldn't know that no one blamed him. John must have been mortally wounded, so he would have died anyway. And in a way, with the arrival of poor Franks, it did all catch up with him. Franks just stopped at Harris's to find the way to where Elizabeth Harris, his mother, had come from, or maybe to find his father. He must have asked for where Harris lived, and then said, according to what Harris confessed to Kenny, 'It's all right, I'm from the British government,' or something, showing him his identity card because Harris seemed so horrified about being asked for by someone with a British accent. I suppose we'll never know exactly why Harris struck him. He only said he did." She shuddered. "It's the war, isn't it? What are we all carrying around from that? I get very bad dreams sometimes. Dreams of fire and darkness; I'm there again, only I can't remember what I'm supposed to be doing; the numbers of the codes are muddled. What ghastly thing is going to suddenly pop up years from now?"

Lane could hear Darling move in his chair and looked over to where he sat, eyes illuminated by the flickering firelight, watching her thoughtfully. It won't do, she thought, this suddenly intimate confessional atmosphere. It won't do at all, and she got up and walked to where the desk lamp stood on the side table and pulled the chain, lighting the room. "I'm about ready to have an omelette and a piece of toast; very French, will you join me?"

They sat in the armchairs eating the omelette off their knees. The preparation of it had steadied Lane's sudden emotional tumult. After a brief silence Darling returned to the case.

"There is a kind of tragedy here that reminds me of some Greek play. All the roots of a later evil planted inadvertently in the past . . . John Armstrong falling on a battlefield long ago and far away; Franks cursed from his very conception to die on a distant shore."

"Literature has lost a star, Inspector, by your choice of policing! But yes, the story of Franks is astonishing . . . According to Eleanor there had always been a story about Reginald Mather and Harris's wife, Elizabeth, floating around, but her disappearance, the war, the devastating fire of '19, and just the passing of the years made the whole thing fade away, until Alice got hold of it somehow, and told Harris. And of course the embarrassing and near-fatal coincidence that Franks and I were in the same business, as it were."

Darling scooped a last buttery morsel of omelette onto his toast and munched thoughtfully. "You know, it's always a relief to solve a case, to understand how the story unfolded. This whole thing could have had several other outcomes; Harris could have killed Mather, when he discovered he'd been made a cuckold; Alice could have poisoned Mather's dinner when she discovered she'd been betrayed. Your pal Sandy could have killed Franks for being a long-lost son, come to take away his inheritance."

A combined laugh and shudder escaped from Lane. "He's not my pal," and then she hesitated. Darling didn't know about that awful fishing trip and he wasn't about to, she decided. She was embarrassed to her core just thinking of it. "But he did end up killing poor Franks, didn't he, without realizing it, no doubt, knowing his turn of mind, thinking he could get something out of Harris . . . 'Here, I'll take care of this body if you finally concede and sell me the land you've refused to sell my dad all these years.' In a way, to get back to your Greek tragedy analogy, he was Fate's unwitting tool."

"So much for the peacefulness of country life," sighed Darling, pushing himself out of his chair. "To be honest, it seems to me there is still enough bitterness left in this community to erupt again. Are you sure you're entirely safe living out here?"

That question having been greeted with only a smile, they stood now at the door. Holding his hat, Darling went out and stood on the doorstep, and after a long moment said, "You are staying then?"

"In spite of the dangers you have raised, I shall have to, I suppose, to take care of those blasted raspberries," Lane said, with what she felt must be an absolutely transparent breeziness.

Darling put his hat on, and turning into the night said, "Ames will be pleased."

ACKNOWLEDGEMENTS

It is my husband, Terry Miller, who brings his intelligence, wisdom, and understanding of human nature to bear on our many discussions, during long walks, about the behaviour and lives of my characters. His support and delight have been unfailing. A written acknowledgement on its own is inadequate—but even so, I offer him my deepest gratitude.

I would like to thank Sasha Bley-Vroman, Lorna Duncan, and Ruth Chaulk, the readers of this book's first incarnation. I must also extend my gratitude to my many readers who have been so encouraging. It is for you I write.

Thank you also to the wonderful staff at TouchWood Editions for bringing this dream into being.

PHOTO BY ANICK VIOLETTE

IONA WHISHAW was born in British Columbia, and, after living her early years in the Kootenays, spent her formative years living and learning in Mexico, Nicaragua, and the US. She travelled extensively for pleasure and education before settling in the Vancouver area. Throughout her roles as youth worker, social worker, teacher, and award-winning high school principal, her love of writing remained consistent, and compelled her to obtain her master's in creative writing from the University of British Columbia. Iona has published short fiction, poetry, poetry translation, and one children's book, *Henry and the Cow Problem*. *A Killer in King's Cove* is her first adult novel. Her heroine, Lane Winslow, was inspired by Iona's mother who, like her father before her, was a wartime spy. Visit ionawhishaw.com to find out more.

Turn the page for a preview of
the next Lane Winslow mystery,

DEATH IN A DARKENING MIST

CHAPTER ONE

December, 1946

THERE WAS A FAINT DUSTING of snow on the treacherous road, but even more threatening were the dark clouds banking along the mountains. The road to Adderly wound sharply, so narrow in places that only one car could go through, and, for one long stretch, it was carved out of a seeming sheer cliff that dropped hundreds of feet to the lake below. Angela drove it clutching the steering wheel and leaning forward, as if this action would keep the station wagon anchored on the dirt road and heading in the right direction. Lane Winslow, who'd agreed to this trip on the grounds that it was to be a lovely day out at the local hot spring, wished she'd offered to drive—indeed was wishing she'd stayed safe at home. But that, she reflected, was because they'd reached the most terrifying section, and at the moment she was on the side that dropped over the cliff. Even Angela's three rambunctious boys, Philip, Rolfie, and Rafe, were sitting quietly in the back, as if they knew their stillness was critical to everyone arriving alive at the swimming pool. Though it was barely ten in the morning, the lake below was dark and brooding, as if night were already coming on. Lane dared herself to look toward the edge of the cliff, just under her, and hoped that this was not the day she would die. What she didn't yet know was that it would be someone else's day to die.

She forced herself to admire the number of shades of deep blues and greys that were represented in the roil of dark clouds, the water, the mountains, so that she would not think about whether they might encounter someone coming the other way and be forced into a dangerous standoff on this narrow road. The faint overnight snowfall had barely covered the ground, and clearly a vehicle had already been along here earlier. She shuddered to think about this road covered in a deep, slippery layer of snow.

It was at this moment that Angela chose to glance at Lane and say, "Has that nice Charles Andrews from the bank come out to see you again?"

Wanting to cry, "Keep your eyes on the road!" Lane said through tight lips, "Yes. No. I mean, he's been out twice. Oh God!" They rounded one last long curve and then she let out a long slow breath of relief when the precipice was exchanged for ordinary deep pine forest on either side. "Crikey! How do you drive that without losing your nerve?"

"Don't try to change the subject. Is he as nice as he looks? All that wavy blond hair must mean something."

"He's perfectly pleasant, but you are making something out of nothing. His aunt lives nearby and he stops out to say hello. I feel a bit sorry for him. He got some sort of shrapnel in his leg, and he limps. He was in the 4th Infantry and got wounded just near the end. He used to be an athlete. It's hard to live with the loss of your powers."

"That's how it starts! You feel sorry for a guy, and then one thing leads to another." Angela was actually winking. Even on this perfectly straight bit of road, Lane wished Angela would keep both eyes open.

"Nothing is leading to anything, I assure you. He is not my type." Lane was pretty sure this was true, though she could not precisely say why. He had come only a few days ago, before the snow, on a crisp, sunny day. She'd been raking leaves with a bedraggled bamboo rake she'd found in her barn when she'd seen his deep blue Studebaker pull up and stop outside her metal gate. He was wearing a long camel coat, and he removed his grey hat to wave at her. He reminded her of a well-cared-for cat. Things must be going well at the bank, she'd thought. It was not entirely kindly meant, she realized immediately, and was sorry. "Mr. Andrews, how nice of you to take the trouble!" she'd called.

On his first visit a few weeks before, he'd just stopped by to say hello, and looked admiringly around her beloved house, but this time she had invited him in, and made them both cheese sandwiches. It had given her a chance to experience how truly charming he was. He had expressed a flattering interest in her, and had been large and comfortable in her kitchen in a way that made her think of his physical presence after he had gone.

"Well, I think he is gorgeous," Angela said.

"That's only because he's always giving you money."

At last a small cabin appeared on their left, and then a wooden house, and finally a tiny main street that, were it not for a few parked cars, could have been the main road of a ghost town. Not a single person was in evidence.

Their destination was the hot springs in the little mining town. The boys, the dangerous road behind them, began to jostle and pummel each other as they approached the town.

"Can we go in the store?" they asked. They were passing a wooden building called Fletcher's Store, but Angela drove on and turned up a steep incline where she pulled the car to a stop in a clearing.

"After our swim," she said.

Lane got out and breathed away the tension of the drive, amazed at how relieved she was to be standing on solid ground, reminded, not for the first time, how being in a war, being dropped out of airplanes, does not take away the ordinary day-to-day fears that life serves up. Just below the parking clearing, through a bank of bare birch trees, she could see the quiet street laid out before her.

"It's like those pictures in magazines. It's the Platonic perfection of a Canadian mining town. That store looks to be from the last century," Lane said.

The boys had run ahead, their towels trailing from the bundles under their arms, and were pounding up a long, trestled wooden stairway that took visitors from the parking area to the outdoor pool. They'd reached the first landing and were shouting at Lane and Angela to come *on*.

"I'll take us into the store after," said Angela. "It's very quaint. That and one other building, the hotel, were practically the only buildings to survive a big fire in the nineties. The boys like to buy chocolate bars there. You wait. We'll be completely enervated after this and will need chocolate."

Feeling doubt that Angela's troop would be enervated

by anything, Lane followed Angela up the stairs. At the top landing Lane saw, through a thick miasma of steam, the swimming pool and a long wooden building at one end. Change rooms, she supposed. Just dimly visible through the steam over the pool were one or two dark shapes decorously doing a breast stroke. Angela knocked on the wooden frame of a window labelled *Tickets*. After a brief struggle and an uttered obscenity, a short, cheerful, artificial blonde finally managed to shoot the window open.

"I should get Frank to oil the damn thing. Hello, dearie! I haven't seen you and yours here for a good while! Who's this?"

"Hello, Betty," said Angela. "This is Lane. She moved to the cove in the summer. Lane, Betty—the doyenne of Adderly Hot Springs."

"How do you do?"

"Ooh—you're English. You must fit right in with them others up at the Cove."

Lane, who, because of her international upbringing, wasn't sure she really fit in anywhere, smiled at the middle-aged woman, squeezed into the brown wool jacket she wore against the cold. "That'll be ten cents all round, dears."

The change rooms were a series of little cubicles smelling of damp wood and lit only by two bare light bulbs in the passageway. The floor was slatted wood—to aid drainage, she imagined—but she wished she had brought plimsolls to wear out to the pool area because the wood had a damp, unwholesome feel on her bare feet. As she hung up her clothing, Lane could already hear the boys splashing into the water and shouting. She wondered how the decorous swimmers were taking the addition of noisy children to their quiet, misty winter morning.

She slid gratefully out of the freezing air into the white, murky depths of the warm pool. The air had a pleasantly sulphurous quality that made the experience seem vaguely medicinal. The miasma of steam was so thick that though she could hear the children, she could not see them across the pool.

"This is heaven!" she exclaimed.

"I told you," Angela said.

"And this is just directly out of the ground?"

"I think so. You can't see them, but the caves I told you about are over there. The water is much hotter in the caves. When we get too used to this we can go sit in there and parboil like a couple of eggs. Perhaps they add a bit of cool water to bring the temperature down in the pool. We've been here when the snow is a foot deep, and we get all heated up and then roll in the snow."

"It's a good thing your lads are such good swimmers. I can't see my hand two inches under the water. If anyone drowned here you'd never find them!"

It wasn't, Lane decided, a pool for doing exercising laps. The steam prevented one from seeing far ahead, and in any case the temperature suggested a regime of just floating about. So she did, on her back, looking upward through the mist at the grey textures of the sky.

"Come on. Let's go to the caves." She heard Angela from somewhere behind her.

They climbed out of the pool up a calcium-encrusted ladder at the deep end, and stepped over a thigh-high ledge into the mouth of a cave. The experience was like getting into a slightly too-hot bath. There was a ledge to sit on just at the entrance, and the two of them sank onto it, looking out at the winter morning behind them.

"How far back does it go?" Lane asked. It was pitch dark only a few feet from the entrance. Water dripped from the ceiling. Somewhere she could hear a cascade splashing onto the surface of the water.

"It goes all the way around and connects to the other cave opening. Maybe twenty feet to the back wall. You have to mind how you go, because it narrows toward the back and you can bump your head on the pokey bits. You can't quite stand up, and it's shallow, so you sort of float along on your belly. I've only done it once. You have to feel your way along. I'm always afraid of grabbing someone's knee in the dark." Angela stood up. "I'd better go see how the boys are. It unnerves me when I can't hear them. You stay here and bask. I'll be right back."

Lane watched Angela disappear into the mist, calling out the names of her brood, and then she tentatively moved away from the mouth of the cave and came to rest in the dark at what she assumed was halfway along. The mouth of the cave shimmered, throwing light only a few feet in. The droplets from the roof of the cave fell with tiny echoes in the silence. Alone in the dark with her musings, her mind turned backward, as if the darkness pulled her into her childhood. Newfangled psychological claptrap, she scolded herself lazily. But there she was, in the Latvian winter, visiting a hot spring. Where? She closed her eyes to picture where she had been. She must have been very young.

Who had taken her? Not her father. He was always away on "diplomatic" business. Madame Olga?

"*Da. Zdyes.*"

Lane's eyes flew open and she peered into the darkness. Was she imagining that someone had said, "Yes. Here" in Russian? There was only silence. Her memory was a bit too vivid, she thought. She supposed someone could come here for some good, old-fashioned Freudian regression. She began to move back toward the entrance, unwilling to regress just at the moment, when she heard it again, in Russian: "*Ya zdyes*"—I'm here.

Lane moved back to the entrance of the cave and sat on the ledge to see if the speaker would appear. The voice had sounded closer the second time. Outside by the pool, she could hear the children, and Angela exhorting them not to bother people and to stay at the shallow end. Through the mist they sounded far away, as if shouting from a dream.

"Aha, Piotr, there you are. I'm going out now. I will see you at the café," said the same voice in Russian, and simultaneously a bearded man with short, pale yellow hair rose directly in front of her, making for the entrance. From somewhere behind him she heard another voice.

"Fine. Ten more minutes and I'll be there."

The bearded man, as he emerged into the light, looked to be in his late forties, with a worried cast to his eyes. Or was it just the effect of adjusting to the light? He was muscular, and, perhaps because of the temperature of the water, a scar across the top of his arm stood out, a great red welt.

"Excuse, madame," he said in heavily accented English, climbing past her, out of the cave.

For a moment Lane considered talking to him in his own language. It had unleashed such nostalgia in her to hear him speak the language that had surrounded her in her childhood. But she held back. He could prove to be someone she didn't want to know, or she might hold him up if he was in a hurry. Besides, if he were an English speaker, she probably would not have talked to him. Thus she sat, watching him splash along the edge of the pool, stopping halfway back to the dressing area to lift a handful of the sparse snow from the raised bank that formed that edge of the pool, vigorously rubbing his limbs with it.

When he had disappeared into the mist between her and the dressing room, she sank back into the hot water until her chin rested on the surface. With her eyes closed, she gave in to the nostalgia of her childhood, of the Latvian winters and the saunas. That time suddenly felt more intensely real to her than the Charles Edwardses, or all the things that had crashed about her life since she had come to King's Cove the previous June.

She remembered the vast stretch of white country where she used to cross-country ski with her friends. Winter was her favourite place and time. The cleanliness and distance, the silence, and the aura of possibility that only the young could feel. Would she ever feel that again? She was barely twenty-six, but she felt old against the memories, as if the war had wrung her out and left only this shell that required her to sit, like an old woman, in a hot spring to ease the aches. Lane had worked for the British Secret Intelligence Service from the age of nineteen till the end of the war. There was plenty to be weary about, which was why she'd moved out to the middle of British Columbia. Here in the middle of nowhere she was free to be herself, she thought, with no tiresome, blond bank clerks to bother with.

Her melancholic reverie was interrupted by Angela, suddenly blocking the light as she climbed into the tunnel with a shudder. "Oof. I still have three boys, and they aren't quite tired enough yet. If I sit in here and don't interfere, another fifteen minutes should do it."

Lane was going to ask Angela about why there should be people speaking Russian, but then worried that the second man, Piotr, might still be nearby, somewhere in the darkness of the cave, so instead she settled back in, and sat with her friend in companionable silence. The boys were still audible in the pool, accompanied by the occasional splash, as one of them cannon-balled into the water, to cries of indignation by his brothers. When the sounds of the boys began to die down, Angela said, "Good. Now we can go. It's going to take me ages to cool down!" They climbed over the ledge, and Lane looked back at the other entrance to the cavern, thinking that next time she would go and sit at that end. She wondered what had happened to the second man. Perhaps he'd walked by toward the change rooms when she was in her reverie.

After an unpleasant struggle to pull her clothes on to her damp body—the towel was unequal to the task of drying her properly in the wet confines of the dressing room—she emerged and listlessly waited for Angela and the boys. Angela had them in several cubicles of the ladies' side and was telling them to get a move on. Lane dried her long hair, more or less, and tied it back, slipping it under her scarf.

She was still hot from the water, and wanted to leave her jacket undone, but she knew that the cold would win out, and she ought to preserve some of the heat. Putting her bag down, she leaned on the railing, looking out at the parking area and the little street below, enjoying the crisp coldness of the air on her face. She imagined gold miners—is that what they mined here?—trudging out of the hills with their little bags of loot, looking for a drink at the bar. Suddenly she heard banging, and she turned to see a man pounding his fist on the wooden window. At first she couldn't hear what he was shouting, and then she understood all too well.

"Help, somebody, quickly—*help!*"

The wooden window flew open and Betty was there, looking alarmed by the wildness of the man yelling at her.

"I don't understand you, lovie, you must speak English."

But the man continued to shout in Russian. Lane bolted to the window and said to the man, in his language, "Can I help you? What has happened?"

The old man, still in his bathing suit, his white belly hanging over the waist, turned to her as if someone here speaking to him in Russian were the most natural thing in the world. "My friend, in there . . . there is something wrong. I think he is dead!"

Lane looked toward the men's changing area where the door hung open, and then glanced back at Betty. "He says that there is something wrong with his friend in the dressing room. He thinks he is . . . ill. I'm going to check. If there is a doctor in the village, can you get him?" Lane hurried along the walkway toward the open door.

Behind her, Betty muttered, "I warn them. I tell them.

They're too old to sit for a long time in hot water. It's bad for their . . ." But Lane was into the passage of the dressing room now, saying to the old man, "Where is he? Which compartment?"

"There, at the end!"

Once inside, and accustomed to the dimly lit area, she could see at the end that the cubicle door was closed, but there was a figure stretched out, the top half of his body hidden inside, his legs splayed out under the high door in the passage. She flung the door open and saw that the man was naked, lying supine, his head on one side. She could see instantly that this was the same man she had seen coming through the tunnel. She knelt down and gently shook him.

"Sir, sir . . . are you all right?" she said in Russian.

He did not move, and even with the gentle shake, his head flopped ominously. She brought her hand to her mouth, unconsciously quelling her physical response. He was dead; she knew this with certainty. But how did he die?

"Lane, darling, what's the matter? What's happened?" It was Angela in the door of the passageway. "Be quiet and go wait by the car!" she added, this last to the children, who had also begun a rising chorus of questions.

Lane reluctantly pulled her eyes away from the man's face. "Angela, get a warm blanket from Betty right now. And find out if she's contacted any kind of doctor," she called out, past the large body of the distressed friend. He was still standing helplessly outside the cubicle, and seemed to be blocking the whole of the narrow passageway. The "warm" blanket was nonsense, she knew, but she felt part of her mind lagging behind, to some moment when he was still alive. She wished now she'd said something to him after all, as if that delay would have kept him from this meeting with fate.

"He was like this when you found him?" she asked.

"Yes, just like this. He didn't move. I tried to wake him." He sounded close to tears now, and looked nervously behind him, as if expecting that whoever had done this to his friend might pop through the door at any moment.

"Sir, go and get dressed. You will become sick in this cold. I have sent for help."

The man shuffled nervously backward, then turned, and Lane heard the door of a cubicle shut, further down the passage. She swore at the darkness. This back cubicle was far from the bulb that hung halfway along the passage. She turned back to the figure, and, craning forward, looked closely at him, thinking perhaps he'd had a stroke and banged his head. When she saw the wound, she frowned, glancing upward to see if a protruding nail could have caused it, but knowing already it was impossible—no nail was that big. Near the top of the back of his head was a dark spot. She reached out and touched it gently, feeling her finger dip sickeningly into the damp wound in his skull. She brought her finger away, shuddering at the dark stain on it. Blood. At that moment, Angela was coming along the passage with a thick grey blanket.

"What's the matter with him? Has he passed out?"

Taking the blanket, and spreading it over him, in some unconscious and superfluous bid to keep him warm until help arrived, she said, "I'm afraid he's dead."